AFTER THE
FIRE

JANE CASEY

AFTER THE
FIRE

EBURY
PRESS

1 3 5 7 9 10 8 6 4 2

Ebury Press, an imprint of Ebury Publishing
20 Vauxhall Bridge Road,
London SW1V 2SA

Penguin
Random House
UK

Ebury Press is part of the Penguin Random House group of companies
whose addresses can be found at global.penguinrandomhouse.com

First published in 2015 by Ebury Press

www.eburypublishing.co.uk

A CIP catalogue record for this book is available from the British Library

Hardback ISBN 9780091949693
Trade paperback ISBN 9780091948313

Typeset in Palatino LT Std by Palimpsest Book Production Limited,
Falkirk, Stirlingshire

Printed and bound in Great Britain by Clays Ltd, St Ives PLC

Penguin Random House is committed to a sustainable future for our
business, our readers and our planet. This book is made from Forest
Stewardship Council® certified paper.

MIX
Paper from
responsible sources
FSC
www.fsc.org   FSC® C018179

For Michael and Bridget

Author's note

For those readers who are coming to this series for the first time, I promise you that you don't need to have read the other books to understand what takes place in *After the Fire*. However, there are references to past events and storylines that run through several books. The Maudling Estate featured in *The Kill*, as did some minor characters who assume greater importance in *After the Fire*. And if you would like to read more about Chris Swain, he first appeared in *The Reckoning* and recurs throughout the series.

JC

Glossary of Police Terminology

ANPR: Automatic Number Plate Recognition; a network of cameras that read and record the registration plates of all vehicles passing them, and check them against various databases (including the PNC) to identify those of interest to the police.

CID: Criminal Investigations Department; detectives in plain clothes responsible for investigating more serious offences in a police area. In London there is one CID per borough, known as the 'main office'.

CPS: Crown Prosecution Service; responsible for assessing the evidence gathered during police investigations and deciding what, if any, offence a suspect should be charged with; also responsible for the prosecution of defendants in the criminal courts.

CRO number: Criminal Records Office number; the unique number allocated to someone when they are first convicted of a crime.

PC: Police Constable; the lowest rank in the British police.

PM: Post Mortem examination; medical examination of a body intended to establish, among other things, a cause of death.

PNC: Police National Computer; the main police computer database, housed in Hendon and containing criminal records, details of wanted and missing people, and information about all UK registered motor vehicles.

Public order offence: an offence contrary to one of the Public Order Acts involving offensive behaviour in public places, including serious public disorder.

Response Officer: uniformed police officer attached to a team that responds to 999 calls from the public.

SOCO: Scenes of Crime Officer; civilian police staff who gather forensic evidence; officially known as Forensic Practitioners in the Metropolitan Police.

TSG: Territorial Support Group; uniformed unit mainly tasked with preventing and responding to incidents of public disorder. TSG units are routinely used to support local officers dealing with large-scale violence.

And among other things, the poor pigeons, I perceive, were loth to leave their houses, but hovered about the windows and balconys till they were, some of them burned, their wings, and fell down.

Samuel Pepys' diary, 2 September 1666

I

There were 224 residents of Murchison House on the Maudling Estate in north London, and on a cold grey late November day not one of them was expecting to die. Some were hoping to die. Some were waiting to die. But no one actually expected to die that day.

Murchison House stood eleven storeys high, an uncompromising slab of cement social housing that dated from the seventies and looked it. Five other tower blocks of varying sizes stood around Murchison House like siblings in an unhappy family. The estate loomed over the surrounding houses, the narrow streets of Victorian terraces built for the working classes that had been slowly, painfully gentrified. Murchison House was never going to be gentrified. Bulldozed, perhaps. In another city, another country, the views would have made it a desirable place to live, but it had taken Londoners a long time to embrace high-rise habitation. Apart from the Maudling Estate, there wasn't a tall building for miles. That meant the inhabitants of Murchison House could see a great deal of London, and a great deal of London could see Murchison House, and to at least one person in the building it felt a lot like torture.

Drina was very familiar with torture.

It was afternoon, around four, she guessed. She sat in the corner of a room in a flat on the top floor, as the grey sky darkened outside the window and the day slid away. She sat on the floor, on a mattress, with her legs stretched out in front of her, because there wasn't anywhere else to sit. There was the mattress, and a lumpy duvet without a cover, a hook on the back of the door and a mirror nailed to one wall. There was a big window with an aluminium frame that didn't fit properly, leaving gaps for the wind. The window itself was locked. All the windows in the flat were locked. Every now and then Drina reached up and tried to open one, almost as a reflex. Someone might have forgotten. Or the window might have broken. These things happened, she'd heard. Mistakes.

Opportunities.

These things happened to other girls, though. Drina was never that lucky. Although what she would do if the window was open, she didn't know. Shout? But they would hear her before anyone else did. The flat was bugged. Even when they weren't actually inside the flat with the girls, someone was nearby – in another flat, or in a car parked below. Close at hand. Cry for help, and the only attention she would attract would be the wrong kind. It wasn't worth the risk. What did that leave? Jumping? It was a possibility. Sometimes she felt like jumping, just to be free for a couple of seconds. Just to get to decide one tiny thing in her life.

Drina lit another cigarette from the butt of the one she had been smoking, then ran her fingernails through her hair. It felt brittle. The bleach was killing it. But blonde was popular with the customers.

There were two other bedrooms and two other girls in the flat, but they wouldn't try to talk to her. It was too dangerous to talk. It was too dangerous to be suspected of planning to escape. Drina had heard – the men had told her – the last girl who had tried to escape hadn't made it out of the tower block alive. She'd left it in a suitcase that was carried to the boot of a car and driven to a riverbank near an industrial estate. They hadn't found her body for weeks, the men said, laughing. Months. Her face was gone, eaten away by decomposition and the river rats. Her fingerprints had disappeared along with her flesh. She'd never been arrested, so there was no DNA to match to her remains. No one had reported her to Interpol as a missing person. No one had ever traced her journey back to Murchison House. No one had ever even found out her name.

'What was it?' Drina had asked, because she was young, and stupid, and she still asked questions then. 'Her name?'

They hadn't remembered either. She was gone, the girl, as if she'd never lived. Someone, somewhere, mourned her – maybe. If they knew she was dead.

All Drina had to do, sitting there, was turn her head to see the streets of London, until they disappeared in a grey haze on the horizon. She looked, sometimes. Sometimes she didn't. Sometimes she just sat and smoked. Today was a smoking day, except that it hurt her mouth. Then again, everything hurt her mouth. Drinking from the small bottle of stale water by her side. Eating, if they gave her anything to eat. A day when she wasn't working was a day when she was costing them money, and they weren't generous people. She could work with cracked ribs and bruised limbs and internal abrasions – she had, frequently. She couldn't work with bruises on her face, though. They'd been angry with her. As if it had been her fault.

As if she could have stopped it.

She had to hand it to the men who'd put her in the room; they couldn't have found a better place to hide her. No one could see her, so high above the ground. The flat faced north; the other towers were to the east and west of it, out of her line of sight. The neighbours to the left and the right were invisible, even from the flat's tiny balcony. It was designed for privacy, or the illusion of it. There was no one above them; the men joked that they were in the penthouse. Nothing but the best for Sajmir's girls, one of them said, and took the girl standing next to Drina into one of the other rooms, where she had screamed until, abruptly, she stopped. The flat below seemed to be unoccupied. Sometimes Drina lay with her cheek pressed against the dusty carpet and tried to hear sounds, but there was nothing.

She was surrounded by people, and alone. But she never felt quite as alone as when she was face to face with the men who paid for her body.

Mary Hearn was on the tenth floor of Murchison House, not quite below Drina's flat, and she was also sitting by the window, though Mary had a chair. It was a smaller place, ideal for a woman on her own, the man from the council had said. Her old house wasn't suitable, with all the stairs. Much better for her to move into a newly renovated flat in Murchison House, where there was a lift to take her up and down and she didn't have to worry about the roof leaking, or the garden. Mary had liked the garden in her old house. She had taken care of it, even though it was small. She had hung up birdfeeders and pulled out weeds and got on her knees to clip the small patch of lawn with the old shears that had been George's. The garden caught the sun in the morning and she had often gone to stand outside and lift her face up, her eyes closed, so the light could warm her. It felt like a blessing. It felt like a message from George, who had died thirteen years earlier after a short fight with the cancer that had ravaged him. He'd died quietly, while Mary sat by his bed. He'd said her name, and turned his head, and died. Upstairs. In the room where she slept. It still smelled of him – not in a bad way, but of Brylcreem and Shield, the soft green soap he'd preferred, and the warm smell that was him. His clothes hung in the wardrobe. He was still there, even though his body was gone. He was all around her.

She hadn't liked to say any of that to the man from the council, though. He was trying to help her. Keep her safe. Stop her from hurting herself on the stairs, or in the bathroom that wasn't really suitable for someone of her years, he said. His voice was very loud and he spoke slowly, as if she was foreign, although he was the one who had been born overseas somewhere. India, maybe. She hadn't liked to ask in case he was offended. People didn't like you to ask these days. They were all Londoners. But what if they wanted to talk about home? What if they thought you didn't care enough to ask? It was difficult, Mary thought. Impossible to do the right thing.

He was still talking, while she was thinking, words like bricks walling her into an unwanted new life. She tried to tell him she was happy, but he didn't listen. He was too busy telling her she could do her shopping, that there was a supermarket on the estate that would be much more convenient than the local shops she'd visited all her life, where the people behind the counters knew her and talked to her.

They'd been sorry to see her go, when she went. They'd signed a card. Her neighbours had too. Young Kevin from next door had helped her to pack up her belongings for the move. The big move, everyone called it.

She'd sat up the night before and wept. Howled like a baby. She didn't want to leave her house. She didn't want to leave her friends. She had been happy there, most of the time, except for George's illness.

But they were expecting her to go. She hadn't liked to upset anyone. They had gone to so much trouble with the cards and the send-off. Besides, the council were selling off the house, Young Kevin had told her – not so young any more with his bald head and three big children, but he would always be Young Kevin to her. They would make a lot of money from the little three-bedroom house she'd lived in since her marriage. People wanted them now. They paid silly money for them and then gutted them so they could spend more money doing them up. Young Kevin started talking about school catchment areas but it didn't mean anything to Mary. She and George hadn't had children, so they'd never needed to know about schools.

Eight months she'd been living in Murchison House. Eight months since she'd lost her home. Mary stared sightlessly at the streets below, not seeing any landmarks that made sense to her. From up here, all the roads looked the same. Eight months and the lift had been vandalised three times. The other lift wasn't working. It hadn't worked in all the time she'd lived there, and no one seemed surprised that it hadn't been fixed. Eight months. In eight months, Mary had been mugged twice – once in the corridor, once in the car park. No one had seen anything. The first time, she called the police. Someone came a few days later, a community officer. She took a statement and shook her head at Mary's bruises and said she would be back, but that was the last Mary had seen of her.

Two kind West Indian ladies picked her up the second time, the time in the car park, and took her to a different flat in a different building and gave her tea that was full of sugar and too hot to drink. Mary had tried, all the same. She didn't want to put them to too much trouble. Her wrist hurt and she felt dizzy and she wanted more than anything to go home, but home was the tenth floor of Murchison House now, not Greenlea Road. And all that was waiting for her in her flat was the television, the view over the streets that were suddenly strange to her, even though she'd lived in them all her life, and the crumbs on the ledge of the tiny balcony. She still tried to feed the birds – not that the sparrows and the blue tits and the finches from the old house could find their way to her now. A couple of battered pigeons visited now and then, hobbling on maimed feet. They were sullen, distrustful birds, their red-rimmed eyes fixed on Mary as they pecked at the food. They didn't like her any more than she liked them, but the pigeons were all she had, and she was all they had, so Mary kept shaking her crumbs out on the balcony, and sat, and watched for the flurry of wings that meant she wasn't alone.

On the tenth floor of Murchison House, three flats to the left of Mary Hearn, the Bellew family were eating. It wasn't dinner, exactly. The kids were back from school and they came home hungry, always. Carl Bellew liked to eat when he was watching television, too, and he was always watching television. He was a big man, heavy with muscle that was well covered in fat. His size was his best asset. You didn't need to be clever, or quick-witted, or even quick at moving when you were as big as Carl.

'Still sitting there? What a surprise.' His mother scuttled into the living room, her handbag over her arm like the Queen's.

He didn't look away from the screen. 'Leave it out.'

'You haven't moved all day. All day you've been sat there. What have you done with yourself? Watched telly, that's all.'

'Mum.' One word. A warning. Not that he'd ever hit her. He wouldn't dare. But the kids were lying on the floor watching the telly and even though they didn't seem to be listening, you never knew. He didn't want them asking questions. He didn't want them thinking he was weak, either.

'You're lazy, Carl,' Nina Bellew snapped. 'You need to get up and get going. Bring in some money for your family.'

Carl looked around, eyeing the room. Pictures on the walls. Curtains at the windows. Games consoles stacked up by the wide-screen television. 'We don't need any money.'

'Stupid.' She leaned over and jabbed her finger into the soft flesh that padded the back of his neck and bulked out the top of his shoulders. 'Stupid and lazy. When are you going to call round to number thirty-four?'

'I will, I said.'

'That was two days ago. They'll be wondering if you're ever going to come. Didn't realise you were so well off you could walk away from a couple of hundred quid, Carl. If you don't go, I will.'

'You?' He laughed halfway through lifting a can of Coke to his mouth. 'Yeah, all right. You can go.'

'I'm telling you—'

'And I heard.'

Nina turned, giving up on him for the time being, and screeched, 'Debbie?'

'What is it?' Debbie Bellew leaned into the living room, her face shiny with sweat from the heat of the kitchen, where she had been ironing in clouds of steam. 'Everything all right?'

'Only that I'm dying for a cup of tea, not that anyone cares.'

'Sorry, Mum.' Debbie called her mother-in-law 'Mum'

because she had no choice. Nina insisted. Nina Bellew couldn't have been less like Debbie's round, comfortable mother, who'd died twenty years earlier. Debbie missed her every day. She sometimes wondered if she would have married Carl, had her mother still been alive. She had been lonely, and scared, and young when Carl started to court her. He had seemed like the answer to her prayers.

Carl had been a mistake.

'Have we got any cakes?' Nina demanded.

'Cakes?'

'A sponge. Better for me teeth. I can't be doing with crisps or whatever it is they're eating.' She peered down at the children, who were having a low-level fight. It wasn't vicious or loud enough for anyone to feel they had to intervene, yet. 'You won't want your dinners,' Nina said loudly.

Nathan rolled over. 'What's for tea?'

'Fish and chips,' Debbie replied.

'From the chippy?'

'No, I'm making them.'

'Yuck.'

Nina kicked him, not gently. 'Enough of that. You're lucky to have anything to eat. When I was a girl we got one meal a day. By the evening your stomach'd be wondering if your throat had been cut.' She laughed, though no one else did. 'Sponge cake, Debbie. Got any?'

'No, sorry.' She felt in the pocket of her jeans for some coins. 'Nathan, you wouldn't run down to the shop—'

'Nooooo.' Nathan flopped face down on the floor, burying his head in his arms. 'I'm not going.'

Becky turned and grinned at her mother, waiting for

her brother to get in trouble. She was too young to go and she knew it.

Debbie couldn't face a fight. Not again. 'I'll go myself. I won't be long. I'll make you your tea when I get back, Mum. Unless—'

Carl hunched up one shoulder in a silent message that was at least as effective as his son's howling. No chance.

'I won't be long,' Debbie said again.

'It might take you a while,' Carl said. 'Lift's broken again.'

'Again? But they only fixed it last week.' It had been broken for so long, she'd thought she'd got used to the stairs. Strange how you resented it, though, when it was broken again. It was the disappointment, that was all. The hope and then the disappointment. Debbie had had just about enough of disappointment.

She hurried to the door and lifted her anorak off the hook, wondering if she needed to get anything else. It was no joke, going up and down all those stairs. On the other hand, it gave her time she wouldn't otherwise have. No one would expect her back for ages.

Debbie left the flat with an unusual feeling of freedom. On her own, for once. No one talking to her. No one asking her to do anything or get anything. No one inter-rupting her. She took her time about heading for the stairs. What was wrong with taking a few minutes for herself? Time to think.

Except that her thoughts weren't all that comforting, when they came. And even though she knew she had time, she couldn't enjoy it. She was going to have to run down and back up again to make up for the three or four minutes she'd stolen for herself.

Debbie started towards the stairwell, hurrying past a man who was walking up, his head bent, a cap pulled down low over his eyebrows. She didn't really notice him. Afterwards, she couldn't remember if he'd been carrying anything. She couldn't remember much at all.

In the flat opposite the lift, Melissa Pell listened. Her wooden spoon circled in the pan of baked beans, slowly, as she strained to hear over the hiss of the gas flame. The television was on in the living room, but it wasn't loud. She liked to be able to hear Thomas playing. She liked to be able to hear any other noises too. Anything unexpected. Anything unusual.

The trouble was that Murchison House was full of unexpected and unusual noises. Screaming and shouting in the middle of the night. Footsteps in the corridor, slow or fast. Doors slamming without warning. The hum and whine of the lift lumbering up and down, the judder as it stopped opposite her door. She was on edge all the time.

'Mummy!'

Melissa started, flicking some lurid orange sauce on the cooker. She went to get a cloth. 'You gave me a fright, poppet.'

'Sorry, Mummy.' He sounded it, too.

It was all wrong, Melissa thought, that a three-year-old should know to be really sorry for scaring his mother. She made an extra effort to sound cheerful as she rubbed at the ceramic hob. 'That's all right. I just wasn't expecting you to burst in here.'

'I didn't mean to burf.' The consonants always foxed

him when they came together. It was babyish and she hated correcting him. She wanted to keep him, her sweet-smelling delicate boy, just as he was, for ever.

'Burst,' she said clearly.

'Burft.'

That was as close as he was going to get, Melissa knew. She grinned at him and went to rinse out the cloth. The water rattled into the sink. She could hear his voice, but not what he was saying to her.

'Hold on a second.'

'Is it ready, Mummy?'

She turned just in time to see him grabbing the handle of the saucepan to tilt it towards him. The sauce was heaving with bubbles, hot as lava. She had no breath to scream at him, no time to inhale. She lunged across the small kitchen and grabbed the handle of the saucepan, pushing it onto one of the rings at the back, out of Thomas's reach, where it should have been all along.

It was as if her husband was in the room, leaning close to her, shouting in her ear. *What the hell do you think you're playing at? Careless, that's what you are. And a bad mother. Selfish, too. Do you really think this is the best place for the boy? Even if you can't stand me, don't you want what's best for him? Can't you even cook his dinner without putting him in danger?*

She was never going to get away from him. Even if she was hundreds of miles away from him, he was still there, in her head. She was never going to be free.

Thomas was looking wounded. 'You snatched it.'

'I had to, pet. It's hot.'

'You're not supposed to snatch things.'

'You could have been scalded.' Melissa felt like screaming at her small son, but she worked very hard not to take the rage and the stress and the fear out on him. She took a deep breath, willing her hands to stop trembling. 'It's dangerous to be in the kitchen when I'm cooking.'

'Sorry.' He said it very softly, his face flushed with the effort of not crying. He was a good child, a quiet and obedient child, and he wasn't used to getting in trouble.

'Come on,' Melissa said, putting the cloth down and holding out her hands. 'Come and have a cuddle.'

'On the sofa?' Thomas suggested, clambering into her arms.

'For a little while.' She held him tight as she walked through to the living room, his soft cheek against hers, his arms and legs wrapped tight around her as if he was a baby monkey.

Dinner could wait.

In the flat next door, just under Drina's bedroom, a man stood by the window. He was looking out, passing the time until *she* came. He wouldn't see her crossing the car park – the flat faced the wrong way. He could imagine it so easily though: her lean, tall figure, narrow-hipped and long-limbed. That elegant neck – her easy way of carrying herself. Dignity in every move she made.

The man winced. He'd asked her once what tribe she belonged to, a conversational misstep that had almost cost him everything.

'I was born in London, sweetheart.' Her voice had been heavy with disapproval, a rough edge to it to remind him

she'd grown up on the estate, not in Kensington, privileged like him. She'd fought her way out of the sheets
and sat on the edge of the bed, running her hands down
her arms over and over again. The movement reminded
him of an irritated cat grooming itself.

'I just mean originally.' He'd traced his fingers down
the length of her spine, his skin pale against her shining
darkness. She was all lines and exciting leanness, not frail
and sagging like Cressida.

'You don't need to worry about originally.' She'd
glanced back at him, full lips curving into a smile. 'You
only need to worry about now.'

And then she had turned so he could see her full, high
breasts and he had forgotten everything except her divine
body.

God, she was incredible. And his. His! He barely dared
to speak to girls like her, usually. For various reasons, it
wasn't a good idea. But there she was, offering herself to
him, not once but often.

As if she actually liked him – and liked the way he
worshipped her. How could he do anything else? She
was his goddess.

He'd have to remember to say that to her, he thought.
My goddess. She would like that.

His body was humming with excitement. Anticipation.
He paced up and down, unable to stand still. She was
all he thought about, all the time – her taste, her smell,
the places he was allowed to touch her and the way her
body felt when he did.

The smile on his face faded as the old, familiar,
unwanted thought came into his head, effective as a cold

shower. No one could know. No one could ever know. It would be a disaster.

It would be the end of everything.

A soft tap at the door brought him back to the present. He felt exquisitely aware of his body as he hurried to unlock the door – of his muscles moving, the clothes touching his skin, his heart thudding. He felt powerful. He felt younger than he had for years. He felt like a man.

His last thought, as he reached out to open the door, was that she was right. There was no point in thinking about the past, or the future. There was only now.

II

At twenty-one minutes past five on a cold Thursday evening, a small fire started in Murchison House. No one noticed, at first. The fire consumed everything it could reach, and as it spread it became stronger, hotter. It borrowed all of the oxygen it could find and paid it back in poisonous, choking black smoke. The smoke travelled faster than the flames, sliding through cracks and crevices, spreading to fill every space it found. And the heat of the fire travelled too, building in intensity until everything it touched burst into flames, and soon the small fire wasn't small any more and the smoke was streaming out of windows, under doors, filling the stairwells and flats, until it had taken control of Murchison House.

Carl Bellew didn't hear anything or smell anything or see anything suspicious. He was asleep in his chair. His mother, Nina, was in her bedroom down the hall from the living room, and she didn't notice anything either. It was seven-year-old Becky who heard the sound of some-thing falling – a muffled sound. A mysterious sound. Becky was sitting in an armchair, her feet hanging down over the side, watching television. The unexpected noise got her attention. She swung her legs down to the floor and stood up, walking past her brother and her sleeping father. She didn't say anything to either of them about the sound she had heard. She didn't say where she was going, or why. The kitchen door was closed and she thought nothing of it. The door to the bedroom she shared with her brother was closed and that wasn't unusual either. But when she touched it, the door was warm. Warm as blood. Becky reached her hand out to the door handle, which was metal. It was hot enough to sear her palm and she cried out in pain. The scream was loud enough to disturb her father.

'What's going on?' he called. He was still half-asleep and grouchy as a hibernating bear. It wasn't a good idea to wake him up at the best of times.

'I'm all right,' Becky shouted back, pulling her sleeve down over her hand to protect it. She put her covered hand on the door handle and turned it, then pushed the door open.

And the fire came to meet her.

Debbie Bellew was crossing the car park, carrying a plastic shopping bag, when she heard a shout. Shouts were normal on the Maudling Estate but it was always wise to check it was nothing to do with you. Debbie glanced behind her and saw a man shading his eyes, pointing up at the tower block opposite him. Murchison House. Debbie turned to see what he was looking at. It took her a second to make sense of the fact that the top of the tower had changed shape, widened, swelled. Against the darkening sky, black smoke made parts of the building disappear. It was flowing out of windows on the west side of the tower, and with every second that passed the smoke seemed to move faster, finding new places to escape.

The handles of the plastic bag slipped through her fingers and fell on the tarmac. By the time the sponge cake slid onto the ground, Debbie was already gone, sprinting towards the base of Murchison House, knowing that she was too late. Nothing on earth could have stopped her.

Melissa Pell heard a smoke alarm going off – not in her flat, somewhere else – and one part of her brain considered it, then dismissed it. It was teatime. People were cooking. People burned food. She'd done it herself, many a time.

She sniffed. She could smell something in the air, something acrid. Smoke. Actual smoke. That was dinner in the bin, she thought. No salvaging it.

'Shit!' She jumped up off the sofa, tipping her son off her lap onto the floor.

'Mummy,' Thomas protested as she rushed to the kitchen. She could see it in her mind's eye: the gas flame flickering, the cloth she'd tossed to one side carelessly. Charring and then burning, the flames rising higher and higher.

But the kitchen was fine. The gas was off. The cloth was nowhere near the cooker. Everything was just the same as normal. Melissa stood for a second, letting her heart rate drop. Everything was all right. There was no reason to panic. Panic was a habit. She needed to let it go. She needed to allow herself to believe that she and Thomas were safe at last.

Melissa turned to go back to her son. She'd moved two steps towards him when her smoke alarm began to chirp.

Mary Hearn put the radio on, for company, and dozed through the afternoon play. She wasn't quite asleep but she wasn't awake either. The words got jumbled up and the plot didn't seem to make any sense. Maybe that was her own fault, though, she thought. Maybe she was missing the point. She didn't usually nap so late in the day but she was tired, and she let herself drift, thinking about George.

Drina saw the smoke first. She stood up and pressed her face against the cold glass of the window, peering down. It was belching out of the building on the floor below. The wind caught it and blew it across Drina's view, blotting out London below her. The window frame rattled and she caught the smell of the smoke. It was in the room with her. She stumbled away from the glass and ran to the door, shouting in English and in her own language as she hurried into the dingy living room. The other two girls came out of their room. One was sleepy and yawning, the other hobbling on her heels with cotton wool wedged between her toes. Her toenails were dark red, like drops of blood. She was dark-skinned, African, very young.

'What is it? What's wrong?'

'There's a fire. We have to get out.' Drina ran to the living room window, seeing only darkness where there should have been miles of orange streetlights. 'Are you listening, you bastards? You have to let us out. Unlock the door.'

'They won't come,' the African girl said.

'They have to.' Drina ran to hammer on the door. 'Otherwise we'll be rescued. If they want to keep us, they have to keep us alive.'

She choked a little on the last word. Smoke was catching the back of her throat. Behind her, the other girl started to cough, muttering something in Russian as she clamped a hand over her mouth and nose. Drina spoke some Russian – she'd learned it in Israel, the first place she'd stopped on her journey from her home. She knew enough to be able to translate it for herself.

Dear God, we are going to die.

Carl Bellew gathered up his daughter and his phone, then yelled to his mother to collect every bit of jewellery he owned: watches, rings, heavy necklaces and bracelets. Debbie's jewellery was worthless but his was real gold, real diamonds. Nathan was snivelling with fear and shock and Carl shoved him towards the door.

'Get a move on.'

'Put that over your mouth and nose.' Nina handed him a t-shirt soaked in water. 'Stay low down when we go outside the door.'

Carl looked down at her, worried. 'Ready, Mum?'

'Ready.' She hefted her handbag on her arm, looking small and spindly but somehow unbreakable. 'We'll go straight down the stairs. Easy peasy.'

*

'So we need to go down the stairs very quickly but not running, darling, do you understand?' Melissa picked up the bag she kept by the door, not allowing herself to stop and check that it still contained the money, the passports, the credit cards, the birth certificates, addresses and phone numbers. She'd put them all in there. She'd checked a hundred times.

She had been ready to run. But not from a fire.

Thomas's face was pink, his bottom lip turned down. He held on to Captain Bunbun. 'I'm scared.'

'I know, I do, but you can't be scared now. We have to go. We're going to crawl until we get to the stairs and then we're going to hold on to the handrail and walk down, but not stopping for anything, and if we see a fireman like Fireman Sam we'll ask him to help us.'

'Fireman Sam?' He looked around, his eyes vacant, tuning her out. It was what he did when he was scared or uncertain, and it worried the hell out of her.

'Come on, Thomas.' She snatched up his coat. No time to look for hers. Keys: yes, in case they had to come back, if it was too bad outside. People died in fires because they left their hotel rooms or their flats and couldn't get back in. Escaping could be more dangerous than staying. But Melissa had learned the hard way about staying where she was. The devil you knew could be worse than any trouble you could find elsewhere.

'Just keep moving,' she said to her son. 'Don't stop for anything. Don't wait for me if I get held up. Go down to the bottom of the stairs and go outside and I'll find you in the car park.'

'But I want to stay with you, Mummy.'

'I'll be right behind you. If you can't see me, just wait for me outside. I'll be there.' She knelt down and hugged him, a quick, hard embrace, pressing his head into her neck. 'What's your name?' she whispered.

The answer came back straight away. 'Sam.'

'Sam what?'

'Sam Hathaway.'

'Good boy.' Melissa made herself stand, her knees trembling, and opened the front door a crack. There was no one in the corridor. She ushered Thomas out in front of her, keeping a hand on him, and the two of them ran towards the door that led to the stairs.

She lifted her head off the pillow. 'Did you hear that?'

'It's nothing.' He didn't hear anything, didn't care. 'You're so beautiful.'

'Shut up.' She put a hand on his chest, pushing him away. 'I heard something.'

'It's nothing. Forget it.'

She wouldn't. She got up and walked through the bedroom, disappearing into the living room. He followed reluctantly, and found her standing at the front door, listening. 'There's something going on out there.'

There were noises from outside, footsteps and swearing and an occasional scream. A party getting started, he thought, or an argument spilling over into the estate's grim public spaces. 'Come back to bed.'

'I'm going to look.'

'Don't open the fucking door, you stupid bitch – not with people outside. If I've told you once . . .' He moved fast to stop her and she turned and hit him on the jaw, a punch that had plenty of power behind it. He reeled back, losing his balance, falling. He clutched his face. 'Jesus fucking Christ.'

'I don't like this. I'm going.' She stepped over him, picking up her clothes from the floor. She started to wriggle into them at speed, shoving her underwear into her handbag. She left her boots unzipped. They jangled as she strode past him on her way to the door. He was still lying where he'd fallen. She stopped.

'You all right?'

'No, I'm not. You hit me.' He sounded petulant and he knew it. She tossed her head.

'Well, you rushed me. I've warned you about that before.' A double blink, very fast. 'Seriously, you need to get dressed and get out of here. There's something weird going on.'

'I can't leave if there are people in the corridor. Especially not with my face like this.'

'Give me strength,' she said. Then, more gently, 'Don't leave it too long, will you?'

He shook his head.

'Will I see you soon?'

'I don't know.' He wanted to punish her, to make her feel as bad as he felt. Maybe she didn't care about him at all. He'd have to get back at her some other way. 'I'm not giving you anything for today.'

A shrug. 'Suit yourself. Not as if you got to do anything, is it?'

He didn't answer her. He watched her open the door and disappear through it. Almost immediately, she poked her head back in.

'It's full of smoke out here. I think there's a fire.'

'*Shit*. Go on, get out of here.' He waved her on irritably, getting to his feet as she closed the door. He wasn't worried about the fire. It was the repercussions that worried him. If there was a fire, that meant one thing: London Fire Brigade responding with all the weight of officialdom, which meant form-filling, which would involve answering awkward questions. He didn't want to explain why he was on the Maudling Estate in the first place, let alone in that flat.

As for the fire, well, he had to approach it logically. He couldn't be found in the flat so he had to get out. He had to get out without being seen. He had to avoid, at all costs, a scandal.

He didn't start to be afraid for his life until it was much too late to save it.

Chapter 1

When my phone rang I knew it was bad news, but there was nothing remarkable about that. If your business is bad news, some part of you is always waiting for the phone to ring.

And for once, it was ringing before I had got as far as going to bed. No dreams to shatter. Small mercies. I checked the time – ten past eleven – before I answered it.

'Kerrigan.'

'Have you been watching the news?' Una Burt's voice filled my head and I winced, holding the phone a little bit further from my ear than I would usually.

'No.' I glanced at the television and its fine layer of dust. I had no idea where the remote control was. I hadn't used it for weeks. 'What's up?'

'A fire on the Maudling Estate.'

It felt as if I'd run head first into a wall. I took a second to respond. 'Fatalities?'

'Three, so far. It took out the top two floors of one of the blocks. Gutted them completely. The floors below aren't all that much better.'

'Arson?'

'Possibly. There's a fire investigator floating around here somewhere. He can tell us more.'

I held back a sigh. Una Burt was a Chief Inspector, but she was acting up, running the team in place of my real boss, Superintendent Charles Godley, who was on indefinite leave. That meant DCI Burt was in charge. You queried her actions at your peril, as I had found out before. Still, it was worth asking why she was calling me at that hour of the night on my day off.

Delicately.

'Is there a particular reason for us to be involved with the investigation?'

'Of course, or I wouldn't be calling you.' Offence taken. Great.

'Sorry. It's just that we're not the closest Homicide team.' *And we're already trying to cope with the extra work you've insisted we can handle because* you *can't say no to anyone.* Godley's team usually handled the most complex and sensitive investigations that came to the Met. Since Una Burt had started running the team, we'd taken on a lot more work than usual, and much of it was run-of-the-mill. It was as if she couldn't bring herself to say no when our help was requested. She liked feeling important and we were close to being overwhelmed.

'It's not likely to be a straightforward investigation. Not when one of the fatalities is very well known. Not when it isn't clear how he died.'

'Who?'

Una's voice was muffled, as if she was covering her

mouth so no one around her could lip-read what she was saying. 'Geoff Armstrong.'

'The MP?' The far-right, immigrant-hating, welfare-criticising MP, to be specific.

'Exactly.'

Which meant that the investigation was likely to be both sensitive and complex, I conceded, and felt the first twinge of interest. 'But what was he doing there? It's hardly his natural habitat. Not much point in him canvassing for support on an estate that's largely social housing. There aren't all that many high-earning conservatives on the Maudling Estate, I'm willing to bet.'

'Yes, these and other questions need answers – which is why I would like you to come straight here. I've already contacted DI Derwent. He says he'll pick you up.'

'Really?' I stared into space. 'There's no need. I can get there myself.'

'I don't care if you take a flying carpet to get here,' Una Burt snapped. 'Just hurry up.'

She was gone. I weighed the phone in my hand. *Worth a try.*

No need to collect me. I'll see you there.

I sent the message, put the phone down on the coffee table and stood up. It vibrated.

Already here. Buzz me in.

Great.

Against my better judgement I let him into the building. I had about thirty seconds before he arrived at the door, I thought, and tried to decide where to start. I looked around, feeling helpless. There was so much to do, and no time to do it. I drifted into the bathroom, where the mirror confirmed my worst fears. I stopped looking at myself in it and concentrated on squirting toothpaste on the brush. If I was brushing my teeth, at least I wouldn't have to talk to him.

Unfortunately, nothing would stop him talking to me.

A volley of knocking on the door. I went and opened it, but I checked the view through the peephole first. These were the rules I lived by. Never open a door without knowing who's on the other side of it. Never park somewhere dark and deserted. Never get into the car without checking the back seat and the boot. Know who's walking behind you. Know who's driving behind you. Know where you're going. Never relax. Never forget there's someone watching you.

They were rules that had kept me alive, so far, but they made me feel as if I was dying a little more every day. I couldn't ever allow myself to forget I was a target for someone else's obsession. A creep named Chris Swain had been hunting me for years and he wouldn't give up until I gave in to him.

And that was never, ever going to happen.

'What happened to you?' Derwent demanded, shouldering his way in with all the finesse of someone on a dawn raid. 'You look like hell.'

'Mmph,' I said. *I missed you too.*

He closed the door. We both looked down at the mountain of junk mail that had built up over the two months I'd been living alone.

'God almighty, Kerrigan, you could tidy up occasionally.'

'I'm busy,' I said through the toothpaste. 'I have better things to do.'

'Like what?' He strode past me to the sitting room, where he whistled. 'I hadn't realised Rob was the tidy one. This place is a pigsty.'

I took the toothbrush out of my mouth. 'Shut up.'

'Didn't catch that.'

I raised a middle finger, and my eyebrows. Derwent grinned. There wasn't much he enjoyed more than getting a reaction from me. He stood in the middle of the living room and turned, taking in far more than I would have liked him to. The bin, overflowing. Untouched saucepans hanging in a neat row. Crumbs on the counter. Takeaway cartons stacked by the sink. Papers everywhere. My laptop, open on the sofa. The room said, more loudly than I could: *I can't be bothered.* His eyes came back to me.

'Nice outfit.'

I looked down at myself and shrugged. Leggings and an old t-shirt of Rob's. It wasn't haute couture, but they were real clothes, not just pyjamas. I counted that as a victory.

'Did you even leave the flat today?'

I nodded vigorously. A trip to the corner shop counted as leaving the flat. I must have been out for all of five minutes.

'Did you eat anything?'

Another nod. I was sure I had. I couldn't quite remember what.

'For God's sake, Kerrigan, I can't talk to you like this.'

I shrugged again. *That was basically my plan.*

30

Derwent's expression darkened. 'Okay. Try this. You have ten minutes to get ready. If you're not ready, you're coming with me anyway. You can explain to DCI Burt why you're inappropriately dressed at a crime scene.'

I rolled my eyes but headed back to the bathroom.

'And do something about your hair,' Derwent yelled after me.

In nine minutes and 59 seconds precisely I walked into the living room, suited, booted and with my hair tamed into a bun. Derwent was leaning against the kitchen counter, his hands in his pockets.

'That's better.'

'I'm glad you think so.'

'You need make-up.'

'No one *needs* make-up,' I snapped. 'Especially not at a crime scene.'

'*You* need make-up. Assuming you want to look human.'

'Oh, great, thank you.'

'Halloween was last month.'

'I'm aware of that.'

'So the zombie look isn't really appropriate.'

I opened my mouth to answer him and then shut it again. I held myself very still. *Do not throw up. Do NOT throw up.*

'Kerrigan.'

I ignored him, staring at the floor until the wave of nausea receded. When I looked back at Derwent, the mocking smirk had disappeared. 'Are you all right?'

'Fine.'

'Sure?'

'Absolutely,' I said, trying to sound as if I meant it. Then I frowned. Something was different. 'Did you tidy up?'

'A bit.'

'You emptied the bin,' I said slowly. 'And you did the washing-up.'

'And got rid of the junk mail in the hall, and threw out the food in the fridge that was actually rotting, and plugged in your computer.'

If it had been anyone other than Derwent who tidied up, I'd have been grateful. But Derwent was the king of ulterior motives.

'My computer,' I said. 'Why did you even touch my computer?'

'You only had five per cent of your battery life left.' Derwent shook his head. 'I know you like living on the edge but that's just unnecessary.'

'You must have been looking at it,' I said, fighting to stay calm. 'Why were you looking at it?'

He levered himself off the counter and came towards me, crowding me, getting into my face. I'd seen him do it hundreds of times. It wasn't even the first time he'd done it to me. It was one of Derwent's favourite interrogation techniques. 'What's wrong, Kerrigan? Something to hide?'

'Nothing to hide. I'm entitled to my privacy, though. Sir.'

A minute narrowing of his eyes told me he'd registered the last word and its implications. *You are my boss. You are in my home. Your behaviour is, as usual, inappropriate and*

I have had enough of it for the time being. I held his gaze, my expression stony.

'I'm just looking out for you.' His voice was soft, which meant precisely nothing. Derwent's temper was volcanic, legendarily so, but he had enough control over it, and himself, to shout only when he needed to. And since we were inches apart, shouting would have been excessive.

'You don't need to look out for me.'

'Someone should.'

'I can manage,' I said. 'I *am* managing. So stop patronising me.'

He didn't move for a long moment. His expression was unreadable, at least to me. Then, to my enormous relief, he turned away. 'I was going to carry the bin bag down for you. But if that's too patronising you can carry it yourself.'

I rolled my eyes at his back. 'Thanks.'

He wouldn't have missed the sarcasm in my voice, but he didn't look back. 'Come on, then. Let's go.'

Chapter 2

It didn't take long to get to the Maudling Estate – at least, not the way Derwent drove. It wasn't the first time we'd been there in the middle of the night and I couldn't suppress a shiver at the memory of another visit, a couple of months earlier.

'All too familiar,' Derwent said, echoing my thoughts. He was trying to find a place to leave the car on the street nearby. There was no point in trying to get into the car park at the centre of the estate. The blue lights from police cars, ambulances and fire engines flared on the buildings, reflecting on the windows. Countless people milled about, apparently aimlessly, evacuees from the buildings or just curious onlookers. Inevitably the media were there, TV reporters clutching microphones, caught in a halo of white light from their cameras. Derwent pulled in at the end of a row of vans with satellite dishes mounted on the top.

'As if they have a right to be here,' he growled. 'You know they think they're important. All they're doing is getting in the way.'

'They're reporting the news.'

'They don't know any news. They haven't been told anything yet.'

'They still need to cover the story.'

'A bloody great building caught fire and no one knows why yet. That's the story.'

'And when they hear about Armstrong?'

Derwent grimaced. 'Then life won't be worth living. Come on. At least this time we're not going to a van full of dead coppers.'

'That's something, I suppose.' I got out of the car and looked up at the flats, to identify the tower that had burned. It was easy to see where the fire had been – black shadows clouded around the windows on the top floors and smoke was still seeping out, dark against the orange-tinted clouds that passed for a night sky. Most of the windows were open or broken, holes in the building that reminded me of wounds. The remains of curtains fluttered inside and out, caught by the breeze that was stronger the higher you went. The movement was eerie. I couldn't stop myself from seeing it as people waving, crying for help, but I knew the fire brigade would have rescued anyone up there by now. Water stained the concrete all the way down the outside of the tower. The whole building was glowing eerily, the emergency lighting shining with a greyish glare. It was a long way from the top of the tower to the ground. The remarkable thing wasn't that three people had died. It was incredible that *only* three people had died.

When Derwent spoke, I jumped. I hadn't realised he was standing right beside me.

'All right, Kerrigan?'

'Fine.'

'It's just – well, this isn't your favourite place, is it? Not after what happened here.'

'I haven't even thought about it,' I lied. It was on the Maudling Estate that I'd been trapped for ten minutes in a stairwell with four teenage boys who wanted to hurt me, at the very least. Only ten minutes – but it had changed the course of my life. It had crossed my mind, once or twice.

Derwent nodded. 'Well, I have been thinking about it. And if you see any of the little shitbags who scared you, I want to know about it.'

'Forget it,' I said lightly. 'I have.'

He shook his head. 'Not convincing.'

'I'll have to try harder.'

'You do that.' He stepped back and let me walk ahead of him. 'Don't worry, Kerrigan. I'll be right behind you.'

It was typical of Derwent that it sounded more like a threat than reassurance. I hunched my shoulders against the prickling unease that made me want to run away and stalked into the Maudling Estate ahead of him, hoping I looked as if I didn't know what fear was.

The first person I saw was Una Burt, deep in conversation with two men. One wore the black and yellow London Fire Brigade uniform. He carried a yellow helmet in one hand and sweat had plastered his hair to his head. He was middle-aged, obviously senior and just as obviously fed up to be talking to Una Burt. I could imagine he had more important things to do with his time, like managing the teams of firefighters who were swarming through the building. The other man was in a blue boiler suit with Fire Investigation written across the back and had a white hard hat on his head. Burt was nodding as he spoke. She glanced over his shoulder and noticed us. To say she looked pleased would be an exaggeration but she beckoned us over. The senior firefighter took the opportunity to disappear while Burt was distracted.

'Here are two more of my team, at last. DI Josh Derwent, DC Maeve Kerrigan, this is Andrew Harper, the fire investigator.'

Harper was tall, with very blue eyes under his white hard hat and a weathered complexion. He nodded to us, then turned back to Una Burt.

'So I can't take you up to the affected areas yet – it's too hot and the structure could be unstable. The firefighters are still damping the building down in case the fire flares up again, and the rescue operation hasn't officially ended. It's too risky to have any untrained personnel up there, for everyone's sake.'

'I understand that. Let us know when you can show us the scenes. As soon as possible, obviously.'

'Do we know if it was an accident or deliberate?' Derwent asked.

'Not yet. I'll need to speak to the survivors. It could have been accidental.' He sounded slightly dubious, though, and Derwent pounced.

'But your instinct says it was deliberate.'

'I don't rely on instinct. I'll do a thorough investigation and go from there.' Harper had a slow way of speaking, measured and unflappable, like an air-traffic controller. It was impossible to imagine him losing his temper, even with Derwent. 'But I will say this. There are two stairwells in these towers, one on the outside of the building largely enclosed in concrete and one inside, running up the centre of the tower by the lift shafts. It seems the fire started on the tenth floor. It blocked off access to the external stair-well. The lifts were both out of order. The residents only had one way out, and that was the internal stairwell which was basically acting as a chimney. It was full of smoke and hot air. Anyone who escaped this fire from the tenth or the eleventh floor got very lucky indeed.'

'So if it *was* deliberate,' I said, 'it was meant to kill.'

'If it was.' Harper tilted his head back to look up. 'I'm going to have a look at how they're getting on up there. The sooner I can get in and get started, the better.'

'You can come with me,' Una Burt said to us. 'The one good thing about this investigation is that we have access to one of the bodies already, since Mr Armstrong was kind enough to meet his end outside the tower block.'

'How?' I asked, hurrying to follow her as she barrelled through the crowds surrounding the cordon near the tower.

'Fell, jumped, pushed. Take your pick.' She ducked under the tape and carried on around the side of the building, through a gate, to an area that was obviously where the residents' rubbish ended up. Huge red and blue wheelie bins filled a yard where the ground was disturbingly slick under foot. Half of the bins were so full the plastic lids wouldn't close properly. The place smelled strongly of rotting food and dirty nappies.

In one corner, a familiar figure was standing on a step ladder, taking a photograph of the top of a bin with exquisite care. Arc lights shone on the scene, and a few other people, anonymous in hooded white suits, stood around waiting for the photographer to finish. Kev Cox lowered the camera and began to climb down, stocky in his white overalls but sure-footed.

'Hi, Maeve.' He waved at me. 'This is a bit of fun, isn't it?'

'If you say so.' I was staring at the shattered figure draped over the bin, the body twisted and broken by the fall. The bin lid had splintered from the impact. He was soaked in blood, his head tipped back and misshapen where the back of it had split open. His eye sockets were distorted, his nose and jaw askew. It was hard to work back to how he might have looked in life. In death, he resembled something that had stepped out of a medieval painting of hell.

'Is that Armstrong?' Derwent asked.

One of the white-suited figures stepped forward, pushed the hood back and revealed itself to be the pathologist, Dr Early. She had met Derwent before, and looked appropriately wary. 'We don't have a formal ID yet. To be honest, the level of damage means it's hard to say for certain just on visuals. We'll check the dental records, or fingerprints if they're on file. We should be able to get a sample of his DNA quite easily from his home so we can double-check it.'

'So why do you think it's him?'

She blushed but held her own. 'Because there was an anonymous tip-off that he was in the flats. Someone phoned 999 and mentioned him specifically. He was on the tenth floor, they said, but they didn't give a flat number. The firefighters didn't find him until one of them looked out of a window.'

Derwent pointed at the ladder. 'Can I take a look?'

'Be my guest. But don't touch him.'

That earned the pathologist a glare. Derwent climbed up so he was looking down on the body. It was clad in grey suit trousers and a shirt that had once been white. There was a shoe on the left foot, but the right had a torn sock on it. There was something particularly pathetic about the pale foot sticking out over the edge of the bin. It looked undignified and vulnerable. Derwent leaned in, peering intently.

'What do you think?' Una Burt demanded.

'Could be him. Could be someone else.' Derwent straightened, his phone in his hand. 'No wallet?'

'No wallet,' the pathologist confirmed. 'No ID. Two hundred pounds in twenties in his back pocket.'

'If robbery was a motive for killing him – if his wallet was stolen and he was pushed out of the building – they'd have taken the cash as well,' Derwent said, tapping at his phone.

'If they knew about it,' I pointed out. 'You might assume all the money was in his wallet, if you found that first.'

'Or his wallet could have been stolen after he fell,' Burt said.

'But what about the two hundred quid?'

'It was . . . messy.' Dr Early wrinkled her nose. 'I don't think you'd have gone looking for it in his back pocket. And even if you found it, you wouldn't have taken it. The notes are saturated.'

'What are you doing?' Una Burt asked Derwent, who was still concentrating on his phone.

Please don't say you're checking Tinder, I thought. *For my sake and yours, don't wind her up.*

'Looking for a picture of Armstrong.' Derwent jumped down and held out the phone. 'He's not looking quite as smart now, but that's the same watch.'

It was a heavy gold watch with a brown leather strap. The glass had shattered in the fall, but it was recognisably the watch in the photograph Derwent had found. Armstrong was grinning, his face shiny in the camera flash. He looked sleek and well fed and oblivious to his fate.

'Car keys? Phone?' I asked.

'We found a BMW key fob here.' Dr Early pointed to a marker a few feet away from the bin. 'It could have fallen out of his pocket on the way down.'

'I've run him through the PNC,' Una Burt said. 'He's the registered owner of a 7 Series BMW saloon. I've circulated the details. If it's parked near here, we'll find it.'

Derwent frowned. 'You've checked the car park.'

'No.' She waited a beat so he could jump to the wrong conclusion, then gave him a tight little smile. 'I told someone else to check it. No 7 Series BMWs. No BMWs at all.'

'This wasn't an official visit,' I said. 'He was trying to fly below the radar. Let's say he wasn't robbed. Let's say he chose to jump. He got rid of his ID if he was carrying any. And he dumped his phone.'

'Or it's upstairs in the flat along with his ID,' Derwent said.

'I'll tell the firefighters to keep their eyes peeled for his personal effects,' Burt said, as if she was in charge of them too. 'We can have a look when it's safe for the SOCOs to go in. At the moment we don't even know which flat he was in before he jumped. I'd like to know that. I think it would help a lot.'

'I know a trick or two about that,' Kev Cox said amiably. 'We can work back from here and trace the route he took down the side of the building.'

'How?' Burt asked.

'When you fall out of a building, even if you jump, it's hard to get completely clear.' Kev nodded at the body. 'The reason he looks so battered is because he bounced off the concrete a few times on the way down. If we have a good look on the balconies and protruding detailing, we should find his blood and fragments of skin or bits of muscle. I'll get a couple of lads to abseil down the side and we'll work out where he started off.'

'Lovely.' Una Burt's face was pale. I fought another wave of nausea, tipping my head back to look up at the building as if I was interested in seeing the blood trail. The air was full of smoke, and even though the night was cold the smell from the bins was, briefly, over-whelming. I stepped back, away from the crowd of people around Armstrong's body, into the shadows. It was a long way from the tenth floor to the ground. I imagined him deciding to jump, choosing what he took with him. Hiding as much as he could about what he had been doing there. Keeping secrets, even in death.

I didn't think we'd find ID and his phone in the flat. I didn't think he was that stupid.

I walked away from the building towards the other side of the yard, staying in line with the bin where the body had landed. A spindly hedge grew there, along the boundary between the estate and the neighbouring industrial units. The fence behind it was metal and topped with spikes. I pulled on a pair of blue gloves and took out my torch. Crouching, I moved along the boundary, searching for a flash of metal or a glint of glass.

'What are you doing?' Una Burt was right behind me.

'If he jumped, I think he threw his phone away first.'

'Why?'

'I can't imagine him going anywhere without a phone, can you? He'd have needed it to keep in touch with whatever was going on at Westminster, especially if he wasn't supposed to be here. You can't be uncontactable in his position. He came here with cash and his car key. Maybe he had his wallet – maybe not. But the phone would have given him away.'

'It could have been stolen too.'

Something on the edge of the torch's beam flashed a reflection. It was on the other side of the fence. The casing for an iPhone. I looked further, seeing the screen, electronic components, all shattered and scattered across a wide area.

'Kev?'

He came trotting across.

'Can you send someone to collect this phone and all the bits? In case they belong to our guy?'

'Will do.' He nudged my shoulder with a knee. 'Good thinking.'

'I learned from the best.' I straightened. 'Make sure they look for the SIM card. It might not be with the rest of the phone. He might have disposed of it separately.'

'If it's here, we'll find it.' Kev hurried back to the body, his suit rustling.

'He was about to die,' Una Burt said. 'He would have known he couldn't survive the fall. Do you really think he was that concerned about keeping a secret?'

'I do. He was so concerned about it, he was prepared to die for it.'

'So we'd better find out what it was.'

I nodded. 'As soon as we can.'

Chapter 3

It was a long, cold wait until the firefighters were prepared to allow us into Murchison House. I stood in the car park, huddled in my coat, trying not to scan the crowd for the faces of the boys who'd attacked me on my previous visit. They probably wouldn't recognise me again, not with my hair tied back and a police jacket in place of the long overcoat I'd been wearing the last time. I thought I'd remember them, though. I thought I might remember them for ever.

The other thing I was trying not to think about was the person who I had to assume was watching me, the man who had inserted himself into my nightmares: Chris Swain. He was in my thoughts in public places and wherever I called home. He'd shown me he could reach me anywhere, even if I tried to hide. He'd taught me there was no such thing as privacy. He'd made me aware that safety was an illusion. He'd promised me a visit, two months earlier, because my boyfriend had disappeared and I was on my own. I was still waiting. I knew he'd come.

A promise was a promise.

'Do you think he's watching?'

The question echoed my thoughts so closely that I jumped. 'Who?'

'The person who set the fire.' Liv Bowen frowned at me. 'Who else?'

'No one.' I nodded to where Mal Upton was standing with a video camera, unobtrusively filming the people who were still watching, still enthralled, even though it was two in the morning. 'If there's an arsonist here, we'll get him on film.'

'With any luck.' Liv looked up at the towers that loomed over us. 'Too many places to hide, though. You'd get a good view from any of these. If he's watching he doesn't need to show himself.'

'From what I understand that's part of the fun. They like to get as close as possible. Smell the smoke. See the bodies.'

Liv shuddered. She was pale and thinner than usual, not quite back to her old self, even if she was finally at work after extensive sick leave. Her hair was neatly plaited, her coat immaculate. She looked as if she was in control, but there was something different about her – a fragility that hadn't been there before. I recognised it like an old friend: fear.

'Are you all right?' I asked.

'Are *you*? You look like death warmed over.'

'To think I missed you.' I shook my head.

She handed me a steaming cup of tea. 'I thought you might need this.'

'And all is forgiven.' I held the cup in both hands, warming them. 'Seriously, this isn't too much for you, is it?'

'Not so far.' She put a hand to her stomach. It was a habit with her now, I'd noticed, whenever she thought about the knife wound that had almost ended her life, not to mention her career. When she felt threatened. When she felt uneasy. It was quite a giveaway, once you knew what it meant – a tell, the gamblers called it. I'd been meaning to mention it to her. In our job, giving information away could be a liability.

But when her confidence was so fragile, criticising her felt wrong. It felt like the kind of thing Derwent would do.

Derwent would say it was for her own good, that a weak member of the team put us all in danger. Derwent would say she should find a job in a quieter part of the Met – missing persons, maybe, or working on cold cases. Fraud. Following paper trails, not killers. And it wouldn't be so bad, maybe, if the biggest hazard you faced every day was a paper cut.

I still couldn't do it. I knew Liv well enough to believe she would step aside if she wasn't happy with her work on the murder team. She was her own fiercest critic. I knew her partner, Joanne, and she was a police officer too. She would see the signs if Liv began to crack up. So all in all, there was no need for me to intervene.

Especially since I needed Liv's presence more than ever. She was the best friend I had made in the job. She was reasonable where Derwent was perverse, supportive when he was undermining me. I had missed her very badly when she was on leave. I still hadn't told her all the details of how my life had managed to come apart so spectacularly in such a short space of time. All she knew was that Rob, my handsome, funny, clever boyfriend, had gone on leave after his colleague was killed. She knew that we weren't in touch, but she didn't know why.

The funny thing was, neither did I. I'd have spoken to him, if he'd contacted me. I'd have forgiven him if he asked me to. I'd forgiven him already, in fact.

I still hadn't quite forgiven myself, but that was another story.

'Who are you working with on this one?' Liv asked.

'Derwent.'

Her eyebrows went up. 'Does Una Burt know?'

'It was her idea. She sent him to collect me.'

'I thought she wanted you to stay away from him.'

'So did I.' I'd been thinking about that, off and on. Almost the first thing Una Burt had done on taking over the team was to make a point of telling me I wouldn't be working with Derwent. We were too close, she thought. He impaired my judgement. He slowed me down.

Which, translated into plain English, was: *you keep him on the straight and narrow but I want to get rid of him, so let's see what happens if you're not holding him back from self-destruction.*

To everyone's surprise, not least mine, Derwent had behaved impeccably since Una Burt took over. I wasn't convinced he'd changed, or that he was capable of changing. To me it felt like the false, uneasy peace that comes after a war has been declared, before the first battle. He wasn't ready to fight her yet, but it was only a matter of time.

I looked for Derwent in the crowd and found him almost immediately. He took up a lot of space, somehow, and it wasn't that he was tall or broad-shouldered, although he was both. Even where people were gathered close together, he stood apart. Instinctively, everyone around him gave him plenty of room. Maybe it was the scowl that put people off standing near him, or some subliminal aware-ness of the rage that burned within him. He was alone, as he tended to be these days. No one on the team could have failed to notice that Una Burt had it in for him. Being too friendly with Derwent was a bad career move.

I was never going to be friends with him, but I couldn't stand to see him on his own.

'He's got his brooding face on,' I said. 'I'd better see if he wants me to do anything.'

Liv grinned. 'You complain about him but you love him really.'

'No, I don't.'

'Yeah, you do.'

I shook my head at her but I was smiling as I went over to him. The past two months had been crushingly dull, even though I'd been busier than ever before. Una Burt had made sure I did more than my share of legwork, the routine inquiries that involved endless phone calls and knocking on doors. My colleagues had been pleasant, considerate and professional; three words I'd never applied to Derwent. But there was something bracing about working with him, in spite of the stroppiness and the sulking. There weren't many people who could make you feel as if you'd launched yourself down a set of rapids just by saying hello.

'Hi.' I made myself sound chirpy. Derwent reacted to chirpiness the way most people reacted to stinging nettles. I got a grunt in response.

I cast about for a neutral subject. 'Cold, isn't it?'

'It's the middle of the night and it's November. It should be cold. Where did you get that?' He was eyeing my tea.

'Liv gave it to me.'

He took the cup out of my hand. 'She must have meant it for me.'

'I wasn't drinking it anyway.'

Derwent's eyebrows twitched together. 'Gone off it?'

'No. Too weak for me.'

He tasted it. 'Just right. What do you want?'

I blinked. 'Nothing, really.'

'Then go away.'

Even for Derwent, that was rude. I held my ground. 'What's going on?'

He wouldn't look at me. 'You're still here.'

'Sorry, did I do something wrong? You weren't behaving like this in the car.'

'I've been having a think about a few things, that's all.' He took another mouthful of tea. 'Any sign of your little scumbags?'

'No.' I wasn't going to tell Derwent that I hadn't even looked for them.

'Maeve. Sir.' Liv was hurrying towards us. 'The fire investigator is ready to show us the crime scenes. He says we'll need boots. It's mucky up there.'

'Ten flights of stairs.' Derwent shook his head. 'Onwards and upwards, Kerrigan. After you.'

'Thanks,' I said, surprised that he was being a gentleman.

'Don't thank me. I'm just making sure I've got something nice to look at on the way.'

Chapter 4

'Watch your step.' Andrew Harper was waiting by the top of the outside stairs on the tenth floor. 'The surfaces are slippery up here and there's a lot of debris on the ground.'

In front of me, DS Chris Pettifer was wheezing like a broken accordion. He and Una Burt had set the pace, which was not as quick as I would have liked it to be given that Derwent's face was a few inches from my bottom most of the way. Every time I glanced back, I got a leer from him. Eventually, I stopped glancing back.

There were eight of us from the murder team, all officers I'd worked with before. We followed Harper from the cold, draughty staircase into the corridor, which was still hot and smelled strongly of burning. It was humid, like a sauna, and the ground was covered in wet ashes that were sticky underfoot.

Harper stopped, letting us gather around him and the senior firefighter I'd seen talking to Una Burt earlier. He introduced himself as Gary Northbridge. He looked more tired than he had in the car park, and defensive. I assumed that fatal fires generated more hassle and paperwork than I could imagine.

'Okay, we'll be drawing up proper plans of the building for your reference, but here's what you need to know,' Harper said. 'There are ten flats on each floor, four on the left and six on the right. We have eight occupied flats on this floor, but two of them were empty at the time of the fire – the residents were still at work. The residents on the left side of the corridor who were present at the time of the fire had enough warning to evacuate. The left side is also where the internal stairwell and the lifts are accessed, which is why there are fewer flats on this side. On the other side we have six flats, two of which are not in use at the moment according to the management. Some are in private hands but most are council-owned. The flats are not numbered consecutively throughout the building – numbering restarts on each floor. So flat 101 is here on the right, opposite flat 107.'

'That caused some problems for the fire crews,' Northbridge said. 'They knew there was a vulnerable person in 104 but they had to find the flat before they could find her.'

'Is she one of the fatalities?' I asked.

'Not so far. She was taken to hospital. We have sixteen in hospital at the moment, mainly with smoke inhalation, minor injuries, a couple of broken bones, one with serious burns. I can't tell you who they are or where they lived yet, but we're working on it. A few of them were unconscious or confused when we picked them up, so we don't have a name for everyone.'

'More injuries than I'd have expected,' Derwent said. 'Sounds more like a fight than a fire.'

'That happens in serious fires,' Northbridge said. 'It's

not just the smoke and the flames you have to worry about. Crush injuries and falls kill just as many people.'

'Where were the bodies?' Pete Belcott asked. He was abrupt, as usual. Charm was not one of his qualities.

'There were two fatalities up in 113 on the next floor, and your gentleman outside.'

'So everyone else escaped from this floor.'

'They escaped or they were rescued by firefighters,' Northbridge said. 'We had a 999 call from flat 101. There were two adults and two children. They were advised to make their way to the internal stairwell and progress down if it was safe to do so. That is where they were located when the first crews came in.'

'Was that the first call you had about the fire?' I asked.

'That's what our records indicate,' Northbridge said.

'So they were the first people to notice the fire. Did it start in their flat? Or nearby?'

'We don't know yet,' Harper said. 'It's possible. The level of damage along this side of the building is considerable. It will take some time to work out where the fire began and how.'

'So it could have been an accident,' Belcott said, and I could see from the look on his face that he was losing interest.

'It could have been an accident. It could have been arson,' Harper replied patiently.

'What makes you say that?' Una Burt asked.

'With this level of damage we can tell that the fire burned extremely hot and it took hold very quickly. That makes me suspicious. Fires that begin accidentally often start slowly, then gather pace as they increase in size. This was overwhelming in minutes. It generated a lot of smoke that seeped into the corridor and vented itself via the outside stairwell, effectively making it unusable for the people on this floor and the floor above. The fire burned through into flat 101, where it caused a great deal of damage in the kitchen and one bedroom.'

Harper led us through the front door into the flat. Everything inside it was blackened by smoke and the carpet felt squelchy underfoot. Nothing looked salvageable. I could make out metal-framed shapes that had once been a sofa and a couple of armchairs, and the television was still recognisable, but the rest of the furnishings were essentially gone. A cut-glass chandelier still hung from the ceiling, incongruous in those surroundings anyway but doubly so when it was streaked with dirty water. The residents had cared about their home, I thought. The fire would be devastating for them in every way, not just the material loss.

'The internal doors were closed, initially, which was lucky,' Northbridge said. 'One of the children opened the bedroom door and discovered the blaze.'

There were scorch marks around the door and across the ceiling.

'These are from the flashover that occurred when the door was opened,' Harper said, playing his torch over them. 'Fire is hungry. It needs oxygen. Any firefighter will tell you not to open a hot door. The little girl didn't know any better. They were lucky the grandmother was nearby and managed to get the door closed before the fire could take hold out here. She gave the child first aid while the dad was on the phone to 999. That call came in at 17.36.'

'Hold on. Shouldn't there have been a smoke alarm in the flat?' Una Burt asked.

'It wasn't working.'

'What about in the hall?'

'It was vandalised.' Northbridge pulled a face. 'Not all that unusual here. The alarms are linked to a main control centre in the estate's management office and they're supposed to inform us straight away when one of the alarms goes off-line, as well as getting it repaired.'

'But they didn't,' I said quietly.

'It happened this morning. No one got around to fixing it before this afternoon.' Northbridge shook his head. 'If everyone didn't persist in thinking fire regulations are just there to annoy them, my job would be a lot easier.'

'The real problem with this fire,' Harper said, leading us out of flat 101 into the next-door property, 'was the smoke. We had a lot of thick, black smoke and it made it very difficult for the residents to make their way to the exits safely. I gather there was a lot of confusion. The call-centre operators in our command centre encouraged people to use their own judgement about whether it was safer to remain where they were or risk making an attempt to escape.'

Flat 102 was significantly smaller than its neighbour, but it was just as thoroughly destroyed. I nudged a jumble of wires and melted plastic with the toe of my boot. 'How did the fire pass into this flat from next door?'

'There's a ventilation system running overhead. The hot air and smoke from the fire spread through the pipes. It was hot enough to ignite materials wherever it found an outlet.' Harper smiled. 'You shouldn't assume the fire started in flat 101. The ventilation system could just as easily have passed it the other way.'

'Who lived here?' Derwent asked.

Northbridge checked his notes. 'It's registered to a Mrs Edmonds. Someone made a 999 call from here at 17.37, saying that her flat and the corridor were full of smoke, but she broke off contact with the operator almost immediately. She said she was planning to use the internal staircase to escape.'

'Did she say anything else?' I asked.

'She said she was scared.'

There was a short silence and then Harper guided us back out to the corridor, to flat 103. 'Now this is where it gets interesting. The fire went up from 102 to 113 on the floor above via the ventilation system. It caused significant damage. We've found two bodies up there. No ID on them yet. This flat, 103, was supposed to be empty. But when the firefighters got here, the door was open. All of the windows were open, not broken. Someone was here, and that person was desperately trying to get air. Smoke doesn't just kill through suffocation. People start making bad decisions. They can become illogical or uncoordinated.'

He led us through the flat, which was empty apart from debris from the ceiling and walls. 'This was a bedroom and that was a bed.'

'How can you tell?' Liv sounded confused and I flashed her a smile. I couldn't see it either in the rubble of charred planks and ashes that filled the small room.

Harper crouched and dug in the rubbish on the floor. 'This is a wire spring,' he said, holding it up in a gloved hand. 'It's likely to have been from a mattress.'

'So there was a bed in the uninhabited flat, and someone who opened the windows.' Derwent headed to the bedroom window and looked down. 'Are you thinking of Armstrong?'

'It's a possibility.'

'His body was a bit to the left of this window.' Derwent was leaning out at a perilous angle. I had to restrain myself from grabbing the back of his coat and hauling him back.

'I'd say it bears further investigation.' Harper's voice was as calm and reasonable as ever.

We followed him out to stand in the corridor. 'From here on the fire was largely contained by the firefighters.' He pointed. 'Flat 104, the firefighters rescued the elderly resident without too much trouble once they found the flat. The main issue was gaining access. She was barricaded inside and it took a while to persuade her to open the door.'

'Lucky escape,' Una Burt commented.

'Very.' Harper sighed. 'Not the case upstairs, unfortunately. If you'd all like to follow me, I can show you flat 113. Whoever they were, they had no luck at all.'

Chapter 5

Soberly, I walked downstairs with Derwent.

'I'm never going to live anywhere higher than the first floor,' he said.

'Me neither.'

'What a fucking horrible way to die. Locked in.' He shuddered. 'Give me Armstrong's death any day.'

It didn't seem to me that Armstrong's ending had been a whole lot better than the two people who had been located in flat 113, but I could understand why Derwent was so unsettled. Flat 113 had been a horror show, a nightmare made real. The smell had hit me first and I wasn't the only one who struggled with the dark, awful stench of charred meat. I'd seen plenty of dead bodies – I'd even seen burned bodies before. These were different, though. The fire had seared through the flat with tremendous speed and heat. I'd never seen destruction like it. Even the front door was warped and buckled. Harper had shown us the lock, proving that the door had been locked at the time of the fire.

'Locked from the inside or the outside?' I'd asked.

'We don't know. We haven't found a key yet.'

'Let's not jump to conclusions,' Una Burt said, her voice firm. 'They might have been waiting for rescue. They might have been scared to leave. It'll take time to search for the key in this mess, but that doesn't mean it isn't here.'

But it was hard to imagine why you would allow yourself to be trapped in an inferno if you had a choice in the matter. The corpses were distorted and black, charred to the bone, huddled in a cupboard where they had tried to hide. They looked like specimens from a museum, bog people dug out of the ground, withered, alien. You had to remind yourself these had been people, once. Recently.

Everyone else on the eleventh floor had escaped, though several had suffered injuries that ranged from very minor to serious. If the two people hadn't been locked in, or if the fire had broken through in a different flat – even if the fire crews had known they were trapped there – the outcome might have been different.

'We'll be looking at the building regulations and whether they were correctly observed,' Northbridge had promised.

'I'm sure that'll make all the difference to them.' Derwent had walked out, as if he couldn't bear to stay there for another moment, and after a nod from Burt I'd followed him. I'd caught up with him on the stairs, aware that he wouldn't want to discuss the fact that he'd walked out. I sometimes wondered why I bothered being tactful around Derwent when he was so absolutely not tactful in his dealings with me.

'So what do you think?' I asked.

'About what?'

'Armstrong. Did he fall, did he jump or was he pushed?'

'Pushed. Definitely.' He was going faster as he got further away from the top of the flats, shedding the gloom that had come over him in the charnel house of flat 113.

'What makes you say that?'

'If anyone was going to be murdered, ever, it was him. He hated everyone who wasn't white, English and wealthy, and that's a lot of people. Especially here on this estate. Frankly, I was surprised he wasn't lynched two months ago when he was wandering around talking shit about that young black kid who was shot.'

'Shot by the police,' I said as quietly as I could. I wasn't prepared to shout about Levon Cole. It was a very raw and recent death, and the last time I'd seen Armstrong he'd been scoring political points as a result of the shooting. It wasn't something I'd found endearing.

Behind us, I could hear the others starting to come down, their voices echoing in the stairwell. Otherwise the flats were silent. The residents had been evacuated to the local school for the night. There was something chilling about the empty corridors on each floor we passed, strewn with bags and belongings that people had dropped as they fled. Disaster had come to find them.

I suddenly, quite desperately, wanted to get out of Murchison House and as far away from the Maudling Estate as I could go. I picked up speed, passing Derwent before he realised that was my intention. He couldn't catch up with me on the last flight, though he tried, and I was the one who made it to the main door first. I shoved it open and stepped outside. As I passed through the door I slowed right down, walking calmly and with

61

composure. There were still people hanging around, even at that late hour. There would be television cameras too. Police officers didn't run unless there was a good reason to.

'You should have said you wanted a race.'

I turned my head to answer Derwent and saw a flicker of movement out of the corner of my eye, between two cars. I put out my hand to grab his sleeve. 'What's that?'

'Where?'

I pointed. He looked, ducking sideways, then crouched down. I heard him swearing under his breath and then he motioned to me to go the long way round, behind the cars. He took the shorter, direct route, and I saw him drop to his knees, then onto the palms of his hands, lowering himself so he was almost flat on the ground.

'What are you doing?' Una Burt's voice was loud and shrill behind us as she came out of the building. Obviously she hadn't been expecting to find Derwent lying on the ground, but it wasn't the right moment to explain why. I ignored her as I skirted the cars and I was sure Derwent was doing the same. It was hard to tell when his head and shoulders had disappeared under the Ford Focus that was on the left. I knelt down, ignoring the sharp bits of gravel that dug into my knees, and leaned to peer under the car. I could see Derwent, his head turned sideways. He was holding out his hand to the small figure that was curled up in a ball by the wheel. Derwent was showing him his warrant card, complete with a shiny metal crest.

'Come on, mate. Out you come. I'm a police officer. I promise you can trust me.'

'No.' A small voice but very definite.

'What's your name?'

'Thomas.' His whole body jerked. 'I mean, Sam.'

Derwent looked across at me: had I noticed? I nodded.

'Easy mistake to make,' he said. 'You can't stay under there all night, Sam. Come on out and we'll find your mum. She's probably wondering where you are.'

'Have you seen her?'

'Yeah. I have.' Derwent glanced at me and I nodded again. I'd have said the same thing. 'What are you doing here?' he asked.

'Waiting. She told me to wait for her until she came.' He unfolded enough to show us a dirty, tear-stained face. 'But she didn't come.'

'Come on,' Derwent said again. 'We'll find her.'

'Can you do that?' he asked, his voice very tiny.

'Of course. We're the police. We can do anything.'

'Are the firemen still here?'

'Yeah, but we're better than the firemen,' Derwent said. 'We catch baddies.'

'I don't like baddies,' the boy said, starting to shuffle towards Derwent. 'They're scary.'

'The police are scarier. The baddies are scared of us.'

'And prison.' He eased forward another couple of inches.

'That too. They don't like prison.'

'Why don't you put them all in prison?'

'That's what I keep saying, Sam. Lock them all up. Then we'd have some peace.'

He crawled over the last bit as Derwent wriggled back to make room for him. I stood up and came round the side of the car in time to see the boy stand up. He was small, his shoulder blades sticking out through the thin material of his t-shirt. His ears stuck out too, and his neck seemed impossibly slender for the weight of his head. His jeans were damp where he had wet himself. How long had he been hiding there, terrified? Hours, anyway.

Derwent sat back on his heels, looking at him. 'What's your name, Sam? Do you know the second bit?'

'Sam Hathaway.' In a rush he added, 'Not Thomas. I don't know why I said that.'

'Don't worry, mate.' For a second I thought Derwent was going to hug the boy, but he was reaching out to brace himself on the cars as he straightened up. I heard the groan he was trying to suppress and filed it away to tease him some time he was in a good mood. *Getting old . . .*

'If you lock all the baddies up,' the boy said quietly, 'then Mummy won't be scared any more.'

Derwent looked down at him for a moment, his face unreadable. Then he smiled. 'I'm working on it, Sam. I promise you, I'm working on it.'

Chapter 6

'How is it possible for no one to know who he is or where he came from?' Derwent snapped. I took a step back.

'Don't shout at me. I'm as frustrated as you are. I've been going through paperwork in the management office. There's no one named Hathaway listed as a resident here. I cross-checked with the PNC and the electoral roll. Not a thing.'

'So where did he spring from?' He turned and peered through the back window of his car. The boy lay across it, fast asleep under Derwent's coat, his head on Derwent's suit jacket. I assumed Derwent was cold, standing there in his shirtsleeves, but he didn't show it and I didn't dare ask.

'Illegal sub-let?' I suggested.

'Which would mean no paperwork for us to follow.'

'No.'

'So we have to assume his mother didn't make it out. And she's either one of the injured—'

'Or one of the dead,' I finished. 'They're still searching the flats for bodies.'

'Either way, until we find someone who can identify her for us, he's on his own.'

'Social services,' I started, and Derwent rounded on me with a look that was pure rage.

'Don't even say it.'

'They're on their way.'

'For fuck's sake.' Derwent turned away, clasping his hands at the back of his skull, the picture of frustration.

'There isn't anyone else. You can't keep him.'

'I know that. He's not a puppy.'

But that was exactly what the child had reminded me of, following Derwent around as if he and he alone could be trusted to look after him and find his mother. Derwent hadn't made a fuss of the boy. He hadn't tried to get his attention or gain his trust. I couldn't tell if he was pleased or irritated that he'd acquired a shadow, but certainly he hadn't tried to get rid of him. When Una Burt had arranged for a female uniformed officer to look after the boy, he'd backed away to hide behind Derwent, who shrugged.

'He can stay with me.'

'You have other responsibilities,' Una Burt said tightly.

'I'm aware of that.' He dropped his voice. 'Let's not make it too hard on the poor kid, all right?'

And Una Burt had muttered something under her breath about priorities before walking off. I wasn't totally sure how he'd managed to put her in the position of being the bad guy, but he'd done it.

Derwent had searched the crowd until he found a woman who happened to be a registered childminder and lived in one of the other towers. He'd exerted his charm to convince her to take the boy to her warm, untidy flat and give him a change of clothes, replacing the damp trousers and dirty, torn t-shirt he was wearing. Unprompted, she offered Sam a snack. His eyes had been closing as he ate it, but he had said please and thank you nicely.

'Polite, ain't he?' the childminder said.

'Well brought up,' Derwent said, his face sombre. A nice child, loved and nurtured by a mother who wasn't there to look after him.

'He could stay here,' I said quietly in Derwent's ear.

'No, he couldn't.'

'She's a registered childminder. He's safe enough with her.'

'He's safe with me.'

'Are you just doing this to annoy DCI Burt?'

He turned to look at me, hurt. 'Would I do something like that?'

'Absolutely.'

The corners of his mouth turned up very slightly, but he shook his head. 'I don't know when you turned into such a cynic, young lady.'

'Working with you would make anyone cynical.'

'Oh, blame me.'

My phone buzzed in my hand, so I answered it rather than Derwent, even though it was Una Burt on the other end.

Derwent watched my face as I spoke to her. When I hung up, he asked, 'What does the wicked witch want?'

'Us, down in the car park. She wants an update.'

'An update,' Derwent repeated. 'On what? Whether the kid ate up all his crusts? You can go. I'm staying here.'

'She's not going to like that.'

'I don't care,' Derwent said, and gave me a very sweet smile that told me there was no point in arguing with him.

So it was that I'd been talking to Burt just outside the cordon around Murchison House when she sucked in a breath and expelled it in a long angry hiss.

I looked to see what she had noticed. Derwent was carrying the boy across the car park. His head was lolling on Derwent's shoulder, as if he was more than half asleep. Derwent sent a brief glower in our direction and carried on walking.

'That's not his job.'

'The boy trusts him,' I said. 'Derwent doesn't want to abandon him. And finding out who he is seems like it might be important.'

'Then you'd better get on with it.'

And I'd tried. I really had. But standing beside Derwent's car as the sky lightened on a new day, we'd made no progress.

'We could try the local schools,' Derwent said.

'He's too young. He could be in nursery but it's optional at that age.'

'Child benefits.'

'Worth a try,' I allowed. 'The staff won't be in yet. That'll have to wait until after nine.'

Derwent looked through the window again. 'I don't want to have to drag him around the hospitals trying to ID his mother.'

'That's very much a last resort.' I looked around. 'Here's Liv.'

She was breathless, but she looked pleased with

herself. 'Right. I've been at the local leisure centre, talking to the people who were evacuated from Murchison House. I showed Sam's picture around and a Mrs Jordan said she recognised him. She's pretty certain he was living in flat 102 on the tenth floor with his mother, but she'd never spoken to them. They only moved in a few weeks ago. She'd seen them in the corridor together. She noticed him because he looks like one of her grandchildren.'

'Flat 102 is one of the flats that was burned out completely,' I said. 'We're not going to be able to recover any ID.'

'No, but we can find out who was supposed to be living there.' Derwent shivered as the wind blew some dead leaves around our feet. 'It's a start.'

'If the owner knows the boy's mother, they can ID her for us.'

Derwent nodded. 'Get back to the management office and find a number for the owner, Kerrigan. Don't come back without it.'

I went. I even hurried. But by the time I got back, Derwent was shrugging his coat on and the back seat of the car was empty.

'Did social services take him?'

'Yeah.' He had his back to me.

'Are you okay?'

It was as if I'd never asked the question. 'Did you get the owner's details?'

'Harriet Edmonds. I've got her address. She lives in Islington.'

'Then let's go to Islington.'

'I've cleared it with DCI Burt already.'

Derwent paused, still facing away from me. 'I was going anyway.'

'I know.'

Chapter 7

'Is this the right place?'

'That's the address I have.' I looked up at the neat Georgian townhouse: five storeys of prime London property, facing onto a pretty square that was completely silent at ten to six in the morning. 'Bit of a step up from Murchison House.'

'Let's go and see if they're awake.' Derwent bounded up the steps to the front door, leaning over the railings to peer in through the basement window. 'Someone's up. The lights are on.' He rang the bell and the sound echoed through the house.

'Yes?' The man who came to the door after a longish wait was pink-faced and dishevelled. He was wearing a t-shirt and shorts and had a towel slung around his neck. The t-shirt was too small and clung to a fairly substantial belly. An early morning workout, I guessed, fighting middle-aged spread. Fighting quite hard, if his sweat patches were anything to go by.

'Sorry for interrupting you. Police.' Derwent held up his ID. 'Is there a Harriet Edmonds at this address?'

'There is.' He mopped his forehead. 'I'll get her for you now. Come in.'

He led us down to the kitchen, a long narrow room that ran the length of the house and ended in a small sitting area. There was a rowing machine by the garden doors, in front of a wall-mounted TV. It was on, showing a business news channel. The sound was muted.

'Multi-tasking,' he explained, moving the machine behind the sofa with an effort. 'Sit down. Can I get you anything? Cup of tea?'

'No thanks,' Derwent said.

'Back in a minute.' He wandered out, rubbing his head with the towel until his iron-grey hair stood up in spikes. I could hear his footsteps on the stairs, climbing up and up. I wondered how far he had to go.

Derwent raised his eyebrows at me. 'What do you think?'

'He wasn't surprised to see us. He didn't even ask why we were here.'

'Maybe this is a regular occurrence.'

I looked out at the garden, which was narrow but long, like the house. There was a small studio at the end of it, little more than a shed. 'What do you think that is?'

'An office?'

'If it was my house, I'd turn that into a gym and find space for the office in the house.'

'You're never going to have a house like this. Not unless you marry money.' He hadn't meant it to hurt but I flinched all the same and he saw it. 'Sorry. I forgot.'

He'd forgotten that my boyfriend had been keeping all sorts of secrets from me, including the fact that he was wealthy, even by London standards. It was the betrayal that had wounded me far more than Rob being unfaithful. I could understand how Rob had ended up in bed with someone other than me. I couldn't understand why he'd lied to me.

Except that I hadn't grown up with the kind of privilege he'd taken for granted, and I didn't altogether trust people who had a lot of money. They assumed they could buy their way out of trouble.

'If I cared about money, I wouldn't be a copper,' I said lightly. 'But I could win the lottery.'

'You never buy a ticket.'

'I forget,' I admitted. Then, 'Someone's coming.'

And at top speed. The kitchen door burst open and a slender woman rushed in, tying the belt of her dressing gown. She had curling shoulder-length red hair that was exceptionally well cut, and if she was in her pyjamas she had made time to put on dark red lipstick before she made her appearance. She crossed the kitchen and pulled down a mug from a shelf, then started fiddling with a vast, shiny coffee machine.

'What can I do for the police this fine morning? Can I get you a coffee? Tea? I'm so sorry, I have to have caffeine before I can speak to anyone.'

If this was Harriet Edmonds before caffeine, I wasn't sure I could cope with after.

Derwent introduced himself, and me. 'We're here about—'

'Just a second.' She dived into the fridge. 'Soy milk. Disgusting. I'm a vegan so I'm not allowed to hate it but I do.'

'Mrs Edmonds.'

She stopped. 'Yes.'

'We need to speak to you about the Maudling Estate. You own a property there.'

She put the carton down. 'I own two.'

'And you let them out to tenants.'

'No. Not officially. I have friends who stay there.' She gave a little shrug. 'People who need somewhere to stay indefinitely. Has – has something happened?'

'You haven't seen the news?'

'I only watch the lunchtime news. I don't like to look at the news in the evenings. It disturbs me.' She ran her fingers around her eyes, massaging the skin. 'I have trouble sleeping. I can't switch off.'

'There was a fire, Mrs Edmonds. In Murchison House.'

'Oh my God.' She put a hand to her mouth. 'That's where I put Melissa. What happened to her?'

'Melissa?' I repeated.

'She had a little boy. Oh God, not them.'

'We found Sam. He's fine,' I added.

'Oh . . . yes, Sam.' She closed her eyes for a moment. 'But Melissa? Is she—'

'We don't know. We haven't been able to identify her yet. She may be among the injured. But there were also some fatalities, I'm afraid.'

'The poor, poor girl. As if she hadn't had enough to deal with.' Harriet Edmonds began to cry, quite openly and helplessly.

I hurried over to her and guided her to the sofa. Derwent crouched down in front of her, and it wasn't quite confrontational but he wasn't giving her much space either.

'Why was Melissa living in Murchison House?'

'It was supposed to be a safe place for her while she found her feet.' Harriet dug in her pocket for a tissue and blew her nose. 'That's what I do. I provide safe places for the women I help. I run a charity for victims of domestic violence. Women's refuges are all very well and good but they're not ideal places for women with children. Some women won't consider a refuge. They'd rather stay with their abuser than bring their children there. They want to keep them in a home environment, even if it's not what they're used to.'

'Too good for a refuge?' Derwent said. 'God bless the middle classes.'

Harriet paused for a moment. 'You don't have to be working class to get beaten up by your partner. You don't have to be poor, or badly educated, or stupid, or whatever it is you're assuming.'

'He knows,' I said, glaring at Derwent. He pulled a face at me while Harriet was occupied with wiping her eyes.

'They put themselves under such pressure. They think they can protect the children from knowing about it and keep up the façade of the perfect marriage, the perfect life. And of course they can't. They all break eventually. Or they are broken.' She sniffed. 'I've been doing this for twelve years. I've had a lot of police officers come here and tell me there's no need for me to run my organisation. I've had a lot of condescending advice from people like you. And I've also had hundreds of women thank me for saving their lives.'

'I apologise,' Derwent said. 'I really do.' He sounded sincere, too.

'It's hard to walk out on a life that looks enviable. It's hard to deprive your children of the things they are used to having. The flats aren't luxurious but they are far away from the abusers, and they're free, and private.'

'How long had Melissa been staying there?' I asked.

'I'd have to check. A couple of months, I think.' She glanced in the direction of the garden and I thought I could understand why she kept the paperwork for the charity outside the house. Hundreds of women meant hundreds of stories that Harriet had absorbed. It was a family home: there were photos on the walls of beautiful, accomplished teenagers. I was willing to bet they didn't know very much at all about their mother's charitable work.

'How long do most of them stay?' Derwent asked.

'Not long.'

'Even though it's free?'

'They don't want me to support them. They want to stand up for themselves. They want to prove to them-selves and everyone else that they can cope without their partners. Besides, most of them don't want to stay in one place for too long. It's too dangerous. Most victims of domestic violence are killed by their partners just after they leave them.' She was shivering. 'The men are well resourced and angry. They like to exert control on their partners. They don't like having that control taken away without their agreement. It's easy to hire a private detective. Sometimes they involve the police, or social services. "My wife has run away with our children and all the cash in the house and I think she's unstable." That's enough to get people making enquiries on your behalf, especially if you don't have a criminal record because your wife was too ashamed or scared to report you and you live in a detached house so the neighbours don't hear the screams.'

'Has that ever happened to any of your ladies?' I asked.

'Once.'

'What happened?'

Harriet looked at me, her eyes the colour of cognac. 'He stabbed her. She died in front of their two daughters.'

'When was this?' Derwent asked.

'Eight years ago. That was when I stopped using flats in nice parts of London and bought up some ex-council properties. It's easier to hide where there are a lot of people. Especially a place where the residents come and go frequently. No one notices a new tenant.'

'This is the problem we're having,' Derwent said. 'We don't have anyone who can identify Melissa. She didn't know anyone in the flats, it seems, and we haven't been able to find any ID for her on any of the victims.'

'Is Melissa her real name?' I asked. 'Melissa Hathaway?'

Harriet shook her head. 'No. Melissa, yes. I shouldn't have said it. I gave her a new name. It's easier for me to think up something that has no meaning for her. That makes it more difficult for anyone to guess it. She was called Vivienne Hathaway.'

'And Sam?'

'I think that was the new name she gave him. I don't remember what it was before.'

'Thomas,' I suggested.

She shrugged but I had the feeling she remembered extremely well, that she regretted giving us as much as

Melissa's first name by accident, and cooperation was not on the cards from this point on.

'Did you meet her?' I asked.

'Just once.'

'Do you have a photograph of her?'

'No.'

'What's her real surname?'

'I'm not going to give you that information without her permission.'

'But we can't get that permission if we can't find her,' Derwent said in his very reasonable I'm-near-the-end-of-my-tether voice.

'Do you have contact information for anyone related to her – anyone she trusts? A family member?' I asked.

'Why?'

Derwent straightened up, looming over the sofa. 'Because at the moment her little boy is being looked after by some foster family social services have dug up, if he's lucky. Or he's sitting in an office somewhere waiting to find out if he's still got a mother. The last home he had is gone and he doesn't know where he's going to end up. He's confused and scared and on his own and I'd like to know he's with someone he trusts.' His voice had roughened as he spoke. He walked away a little before he added, 'Wouldn't you?'

Harriet was staring down at her hands, looking stubborn. 'I'm sorry. I find it hard to trust the police. I've been let down too many times. It puts people in danger. That's why I have a rule about not giving out personal information.'

'Even in these circumstances?' I asked.

'I'm sorry.'

'Don't you think Melissa would want to know her son was being looked after? Isn't that why she came to you instead of one of the refuges you mentioned?' I spoke softly, hoping I could persuade her where Derwent's temper had failed. 'She wants what's best for her boy, and the best thing is her. If she can't look after him, who comes next? Not his father.'

Harriet hugged herself, saying nothing.

'If we can identify Thomas or Sam or whatever his name is by some other means – and we will – you know his father will be likely to get custody. Especially if there's no record of domestic violence. Especially if Melissa is incapacitated or dead.'

She dropped her head down on to her chest and shuddered.

'If we have a grandmother or a sister or even a best friend – someone Melissa trusts – we can keep him out of foster care and postpone returning him to his father until the family courts have had a chance to consider the best place for him. So do you have contact details for someone suitable?'

'Yes,' she said quietly.

'And can you give them to us so we can get in touch with them?'

'Yes.'

'Now we're getting somewhere,' Derwent said under his breath and I incinerated him with a glare. Far too risky to assume Harriet was on our side.

A rattle of feet on the stairs announced the return of the man who'd let us in, this time knotting a tie. He was wearing a very well-cut suit and looked sleek rather than paunchy. He'd tamed his hair in the shower and his cufflinks gleamed gold as he whipped the silk tie through his fingers.

'Everything all right?'

'Fine, Matt.' Harriet pulled herself together and gave him a smile. 'I need to help the police with their inquiries but I don't think I'm actually under arrest.'

'It's all voluntary,' Derwent said.

'Try and stop her from volunteering in a good cause.' Matt Edmonds leaned over the back of the sofa and kissed the top of his wife's head. 'Don't put yourself through too much, though.' Without her seeing, he looked at Derwent, then me, and the expression in his eyes was cold. I wouldn't want to cross him, I decided.

'I'll call you,' Harriet said, oblivious.

'Do that. I have meetings all morning but Kendall can interrupt me. I'll be glad of a break.' He strode out of the room, back up the stairs to the front door. When he slammed it shut the sound reverberated through the entire house.

'I'm sure the neighbours loathe us,' Harriet said tranquilly. 'You could set a clock by him. Every day, just the same. The children used to hate it.'

'I assume they're not here at the moment,' I said.

'Moved out. One is at university.' She smiled but her eyes were sad. 'It all went so quickly.'

'That's what my mum says.'

She stood up, tucking her dressing gown around her. 'Do you want the contact details now?'

'Yes, please.'

'And we'll need you to come with us if you don't mind,'

Derwent said. 'I still need to find Melissa as a matter of urgency. You're the only person I've found who could identify her, even tentatively.'

She nodded. 'I understand. Can I get changed?'

'Of course.'

She started to walk towards the stairs, her head down.

'Why do you do this?' The question seemed to surprise Derwent as much as Harriet, who turned, nonplussed, to stare at him. 'I mean, you have it all, don't you? Money, nice house, successful kids. It can't just be to pass the time.'

'No, it's not.' She pulled back her dressing gown a little and we stared at the long, jagged silver scar that ran across her chest from the base of her throat. 'My first husband was a very violent man. I almost didn't leave in time. I didn't want to deprive my daughter of all the things she took for granted. I thought I could stand it, for her sake.'

'But you couldn't.'

'No. I went to a hotel. I took Ruth and I took my jewellery and some money – not much. And he found us.' She touched the scar lightly. 'I was lucky. I try to make sure the women I help are even luckier.'

This time, when she moved towards the stairs, Derwent let her go.

Chapter 8

We were late arriving at the briefing and Una Burt looked distinctly unimpressed. Derwent walked straight past her to find a seat. The room was full of faces, all turned towards us. I tried not to catch anyone's eye and settled down in a seat next to Liv.

'Where have you been?' Burt demanded of Derwent, who was causing maximum chaos by making for a seat at the far end of a row.

'Finding the boy's mother,' he said over his shoulder.

'And?'

'We found her. Her name's Melissa Pell, if anyone's interested.'

'Alive?'

'Sort of.' He eased himself into a seat. 'Fractured eye socket, smoke inhalation. She was asleep and we weren't allowed to wake her.'

We'd found her after touring all of the victims in the hospital. Harriet Edmonds had suffered through it without complaint, gallant and dedicated as she was. I had been expecting – and dreading – a trip to the hospital morgue, where the fatalities were stored, waiting for the pathologist to deal with them. It was a huge relief when Harriet had turned to us and said, 'That's her.'

She had known her straight away, despite the bandages and the bruising to her face. It was hard to tell what Melissa looked like normally but she was slightly built with fine, delicate hands and a profusion of corkscrew-curly fair hair. Once I knew who she was, I could see how her son resembled her in the shape of his face and the colour of his hair.

'But she should recover,' Una Burt said.

'She should,' Derwent said. 'In the meantime, her mother is coming to London to look after the boy.'

'So you can stop worrying about her and concentrate on your actual job.' Una Burt shuffled her papers, not looking in Derwent's direction.

Derwent folded his arms. 'I rather thought it was part of my actual job to find out how she was injured, in case it was deliberate.'

'She fell. We covered this at the scene.' Burt shot a glance at the fire investigator, Harper, who checked his notes.

'That's what we've assumed. It's certainly not unusual to have injuries of that sort in a large fire.'

'Where did they find her?' I asked.

'In the hallway on the eighth floor,' Harper said.

I frowned. 'Why was she there? She lived on the tenth floor.'

'Someone might have helped her out of the stairwell,' Harper said. 'It was full of people as well as smoke. She was in danger of being trampled if she was unconscious.'

'According to the control room's logs, did anyone say

there was a woman in need of assistance on the eighth floor?' I asked.

'Not according to my notes.'

'Not very helpful to rescue her and then abandon her to her fate.'

'There were a lot of firefighters in the building supervising the evacuation. It would have been reasonable to assume they would come across her, as indeed they did.'

'But—' I started to object and Una Burt cleared her throat.

'I think we'd all like to hear what Mr Harper has to tell us about the fire, Maeve, rather than concentrating on creating a mystery around one of the victims.'

I sat back in my seat, my face burning.

'As I was saying,' Harper began, 'we've been working quite hard on trying to find where the fire originated. Ordinarily I would work from the areas of least damage towards the areas that were most damaged to find the place that the fire burned for longest. Because of the way it spread through the ventilation system, this fire didn't burn in a consistent way through the building.'

He had a flip chart on a stand behind him and now he turned to it. There was a rectangular shape on the page, roughly drawn, divided into sections. 'This is a floorplan I drew of the tenth floor and obviously it's just for reference, not to scale. We can say fairly certainly that the fire began on this floor and jumped to the eleventh floor. The ninth floor was smoke-damaged but none of the flats here were involved in the fire directly. So looking at the tenth floor, this is the outside staircase which you came up.' He pointed at a zigzag line, then moved on to the box he'd drawn next to it. 'This is flat 101, 102, and so on. The damage is concentrated in the flats here, at this end of the corridor, and on the north side of the building.'

'Could it have started in one of the flats?' Una Burt asked. 'Or in the corridor?'

'It's possible that it was in one of the flats,' Harper said. 'We need to talk to the residents to find out what they were doing before the fire broke out. It was early evening so people were cooking meals. I found the remains of an iron and an ironing board in the kitchen of flat 101. We joke about leaving the iron on but it's easily done and it can ignite fabric if it's left in contact with it for too long. Hair straighteners are another regular culprit – very hot, very easy to leave switched on and if they're lying on a bed or a carpeted surface you're almost guaranteed a fire. But certain things about this fire make me suspicious that we might be dealing with arson, not an accidental blaze.'

Everyone in the room sat up a little in their chairs, consciously or unconsciously, paying closer attention.

Harper pointed at a small box on the floor plan, near the outside staircase. 'This was once a store cupboard. It was completely destroyed in the fire. The back wall of it had burned through to the flat behind it, which was flat 101. Bear in mind that the fire may have originated inside the flat so we can't assume the store cupboard burned first. However, looking at the burn patterns on what's left in the cupboard, it seems likely that the fire moved from south to north, not the other way. The majority of the damage is on the south side of the objects. Fire consumes what it needs to and moves on, so where you have a half-charred object you can assume the burning started on the more damaged side. But as I say, the destruction was quite comprehensive in this area.'

'Who had access to the store cupboard?' Derwent asked.

'The cleaners and maintenance staff on the estate. According to the management it was kept locked, but there was nothing of particular value in it so I don't think the lock would have kept out a determined thief. We'll sift through the wreckage to try to find it. We should be able to work out if the lock was still engaged when the fire destroyed the door, or if it was damaged before the fire began, or if it was left open.'

'What was in the store cupboard?' Burt asked.

'Floor cleaner, rags, pressurised containers, a floor-polishing machine and an industrial vacuum cleaner – that sort of thing. A lot of it was highly flammable. But it was properly stored, according to the management, and I've had a look at other store cupboards lower down in the same building and found nothing that made me think anyone was careless.'

'Nothing that could spontaneously combust?' Chris Pettifer asked.

'In my opinion, no. There are certain oils that can combust in the right circumstances, such as linseed oil, and we'll test the residue of the fire for the chemical compounds associated with it, but I've checked and there was no reason to store linseed oil in this cupboard. The management said they had no use for it and I didn't find any in any of the other cupboards, all of which were stocked similarly.'

'So if it didn't start accidentally or spontaneously it's got to be arson,' Una Burt said.

Harper nodded. 'Which would fit with the speed of the fire's development and the heat it generated immediately. I can't tell you what accelerant might have been used until we've conducted tests on the chemical residues, but in my experience a fire of this sort will have begun with some sort of accelerant and a naked flame. Whoever set it did a good job of finding a fuel source for the fire. I don't think they could have anticipated how successful the fire was going to be. It shouldn't have gone into the ventilation system, and no one could have predicted that it would, but it obviously did.'

'So who are we looking for?' Derwent asked. 'Someone who gets a kick out of setting fires?'

Harper gave him a grim smile. 'That's the classic arsonist that people imagine – the kid watching the fire crews, cheering at the size and intensity of the flames. No remorse, no conscience, no concept of how dangerous their actions might be – just in it for the thrill. But that's only one kind of arsonist. People set fires for a lot of different reasons. Sometimes it's for profit, for an insurance claim or to wipe out your competitor's business. Sometimes it's to hide a crime. It's a good way of destroying forensic evidence that could otherwise be collected.'

I'd been involved with an investigation into a serial killer who burned his victims' bodies after he'd killed them. I knew all about how destructive fire could be. It still made me shiver.

Harper went on, 'But then you have the fire setters who do it as a way of coping with trauma in their life – it expresses something that they aren't able to put into words. You'll get a run of fires over a short period and then the arsonist recovers, if you like, or whatever has been stressing them passes, and so they don't have that need to set fires any more. Or you have the delinquent fire setters who are usually kids, a bit bored, playing around with matches. They're the kids who don't have good impulse control, who don't think about the consequences of their actions. The police come across them when they have to arrest them for doing stupid, dangerous things for the fun of it. Or you have the kids who set a fire as a cry for help, hoping that they'll get noticed. They're often socially isolated, bullied, or coping with sexual or physical abuse at home.'

'I don't really understand how setting fires would make them feel better,' Derwent said.

'It's a release, like self-harming or substance abuse. The difference is that it's external. A fire isn't a secret.' Harper shrugged. 'I've had a few cases of arson where the fire setter turned out to be a very disturbed teenager and you just hope they get the help they need while they're in custody because otherwise they'll come back out and start again. It's like an addiction.'

'Scary,' Mal Upton commented.

'Not as scary as the revenge arsonists,' Harper said, his voice sombre. 'They're the ones who keep me awake at night. They use fire to get even, to punish people who've crossed them. They're the ones who'll firebomb premises without any concern for innocent people who might get caught up in the blaze. They're ruthless.'

'So what have we got here?' Una Burt asked.

Harper smiled. 'That's something you'll have to work

out. I'll tell you as much as I can about how they did it. *Why* they did it is another problem.'

'It was a trap,' I said, staring at the floor plan.

Una Burt turned, a frown pulling her eyebrows together. 'What was that?'

'Where the fire started. It blocked off the outside stair-case for the people on the tenth floor, and the eleventh. It sent everyone down the internal staircase. If they escaped at all, I mean. The lifts weren't working, even if they'd risked using them during the fire. They had no other way to get out. We should assume the fire was set deliberately, to target someone on the tenth or eleventh floor, and the other victims were just collateral damage. We need to talk to the survivors and find out if they saw anyone hanging around in the stairwell or on the tenth floor. Melissa Pell—'

'Ah, we're back to her. I wondered how long it would take.' Burt's face was mottled with pink patches, even though her voice was calm.

'I think it's relevant. She has a violent ex-partner.'

'Which is so much more likely than the hate-figure politician being a target.'

Sarcasm. Perfect.

'It's more common,' I pointed out. 'But you're right. It could have been Armstrong who was the target. It could have been someone else. The fire could have been designed to kill. It could have been to flush someone into the open. It could have been to scare someone or send a message.'

That was the one thing I appreciated about Una Burt. She was scrupulously fair. I saw her take my point and

I saw her make up her mind. 'We should assume that they were all targets until we can rule them out.'

'What, everyone?' Pete Belcott looked horrified at the impending workload.

'Everyone on the tenth and eleventh floor,' Una Burt said calmly. 'We need to talk to everyone, and we shouldn't assume they're telling us the truth. Not everyone will see it as being in their interests to be honest with us. They need to be investigated as thoroughly as our potential arsonist.'

'We don't even know it is arson,' Belcott protested.

'And if we wait around until we find out for sure, he'll have time to try again.' Burt shook her head. 'I want a guard on everyone in the hospital. I want you to offer advice to the uninjured survivors about their personal safety. They should all be keeping a low profile for the next few days.'

'The press will be looking to talk to them,' Harper observed. 'That's a given. Human interest stories.'

'We have to assume the ones who are aware they might be in danger won't seek to talk to the papers. Mind you, I've known stranger things. People are stupid.' Burt looked surprised as a titter ran around the room. She hadn't been playing it for laughs. 'Priorities, people. We need to get current addresses for every resident of the top two floors of Murchison House. The ones who aren't in hospital who were council tenants will be in temporary housing arranged by the council. Bed and breakfasts, hostels – nowhere very glamorous but better than a burned-out shell. We'll have to trace any private owners through the insurers. And I want someone to review the CCTV from the estate.'

'Looking for?' Derwent asked.

'Someone out of place. And Armstrong, so we can get an idea of when he arrived and who was with him. The arsonist, ideally, although I don't think we're going to be lucky enough to see anyone carrying a petrol can into the building.'

'I can get on with that.' Colin Vale was a glutton for admin, a DS who lived for the long, tedious data-crunching that actually solved many murders. Hours of CCTV made him positively happy. I would have been clawing out my eyeballs at the prospect.

'If we're going to concentrate on the residents I want to allocate the flats to teams of detectives.' Burt flattened out a list on the clipboard in front of her. 'Flat 102 and 105, Pettifer and Upton, flat 101 and 103, Kerrigan and Derwent, assuming we can prove Armstrong was in 103 – I'll reallocate you if he was somewhere else. While we're waiting to hear about that you can interview the family from 101 and the lady from 104. Flat—'

'Hold on a second,' Derwent said from the back of the room. 'I want flat 102.'

'I thought you might. Mal and Chris are handling it.'

'Oh, come on. I've started on it already. And I want to do a good job on it, for the boy's sake. He deserves the best.' Derwent glanced across at Mal Upton. 'No offence.'

'Offence taken.' Mal glowered at Derwent. 'I think we can manage this one on our own, sir.'

'That's my boy,' Chris Pettifer said, just loudly enough that everyone in the room could hear him. Mal was a recent addition to the team and terrified of Derwent. I was impressed that he was standing up to him.

'Concentrate on Armstrong, Josh,' Una Burt said. 'He's an important part of this. It's foolish to think he isn't. This is the most sensitive aspect of the investigation, potentially. It's the one thing that is going to keep the media focused on us and what we're doing at all times. I want someone senior working on Armstrong, and he is going to take up a lot of your time. The family in 101 should be fairly straightforward. Armstrong will be anything but. So get your priorities right.'

The expression on Derwent's face was pure murder.

'Anyway, it shouldn't matter.' Burt smiled at him sweetly. 'You'll all be working as a team. I expect you to share your knowledge. Ask your subjects about the other residents. Find out as much as you can. I want to build up a complete picture of what life was like in Murchison House before the fire. Assume that everyone is lying unless you can corroborate it independently.'

'I think we all know how to conduct interviews,' Derwent spat.

Her head snapped up. 'I've learned not to assume you know the basics, Josh. I'd rather remind you now than pick up the pieces afterwards.'

Wisely, he decided not to challenge her to be specific. I could see it was a struggle. The fact was that he *had* made mistakes in the past. I'd even helped to hide some of them, not that he was remotely grateful.

Burt turned to Harper. 'We all have a lot of work to do, it seems. Thank you for sharing your knowledge with us.'

He nodded. 'I'll be working on this fire for the foreseeable future. I'll keep you informed, of course, if anything else comes up.'

In the general chaos as the briefing ended, I found Derwent at my side.

'What a load of bollocks.'

'Harper was interesting. He knew his stuff.'

'Not him. *Her*.'

I grinned at him. 'I know. I was just winding you up.'

'I'm already wound as far as I can go.' He shook his head. 'She's waiting for me to put a foot wrong. The tension is killing me.'

'If you do what she says she can't complain.'

'She can, and she will.' Derwent rubbed his eyes with his forefinger and thumb. 'Christ, the lack of sleep is catching up with me.'

'You're getting old.'

'Watch it, Kerrigan,' he snapped.

'Okay, okay. You're still young and vibrant.'

Una Burt bustled past us and Derwent gave her retreating back a death stare. 'She fancies Harper.'

'What? Don't be ridiculous.'

'He's exactly her type. An older man, rugged and brave. I'd say she's in with a chance, too.'

'Really?' I was genuinely surprised.

'Absolutely. He's used to studying things that have been set on fire and put out with a shovel. Burt's face probably looks like homework.'

Before I could reply, Derwent leaned across and grabbed Chris Pettifer's shoulder. He turned from his conversation with Mal, surprise darkening to disapproval on both of their faces.

'Listen, sorry about before. I never meant to suggest you two weren't good enough to handle the Melissa Pell investigation. It's just that we'd already started on it and got involved. You know how it is.'

Derwent had turned on the charm for them, giving them the benefit of the honesty I found so disarming.

Apparently I was the only one.

'Fuck you very much,' Pettifer snapped. 'You might have got away with being a princess when Godley was in charge here but you're not going to be able to do it while Burt is running the show. You need to learn some manners.' He and Derwent were drinking buddies, so he could get away with talking to him like that.

'It's got nothing to do with manners. That was Burt looking for something she could use to annoy me. You two just got in the way.'

'Again, fuck you.'

Derwent shoved his hands in his pockets and leaned back against the wall, completely relaxed, or pretending to be. 'Melissa Pell, right? Domestic violence victim. She's run away from her husband and what was probably a pretty nice life to live in a high-rise shithole in north London with her kid. How do you think she feels about men?'

Pettifer shook his head. 'Not relevant.'

'Absolutely relevant. She's going to be scared of you and she's not going to tell you anything.' Derwent elbowed me in the side, pushing me forward. 'You need Kerrigan.'

I blinked, caught off guard. 'What? Why are you putting me in the middle of this?'

'Because you're a bird and they aren't.' Derwent smiled thinly at Pettifer and Mal. 'Look at them. Not the gentle sort, are they?'

Pettifer had played rugby until his knees gave out and

he had the face to prove it. Mal was shaggy-haired, untidy and as clumsy as a Great Dane.

'I wouldn't say Kerrigan was exactly gentle either,' Pettifer said.

I folded my arms. 'I don't know whether to thank you or tell you to piss off.'

'You didn't get your reputation for being sweetness and light.'

'What reputation?' I demanded.

'Nothing.' Pettifer started to back away. 'Absolutely nothing.'

'Come back and explain yourself.'

'Nope. Too scared.'

'Oh, come on,' I said, disgusted. 'As if you're really scared of me.'

'Yeah, you're right. Try terrified.' Mal was shuffling away too.

'So you're too scared to leave her behind when you go to speak to Melissa Pell,' Derwent said. 'You couldn't take that kind of risk.'

Pettifer stopped. 'You never give up, do you?'

'Not really.'

Pettifer pointed at me. '*She* can come. You'd better stay away.'

'That was my plan.' Derwent grinned. 'Thanks, mate.'

'Don't thank me.' He walked away, shadowed by Mal.

I turned to Derwent. 'Where's my thank you?'

'Don't push it, Kerrigan.'

'You heard what Burt said. We're going to be busy. When am I supposed to have time to speak to Melissa Pell?'

95

'Whenever they need you. I'll let you go,' he said, magnanimous as ever.

'Burt will rip off my head if she finds out.'

'I'm sure that's not what they taught her on her management course. She's all about people skills now. She'll just tell you she's very, very disappointed in you.'

'Oh, great.'

'Enjoy it.' Derwent stretched. 'Your trouble is you're a people-pleaser. You want to make everyone happy.'

'Is that a bad thing?'

'It is for you.'

'Okay,' I said. 'I like to make people happy. You like to make them miserable.'

He grinned. 'If I have to.'

'Or for fun.'

'Or, indeed, for fun.'

'So, this Melissa Pell thing,' I said. 'It's because you know it will annoy Una Burt that I'm involved.'

The grin disappeared. All of a sudden he was as serious as I'd ever seen him. 'Not at all. I meant what I said in the briefing. I want the best copper I know to investigate her case.'

I felt a warm, unfamiliar glow of pride mingled with surprise. 'Oh. That's—'

'And if they can't have the best,' Derwent said, 'you'll have to do.'

Chapter 9

The relatives' room was overheated and the windows were clouded with condensation. It was a small, miserable space, furnished with wooden-framed armchairs that seemed to have been designed to be not quite comfortable enough to sleep in.

It didn't help that there were so many people in the room – nine, including me and Derwent. We stood with our backs to the door, largely ignored, as a wizened woman blew her nose into a giant handkerchief. Two large men sat on either side of her. One was bearded, the other clean-shaven but you would have known them as brothers straight away by the shape of their heads, the breadth of their shoulders and their shovel-like hands. They were dark-haired, with sallow skin, and reminded me of storybook gypsies – I half expected them to have gold hoop earrings glinting among their curls. Beside them sat a plump fair woman with small eyes and petrol-blue nails. She looked up when we came in but didn't speak, returning her attention to the two little girls who were squabbling over a colouring book on the floor. A boy sat beside the woman, staring into space. He was overweight, his t-shirt riding up to expose a half-moon of white stomach. I recognised the unseeing gaze: shock.

'Sorry to interrupt,' Derwent said. 'I'm looking for a Carl Bellew.'

There was a pause before the clean-shaven man said, 'That's me.'

Derwent introduced us and explained that we were investigating the fire. 'You are the owner of flat 101 on the tenth floor of Murchison House, is that right?'

'That's right.' He was surly, not making eye contact with us. The older woman was watching us, holding the handkerchief up to her face so I couldn't quite see her expression. Her eyes were shrewd, though, and I felt she was missing nothing. It was clear that the men got their colouring from her, even if her hair was now dyed a shade of blue-black that didn't exist in nature. She was sallow, like her sons, but a quarter of their size. Her face was thin, the skin lined and cracked like a dried-out riverbed. Her nose was too big for the rest of her features and curved like a beak. She had a big black handbag on her lap and she held on to it with one claw-like hand that was wrapped in a white bandage. She wasn't old so much as desiccated. She could have been any age from fifty to eighty.

'And you live there with your family,' Derwent checked.

'Yeah. The kids, the wife and Mum.'

'Are all of these yours?' Derwent indicated the two girls and the boy.

'No. Just the lad. My daughter is in intensive care.'

'That's why we're here,' the older woman said.

I frowned. 'Isn't intensive care on the next floor?'

'Yeah, but there isn't a room we can use there.' She pulled her handbag closer to her chest. 'It's not as if we have anywhere else to go.'

'Mum, you can come home with me, I told you.' The bearded man patted his mother's arm with a giant hand. She shook him off without looking at him.

'Leave it for now, Rocco. Now's not the time.'

I caught the tail end of an expression that passed over the fair-haired woman's face: pure horror. Not the easiest mother-in-law, I guessed.

'Who exactly was in the flat at the time of the fire?' Derwent asked.

'Me. Mum—'

'Nina Bellew,' she said. 'That's my name. Nina.'

'Yeah,' Carl said, giving her a wary look. 'Nina Bellew. Becky, my daughter – she's seven – and Nathan. Nathan's ten.'

At the sound of his name the boy's eyelids flickered but he didn't really come out of his stupor.

'Anyone else?' Derwent asked.

'Debbie, my wife.'

'No, she wasn't there. She'd gone out, remember? Down to the shops. She wasn't there at the time of the fire. That's what he asked. Not who lives in the flat. Who was there at the time of the fire.' Nina Bellew reminded me of a crow, with her harsh voice and staccato delivery. The words rattled out of her like machine-gun fire.

'Yeah, all right, Mum. Debbie had gone out.'

'Did she go to the shops on the estate?' I asked.

'Yeah.'

'So she hadn't been gone for long.'

'No. Ten, twenty minutes?'

'The bloody lift was broken again, wasn't it? She had to walk all the way down and all the way back up again. Takes bloody ages.' Nina sniffed. 'She's not one to hurry herself, is she?'

If Nina was waiting for her on her return, I was inclined to feel Debbie had every right to dawdle.

Before Derwent could ask his next question the simmering tension between the two small girls boiled over. Twin screams of rage tore through the air. It was all I could do to stop myself from putting my hands over my ears. Nina looked disgusted. Nathan drew his knees up and tried to curl into a ball on the chair, like an armadillo. He pulled his hoodie over his head and tightened the strings so his face was hidden.

'Lola, stop it. Tansy, you too.' The fair-haired woman spoke in a high, wispy voice, her words barely audible from where I was standing.

'Come on, Louise, can't you keep them quiet for five minutes?' Rocco demanded.

'I'm trying,' Louise whispered. 'It ain't easy. They've got the hump because we've been stuck in here all day.'

'Supporting my family in their hour of need.'

'That doesn't matter to *her*,' Nina said venomously. 'She'd see us on the street sooner than offer to take us in.'

'That's not true.' Louise looked wounded. 'I'd never leave you with nowhere to go.'

Derwent had obviously judged that the family squabbling could go on all day. He raised his voice so he could be heard. 'Where is Debbie?'

'She's with Becky,' Carl said.

'No, she's not,' Nina snapped. To us, she said, 'She wanted to stay with her but she's not allowed. They let her wait in the hall, by Becky's room.'

'We'll go and speak to her in a minute.'

Nina snorted. 'She won't be able to tell you anything. Never pays any attention to what's going on around her. She's in a dream half the time.'

'You never know. Sometimes people see things or hear things that don't seem significant at the time but they're important for us to know,' I said. 'And on that point, did any of you see anything suspicious yesterday? Or hear anything?'

Carl and Nina shook their heads in unison. Nathan was invisible.

'Do you know of any reason why anyone would want to harm you or anyone in your family?' Derwent's tone was matter-of-fact and the question was routine but the effect on Carl Bellew was striking. He went pale and started opening and closing his mouth like a recently landed fish.

'Course not.' Nina shot a look at her son. 'There's no reason, is there, Carl?'

'No.' He shook his head again, this time so violently that his jowls rasped on the collar of his shirt.

'Why are you making out this was something to do with us?' Rocco leaned forward, his hands balled into massive fists that he braced on his thighs. 'We've done nothing to bother anyone.'

'We have to ask,' I said smoothly. 'You'd be surprised. Anyone can get into a fight, can't they?'

'People don't fight with us,' Nina Bellew said.

'Not if they know what's good for them.' Rocco said it in a mutter but I heard it, and Nina heard it. She turned and treated her other son to the look she'd given his brother.

'What's your date of birth, Carl?' Derwent asked.

'Seven, seven, seventy.'

'The seventh of July, 1970.' Derwent was writing it down.

'That's what I said.'

'And what do you do for a living?' I asked.

'Handyman,' Carl muttered. Louise couldn't quite keep the look of surprise off her face, I noticed. She bent her head over one of her daughters so I couldn't see her expression any more.

'You must be doing well,' Derwent said pleasantly. 'You bought your flat, didn't you?'

'Yeah.' He looked shifty. 'It was a right-to-buy type of thing. The council was selling so we bought it.'

'We?'

'Me and Mum.'

'You're not on the paperwork, Mrs Bellew,' Derwent said.

'I gave him some money. So what? It was a family matter.' She smiled at her son, revealing shining white dentures that were as even and unsettling as the teeth of a ventriloquist's dummy. 'He knows better than to try and kick me out.'

'I wouldn't want to even try,' Carl said. Sweat glinted on his upper lip and across his forehead.

'Have you lived there long?' I asked.

'Only since it was built; 1966, I moved in,' Nina said. 'Never lived anywhere else as a married woman. Never wanted to.'

'And you were all right with your son and his wife living with you?'

'Course I was. Family's family. Anyway, he was always my favourite.'

'Oi!' Rocco looked genuinely upset. 'Leave it out, Mum.'

She cackled. 'I'm only pulling your leg.'

Derwent turned to Carl. 'Where did you keep your tools? In the flat?'

He looked cagey. 'Why do you want to know?'

'We're looking for anything that could have started the fire accidentally. If you had a drill charging or if you had paint or varnish it would help us to know about it.'

'No. Nothing like that.'

'So where do you keep your tools?' I asked.

'In a lock-up garage behind Barber House.'

'That's one of the other tower blocks,' I said to Derwent.

'That's lucky, isn't it? You won't have lost anything.' Derwent's tone was deceptively light.

'Yeah. Of course.' Carl glanced at his mother, looking for help, and got only withering scorn. 'Is there any chance we can get back into the flat?'

'No. It's too dangerous,' Derwent said firmly.

'There's something I've got to get.'

'If it was in the flat, it's gone.' Derwent shook his head. 'Smoke damage, fire damage, water damage. Whatever it is, it's had it, mate.'

'No, I understand that. But it's of sentimental value, you know.'

'There really wasn't anything left,' I said, thinking of the scorched chandelier hanging over the wreckage in the living room. 'I'm so sorry.'

'There was a safe. In my room.' Nina Bellew blinked very rapidly. 'Behind the bed. Not big. Thirteen inches by ten by ten.' She sketched out the size with her free hand. The other was still clinging to her handbag. 'The safe was supposed to be fireproof. There are things in it that I should have.'

'I can ask the fire crews and scene of crime officers to look out for it,' I said.

'They can't touch it. It's mine.'

'Mrs Bellew, they'll be clearing out the contents of your flat. If they come across anything that can be salvaged, including the safe, it will be returned to you.'

'They'll nick it now they know it's valuable. But it's not money or jewellery. Nothing like that.' She blinked again, and I realised it was a sign she was agitated. 'It's personal. Sentimental value, like what Carl said.'

'I promise you, they won't steal anything,' I said. 'They'd get fired immediately if they were caught. It wouldn't be worth it.'

'That's what you think,' Nina croaked.

'It's what I know.'

'I'll tell them to look out for it. Whatever they recover, you're welcome to inspect it. If they find it and the contents have been destroyed, you'll be able to reassure yourself that the safe was fire-damaged, not emptied.'

'Listen, missy, I know they can make it look as if it was burned and everything was destroyed. I wasn't born yesterday.'

'When were you born, Mrs Bellew?' Derwent asked, his pen poised over his notebook.

She looked horrified. 'That's not something I tell my nearest and dearest, young man.'

'Yeah, but I'm not near or dear. I'm a police officer and I'm asking for your date of birth.'

'Fifteenth of February.' Her normal rasp was muted to a mumble.

'Year?'

''46.'

'1946,' Derwent said clearly. 'Thank you, Mrs Bellew. And what was your maiden name?'

'Hayes.'

'Thank you.'

'Piss off,' she muttered.

'What was that, Mrs Bellew?'

'Nothing. Here, haven't you asked us enough questions? We're very upset, you know. We've lost our home and our belongings and my little granddaughter is very ill. Can't you leave us in peace?'

'Almost done,' Derwent said with a sympathetic smile that didn't reach his eyes. 'I need an address for you in case we need to contact you again.'

'They'll be living with me,' Rocco said, and the two girls sat bolt upright, stricken.

'What – all of them?' Louise laughed. 'Where are we going to put them?'

'We'll manage, all right?' To Derwent, he said, 'It's 24 Eastfield Lane.'

'And a telephone number for each of you.' Derwent passed his notebook around, turned to a fresh page so they couldn't see what he'd written down about them. Nina didn't even glance at it.

'Ain't got a phone. Don't like mobiles. The radiation cooks your brain.'

'You can get hold of Mum through me,' Carl said. 'She won't be far from me.'

'Or me.' Rocco scowled at his brother. 'We'll be right beside her.'

'Aren't I lucky.' Nina Bellew winked at Derwent and it was impossible to tell if she meant what she was saying, or if we were supposed to understand the exact opposite.

Chapter 10

'I have questions.'

'So do I,' Derwent said. I followed him down the hospital corridor, struggling slightly to keep up with him. A polished floor and heels did not go together, but I liked wearing heels. I was tall anyway. I never minded being taller still, especially at work. There were men who had decided against causing me trouble, purely because I could look them in the eye.

One of them was walking a stride ahead of me.

'Why did you ask Mrs Bellew for her date of birth?' I asked.

'I want to run her through the box.' He meant the PNC database.

'Do you think she has a record?'

'I'm sure of it. And her sons definitely do.' Derwent sidestepped a young nurse, then turned to watch her walk away. He gave a soundless whistle. 'I love hospitals.'

'You're a cliché.'

'Oh, come on. Who doesn't fancy nurses? Young and pretty, eager to please, nice little uniform . . .'

'She was wearing scrubs, which are not exactly designed to be titillating.'

'Titillating,' Derwent repeated, grinning. '*Titillating*.'

I ignored him. 'Just because she's a nurse that doesn't mean you can leer at her.'

'You're jealous.'

'I hardly think so.'

There was a police officer on duty outside the intensive care unit where Becky Bellew was being treated. We showed our credentials to her and Derwent checked that nothing had happened since she'd been on duty.

'No journalists hanging around? No one strange asking questions?'

'Nothing, sir.' She sounded definite.

'Bored yet?'

'No, sir.' She was probably in her early twenties but she was the sort of person who seemed to have been born middle-aged, from her sensible haircut to her no-nonsense manner.

'Keep up the good work,' Derwent said, and held open the door so I could pass through. I waited until he'd closed it again.

'What are you, the Queen? "Keep up the good work"?'

He looked defensive. 'What was I supposed to say to her?'

'I don't know. Apparently there's nothing in your repertoire that isn't flirting or patronising.'

His expression darkened. 'There's intimidating.'

'Yeah, you're really scary.'

'I can be.'

'Of course you can,' I said sweetly. 'You can be anything you want to be if you just believe in yourself.'

'There was a time you were afraid of me,' Derwent complained.

'I got over that.'

'Don't tell me.' That slow grin spread across his face. 'You've been imagining me naked.'

'I don't have to imagine that. I've seen it.' In the most unromantic circumstances possible, naturally.

The grin widened. 'Of course you have.'

'But don't worry about that.'

He frowned. 'Why would I worry?'

'You were cold and hurt. I'm sure it wasn't your most impressive showing. I'm willing to give you the benefit of the doubt.'

'Kerrigan.'

'Sir.'

He sucked in his cheeks, trying not to laugh, then settled for shaking his head. 'Back to work.'

'Yes, sir.' I headed to the nurses' station so I could ask where Debbie Bellew might be. An Irish nurse who reminded me of my mother gave us directions.

'You'll find her in the corridor outside her daughter's room. Poor lady. She's very upset. She hasn't slept. She won't eat anything and I only just got her to take a little drink of tea a while ago.'

'How's her daughter doing?' Derwent asked.

'Ah, you know. We can't say for sure yet. All we can do is wait.'

Debbie was sitting with her head in her hands, her hair falling down on either side of her face so I couldn't tell if she was sleeping or crying or just thinking.

'Mrs Bellew?'

Her head snapped up, anxiety corrugating her brow. 'What is it? Is it Becky?'

'We're police officers, Mrs Bellew. We're investigating what happened at Murchison House yesterday.'

'Oh.' She looked past us, as if she was expecting to see someone else. She looked uncertain, and also – strangely, in the circumstances – guilty. 'What do you want me to say?'

'We'd like to ask you some questions about yesterday evening,' Derwent said. 'Firstly, you weren't in the flat at the time the fire broke out. What time did you leave?'

'Oh . . .' She blinked up at us. 'I don't know. After five, I suppose.'

'Why did you leave?'

'I was buying cake for Nina. My mother-in-law,' she clarified. 'She sent me down to the shop. I was only gone twenty minutes. Half an hour at most.'

'Sent you,' I repeated.

'I didn't mind.' Debbie pulled her sleeves down over her hands, a gesture that I'd have expected from a teenager more than from a grown woman. 'I never mind going out to the shops.'

'Even though the lift was broken,' Derwent said with a smile.

'Keeps me fit.'

'Did you see anyone suspicious on your way to the shops?' I asked. She shook her head.

'What about anyone you didn't know?'

'There was a man.' Debbie sounded vague. 'I can't remember much about him. He was on the stairs and he walked past me.'

'Age?'

'I don't know.'

'Younger than me? Older than me?' Derwent was really trying not to sound impatient but it edged his voice and Debbie shrank a little.

'Maybe the same? I don't know.'

'Build?'

'Normal.'

'What does that mean?' Derwent asked.

'I don't know. Normal.' She flapped her hands, agitated. 'I didn't know he was important.'

'He might not be.' I gave Derwent a warning look. To Debbie, I said, 'What about his face? Could you describe him?'

'He was white.'

'Is that it?' Derwent demanded.

'I couldn't see him very well. He had a hat on.'

'Hair colour?'

She shook her head.

'Eye colour? Glasses?'

'I just saw the hat.'

'What was it like?'

'I don't know.' Debbie started to sob. 'I can't remember.'

'Was it a baseball cap?' I asked. 'With a peak? Or a hat with a brim?'

'Baseball cap.' She gave a couple of sniffs. 'Red.'

'Any logos on it? Or other colours?'

'No.'

'What about his clothes?'

'Jeans, I think, and a dark jacket.' She ran her finger down the centre of her torso. 'It had a zip.'

'Shoes?'

'Trainers?' It was a guess and we all knew it.

'That's very helpful,' Derwent said. 'If you think of anything else about him, do tell us.' He handed her a card. 'Call that number any time. Day or night.'

It was my telephone number on the card he'd given her, I saw.

'I won't remember anything else,' Debbie said. 'I barely saw him.'

'If you do, you know where to find us,' Derwent said easily. 'How's your daughter?'

'Not good.' She sounded bleak.

'I'm sorry.' For once, Derwent was completely sincere. 'Would you like me to get someone to keep you company here? Your husband—'

'No!' It was pure instinct. I saw her try to get herself under control. 'No. Thank you. He's got Nathan to look after.'

I thought of the stunned boy curled up on his chair, being roundly ignored by his family.

'Were you scared of anyone outside the family?' I asked.

'Not outside.' It was an unguarded comment and she caught it just too late, putting a hand over her mouth.

'Mrs Bellew, if you feel unsafe—'

'No. No, it was a joke.' She tried to smile. 'Just a joke.'

I'd come back to it, I thought. Some time when she was less upset, less wary. I'd help her, if I could.

'Do they think it was deliberate?' she asked. 'The fire?'

'They don't know yet,' Derwent said. 'That's why we're trying to work out if there was a reason for it to be arson.'

Her face was grey, like dirty ice. 'But it could have been an accident.'

'It's possible. Why do you ask?'

'I just can't remember.' She squeezed her hands together in her lap. 'I keep trying, but I can't.'

'Remember what?' I asked.

'I was ironing, before I left.' She put a hand to her head, distraught. 'And I don't remember. I don't remember turning the iron off.'

'They found an iron,' Derwent said. 'The investigator said. They'll be able to tell if that was where the fire started.'

'They can work it out?' She looked even more worried. 'But if everything's burned . . .'

'They're used to studying fires. They can find out a lot more than you or I could.' Derwent smiled. 'But you really shouldn't worry about it.'

'My daughter is lying in that room suffering and it could be because of me. I can't help worrying.'

I felt very sorry for her. 'I can ask the investigator, if you like. I'll let you know what he says.'

'I'd just like to know.' Debbie's eyes were full of tears.

'I understand.'

'Do you know if anyone had a reason to threaten you or your family?' I asked.

'Threaten them? What are you talking about?'

'We're trying to find out if anyone had a motive to set the fire, Mrs Bellew. If anyone had a grudge against your family or wanted to scare you, that would be useful for us to know.'

Her eyes were huge. 'I – why would you think anyone would be angry with us?'

'We're asking everyone,' Derwent explained. 'It's not just you.'

'Oh.' She looked down at her hands. 'What did Carl say?'

'Why is that important?' Derwent asked.

A tiny shrug. 'Whatever he said is what I think.'

'That's the rule, is it?'

'It's the truth.' She was still looking down, sullen. We'd lost her. Derwent caught my eye and nodded towards the exit.

'We'll leave you in peace, Mrs Bellew,' I said. 'Remember, you can call me any time if you have any questions or if you remember anything at all that was strange about yesterday, even if you don't think it's relevant or important.'

She nodded. Derwent and I had started to walk away when she spoke again, to ask the same question she'd asked before.

'What did Carl say?'

Derwent glanced at me. I shrugged.

'He said no one had any reason to harm you.'

'Did he?' She said it softly. 'Was his mum there?'

'Yes.'

'I wonder what he'd have said if she wasn't there.'

'Why's that?'

She shook her head, still not looking at us. 'Just wondering, that's all.'

We turned away. Derwent stopped once we were out of range. 'We need to talk to Carl again.'

'I'd say so.'

'On his own this time.'

'As a priority.'

'And see if any CCTV cameras got footage of a man in a cap.'

'He might not have been wearing the cap all the time,' I pointed out.

'What does that leave? A man in jeans and a zip-up jacket.'

'Yeah, because I'm sure there was only one of them hanging around.'

'It's a start,' Derwent said grimly. 'At this stage, that's all we need.'

Chapter 11

We walked back down the stairs together, avoiding the lifts, because hospital lifts were slow and full of people who needed to use them, unlike us. I was always embarrassed to cram myself in alongside a patient on a trolley, and Derwent was paranoid about catching some sort of virus. That, in a nutshell, was the difference between us.

'What's next?'

'The lady from flat 104,' I said, checking my notes. 'She's the one who was rescued by the fire crews.'

'A housebound little old lady.' Derwent rolled his eyes. 'She's not going to be much use to us, is she? She won't have seen anything. Or heard anything, probably. I bet she's deaf.'

'I'm sure you'll manage to communicate with her. You have a loud enough voice.'

'You can handle it. I'm going back to Carl Bellew.'

'He'll still be with his mother. You can't call him out of the room in front of her – she'll know exactly what you're up to.'

'He's got to piss some time.'

'You might have a long wait.'

'I don't mind. I'm disciplined, you see.'

'Una Burt would say you were wasting your time.'

'She says a lot of things about me, and most of them aren't true.'

'I think,' I said, trying to be diplomatic, 'she just doesn't give you much credit. She doesn't actually lie about what you do or how you do it. But she definitely doesn't approve of you.'

'Then I must be doing something right.'

We walked down the corridor, Derwent a little in front of me. That meant he went around the next corner first, and collided with a woman who was walking the other way. 'Whoops.'

'A fucking apology wouldn't go amiss, thank you very much,' she snapped. She was tanned to a leathery orange that clashed with her pale pink lipstick. Her hair was in the matted rat's tails I associated with cheap extensions.

'A fucking apology?' Derwent repeated slowly. 'I'm very fucking sorry. Your turn.'

The answer was a raised middle finger. She walked off, giving us the benefit of her backside in very tight, very stonewashed jeans that had a few strategic rips so her neon-orange skin could show through.

'How many coats of Ronseal do you think that took?' Derwent's nose was wrinkled in disgust.

'I don't know but I'd say she's fully protected for winter.'

'She looks dirty.'

'I thought that was your type,' I said.

Derwent looked appalled. 'There's dirty and dirty.

You'd need a trip to the STD clinic every time you held her hand. Anyway, I prefer the natural look.'

I snorted. 'I bet you're one of those men who says they love women who don't wear make-up when you actually don't have any idea what we look like without it.'

'It can be a surprise the morning after,' he admitted. 'You never know what you're going to get in the cold light of day.'

'Maybe you should try to find someone you're prepared to see more than once.'

He grinned. 'Where's the fun in that?'

'It's all about the thrill of the chase for you, isn't it?'

A shrug. 'I only go after the ones who want to be caught.'

'Which is every woman, according to you.'

'Not every woman.' He turned away. 'Just most of them.'

The annoying thing was that I knew he didn't have any trouble getting women to sleep with him. He was attractive enough, but it was the fact that he was a pure predator about it that made him so effective. He was ruthless, and determined, and he liked women – at least, he liked having sex with them. I'd seen it work time and time again.

He headed towards the waiting room where the Bellews had been, and I went in the opposite direction, towards double doors guarded by another uniformed officer. This one was slouching in his chair, looking at the ceiling. He was young and clean-cut.

I stopped beside him. 'Is this where they took the victims from the tower block fire?'

'Yep.'

'Thanks.' I opened the door and went through. After a second I opened the door again. 'Did you want to check if I was supposed to be here, or what?'

'Huh?'

I held up my ID and watched the colour leave his face.

'Sorry. I should have—'

'Yes, you should.' *But you looked at me and you didn't think 'cop'. You definitely didn't think CID.* 'Why do you think you're sitting here?'

'To stop people bothering the victims.'

'Bothering – or harming them. We still don't know why the fire happened, or if it was deliberate. These people are witnesses at the very least, even if they aren't targets. And there'll be journalists coming and going, pretending to be hospital staff or counsellors or just visitors.'

'I know that.'

'Do you? But it didn't ring any alarm bells for you when you heard me ask specifically about the fire victims?'

'There've been quite a few people asking,' he said lamely. 'They're curious. Other patients, you know. I haven't let anyone through the doors who didn't have proper ID.'

'Anyone else, I think you mean. That's something, I suppose.' I gave him a hard stare. If it had been Derwent who'd encountered this idiot he'd have left him in tatters. I hadn't the heart – not quite. But I didn't want him to think it didn't matter. 'You're the last person between these people and harm. Your job is to keep them safe. You have to be alert, and wary of every single person who passes you, even if they look like legitimate hospital employees.

You're not going to get in trouble for being too careful. You're going to get in trouble if you sit there and let someone through those doors who shouldn't be there.'

'But you're a police officer.'

'And you had no idea that was the case when I walked through that door.'

'I'm sorry.'

'Be honest. Have you let anyone else go through there without checking their ID?'

He shook his head earnestly. 'You just moved so fast.'

'Yeah, I really didn't give you a chance.'

He looked as if he was about to agree with me before he detected the sarcasm in my voice.

'Do better,' I said quietly, and went back through the doors again without waiting for an answer.

Mrs Mary Hearn had a room to herself, a sunny room that was already filling up with cards and balloons. She looked small in the bed, her slight frame propped up on stacks of pillows. Her fluffy white hair was untidy, her face lined and thin. I could smell smoke when I walked into the room, the acrid smell I'd noticed at the crime scene. A stocky man was sitting on a chair beside the bed. He stood up when I introduced myself.

'Do you want me to leave?'

'I don't mind if you stay. Are you Mrs Hearn's . . .'

'Neighbour.' He corrected himself. 'Ex-neighbour.'

'This is Young Kevin.' She smiled at him. 'I don't know what I'd do without him.'

'I've lived next door to Mrs Hearn all my life. Until she moved.' He smiled. 'Still can't get used to not having her there.'

'When did you move, Mrs Hearn?'

'Eight months ago.'

'Is it that long?' Kevin ran a hand over his balding head, embarrassed. 'Where does the time go?'

'You're busy, you see, with the children. You wouldn't notice.'

'I meant to come round and see you.' To me, he said, 'My parents were Mrs Hearn's neighbours. They all used to look after each other and the rest of us. My parents are dead, but Mrs Hearn was like another mum to me.'

She smiled. 'That's how I thought of it too.'

'Mrs Hearn knew everyone on our road,' Kevin said. 'She never missed anything that happened. If you wanted to know what was going on, Mrs Hearn was the one to ask.'

'You make me sound like a busybody,' Mrs Hearn complained.

'My favourite kind of person,' I said. 'I like people who notice things. I imagine it wasn't so easy for you to get to know everything about everyone when you moved to your flat.'

The reply was instant. 'Well, it was more difficult. No windows, you see, except the ones looking out over the streets and I was too high up to see much. No, that was no use. But I did get to see people coming and going. And the great thing was that they couldn't see me.'

'How was that?'

She nodded at Young Kevin. 'He set up a camera for me.'

'Just so she could see people calling to the door.' He looked worried. 'It wasn't wrong, was it? But the peephole was bloody rubbish and I'd heard about old – older people being attacked when they answer the door, so I wanted her to be able to see who was standing outside.'

'Do you mean a CCTV camera?'

'All I had to do was look on the television. Channel 773.' She smiled. 'Young Kevin is so clever.'

I turned to him, my fingers crossed. 'Did it record to tape? Or disc?'

'It was a live feed.'

'Nothing recorded?' I said, hope fading.

'No.'

Which left what Mrs Hearn had seen.

'What sort of view did you have?' I asked, trying not to betray too much interest in case it made her nervous. 'Just in front of your door?'

'Oh no. I could see the whole corridor. Everyone coming and going.'

'It was a fisheye lens,' Young Kevin explained.

She smiled. 'It was like having my own television programme. Better than *EastEnders*. I got to know everyone.'

'I can imagine.'

'I had to give them nicknames. I didn't know who they really were. But I felt as if I was getting to know them.'

'Who did you see? The people who lived there?'

'And their visitors. And the people who seemed to come now and then but didn't live there.'

'Like who?'

'Well, like the boy and his mother who moved in a little while ago. I called her Judy and I called him Luke because he reminded me of Luke – do you remember,

Kevin? Luke who used to live at number eight? Gorgeous little lad but he was killed by a car.'

Melissa Pell and her son. I nodded, encouraging her. 'What did you notice about them?'

'She always checked the corridor before she let him out of the flat. She'd come out and look around – check the stairwell and so forth – and then she'd call him if the coast was clear.'

'If the coast was clear,' I repeated.

'I don't know what was worrying her,' Mrs Hearn said, 'but she was afraid of something. Or someone. I was mugged myself so I didn't blame her for being careful. Luke was so good – such a well-behaved little fellow. Always muffled up with scarves and hats so you could barely see him.' She chuckled. 'He liked to press the button for the lift. Just liked pressing it. He knew it was broken.'

'Who else did you notice?'

'The gang at the end. The gangsters.'

'In which flat?' I checked my floorplan.

'The one at the end on my side. They weren't really gangsters – it's a family. Granny and parents and children.'

'The Bellews.'

'I don't know their name.'

'Why do you call them the gangsters?'

'All the coming and going. People calling to the door at all hours. And him and his brother going out late and early, looking for trouble.' Her eyes were bright. 'I'm making it up, you know.'

'You're not in court,' I said with a smile. 'Your impressions are a great help to me – you don't have to have proof. What else did you notice?'

What hadn't she noticed? She'd seen the man in 106 feeling up the woman from 109 in the hallway, late one night when they'd been having a party in 107. She'd seen the young mother in 108 with a new boyfriend every week. She'd seen the man in 104 come and go once a week, every week, regular as clockwork.

'I don't know what he was doing on the Maudling Estate. He looked too rich for the likes of us. Beautiful suits.' She ran a hand over the sheet that covered her. 'You could tell. Quality.'

'Did you recognise him?' I asked.

'No. I'd never met him.'

I showed her a picture of Armstrong. 'Could this be the man?'

'That's him.' She nodded. 'Who is he?'

I didn't answer her. 'Did you see who he was meeting?'

'Someone who didn't want to be noticed. She always had the hood up on her coat or a shawl over her head.'

'Can you describe her?'

'Tall. Dark complexion. Elegant – you know. Slim.'

'When you say a dark complexion, do you mean she was black?'

She nodded. I sat back on my chair. That would explain a lot, including why Armstrong had wanted to keep his visits a secret.

'What sort of age was she?' I was expecting her to say the woman was young, but she frowned.

'Maybe . . . thirty-five? Forty?'

'What makes you say that?'

'Just the way she carried herself. Like she was thinking about how she moved. Young people just . . . go. She always seemed very aware of how she walked.' Mrs Hearn shook her head. 'This is such rubbish, isn't it? A lonely old woman, inventing stories about people.'

'It's very useful indeed,' I said. 'Was there anything else you noticed about your neighbours?'

She thought. 'Nothing that stands out.'

'Can I ask about yesterday? Did you notice anything strange or unusual before the fire?'

'I wasn't watching what was going on in the hall. It was a nice day and I read for a while. I dozed.' She looked apologetic. 'I didn't know it was going to be important.'

'That's okay. Did you hear anything? Any arguments?'

'No. I heard people coming and going. The door to the stairwell always banged, you know, and I'd hear them going in and out. If they were talking they made a lot of noise. The voices echoed in the stairwell. It woke me up sometimes.'

Young Kevin shook his head. 'Thoughtless.'

'They were living,' she said, with a forcefulness that surprised both of us. 'They were falling in love and being families and making friends and fighting. What was I doing that couldn't be interrupted? Waiting to die?'

'Mrs Hearn,' Young Kevin said, and it was a reproach.

'I'm sorry, Kevin, but it's the truth. Since George died I've been existing. There's nothing left for me. You don't need me.'

'I do.' He put his hand on hers. 'We all do.'

I waited for a minute before I interrupted them. 'When did you become aware of the fire?'

'I heard running in the corridor. That wasn't unusual. But there was someone shouting too. And then the alarm went off.'

'The smoke alarm?'

'In my flat. And then of course I smelled the smoke.'

'Did you think about leaving?'

'I looked on the television and I saw people going to the stairs, but I couldn't see much. The hall was full of smoke. I can't even tell you who was there and who wasn't.'

'That's all right. We're working that out.' I smiled at her. 'Did you try to go out?'

'No. I thought I'd be too slow. I'd get in people's way. Maybe get knocked over.' She clutched the sheet. 'I don't like big crowds of people. They don't care about you. They don't notice if you're not too steady on your feet.'

'So you called the fire brigade.'

She nodded. 'They told me to stay where I was. They said they'd come and get me and they did. So it all worked out perfectly. Except that they wouldn't let me bring much with me.'

'They don't, as a rule.'

'I just took my handbag. That's all I have.' She looked very small in her hospital gown. 'When do you think I can go back?'

'Not for a while,' I said, thinking of the damage to Murchison House and how it would be a prime opportunity to demolish the whole thing. 'But you won't have to stay in hospital. They'll find you somewhere else to go.'

'You can come and live with us,' Young Kevin said.

'You don't have room for me.'

'We've got a spare room and no one's using it.'

Mrs Hearn smiled, although I thought she was on the verge of tears. 'I'd love that. It would be like going home.'

When I left, Young Kevin followed me into the corridor.

'Have you seen the flat? Mrs Hearn was wondering about her things. Photographs, you know. Her jewellery. I didn't want to ask you in there in case it was bad news.'

'There was quite a bit of smoke damage but I don't think the fire took hold in her flat. I'm sure some of it will be recoverable.'

'Can I go and take a look?'

I shook my head. 'The fire investigator is still working there and I'm not sure if it's safe for civilians at the moment.'

'Can you let me know? It's just' – he glanced back at the hospital room – 'she doesn't have much. I helped her move and she had almost nothing left. She kept the things that really mattered to her. I want to get them back for her, if I can.'

'I'll do what I can,' I said. 'You're very good to help her out like this.'

Kevin leaned against the wall. 'I feel like I let her down.'

'She doesn't think that.'

'She's had a hard life. No kids. And her husband dying—' He sighed. 'She wasn't the same after.'

'These things happen,' I said, knowing I sounded patronising. Husbands died, though. People had to deal with their tragedies. No one got out of life unscathed, in my experience.

Young Kevin was still wallowing in guilt. 'I left her

127

there on her own and I never checked to see she was all right. She'd been mugged, did you know that? I didn't know that. Broke her wrist. No wonder she was too scared to go into the corridor. Watching them all on the telly.' He shook his head. 'She was in prison, basically. And I helped to put her there. She's not going back.'

'It will be a long time before the flat is habitable.'

'She's not going back,' Young Kevin repeated, looking as fierce as his rounded features would allow. 'I don't know where she'll end up, but not there. Not if I have anything to do with it. I'm all she has left and I'm not going to let her down again.'

Chapter 12

I was in two minds about whether to go and find Derwent, to relieve him from his lonely vigil. Mrs Hearn's impression of the family suggested pretty strongly that Carl Bellew wasn't a simple handyman, that he was up to no good and that Debbie had been right to have her concerns about the fire. On the other hand, I hadn't found out anything substantive. I was wondering about drug-dealing. I was wondering if Carl and his brother were professional burglars. I had more questions than answers as a result of talking to Mrs Hearn, and Derwent was perfectly capable of asking the right questions himself without any input from me.

But I desperately wanted to share with someone – anyone – what I had learned about the woman who was presumably Geoff Armstrong's girlfriend. I headed for the double doors that led to the corridor, and had almost reached them when one of them burst open. I stepped back out of the way, as Mal Upton came through the door, looking flustered. Chris Pettifer followed, his face lighting up when he saw me.

'Just the girl I wanted.'

'What can I do for you?'

'You're coming with us to see Melissa Pell, aren't you?'

'Is she awake?'

'So I'm told.'

I fell into step beside them. 'Then yes. Thanks for including me.'

Pettifer snorted. 'Like I had a choice about it. Derwent would flay me alive and wear my skin as a coat if I didn't.'

'Picturesque,' I said. 'I'll try not to get in your way.'

Mal was still looking upset. 'What was all that about?' he asked Pettifer.

'What – the kid on the door? Just taking his job seriously, I should think.'

I started to laugh. 'Did he give you a hard time?'

'I didn't think he was going to let us in.'

'That would be my fault. I gave him a bit of a lecture earlier. I didn't think he was being strict enough about people who were coming and going.'

'Well, he sure as shit is now.' Pettifer grinned. 'And Mal got the worst of it.'

'That makes a lot more sense.' Mal glanced at me. 'No wonder he was scared if you shouted at him. You're terrifying.'

'This is a total myth,' I said. 'I'm not scary.'

'That's what you think. If you told me to jump, I'd ask how high.' Mal's face was very serious.

'I'm so tempted to try.'

'Please do.' Pettifer folded his arms. 'This I would pay to see.'

'Some other time.' I stopped. 'This is Melissa's room.'

'How do you want to play this?' Pettifer asked.

'Let me take the lead, at least at first, in case she's wary of men. Let's see how she is. She's been injured so she might not be feeling too bright.' I bit my lip. 'I don't want to push her too far today. But I do want to know how she ended up with such serious injuries when Thomas walked out of the building unharmed.'

'Anything else?'

'I want to know why she had to run away in the first place.'

Melissa had her eyes closed when we walked in. The room was dim, the blinds drawn. I glanced back to warn the other two to be quiet. By the time I looked back at the bed, she was staring at me with one eye. The other was still swollen shut. Her eyelashes were dark but her hair was very fair, the curls far more delicate than mine. She was astonishingly pretty, allowing for the bandage on her head and the bruising.

'Who are you?'

'Maeve Kerrigan. I'm a detective constable. These are my colleagues.' I indicated Upton and Pettifer, who were doing their best to look small and unthreatening. 'We're investigating the fire at Murchison House, Mrs Hathaway.'

'Oh.' She looked up at the ceiling, drifting a little. Then she snapped back to full attention. 'Have you seen my son?'

'I saw him after the fire,' I said carefully. 'He's being very well looked after.'

'Who's got him?' She reminded me of a cornered animal, halfway between angry and terrified.

'Social services at the moment. But we've been in contact with your mother.'

Melissa coughed, her whole body shaking, before she could speak again. 'Is she coming?'

I nodded. 'As soon as she can.'

'She knows where we are?'

'We had to tell her.' I hesitated. 'Mrs Hathaway, do you want me to keep calling you by that name? Or should I use your real name?'

'My real name?' she said, making it a question.

'You were Melissa Moore before you got married in 2009, when you became Melissa Pell. And your son is Thomas, isn't he? You changed his name when you ran away. You became Vivienne Hathaway and he became Sam.'

'You must have found my handbag.'

I actually didn't know if we had. I looked to see Pettifer shaking his head. 'No,' I said. 'We tracked you down through Harriet Edmonds.'

Tears filled her eyes. 'She promised me I could trust her. I believed her.'

'She took some persuading.' I sat down in the chair beside the bed, conscious that I was standing over her. 'We thought you'd want us to find someone to look after Thomas. In case you weren't well enough.'

'I'm getting out of here today,' Melissa said, sitting up and starting to unpeel the tape holding the IV needle in place. 'I'm going. And Thomas is coming with me.'

'Mrs Pell, you're not well enough.' I put a hand out to stop her and she flinched away from me.

'You don't understand. I have to go. I can't leave him.'

'But your mother—'

'She doesn't get it. She doesn't understand. She believes *him*, not me.'

'Him?' I could tell she didn't mean Thomas.

'My husband.' Melissa looked as if she was about to be sick. Her eyelashes fluttered against her cheeks, which were lacking all colour. 'Mark Pell. I have to keep Thomas away from him. He's dangerous.'

'Did he hurt Thomas?'

'Not yet.'

'Did he hurt you?'

She looked straight at me, daring me to doubt her. 'Over and over again.'

'Why doesn't your mother believe you?'

'Because he's so fucking good at persuading people he's a good man and I'm insane,' she spat. 'He's been halfway to getting me sectioned before now and no one ever believes you if you're mad, do they? Mental people can't possibly be telling the truth about their handsome, rich husband, and how he manipulates everything they say.'

'Did you report him to the police?'

'I tried. They thought I was doing it to myself – pretending he hit me, or pushed me downstairs, or burned me, or pulled out my hair. I mean, that's what he told everyone. The police, everyone. No one believed me, because how could it be true? Mr Perfect doesn't hit his wife. Even if she really, really deserves it for being a lying bitch. I accused him of all of these things, you see, and no one could believe it, so I had to be lying. And I had to be evil, too, to try to take his son away.' Two tears streaked down her cheeks. 'All of our friends. Our neighbours. Our families. He persuaded them all that I'd stolen Thomas. They're all sorry for him – can you imagine that?'

'You must have felt very much alone.'

'He made it so I couldn't even trust my own mother.' She corrected herself. 'I *can't* trust her. That's why I have to get out of here.'

'I spoke to her.' Pettifer sounded guilty. 'We wanted to get in touch with her because of Thomas. So she could help with him, I mean.'

'What did she say?'

'She said she'd come. She said she wished she'd supported you. She cried.'

Melissa covered her face with her hands so we couldn't see her weep. I glanced back at Pettifer. He mouthed, 'Ask about the fire.'

I pulled a face which was supposed to imply, *I had thought of that, thanks*. He shrugged.

Melissa's voice was muffled when she spoke. 'When is she coming?'

'Soon, I think.' I leaned forward. 'Mrs Pell, I need to ask you about what happened yesterday.'

'The fire.'

'Exactly.'

She sniffed, gathering herself together. 'I don't know what to tell you.'

'Did you see anything suspicious? Or hear anything?'

'Not really.'

'What do you mean by not really?'

She managed a half-smile. 'That's the trouble with being scared all the time. Everything is suspicious. Every sound is terrifying.'

I did actually know what she meant, but I didn't think I'd try to join in. *Let me tell you about my stalker . . .* 'Was there anything in particular that seemed different yesterday?'

She thought for a moment, really considering the question. 'It was just the usual sorts of things. Footsteps. Voices. People coming and going all the time. I'd never lived anywhere so noisy. You know, when there's someone above you and someone below you and someone on either side, you feel like a battery hen.'

'Especially if you're used to a detached house,' Mal suggested. His tone was gentle but it inspired pure aggression in Melissa Pell.

'You don't know anything about what I'm used to.'

'No, I'm just saying—'

'Think back,' I said, interrupting. 'What sounds did you hear that made you scared before the fire?'

She closed her eyes. 'Voices from the flat beside us. I thought I was hearing things. There wasn't anyone living there, as far as I knew. But I could hear voices.'

Armstrong and his girlfriend. 'What else?'

'A few random screams and shouts from upstairs – they were always noisy – and doors banging. But none of that was unusual. It was a noisy place.' She laughed. 'I was probably the only person who was glad when the lift was broken. It terrified me when it was working. The doors shake. They rattle when they slide back and I always think – thought – it was someone trying to break in to my flat.'

'That someone being . . .' Pettifer prompted. She gave him a clear, cold stare.

'My husband, obviously. It wasn't a great place to live but I never felt unsafe in Murchison House. People were kind. They were nice to Thomas.' She smiled a little. 'Maybe I was naïve but I thought they wouldn't bother trying to break into our flat. It was so obvious we had nothing much to steal. My clothes—' she broke off to look around the room. 'I don't know what happened to them. But they were cheap. My bag was from Primark. Thomas's clothes were nothing special either, and he didn't have a scooter or a bike. We had an old TV that was basically worthless and a tiny amount of cash and I never wore any jewellery or anything – I mean, I left it all behind. I left everything behind. I didn't want him to be able to say I'd stolen anything.'

'Did you call 999 when you realised there was a fire in the block?' I asked.

'Yes. They told me it was up to me if I waited or if I tried to leave.' She frowned. 'That wasn't fair, I thought. If I made the wrong decision it was on me, wasn't it? If we stayed and the fire got to us before the firefighters, we were screwed.'

'It's because of what happened in Camberwell in 2006,' I explained, having had a lecture from Northbridge on it the previous evening. 'There was a fatal fire in a block of flats. The coroner found that some of the victims could have escaped if they'd been encouraged to go. The people in the control room aren't always in the best position to decide what's safest.'

'Well, *I* didn't know.' She coughed again. 'I didn't want to have to leave. I just didn't feel we had a choice.'

'Having seen your flat, I think you made the right decision,' I said.

'Is it gone?'

'Pretty much.'

'We couldn't go back there anyway.' Her voice was flat. 'And I had everything important in my bag.'

'Your bag – what did it look like?' Pettifer asked.

'It's a green shoulder bag. It's not leather but it's supposed to look like it. It has a navy blue tassel on the zip and a navy strap. Primark, as I said before.'

'We haven't found it,' Mal said.

She looked confused. 'I had it over my shoulder.'

'There was no ID on you or near you when they found you,' I said. 'That's why it took us a while to work out who Thomas belonged to. You were on the eighth floor and you were unconscious.'

'How did I get there?' She looked from me to Pettifer, then Mal. 'I was going straight downstairs. Thomas was in front of me. I let him go first so I could watch him walk down. I didn't want him behind me in case we got separated.'

'Was there anyone in the stairwell?'

'Not on our floor,' she said instantly. 'There were people coming down from the eleventh floor – I heard them coming through the door, coughing. And other people were ahead of us. But we were on our own.'

'Do you remember someone attacking you?'

'No.'

'Someone grabbing you?'

'No.' She frowned. 'I remember someone running down from behind us, very fast. I told Thomas to hold on to the handrail in case he got knocked over.'

'Do you remember anyone speaking to you, or passing you on the stairs?'

'No.'

'What about a man in a black zip-up jacket and a red baseball cap?' I asked, and saw her eyes flicker as it triggered something.

'I don't— why are you asking about that?'

'Does it ring any bells?'

'Not from yesterday.' Her face was as white as the hospital pillows. 'My husband wears a red cap. It's his favourite.'

I felt the familiar rush, the moment a shape began to emerge from the darkness that surrounded the case. A pattern. A connection. A witness and a suspect.

A killer with a face and a name.

Maybe.

'Melissa, does your husband have a black zipped jacket?'

'Probably.' She rolled her head on the pillow. 'I don't know. He has lots of jackets.'

I leaned forward a little more. 'Melissa, this is important. I need you to think about this and answer me honestly. Do you think – if he found you – he'd do something as reckless as set a fire to make you leave your flat?'

She nodded.

'Did he ever do anything like that?'

'He likes fires.' She licked her lips. 'He burned my things in the garden. Clothes he didn't like. Pictures. Letters.'

Better and better.

'Hold on a second,' Pettifer said. 'He knew you had Thomas with you, didn't he? Thomas is his kid. Is he really going to put him in harm's way – risk his life in the fire, or even just leave him on his own in a car park for hours – to get back at you?'

I could have killed him. The hurt on Melissa's face was obvious.

'I thought you were different.'

'We're not saying we don't believe you. We just have to test every theory,' I said, talking quickly. 'It's what we do. It's how we get to the truth, and that's what we want in this case. We'll talk to your husband, Mrs Pell. We'll find out if he had an alibi for last night and we'll turn his life upside down if he looks like being a suspect. But we have to ask these questions first.'

She was tired, and injured, and she'd been under strain for a long time, but Melissa Pell had an inner strength that hadn't yet deserted her. 'I understand,' she said, her voice low. 'All I can tell you is what I know. You asked if he was capable of putting his son in danger.'

'That's right.'

She looked up and there was nothing but certainty in her eyes. 'Mark Pell is capable of anything.'

A knock on the door made us all jump. Mal muttered as he hurried to open it, obviously intending to send the intruder away. Instead, he fell back as Derwent strode into the room, followed by an older woman who bore a striking resemblance to Melissa Pell. It didn't take a huge leap of imagination to think she might be her mother. Derwent was carrying Thomas, whose arms were wrapped around his neck, his head buried in Derwent's shoulder again. This time he was hiding rather than asleep. I stood up, moving out of the way as they approached the bed.

'Here she is,' Derwent said. 'Look.'

Thomas risked a peek as his mother said his name. She'd sat up in bed, and the expression on her face made me catch my breath. The boy twisted once he saw her, wriggling to get down, a grubby rabbit clutched in one hand. Derwent dropped him on the end of the bed.

'Mummy.' He scrambled up the bed into her arms, fitting his head in under her chin as she held on to him tightly.

I turned away, clearing my throat, to see Mal rubbing his eyes surreptitiously. Melissa's mother was in floods of tears, not for the first time that day if the redness of her eyes was anything to go by. Pettifer was beaming paternally. I glanced in Derwent's direction, wondering if the emotion of it all was getting to him too. He stood at the end of the bed, his expression remote, his arms folded, as cold and stern as if he was carved from stone.

Some things never changed.

Chapter 13

Geoff Armstrong hadn't been looking all that great the last time I'd seen him. It was safe to say he looked a lot worse after his post-mortem. The incisions the pathologist had made in his body were the least of it. Now that he'd been stripped and washed, the damage he'd sustained was impossible to miss. The blood had hidden the worst of it, ironically. Now he was naked, flat on his back, his skin pale where it wasn't livid or lacerated or torn away completely.

Dr Early was just stepping back from his body when Derwent and I walked into the morgue. She pulled her mask down, revealing a disapproving look on her narrow face.

'You missed the show.'

'Sorry about that,' Derwent said, as if he hadn't been dawdling the whole way there. Neither of us was exactly squeamish – not any more – but Armstrong's post-mortem was unlikely to be a spectator sport, we'd agreed. Besides, it was all so straightforward, compared to the other deaths in Murchison House. He'd been with a woman who was definitely, emphatically not his wife, and his constituents

141

would have been outraged at the idea of their MP in a mixed-race extra-marital affair. Public humiliation, resignation, the end of a promising career as a political pundit, accusations of hypocrisy . . . he'd deserved it all, and more. But I could see why he'd been desperate to avoid it, why he'd gambled on escaping unnoticed, or why he'd given his life rather than face his future. I hadn't had much time for him, but arguably he hadn't deserved to die in a fire. I'd do a decent job of finding out what had happened, close the case, and never think about Armstrong again.

'Maybe you could just give us the highlights,' Derwent suggested to Dr Early. 'That should be enough to get DCI Burt off my case.'

'I could make you wait for my report.'

Derwent winced. 'You wouldn't do that to me, would you?'

'Watch me. I have other work to do. Armstrong was first but he's had his moment in the sun.' She turned away, and inwardly I cheered. Derwent had made a habit of unsettling her from the first time they met. It was nice to see her being more confident now that she was on her own territory.

Still, we had Una Burt to deal with. And whenever Derwent was in trouble, so was I.

'Now would be a great time to switch on the charm,' I said to him.

'I'm trying.'

'Try harder,' I said, and it was pure joy to use one of his own lines on him.

'I'm disappointed,' Dr Early said over her shoulder. 'I

was led to believe the Derwent charm was irresistible when you bother to use it.'

Derwent shrugged, but it was apologetic rather than arrogant. His hands were jammed in his pockets, his posture a slouch. 'No one's perfect.'

'Wow. Remember where you were when DI Derwent admitted he wasn't perfect after all, because it's a historic moment,' I said.

Dr Early glanced at the clock. 'I really don't have much time to give you. I've got a suspicious head injury to examine. I'm considering whether I need to remove the flesh altogether – get it down to the bones. But that would take quite a bit of boiling.'

'Doc.' Derwent looked appalled.

'I don't know any pathologists who like soup,' Dr Early said with a grin. 'And you definitely shouldn't have any they've made.'

It was graphic but not the most gruesome thing I'd ever heard. Still, I felt a sudden rush of coldness followed by heat, sweat prickling down my back. My hands were wet and saliva filled my mouth. I turned away sharply, knocking into a trolley with a clatter.

'Kerrigan?'

I waved a hand in Derwent's direction, breathing hard through my nose. If I was sick, Dr Early wouldn't think anything of it. It wouldn't be the first time a police officer lost their breakfast in her morgue, and I had a good enough working relationship with her that she'd forgive me.

Derwent, as ever, was a different story.

I closed my eyes and kept breathing, swallowing,

concentrating very hard on whatever was happening in my stomach. I was clenching muscles I didn't even know I had, fighting my body.

'Do you want to go outside?' Derwent's voice was soft in my ear. He took hold of my elbow and I shook him off.

'I don't need any help.'

Instant withdrawal of sympathy. 'Pull yourself together, then.'

I heard his footsteps as he returned to Dr Early. I wiped my palms on my trousers and took a moment before I turned back.

'Sorry.'

'Don't be silly. It happens,' Dr Early said, and her eyes were kind. It was another reason to be glad we weren't working with her senior colleague, Glen Hanshaw, who was as bitter and unsmiling as he was knowledgeable. He was working less and less now, weakened by the cancer treatment that was keeping him alive. I'd never warmed to him but I liked Dr Early. She was a fast talker, quick to give her opinions, friendlier now that she'd got the measure of us too.

'I'll tell you what I can. There are a lot of things that should become clearer once we have the test results back. But I can be fairly confident about one thing. He definitely fell out of the building.' She snapped off her gloves and dropped them into a yellow bin for medical waste. 'He's got multiple broken bones. We X-rayed his whole body, so you can have a look in due course. In the meantime it would be easier for me to tell you what he *didn't* fracture.'

'Not a surprise, is it? Assuming he fell from the tenth floor,' Derwent said.

I was thinking about what the pathologist had said, and what she hadn't said. 'Is that what caused his death?'

She grinned. 'And that was exactly the right question to ask. I don't think it was.'

Beside me, I was aware of Derwent straightening up, suddenly interested. 'Go on.'

'He was already dead when he fell.'

'How do you know?'

'I think he was strangled. I found bruising on his neck – I missed it at the scene because it was under his shirt collar, and anyway I think the ligature was something soft like a scarf or a pair of tights because there isn't a clearly defined injury. I was suspicious because I'd have expected to find a lot more bleeding into the tissues around his injuries.'

'There was plenty of blood at the scene,' Derwent pointed out. 'He was coated in it. So was the bin. Whatever was in him spilled out somehow.'

'When you fall from that sort of height, you're likely to bounce. Depending on the distance you fall and the flexibility of whatever you land on, you can have a significant impact second time round. Sometimes people survive the first impact and die from injuries sustained the second time.' The pathologist smiled. 'Worth remembering if you're ever falling from a high building. Try to land on your feet and fall forward, not back.'

'I'll keep it in mind.' Derwent's voice was dry. 'But I don't understand why two impacts would make a difference.'

'That gives us two opportunities for the blood to be pushed out of his body by force. It doesn't mean his heart was still pumping it through his arteries. When you look closely at the injuries, there isn't the physical reaction I'd expect.'

'Could he have died on the way down? A heart attack or something?' I asked.

She shook her head. 'Maybe if he'd fallen from a plane he'd have had time for that. He was ten floors up. Definitely high enough for the fall to kill him but the actual descent wouldn't have taken long at all.' Dr Early pointed to Armstrong's knees. 'He has scrapes here that correspond to rips in his trousers, but again, there's no bruising, no significant bleeding. I think someone shoved him out of the window and he got caught on the sill as he went.'

'He was murdered,' Derwent said. '*Fuck.*'

I knew what he meant. A straightforward case, albeit with a high-profile victim, had just turned into a nightmare. Una Burt couldn't have known it in advance, but she'd handed us a disaster wrapped in a scandal. If we didn't solve it, the fault would be ours and ours alone.

And we currently had absolutely no suspects.

'Right, Kerrigan, give me the benefit of your famous intuition. Who did it?' Derwent said.

'The girlfriend? If she *was* a girlfriend.'

'What do you mean?'

'He had two hundred quid in his back pocket.' I turned to Dr Early. 'Did you find anything else on him?'

She shook her head.

'There was that phone on the other side of the fence.

146

I bet we'll find it was Armstrong's. I can see how he'd have needed that – he couldn't afford to be out of contact for an hour or two. He brought what he needed to Murchison House and nothing more. So my guess would be that he needed two hundred pounds for whatever little meeting he had organised.'

'Imagine someone so delightful having to pay for sex,' Derwent said. 'What about the wife?'

'We'll have to see. What about any right-thinking member of society?'

'Definitely anyone on that estate who recognised him. Armstrong wouldn't have had many friends there.'

'So actually we have plenty of suspects,' I said. 'Everyone and anyone.'

Derwent jammed the heels of his hands into his eye sockets and groaned. 'I should never have come to work today.'

'What about the fire? Could they have set it to – to distract everyone? Or to provide a reason for him to have jumped?' I was thinking it through as I said it. 'Did he die before the fire started?'

Dr Early shook her head. 'He was alive for at least some of the fire. I found smoke staining in his trachea and particles of soot throughout his respiratory system, so he was breathing in smoke before he died. And I took his temperature when I arrived at the scene. It was cold out last night and we don't know how long he'd been lying outside, but his temperature was only a couple of degrees below normal. He hadn't been dead long.'

Derwent's shoulders dropped a millimetre or two. 'What else can you tell us?'

'I've swabbed him, taken nail scrapings – we just need to wait for the lab results to come back. One other thing for you to look for – whoever punched him in the face.' She tilted his head so the light shone on his jaw. A bruise bloomed under the skin. 'There was a lot of force behind it and it happened some time before he actually died.'

'Could it have been a woman?' I asked, thinking of the girlfriend.

'It could, if she was big enough and strong enough. Most women won't punch with a closed fist unless they're trained to do it – if they box or if they're really into self-defence classes. Women tend to scratch and gouge. They might resort to open-handed slaps, or they use an object to inflict a blunt or penetrating injury. But anything is possible.'

'I mean, this is Geoff Armstrong we're talking about. The line of people waiting to punch him wasn't short,' Derwent pointed out.

'Well, you're looking for someone who was strong, probably right-handed, with big hands.' She fitted her own fist over the mark on Armstrong's jaw, showing a clear border of bruising. 'Bigger than mine, anyway. But mine are tiny.'

Derwent held his hand in the same place. 'Not as big as mine. Kerrigan, you have a go.'

I did as I was told.

'Ah,' Dr Early said. 'That's a lot closer. More or less right.'

Derwent nudged me. 'Man hands.'

'Shut up.' I leaned over to look at the body more closely. 'Did he fight back?'

'I can't tell you.' She turned his hands over so I could see the cuts and bruises across his knuckles. 'He might have. He might not. He could have got these injuries from fighting someone off, or from falling. I took scrapings from under his nails and I swabbed his mouth, his hands, his genitals – everywhere I could think that we might find DNA from someone he was with. You'll have to wait to see if we get anything from that.'

'He was fully dressed when he was found,' Derwent pointed out.

'Except for his shoes, one sock and his suit jacket.' They both looked at me. 'What? I noticed.'

'He lost the shoes on his way down. Kev Cox found them in the bin yard. No one found the missing sock,' Dr Early said. 'I'd say he got dressed in a hurry. Maybe he couldn't find it.'

'Or someone dressed him,' I suggested.

'Mmm. I don't think so. Have you ever tried to dress a dead body?'

Derwent and I shook our heads in unison.

'They're awkward as hell. They're heavy – the expression "dead weight" is absolutely accurate. A dead body won't help you push a hand through a sleeve, or a leg through trousers. You get twisted seams. The clothes don't sit right on the body. The waistbands are too high or too low.' She shrugged. 'I know it when I see it here in the morgue, basically. Armstrong wasn't fully dressed but I'd lay money he put his own clothes on, cufflinks and all.'

'So what do we know? He went to Murchison House for his regular meeting with a lady who was apparently black and possibly paid for. He took off at least some of his clothes. He would have known there was a fire because of the smoke and the alarms. He got dressed. He got into a fight with someone. He died. Then someone pushed him out of the window.' Derwent looked down at him. 'I almost feel sorry for him.'

'Don't waste your time feeling sorry for him. His troubles are over.' I patted Derwent on the shoulder. 'Ours are just beginning.'

Chapter 14

Like a lot of politicians, Geoff Armstrong had lived in
London – where he worked – rather than where his
constituency was. Derwent pulled up on the quiet street
in Hampstead and looked at the house. It was set back
from the road: red-brick, double-fronted, immaculate
gravel on the drive, clipped box trees by the front door.

'Well, he wasn't short of a few bob.'

'Armstrong's dad left him a fortune.' I'd been reading
up on him on the way over. 'He inherited about fifty
million pounds when he was twenty-three.'

Derwent snorted. 'And then had the cheek to lecture
the rest of us about not relying on hand-outs.'

'There's nothing like being rich to make you unsym-
pathetic to the poor,' I said. 'He believed in people
standing on their own two feet. In his case, in handmade
shoes.'

'And he hated us because we're part of the nanny state.'

'We interfere with people's privacy.'

'Yeah, but they're mainly criminals. And if they're not,
what do they have to hide?' Derwent shook his head.
'Privacy is a privilege, not a right. If you can't trust people

to behave themselves, which you can't, you have to keep an eye on them.'

'That's your view.'

'Isn't it yours?'

'There must be a middle ground,' I said.

'Armstrong wasn't interested in the middle ground. He wanted us to be weaker. He wanted to limit our powers, which are already fairly pathetic if you ask me.'

'You just missed your calling. You'd have thrived in a police state.'

Derwent grinned. 'Sounds like heaven to me. As long as you're on the right side.'

'That's the trick, isn't it? Picking the right side.' I looked sideways at him. 'Are we going to sit in the car and talk politics or go and talk to the grieving widow?'

He groaned. 'This is going to be the most enormous ball-ache.'

'All part of the job. At least we're not breaking the news to her. The best thing about not being in uniform is not having to do the death message.'

'Yeah, but it's tricky, isn't it? Because we've got to ask her about her husband's extra-marital activities, which she may not even know about.'

'Go gently,' I said. 'Try not to blurt it out.'

'I was thinking you could do the talking. Woman to woman.'

'And I was thinking you were the senior officer and she'd wonder why you were standing around saying nothing.'

He swore under his breath. 'Get out of my car.'

It was a woman in a fitted, knee-length black dress

who answered the door. She had iron-grey hair cut in a perfect Vidal Sassoon bob: it was a deliberate choice not to dye it, not neglect. A complicated silver bracelet twisted around one arm; that was all the jewellery she wore apart from an ornate ruby engagement ring and matching wedding band. There was no expression on her face: I recognised the blankness of shock. She had strong features, heavy eyebrows: it was the sort of face that couldn't be softened or made prettier with make-up, and she hadn't tried.

'Police.' Derwent held up his ID as I did the same. 'Mrs Armstrong?'

'She's not seeing anyone.'

Which meant that the woman in front of us was not Mrs Armstrong. 'We need to interview her, I'm afraid.' I kept my tone polite, but firm. 'We did try to ring to let you know we were on our way.'

'Oh, how irritating.' The woman looked back over her shoulder as a young man strode down the hall towards us, taking over the conversation without reference to her, or us, or anything else. He was thin, tall, nervy and very slightly camp. 'We've had to take the phone off the hook. It was absolutely unbearable to have it ringing all the time. So many journalists, and Geoff's friends. What they think we can tell them, I don't know.'

'Are you Mr Armstrong's secretary?' Derwent asked.

'I'm his *assistant*,' the young man said. 'John Grey. I should say I was his assistant, shouldn't I? I handled Geoff's political and media strategy. Elaine was his secretary.'

The grey-haired woman nodded. 'Elaine Lister.'

'Did you keep track of Mr Armstrong's schedule?'

'Yes. He was useless at being organised.' She bit her lip. 'I probably shouldn't criticise him now that he's gone.'

'We'll need to speak to you as well.'

'Of course. What do you want to know?'

'We need to get a picture of his usual routine, Mrs Lister,' I said. 'We'd appreciate any help you can give us at all.'

'I'll tell you whatever I can.'

'Do you need to speak to me?' John Grey demanded.

'That depends,' Derwent said. 'Do you know anything that you think we should know?'

'About Geoff? I can't think of anything.' Grey leaned against the wall, his hands in the pockets of his suit trousers. His shirt was so fitted I could see the outline of his pectoral muscles, and his tie looked expensive. Everything about him was immaculate. 'We had a good working relationship but he didn't confide in me or anything. I just want to make sure none of this damages the message that Geoff was trying to communicate. He may be gone but someone will come after him and build on what he started. So protecting his reputation matters.'

'That sounds cold.' I couldn't help saying it.

'All political careers end in failure.' He shrugged. 'Some of them end more spectacularly than others.'

'Do you want to come in?' Elaine Lister was pale.

Derwent was through the door before she'd finished asking. He wiped his feet very thoroughly on the doormat. *Look how house-trained I am. You can trust me to behave myself.*

'Where's Mrs Armstrong?'

154

John Grey laughed. 'As if she'll be able to tell you anything useful.'

'Why's that?'

'I've never seen her sober, put it that way.' Grey was showing off, I thought, and disliked him for it. 'Most of the time she doesn't know what's going on.'

'Are we talking alcohol or drugs?' Derwent checked.

'Both?' Grey shrugged. 'I don't really know, to be honest with you.'

'But that hasn't stopped you from throwing accusations around,' Elaine Lister said tightly, and I tried not to smirk as John Grey looked uncomfortable. He muttered something and went away, taking the stairs two at a time. Elaine waited until he was out of sight. 'Cressida is in the drawing room. Perhaps I could just go and let her know you're here . . .'

'In here?' Derwent was opening the door already. 'Mrs Armstrong? Could we have a word?'

She was standing by the fireplace, small and fine-boned in a grey dress that clung to her body. Her hair was honey-coloured, swept back from a high forehead. She must have been stunning when she was young, with high cheekbones and a wide mouth, but the overall effect now was of tremendous fragility. At least one facelift, I judged, and a serious Botox habit that left her forehead as smooth as an egg. The skin on her neck and hands gave away her age, but her eyes were bright under arched eyebrows. Her mouth parted in surprise and, I thought, anger.

'What is it? Elaine?'

'The police. I did try to say you weren't seeing anyone, but—'

'I'm sure you appreciate that we need to speak with you sooner rather than later,' Derwent said to Mrs Armstrong. He crossed the room and took her hand, his voice low as he said, 'I'm so sorry for your loss. And I'm sorry to impose on your privacy at this time. I wouldn't if there was any other way.'

'Oh – well, of course.' She looked past him to Elaine, who was still standing in the doorway. 'I certainly didn't mean I wouldn't speak to the police, Elaine. You should have known that.'

Elaine's head went up. I saw her fighting the impulse to snap, but she didn't give in to it. 'I'm sorry,' she said.

'Thank you, Elaine.' It was a dismissal. I half-expected to be sent packing too, but I got a flick of a glance through narrow eyes before she returned to Derwent.

'Please, sit down.'

He folded himself onto the sofa she had indicated, as she perched beside him. Her back was towards me, so I crossed the room and sat where I could see her.

Derwent introduced us both, emphasising his rank. I thought she probably didn't have a very good grasp of police hierarchy but she could tell he was a senior officer. She could also tell he was a reasonably well-made specimen, I thought, from the look on her face as she stared at his thigh, so close to hers.

'I'll try not to take up too much of your time,' Derwent said.

'Thank you. It's just been a tremendous shock.'

'I can imagine. Did you know your husband was planning to visit the Maudling Estate yesterday?'

'No.' She smoothed her skirt over her lap. 'We led very

separate lives, Geoff and I. It was impossible for me to keep track of where he was and when. He was always at the House when he was in London, or on television. Sometimes I only knew where he was when I switched on *Newsnight*, and there he was.'

'He was a very high-profile man.'

'He was unusual for a politician because he was willing to say what he thought. Straight talking got him plenty of loyalty. There are so many people who think the way Geoff did, but they get shouted down all the time. The left just bullies and harangues anyone who disagrees with them.'

Yes, it was tough being privileged, I thought. Derwent was nodding, very serious, not catching my eye.

'He had a lot of supporters but he had enemies too, didn't he?'

'Of course. Anyone who takes a stand is going to attract attention from the wrong sort of person.'

'Did he get death threats?'

'I believe so.' She waved a hand. 'He didn't share them with me. He protected me from that sort of thing. But he did warn me now and then to take care when I was driving, in case someone followed me. And he told me to check under the car for anything suspicious if I'd left it parked on the street or in a car park.' She laughed. 'I can't say I did it every time. Grovelling on the ground is not my style.'

'Was this recent?' Derwent asked.

She shrugged. 'It was fairly constant. I think he said something about it when we were on our way back from Paris the last time. That was three weeks ago. No – four.'

'But you weren't particularly scared.'

'Nor was he.' She smiled. 'It made him feel important, I think.'

'Are you aware of any specific threats that were made to him? Was there anyone who scared him?'

'No.'

'Do you know what he was doing on the Maudling Estate?'

'No idea.'

'It's not exactly his constituency, is it?'

'Geoff was always involving himself in other people's problems. Some people are like that. They have a vocation to help others.' She shot Derwent a languorous glance. 'Like the police. I must say, I've always been drawn to selflessness.'

'It's a good quality.' Derwent's voice came out about an octave lower than usual. I was trying very hard not to laugh. 'Mrs Armstrong—'

'Cressida,' she said quickly.

He cleared his throat. 'Um – Cressida. It's never pleasant to ask these questions and you'll have to forgive me for bringing it up, but you said you and your husband led separate lives. Did that apply to your private lives as well?'

She blinked. 'What do you mean?'

'Did you have an open marriage?'

'No. Nothing like that.'

'As far as you know, he was faithful to you.'

'Of course he was.' A pink patch had formed high on each of her cheeks. 'He wouldn't have been anything else. Partly because our marriage was very strong – *very* strong,

Inspector. But also because he'd never have taken the risk of being found out.' She leaned forward. 'Most of the MPs Geoff's age have pretty young secretaries, unless their wives are prepared to do the donkey work. They're all having affairs, all the time. Geoff was different. He was focused on his job.'

'So he wouldn't have been on the Maudling Estate for personal reasons.'

'I don't know what you're implying.' Her voice was flat. 'He didn't want to mess around with anyone. Why would he?'

'Why indeed?' Derwent said weakly. He looked in my general direction, not meeting my eyes – which was wise, because I wasn't sure either of us could have kept our composure. 'Was there anything else we wanted to ask?'

'I think that covers it,' I said, closing my notebook. 'Thank you, Mrs Armstrong.'

'You're welcome,' she said without looking at me, the response automatic. She reached out and put a hand on Derwent's arm, pushing his sleeve back and turning his wrist towards her, which meant she was stronger than she looked. 'What time is it?'

'Coming up on one o'clock.'

'I must watch the lunchtime news. There should be a lot about Geoff. I'd like to see it.'

'Stop smirking.' Derwent's shoulders were hunched. He leaned back against the wall, shaking his head.

'I'm sure I will. Not immediately, obviously.'

'It was necessary.'

'I'm not saying it wasn't.'

'Well, then.'

'You can't expect me not to rip the piss.' I put a hand on his arm and purred, 'I've always been drawn to self-lessness, Inspector.'

Before he could reply, a door at the end of the hallway opened and a face poked around it.

'I thought I heard voices.'

Derwent straightened up. 'Mrs Lister. Just the person we wanted to see.'

'Are you finished with Cressida?'

'For now. Can we speak with you?'

'Of course.' She stood back and the two of us filed into a big, warm kitchen. John Grey sat at the table, sipping coffee from a bone china mug. There was no sign of his earlier loss of composure. He raised his eyebrows at me, which I was free to interpret as *hello*, or *isn't this strange*, or *what are you looking at*. A uniformed housekeeper was standing at the stove, stirring a pot of soup. That brought back unpleasant memories of Dr Early, which I forced to the back of my mind. Throwing up all over Geoff Armstrong's kitchen would be a quick way to lose my advantage over Derwent.

'Would it be possible to speak with you two alone?' Derwent asked, glancing at the housekeeper's broad back.

'Hanna is completely discreet,' Grey said, not even bothering to lower his voice.

Derwent wasn't happy, I could tell, but I sat down at the table and Elaine took a seat opposite me, beside Grey. Tension was pulling at the corners of her eyes and mouth, and two deep wrinkles cut into the skin between her eyes.

'Are you all right? Can I get you a glass of water?' I asked.

'I'm fine.'

'It must have been a dreadful shock when you heard the news about Mr Armstrong.'

'It was, for both of us.' John Grey glanced at Elaine. 'I couldn't believe it when Cressida called me. She was in hysterics – I couldn't even understand what she was saying at first. Then I thought she must have made a mistake, or someone else had.'

'I couldn't believe it either,' Elaine said quietly. 'I'd known him for such a long time. We were at Cambridge together. I can't imagine life without him.' She fumbled for a tissue in her sleeve and dabbed her nose for a second, buying time. I could tell she didn't want to cry in front of Grey.

'It's natural to hope the bad news isn't true,' I said. 'Especially in the circumstances. Mrs Armstrong didn't even know her husband was visiting the Maudling Estate yesterday.'

'Oh, well, she doesn't pay much attention to his diary.' Elaine balled the tissue up in her hand absent-mindedly.

'Did you know he was planning to be there?' Derwent asked.

'Of course.'

'What was he doing there?'

Elaine opened her mouth to answer but John Grey got there first. 'He was attending a meeting of Justice for Levon. You know, the group set up by Claudine Cole. Levon Cole's mother.'

Levon Cole was the teenager shot dead by armed

Metropolitan police a few months earlier. The last time I'd been on the Maudling Estate, Armstrong had been giving interviews about how Cole had deserved what happened to him, apparently because he was poor and black and unlucky.

'I wouldn't have thought he'd be exactly welcome at that sort of meeting,' I said.

'No, no. He was very involved. He went every week.'

'When did he start going?'

'Two months ago? After those police shootings on the estate. He became interested in the group and their work. He invited Mrs Cole and her friends to the House of Commons last month, but they turned him down. He found them inspirational, he told me. Their willingness to change their community from within was very much in line with what he believed was important. They didn't want help from him but he persuaded them he could spread their message more widely than they ever could.'

'How was he spreading their message? No one had any idea he was involved with them,' Derwent said. 'Even his wife didn't know.'

'Geoff was working up to an announcement about it,' Grey said, his tone condescending. Of course we couldn't be expected to understand how politics worked. We were only simple police officers. 'These things have to be choreographed. He had to work with the party to decide on how to present it to the public, and when. He was an important figure, so what he did mattered.'

'He was just a backbencher.' Derwent didn't quite manage to keep the scorn out of his voice.

John Grey bristled. 'He was far more than that.'

'Mrs Armstrong tells us her husband warned her to take security precautions,' I said, changing tack as I willed Derwent to shut up. 'Were you aware of any threats he'd received?'

'I didn't keep track of them.' Grey turned. 'Elaine?'

'I opened his post,' she said quietly. 'I read his emails. I knew about all the threats.'

'Were there many?'

A nod.

'Did you ever mention them to the police?'

'No. Geoff thought it was a waste of time. He told me to throw them away. He didn't think the people who made the threats were the type to attack him. It was all bluster, he said.'

'So who did he think might attack him?' Derwent asked.

'Extremists.' John Grey saw the look on our faces. 'I can't be more specific, I'm afraid. People from very different walks of life objected to Geoff's stance on politics and the economy.'

'Because he wanted everyone who wasn't rich and English to disappear,' Derwent said.

'Because he wanted the government to stay out of people's lives, and stop interfering with doing business. He wanted us to leave Europe. He wanted to call a halt to immigration. He wanted everyone in the UK to wake up. He wanted us to grow up and stop expecting hand-outs.'

'He wanted to dismantle the NHS and the welfare state, the two greatest post-war achievements of any government,' Derwent said.

'He wanted to take away the safety net for people who

used it as a trampoline. He hated anyone who worked the system to their advantage.' John Grey spun Armstrong's line effortlessly; it was like hearing him talk again. He smiled. 'I gave quotes on his behalf when he was too busy. I used to think I shared his brain.'

'Did you believe in his policies too?' I couldn't help asking. 'Or was it just work?'

'I believed his policies could have led him to electoral success.' Grey held my gaze for a second. 'It's all about winning, you see. There's no point in being worthy and politically correct if the voters don't want that. Geoff knew it and I knew it. It was my job to get him to the top of his profession, not to worry about how he'd done it.'

'Was he really going to get to the top, though? People hated him,' Derwent point out.

'More people voted for Geoff than would ever admit it. The figures didn't lie, even if the voters did.'

'Did either of you ever think that Mr Armstrong was having an extra-marital affair?'

Grey's response was immediate. 'No. He wasn't like that.'

'It's just a theory at the moment.'

'It's impossible,' Elaine said. 'He was devoted to Cressida. His career mattered very much to him, as did his marriage.'

'When did they meet?'

'When we were at Cambridge. She wasn't an under-graduate. She just came to a ball. They'd been together ever since. Hardly a day apart.'

'And you were there too.'

'I was there too.'

'Were you ever romantically involved with Geoff Armstrong?' Derwent said, jumping in feet first.

'No. It was never like that.' Elaine Lister frowned. 'Geoff and I were friends and colleagues. Nothing more. Please tell me you're not so unimaginative that you believe a man and woman working together must be romantically or sexually involved with one another.'

'If it helps, I can imagine that quite well,' I said. Derwent's expression didn't change but he shot me a look out of the corner of his eye: *touché.*

'I met Miles – my husband – when I was at Cambridge, before I met Geoff.'

John Grey gave a short, cruel bark of amusement. 'How could Geoff begin to compare to Miles?'

She flushed. Consciously or not, she was fiddling with her rings. 'Miles is a philosophy professor. He's not like Geoff. He lives in his own world a lot of the time. But he's an excellent husband.'

'He never minded her spending all her time with Geoff,' Grey said. 'We should all be so lucky with our partners.'

'Geoff and I were friends for a long time. We worked together very closely. He was part of my family and I was part of his.' Elaine pressed the tissue under her eyes carefully once again. 'People saw him as a monster but he wasn't. He was a good man. He wanted to make a difference.'

'We'll never know what he could have achieved if he'd had the time,' John Grey said. 'Ah well. *C'est la vie,* as they say.' He drained his coffee and set the mug down on the table with a bang.

Chapter 15

This time round I walked into the meeting room and found Derwent had got there first. He was sitting in the middle of the front row, right in front of Una Burt. His hair was suspiciously neat, his tie pushed right up to his collar. Immaculate. Irreproachable.

Up to something.

Una Burt had her back to him. She was busy writing on the whiteboard, her marker squeaking as she went. I took the seat behind him, close enough to risk nudging him if I thought he was going too far. I liked working with Derwent and I had missed him more than I'd expected when Burt had kept us apart but he wasn't the hill I was going to die on. If he fought Burt and lost, he was on his own.

The whiteboard was filling up: names, times, lots of question marks. Armstrong's name was in the centre, blocked from my view by Burt's square body. Time to tell the class what we'd found out, I gathered. It was unintentionally revealing of how Burt thought about this case: Armstrong at the centre, the other victims incidental. And if I wasn't sure she was wrong, I wasn't altogether sure she was right.

The rest of the team filed in, all tired faces and crumpled suits. The initial investigative rush was slowing, the fast-time enquiries winding down as the tedious painstaking work reasserted itself. So many cases unravelled for us because of something as mundane and administrative as reading phone records or checking CCTV or analysing automatic number-plate recognition, not to mention the old routine of door-to-door inquiries that eventually turned up a witness who didn't realise the importance of what they'd seen. That was our job, and knowing it could solve a crime was what kept me going when I was ready to come apart at the seams from the dreariness of it all.

'Okay,' Burt said, eyeing the latecomers as they hurried to fit themselves into the last remaining spaces. 'The purpose of this meeting is to focus our inquiries now that we've started on this investigation. There's a big picture here and you can't see all of it at once, so this is your opportunity to stand back and see how your part of the puzzle fits into the rest of it.'

The door opened to admit a man I didn't recognise. He murmured an apology and leaned against the wall rather than trying to find a place to sit. He had untidy dark hair and soft brown eyes.

'I know you're all tired,' Una Burt went on, 'so we'll keep it brief. But we have a lot of ground to cover. Let's start with the fire. Colin? Anything on the CCTV?'

'I've only just started looking at it,' Colin Vale said apologetically. 'It took us a while to get it from the estate. I've got footage from ten cameras to review and obviously we can widen that out beyond the estate once we know what we're looking for.'

'So nothing useful so far,' Burt said, her manner impatient.

'The opposite of useful.' Colin gave us a lopsided smile. 'As luck would have it, a lot of the footage from Murchison House is unusable. The camera on the tenth floor hadn't been working for months. They were waiting for a part, they said.'

There was a groan from the officers in the room, but there was no surprise in it. CCTV was often far more useful as a deterrent than as an investigative tool. The image quality was wildly variable, and that was assuming it was working in the first place.

'The camera above the entrance that should have shown us everyone coming in and out of the building had been vandalised more recently.'

'Who by? When?'

'Kids, last week.' Vale shrugged as a general mutter arose. 'I know. I was hoping it would be our arsonist too.' It wasn't unheard of for a criminal to give us a perfect shot of their faces as they tried to deal with a security camera. 'I don't think it's connected, I'm afraid. They've had a problem with kids damaging the cameras for a while. They know who did it and I've had a word but it doesn't lead us anywhere. No one asked the boy to do it. He was just bored. He's eleven and a very promising fast bowler, apparently. He hit it with a cricket ball and it was all over.'

'So what have we got?'

'Bits and pieces. The usual.' Colin smiled. 'There's a camera in the car park that should show us most of the people who came out from a distance, and I'm trying to match up the footage with the rest of the material we have. I'll be able to patch it together but we might not have the best quality images at the end of it all. Enough to give us some direction, though.'

'What about local petrol stations?' I asked. They generally had very good CCTV so they could trace drivers who try to drive off without paying. 'Isn't it worth getting hold of the footage in case our arsonist bought a can or two of petrol?'

'Already done,' Vale said. 'What I'd like is to know what I'm looking for. If I see someone I recognise, we're home and dry.'

Burt stood back and used the end of her pen to tap Armstrong's name. 'What have you found out, Josh?'

Quietly, calmly, Derwent explained what we'd found out at the post-mortem and from Armstrong's wife, not to mention his secretary. We had briefed Una Burt first so she knew it was murder already. She nodded while everyone else muttered.

'It does complicate matters for you.' *For you*. I got the hint. 'I still wouldn't rule out the fire being set to target Armstrong.'

'But they couldn't have known how he'd react,' I objected. 'If he'd evacuated the flat along with his girl-friend, he'd be alive now. Embarrassed, but alive.'

'So it's just a coincidence that he's there and he ends up dead. That seems more likely.' Her voice was dripping with sarcasm.

'That's not what I said. But I don't think it's necessarily all about Armstrong either. There are other victims of this fire, other people on the tenth floor who might have been targets. Without the fire, Armstrong might not have been murdered, but that doesn't mean whoever set the fire even knew he was there. No one else did.'

'Except his secretary,' Burt pointed out.

'She didn't know where he was. She thought she did, but she was wrong. He'd told her he was at a meeting with Levon Cole's mother and her supporters. I rang Mrs Cole to check and there was no meeting yesterday. More to the point, she said Armstrong had never been at any of their meetings and he wouldn't have been welcome if he'd turned up.'

Derwent turned round in his seat to give me one of his hard stares. 'I thought he was their biggest supporter.'

'Not according to Mrs Cole. She said he'd been hanging around after the TSG unit got shot up on the estate in September but she'd made it absolutely clear she wasn't interested in being whatever Armstrong wanted her to be. A figurehead for a people's revolution, he'd suggested.' I rolled my eyes. 'What a user.'

'Why was he so interested in Claudine Cole's campaign?' Una Burt asked, puzzled.

'If I had to guess, it's was protective cover for him. It was a reason for him to be on the estate. We know he was with a woman in the flat and according to Mrs Hearn, that woman was black. Where do you think he might have met her? Probably not at his club, I'm guessing.'

'Someone involved in the Cole campaign,' Derwent said.

'That's what I'm thinking.'

'So we can get a list of names from her.'

I laughed. 'Yeah, right. Because Claudine Cole has so

many reasons to cooperate with the police. I barely got her to speak to me on the phone once she heard who I was. The only reason she gave me any time at all was to make it clear that she'd had nothing to do with Armstrong and she was adamant he'd never worked on the campaign. If I tell her I need names, she'll tell me to back off.'

'Try in person,' Una Burt said. 'You might be able to convince her if you're face to face. It's easier to say no on the phone.'

I made a note. Another visit to the Maudling Estate. I could hardly wait.

'We might be able to get something from MI5,' Burt went on. 'I'm sure they're monitoring Claudine Cole and her supporters in case their activism takes an illegal turn.'

I nodded. 'And Dr Early has sent swabs off to the lab to check for DNA. We might get a hit that way. There's more than one way to track her down. We'll find her.'

'Speaking of finding people, any update on Melissa Pell's husband?' Derwent's voice was casual but he was pressing his thumb on the top of his pen so hard that it had bleached white.

'Why should we care about him?' Una Burt's voice was tight.

'Because she was hiding from him in Murchison House.'

'He was possibly abusive,' Pettifer added. 'So we should keep him on the list as a potential suspect.'

'*Possibly*,' Derwent exploded and I kicked the seat of his chair as hard as I could without being observed.

'Yeah, possibly.' Pettifer stared Derwent down. 'We've spoken to the officers who dealt with the family in Lincolnshire. They said it was a difficult situation. Mark

Pell struck them as a decent bloke struggling to cope with a wife who'd basically lost the plot. She accused him of all sorts of things but then backed out of pressing charges. She suffers from depression, apparently.'

'Hardly surprising, if her old man was beating her senseless.' Derwent's jaw was tight. 'Did they investigate whether she was telling the truth with her original allegations?'

'They didn't find any evidence of it. She admitted that she self-harmed from time to time. He had no record of any violence. He reported his wife and son missing a few months ago.'

'And it didn't hit the headlines? A vulnerable woman with her son – you'd assume they were in danger,' Una Burt said.

'They'd been assigned a social worker, who backed up Melissa,' Mal Upton explained. Derwent made a small, satisfied noise in the back of his throat. 'According to her, Melissa was a few days away from being sectioned when she took on the case. The social worker didn't see any sign of insanity or instability or whatever her husband alleges. She didn't feel the boy was in danger. And when Melissa left, she contacted the social worker and told her she was going. The social worker did try to reassure the husband, but didn't get very far with him. He complained to her supervisor that she'd become too close to Melissa and wasn't behaving in a professional way. He got her into a lot of trouble.'

'Pell's spent a fortune on private investigators trying to track his wife down,' Pettifer said. 'Like I said, he seems like a nice bloke.'

'Or a husband trying to get control of his wife after she's run away from him,' I said tartly. 'I don't know why you're taking him at face value.'

Pettifer glared. 'And I don't know why you aren't.'

'Because when I spoke to Melissa Pell in the hospital she was terrified of him. Not faking. Not insane. Terrified.'

'Why were you talking to her?' Burt was frowning. She was speaking to me but looking at Derwent. 'I thought I told you—'

Pettifer's innate sense of fairness resurfaced in the nick of time. 'Kerrigan helped us out. Mrs Pell wasn't all that keen on talking to two men.'

'It didn't take long,' I added, lamely.

'Can we find out if the husband has an alibi?' Derwent was still very tightly wound. 'Or if he knows a bloke who knows a bloke who's good at setting fires?'

'It's worth a look,' Pettifer admitted. 'You can see a motive there. Make her feel unsafe, make it clear the boy's better off at home – get custody, if it comes to that.'

'And her injuries?' Derwent looked round. 'Maybe it was a good way to get rid of her for ever so he could have the boy to himself.'

'Assuming he knew where she was,' Burt pointed out. 'Assuming he knew someone who was prepared to attack her and start a fire that killed three people. I know a lot of bad guys and I'm not sure I could find someone to do that all that easily, even if I could afford to pay them what I'd need to.'

'I don't get the impression money is a problem,' Pettifer said. 'We're going to Lincolnshire to speak to him tomorrow. We'll see what we can find out.'

'Okay, who else?' Burt said. 'Oh, the family in 101.'

'The Bellews,' I said. 'There's something strange about them but we haven't got to the bottom of it yet. The dad says he's a handyman but he was a bit vague on the details. They seem to have plenty of cash. The granny was worried about a safe in her flat, but wouldn't say what was in it.'

'Proceeds of crime?' Burt suggested.

'I wouldn't put it past them. You thought the same, sir, didn't you?'

Derwent had been staring into space. He came back to the present with a start. 'Yeah. They're on my list. Can't forget the fire started beside their home.'

'How's the little girl?' Burt asked.

'The same. Still in intensive care. We haven't gone near her,' I said. 'We did speak to her mother.'

'This is where we got the description you gave me,' Colin Vale said. 'The man with the cap and the zip-up jacket.'

'That's the one.'

'I haven't found him yet,' Colin said. 'I have a few possibles, but nothing definite. No caps at all.'

'Give us whatever you've got and we'll show it to her,' Derwent said. 'I don't think she's a great witness but the sooner she has a look the better.'

'Right.' Una Burt looked at her board. 'I want to talk about the eleventh floor. Who's been dealing with the bodies in flat 113?'

Ben Dornton raised a hand. 'That would be me. And Liv and Pete.'

'Has Dr Early done the posts yet?'

'Yeah.' Dornton looked sick at the memory. 'For some reason I've gone right off barbecue.'

There were worse things than a body that had fallen out of a tall building I thought, staring at my notebook. At least I hadn't had to get through a PM on burned bodies. I'd never have made it.

Dornton was still talking. I tuned back in to hear him say, 'The fire actually splits bones if it's hot enough. The doc said their brains would have boiled. I wouldn't wish it on my worst enemy.'

'Did she find anything suspicious about the bodies?'

'Two things,' Liv said, composed as ever. 'They were both young women who hadn't had children. Both had a number of old injuries – broken ribs, a broken arm in one case, a fractured jaw. She noted it but she couldn't really tell us very much about the injuries or how recent they were because of the heat damage to the bones. They were definitely old, healed fractures, but the broken arm hadn't been set properly, she said.'

'Okay. What else?'

'The dental work. Dr Early called in a dentist friend of hers who had a look. In her opinion, one of them was Russian or had spent time there. They looked at the second victim too. From her skull shape and the condition of her teeth, they were fairly sure she was African.'

'You mean she was black. That doesn't mean she was African,' I pointed out. 'Plenty of British people with African ancestry.'

'Yes, but the dentist said the wear pattern on her teeth was distinctive. He said she was probably from some-where in West Africa – Nigeria, somewhere like that.'

Two young women from very different backgrounds, living together in a small flat where the door was locked from the outside.

'Trafficked,' the man by the door said. His arms were folded and he had one foot braced against the wall behind him. He looked completely relaxed to be addressing a room full of strangers, his voice pitched just loud enough to carry to the back. 'Almost certainly trafficked. Brought to the UK to work in the sex industry but the chances are they don't see a penny of what they earn. They'll have started out as economic migrants and more than likely the UK won't be the first place they've worked as prostitutes or strippers or whatever these girls were doing.'

'Sorry, everyone, I should have introduced Tom Bridges,' Dornton said. 'I asked him to come along because he knows a bit more about people-trafficking than I do. He's a DS on the human traffic task force the commissioner set up last year.'

'The fact that your victims weren't known to their neighbours and they were locked in the flat tells us they were effectively imprisoned,' Bridges explained. 'Their movements were strictly controlled by whoever was using them to make money.'

'How can you tell they were working in the sex trade?' Liv asked. 'Just because they were young women, that's not a safe assumption, is it?'

'It's more than likely.' He sounded apologetic, which was nice of him as it certainly wasn't his fault. 'The majority of people trafficked into the UK are here to work in the sex industry, and the majority of them are women.

Women also work in domestic slavery – housekeeping roles, but they aren't paid. These women were at home in the middle of the day. They worked at night.'

'Somewhere there's an empty street corner or a deserted pole,' Belcott said. 'What a waste.'

I whipped around. 'They weren't just sex workers. They were people.'

'People who could have told a customer they didn't want to do what they were doing. If they were walking the streets they could have walked away. They made their choices.'

I couldn't believe he was actually arguing with me. 'They were locked in. They died in screaming terror. That wasn't a choice.'

'We find the women who escape traffickers are very reluctant to trust anyone,' Bridges said. 'Especially us. They're not used to police forces they can rely on, for the most part. They expect us to be corrupt at best, involved at worst. And they don't know if any interaction is a test. If they ask for help from someone who seems kind and he tells their pimp, they get a beating. If they try to run away and they get caught, they get killed. If they get away, the traffickers go and find their families in Nigeria or Romania or China or wherever they started out, and they beat *them* up. They rape their kids, their siblings. They kill their parents.'

'Why bother?' Belcott asked. 'Why don't they just grab a new girl and move on?'

'Because it's hard to move humans across borders legally, and even harder to do it illegally. A bird in the hand is worth at least two trying to enter the country.

Humans are worth more than drugs. A girl can make tens of thousands for a gang. But they need to keep them scared. That makes the girls obedient.' Bridges shrugged. 'It's worth their while. They hurt one girl or her family, the word spreads to the others. I promise you, I'm not exaggerating how they operate. They bring the women here or wherever they start out – Germany, France, Russia – and the women cooperate all along the line, thinking they're coming to a new life. And they are. It's just not the one they were promised.'

'How do we find out who they were?' I asked Bridges. 'We don't have faces for them, let alone names.'

'We probably won't ever know. Not unless Interpol sends us a missing person report that matches the details and we can test familial DNA. For now, we have nothing on these women. We don't know who was running the show. We don't know what they were even doing, or where they were working.'

'There's one other thing we don't know,' Dornton said. 'There were three of them in the flat, according to the neighbours. Three bedrooms in the flat. Three sets of belongings. Three toothbrushes in the bathroom.' He looked around the room, knowing we couldn't answer him, asking anyway. 'So where is she? Where's the third girl?'

Chapter 16

'Coming out?'

I straightened up from where I'd been kneeling by my desk, unplugging my mobile phone from its charger. 'Oh, Mal, I don't know. I'm a bit tired.'

His shoulders sagged a little. 'Yeah, I know. Everyone is. Next year I'll try and have my birthday on a day we aren't dealing with a massive arson.'

'I think we'd all appreciate that.' I bit my lip. 'I'm sorry.'

'Another time.' He managed a smile as he moved away and I remembered with a pang what it was like to ask the team to come out for a drink for the first time – the first test of whether you were popular and valued or just that new DC who no one really knew.

'I'll come for a bit,' I said, impulsively.

He turned, transformed by delight. 'Really?'

I'd had some sleep. About three hours, total, before Derwent had collected me to go to Armstrong's post-mortem.

To be perfectly honest, that was about what I averaged on a normal night.

'I'm sure. I might not stay for very long,' I warned.

'That's fine. Brilliant.' He gave me two thumbs up, grinning widely, then headed off with a noticeable spring in his step. It was so easy to make people happy, I thought, pawing through my bag to find some lipstick. And at least I had everything I needed with me.

'Kerrigan . . .' The word was drawn out, the tone silky and dangerous. Derwent was sitting on his desk chair, leaning well back, rotating a few inches to the left, then the right. 'What are you doing?'

'Getting ready to leave the office.'

'That's not what I mean.'

I brushed blusher onto my cheeks, then smiled at him. *If you think I'm going to ask you what you do mean, you must not know me very well.*

He sat forward, leaning his elbows on his knees. 'Playing a little game?'

'Nope.' I was concentrating on my mouth. The margin for error with red lipstick was too small to take risks.

'Why are you going out for a drink with him?'

'I'm going out for a drink with the team. Are you coming?'

A frown. 'Haven't decided.'

'Think fast. The clock's ticking.'

Around the room, people were pulling on their coats. Liv was plaiting her long dark hair, her fingers flying. She looked surprised, then pleased when she realised I was getting ready too.

I threw my make-up into my bag and picked up my phone, thumbing through screens, tapping in one quick update after another on various sites. *Heading out for team drinks in the local! Mine's a gin.* The chirpy tone set my teeth on edge. *Heading to Red Velvet later for dancing. Who's with me?*

Derwent was still watching me. 'If you're expecting me to do something exciting, you're going to be disappointed,' I said mildly.

'What's going on?'

'Absolutely nothing. Goodnight.' I picked up my bag and crossed the room to where Liv was waiting for me. I didn't have to look back to know that Derwent was still watching me as I left.

I stood in the corner of the pub, half-listening to Dave Kemp telling me about an arrest a friend of his had made.

'The mum keeps going on about how he's not there. She says he's in Spain, says she hasn't seen him for two weeks. And the whole time the kid is standing behind her in the hall.'

'Ha ha,' I said, because it was expected. Three drinks in. More people were arriving, letting a rush of cold air into the pub every time the door opened. It had started raining and my enthusiasm for heading out into the night was low. The trouble was that I couldn't stay. Mal was at the centre of a crowd, his eyes shiny from pleasure and a lot of alcohol consumed much too quickly. His shirt had pulled out from his trousers on one side. I needed to fight through to the bar and buy him a drink before I left, but Dave was blocking me in, whether he knew it or not. I stared over his shoulder, nodding when he paused for a response. The door opened again and Derwent prowled in like the Prince of Darkness he fondly believed himself to be. Raindrops sparkled like stars across the shoulders of his coat. He passed through the crowd, acknowledging greetings, muttering a comment that made Chris Pettifer throw his head back with a shout of laughter. He clapped Mal on the shoulder and leaned past him to order from the barman, who hurried to get him his round. I glanced down the bar, seeing frowns from customers who'd been waiting to be served. It would take more than a frown to shame Derwent into behaving himself.

But this was England. And the worst Derwent had to fear was someone saying, quite clearly, 'Wanker.'

It might have been possible for him to ignore it completely, but of course Derwent wasn't that person. He stopped in the act of getting his change and turned. 'Sorry?'

'I said, "Wanker".' It was a guy with artfully tousled hair, a media type if I had to guess from his t-shirt and his designer jeans and the trainers that were too ridiculous to be anything but a cult brand. The girl he was with looked away, her expression pained. She ran a hand through her hair and licked her lips and Derwent glanced at her, then stared with that single-minded focus I knew too well. Skinny jeans, tight top, cascading hair. Subtle as a manicured brick. Derwent's type in more ways than one.

'Oh shit,' I said, moving even though Dave was in the middle of a sentence. I couldn't afford to be polite just at that moment. 'Excuse me.'

'Have you got a problem, *mate*?' the man asked, beginning to shift from foot to foot, as if all he needed was the right angle to punch Derwent into the middle of next week. He didn't stand a chance.

'I don't have a problem. Have you?' Derwent demanded.

'Did you get me a drink? I'm dying of thirst.' I leaned in between the two men, facing Derwent. 'Don't tell me you forgot me.'

'I couldn't see you.'

'I was in the corner with Dave Kemp.'

It was like waving a squeaky toy in front of a German Shepherd. Derwent frowned, distracted from the fight he'd been fully prepared to start. 'What were you doing with him?'

'Talking.'

'Just talking.'

'Listening,' I admitted. 'He was doing most of the talking.'

Derwent glowered in his direction. Dave was very conscious of his own good looks – not something that Derwent trusted, even though he had more than his fair share of vanity.

'Why are you wasting time with him? Are you missing Rob?'

'That's none of your business.'

'It's absolutely my business if you're going to start boring me with stories about Dave Kemp.'

I leaned back as far as I could go, which wasn't very. The pub was heaving with Friday evening drinkers celebrating the end of the working week, and the crowd had swallowed the angry man. The noise level meant we might as well have been alone. 'When have I ever told you anything about my love life? Willingly, I mean?'

'Never.'

'So why would I start now?' Someone jostled me and

I swayed towards Derwent, a little closer than I would have chosen to be. He looked at my mouth for a long moment, then took the glass out of my hand and sniffed it.

'What's this?'

'The usual,' I said tightly.

'Gin and tonic.' It wasn't a question. He'd bought it for me himself more than once. He tilted the glass and drained it, pulling a face as he put the empty glass on the bar.

'Thanks,' I said. 'Thank you very much indeed.'

'I'll get you another one.'

'Don't bother, I—'

'They put too much ice in it. I couldn't even taste the gin.' It was a throwaway remark, unless you realised he was watching my reaction in the mirror over the bar.

That was it. I had to go.

'I'm going to the ladies.' I walked away from him, pushing through the crowd until I fetched up by Liv's side. 'Hi.'

'Hi yourself. What was that about?'

'Getting between Derwent and an argument.'

'That was nice of you.'

'I don't want to ruin Mal's birthday.'

'Ruin it? I think you made it. He was so pleased you came.'

'I haven't even had a chance to speak to him.'

'You're not the most sociable person on the team,' Liv said. 'It's like seeing a white rhino when you're on safari.'

'A white rhino. Charming.'

'Because they're rare,' she protested, pulling me in for

a hug. 'Seriously, it's good to see you out. I've missed you.'

'I haven't been anywhere. You're the one who was away.'

She shook her head. 'You know what I mean. You've been missing. Present but not present.'

'I've been doing my job.'

'And that's about it.' There was real concern on her face. 'If you need to talk—'

'There's nothing to talk about.'

'You don't look well. Are you eating? Are you sleeping?'

'Liv, I'm having a night out. A rare one, as you pointed out. Do me a favour and back off, will you?' I went past her and pushed through the door that led to the toilets. I felt cold, numb, aware in an anaesthetised sort of way that the row with Liv had hurt – and would hurt more later. What else was I going to break? What else was I willing to sacrifice? And still I was dry-eyed, full of purpose. The ladies' room was a symphony of patterned brown carpet and pink sanitary ware, most of it cracked or chipped. The lavatory in my cubicle was alarmingly stained. The air freshener was strong enough that I could taste it. I took out my phone and tapped in a status update on every social media site I could think of, then ransacked my bag. Hairbrush. Blister strip of pills. Make-up. Mirror. Perfume. Heels. A dress that was barely worthy of the name.

Nothing I would ever wear normally. Nothing I would ever wear in front of someone who knew me. I applied it to myself like armour, humming under my breath so I couldn't hear the voice in my head that was shouting a warning.

I walked back out into the pub a few minutes later. Out of the corner of my eye I saw Liv falter and stop talking, her face set.

'Fucking hell,' Pettifer said as I moved past him. 'I didn't know you were the entertainment, Kerrigan. Bit of a tip for you. Usually the strippers start off dressed and then take their kit off, not the other way round.'

I ignored him, leaning in to kiss Mal on the cheek. 'Sorry I have to go. Have a great night.'

He half said something, his eyes round. I couldn't stand to look at him, or the other members of the team who were standing around him.

I couldn't even stand to catch my own dark-rimmed eyes in the mirror behind the bar.

As I moved towards the door, I saw Derwent. I was completely unsurprised to see that he was talking to the girl who'd been with the man who'd called Derwent a wanker. *Insult me and I'll take your bird. Whether I want her or not.*

Then again, maybe Derwent did want her. She was sitting on a bar stool as he stood in front of her. He bent to say something into her ear that was only meant for her to hear, something that made her dip her head and giggle. His hand was on her thigh and as I watched he moved so his thumb slid between her legs, high up, and he was still talking, words spinning a spell, binding her to him. I saw her react, half-resisting at first, then giving in. He could do what he wanted with her.

He owned her.

I walked out of the pub and the cold night air was like a shot of adrenalin to the heart. I hailed a black cab and jumped into the back, slamming the door behind me. I didn't look to see if anyone had followed. I wasn't planning to wait anyway.

Later – much later – I stretched my arms above my head, not caring that it made the difference between my skirt being brief and indecent. My eyes were half-closed. The music pounded in my chest, blurring out my heartbeat, replacing it with something sharp and fast that made me think I might die there and then. I was hot, my hair damp, my dress sticking to my skin. Around me, bodies writhed, moving in time to the music, in thrall to the DJ. My feet ached, my head rang and I was barely aware of it. I couldn't hear myself think, which was fine by me. My phone purred against my hip, vibrating with a message I should probably have read, but I decided it could stay in my bag for the moment. Half of the people in the club were high; the other half just hadn't scored yet. They were blank-eyed, distant, part of a single organism that was totally devoted to hedonism, or as close to hedonism as you could get in a basement club in King's Cross. I was attracting plenty of attention, which had been my intention all along. Even sweat-smeared mascara and lank hair didn't put them off. I allowed one of the bigger men to grab hold of me around the waist for a second. Then I pushed him away, my eyelids lowered, my expression disdainful. It wasn't him I wanted.

I closed my eyes completely for a second, imagining the man I did want, summoning him with so much concentration, so much desire that it was a genuine surprise when I opened my eyes and he wasn't there. All of the men near me were wrong – their faces, their bodies. The way they held themselves. The way they looked at me.

Abruptly, I stopped dancing and elbowed my way off the dance floor with scant regard for anyone else. I made it past the ring of men who stood around the edge, watching the women with hungry eyes. I made it all the way to the sticky carpeted area by the bar where there was a smoked-glass mirror. I had time to see myself and appreciate for a moment the total transformation from policewoman to party girl. Legs forever, tumbling hair, sulky mouth. It was so convincing if you didn't look into my eyes, at the weariness and self-loathing. *Time to go.* I took a step towards the exit before the big guy who'd grabbed me on the dance floor came up behind me and took hold of me, this time by the neck. He pressed me back against his body, against the damp blue shirt that clung to overdeveloped pectoral muscles. Rugby player, I thought, going limp so he didn't feel he needed to put any pressure on my neck. *It's all fun and games until someone dies of vagal inhibition.*

He said something, his voice a rumble that I felt more than heard. It was too deep for me to pick out actual words, the pitch identical to the bass that throbbed in my ears, in my blood. I locked eyes with him in the mirror and apparently that was enough to count as a yes, because he lifted me off my feet and carried me down the hallway to the men's room.

I was protesting and wriggling, trying to get free as he shoved the door open. The bathroom stank of stale urine, harsh pine air freshener and cheap aftershave. There was an attendant, tall and dark-skinned, Indian at a guess. He threw a single glance in our direction, then turned to rearrange the hand towels, affecting not to see anything.

No help.

'Get off me,' I snarled. My voice seemed too loud in my ears and yet no one reacted. The music throbbed outside but the bathroom was quiet: flushing lavatories, running water. Men, ignoring me. Ignoring the man who held me. Deaf and blind, witnesses to nothing. The ones who did look had a confused, wary expression. *I don't want to get involved. I don't want to get hurt.* Maybe one of them would man up, find a bouncer and mention what was going on.

Or maybe not.

'Fucking let go of me, you twat,' I hissed.

Mr Blue Shirt elbowed a cubicle door and shoved me through it, which was a mistake because I got hold of the edge of the door and whipped it back into his face, slamming it over and over against his arm, his shoulder, his head. He lost his grip on me completely and for a second I was winning, but then he lowered his shoulder and charged the door and I had to jump back or risk getting flattened. I knew a lot about fighting in confined spaces, and I was trained in unarmed combat, but the main bit of relevant training was no help to me. Don't let yourself get trapped. Don't go out without back-up. Don't take on anyone bigger than you. Don't, in short, do any of the things I had done. And I still didn't feel scared, which was stupid. He was a distraction, not the main event. I couldn't quite believe that he was going to get in my way so comprehensively.

I had a fair idea of what Mr Blue Shirt intended to do to me, and I could see from the way the tendons were standing out in his neck that a simple 'no' wasn't going to be enough. I stamped on his instep. He staggered back a pace or two, breathing heavily.

'Bitch.'

'Leave me alone. It's not worth your while.'

'Shut up.' He came towards me again and I punched him in the neck, thinking of Dr Early. It was true, most women didn't punch. Men didn't expect it. This man, his reactions dulled by alcohol, had not expected it in the slightest. He coughed, holding on to his throat, and I worried for a second that I'd fractured his larynx, imagining the 999 call, the ambulance crew, the hospital, the response officers' questions, the possibility that he might actually die, and what an enormous fuck-up that would be. Then he squared his shoulders and came back at me, and this time he slapped me hard enough to make my ears ring. My lower lip stung and I tasted blood.

'I didn't want to have to do this but now I don't have a choice.' I took my warrant card out of my bag.

Mr Blue Shirt saw it, read it, read it again and faltered. 'What the—'

'Don't make me arrest you,' I hissed. 'Believe me, I'd like to, but I'm part of a much bigger operation, and I'm not going to fuck it up so I can spend four hours processing your arrest.'

He backed away, out of the cubicle. I followed him, keeping within a couple of feet of him. It gave me a certain amount of satisfaction to turn the tables on him.

'A bigger operation?' He had walked backwards all the

way to the sinks and now he was edging along them, towards the door.

'Drugs and vice.' I nodded to the pocket of his shirt which was transparent with sweat. 'I'd dump those pills for starters. Unless you want to find out what it's like to be locked up with a load of drug-dealers.'

He swallowed, hard, sobering up. 'Can I go?'

'I wish you would.'

For a big guy, Mr Blue Shirt moved fast. He turned, colliding with a man who was coming in and there was something inevitable about the new arrival being there, something that made it impossible for me to be even slightly surprised, even though he was the last person who should have been there. Derwent's eyes fell on me looking dishevelled, my cheek flaring red where the man had hit me. His reaction was instant. He dropped his shoulder and rammed it into Mr Blue Shirt's chest, pinning him back against the sinks at an awkward angle, with enough force to make Mr Blue Shirt grunt in pain. He braced a forearm high on Mr Blue Shirt's chest and grabbed his right arm, pushing it back against the mirror. Elegant, economical, a masterclass in controlling a difficult prisoner.

'No!' I said. 'Let him go.'

Derwent turned his head far enough that I could see his profile but not far enough to lose sight of the man he was holding down. 'Sure?'

'Sure.'

With obvious reluctance he stepped back, away from Mr Blue Shirt, who fell away from the sinks and by the greatest good luck staggered in the direction of the door. This time, he made it all the way out.

Derwent straightened his suit jacket and smoothed his hair. He scanned the bathroom for cameras, then pointed at the bathroom attendant.

'You saw nothing.'

'Nothing.' A note changed hands, disappearing at the speed of light. Then Derwent turned to me. He walked over, reached into my cleavage and tweaked a crumpled cloakroom ticket out of my bra.

'How did you—'

'No questions now. Go and get your stuff. Meet me outside in two minutes. Go.'

He spun me round and pushed me towards the door and I went, ducking past a very drunk man who was unzipping his flies before he'd even made it across the threshold, who leered approval at me as I hurried out. I saw a couple of bouncers walking down the hallway towards me and looked down so my hair fell in front of my face, looked anywhere but at them, trying to disappear. At the cloakroom I charmed and coaxed and bullied my way to the front of the queue. I got my coat and my other bag, clutching them to me instead of stopping to put them on properly. I kept my head down as I ran up the stairs, hurrying past the door staff, hoping to be ignored.

The car engine was already running when I slid into the passenger seat. I looked across at Derwent, who spared a second to glare back before he moved off.

I racked my brains for something to say. In the end, only one thing seemed appropriate. 'I'm sorry.'

'If you aren't,' he said evenly, 'you will be.'

Chapter 17

My flat was cold and dark, comfortless. I flicked on some lights, threw my bag and coat on the sofa and shook off my heels, leaving them capsized in a corner. Derwent stood in the middle of the living room, watching me. I moved around without looking at him, putting on the heating, filling a glass with water, drinking it in one long swallow. He hadn't spoken to me in the car. He hadn't asked where I wanted to go. He'd taken me home, and without a single word made it very clear that he wasn't just dropping me off, that there was a conversation we had to have. And I was tired all the way to my soul. It was easier to let him in, to let him shout at me if that was what he wanted to do, than to put it off for another day.

But I was damned if I was going to listen to a lecture while I was wearing a dress that put me at a positive disadvantage.

'I'm going to change.'

He nodded.

'Help yourself to a drink. Or make a cup of tea.'

Another nod. He looked tired, I thought, at a low ebb

after the high tide of controlled violence and efficiency that had got me out of the club, to the safety of my home.

Comparative safety.

If I'd been given a straight choice between Mr Blue Shirt and Derwent, I wasn't totally sure which one I'd have chosen.

It took me five minutes to change into a sweatshirt and tracksuit bottoms, to tie back my hair and wipe off the make-up that had smudged around my eyes. That was life, pulling off one personality and putting on another. Dressing to play a part, whether it was the confident police detective or the wayward clubber looking for trouble and finding it. The person in the mirror looked back at me, pale and thin, bare-faced, honest, or something like it. I went back out to the living room, as composed as Anne Boleyn walking to the executioner's axe, expecting more or less the same outcome.

Derwent was standing where I'd left him. He looked me up and down. 'That's better.'

'I thought so,' I agreed, stifling a yawn. 'I hadn't real-ised how late it is. You must be tired.'

The shadows were blue-black under his eyes. 'I'm fine.'

'Did you want anything? A drink?'

'No.'

I ignored him, pulling out a bottle of whisky and two glasses.

'Food?'

'No.' His mouth twitched. 'Not that you have any food here anyway.'

'There's something.' I sounded vague and knew it. 'Toast. I'm sure there's some bread in the freezer.'

'That's okay.' In the same conversational tone, he said, 'What were you doing?'

'What do you mean?' I spun the lid off the bottle and poured a generous slug of the golden brown liquid into each glass. The clear, peaty smell filled my head and I blinked.

'Back there in the club. What were you trying to do?'

'Just having a good time,' I said lightly, and it was like seeing a crack spread and splinter across a dam wall before it collapsed.

'For *fuck's sake*, Kerrigan, what the fucking fuck did you think you were doing? What the hell were you trying to achieve?' He was white with anger, his eyes bright, and I'd made him shout at me for the first time in a long time. 'It's obvious you don't have any sense but I can't believe you don't have any pride. Is that really what it's come to? Shagging a coked-up estate agent in a nightclub toilet?'

'He was on pills, not coke, and I wasn't shagging him. He thought I was an easy target but I made him think again.'

'How did you manage that?'

'I threatened to arrest him.'

He laughed, and it wasn't because he admired my technique. 'Fucking marvellous.'

'Obviously I wouldn't have done it. That was a last resort.'

'What would you have done if I hadn't turned up?'

'Exactly what I did. He was leaving when you arrived. I didn't need you to get involved.'

Derwent shook his head, his expression pained. 'That's not what I saw.'

'You saw a chance to be a hero and that was the last thing you thought.'

'And you wanted to be what? A victim?' He leaned on the counter. 'Listen, darling, I can follow you around for the rest of for ever and beat up guys like that when they won't listen to you, and I'd probably enjoy it, but that's not the point. What were you doing there? What's going on?'

I moved to switch the television on, selecting a channel that wasn't tuned in and played white noise. I turned it up, filling the room with a dull hiss. Then I turned back to him.

'Chris Swain.'

It took him a second. 'That fucking lizard who was hassling you?'

'Stalking me,' I said.

'I thought he'd gone away.'

'Nope. Quite the opposite.' I pulled open a drawer in the kitchen and took out a folded sheet of paper. I sent it skimming across the counter and Derwent pinned it down, then opened it out.

'What's this?'

'It's a list of places I went last week. People I spoke to. Things I bought. I get one every week.'

'Here?'

I nodded. 'Hand-delivered.'

He pointed at the TV. 'And the sound effects are because you think he's bugged this place.'

'I'm sure he has. I just don't know how.'

He looked appalled, stepping back with his hands up so he didn't contaminate the paper in front of him. 'What are you doing about it? Why haven't you reported it? Why isn't this letter in an evidence bag?'

'Because he's already under investigation for hosting child pornography on his website and if he gets arrested I'd be the entertainment. You know what it's like. You don't want to be the story if you're a police officer.'

He nodded. 'People start questioning your judgement.'

'Even if it's not your fault that some creep decided to target you.' I sounded bitter because I was: for years now Swain had been shadowing me and he still hadn't lost interest. Quite the opposite. The longer it went on the more he enjoyed it. 'You know he'd get five years at the most for stalking me. And in the meantime, no one is going to make it a priority. Some overworked detective will turn up and take a statement. They'll take the letters away. They'll tell me to note every incident of harassment. And if he kills me, they'll use it all to build the case against him. But I'll still be dead. If he doesn't kill me, it'll be all over the papers and my reputation will be in tatters. No one will ever take me seriously again. Either way, I lose.'

Derwent frowned. 'So what, you're fitting in as much stupidity as you can before the bitter end? It's an original bucket list, I'll give you that. Most people just want to travel and spend time with family.'

I rolled my eyes. 'Obviously not. I'm not going to waste my time by going the official route. I've been waiting for them to find him for years and they've done nothing. I'm tired of letting him make the running. I'm tired of waiting for him to attack me. I've met him, remember, and he didn't scare me. What scares me is the idea of him. He's made himself into my nightmare and I'm not going to let him control me any more. I'm trying to draw him out of the shadows so I can deal with him once and for all. I want to scare him into leaving me alone.'

'You're setting a trap.'

'Now you're getting it.'

'And you're the bait.'

'If you want to put it that way.'

'No other way to put it, is there?' He shook his head. 'I wondered about the social media updates.'

'So that's how you found me.'

'You made it easy for me.'

'That was the idea,' I said. 'But it wasn't meant for you. How did you know I was putting personal information on the internet?'

'I had a look at your internet history the last time I was here.'

'Damn it. I knew it.' I scowled at him. 'You had no reason to do that.'

'Just natural curiosity. I wasn't keeping tabs on you, though. I promise. Until tonight.'

I folded my arms. 'I'm so sure.'

'It's true.' A grin lit up his face for a second. 'You made me look. I knew you were up to no good when I saw you leaving the pub.'

'I thought you were too busy with your new lady friend to notice me.'

'I—' He broke off to shake his head. 'I noticed. It's not every day you see a colleague come down with a bad case of the sluts.'

'What a shitty thing to say,' I protested.

'Deny it.'

I couldn't. 'Well, it was deliberate. I'm telling Swain where to find me and when. I'm making myself vulnerable. At least, that's what I want him to think.'

'And you haven't told anyone. You haven't asked for help from anyone. Even if you're deliberately putting yourself in harm's way, that doesn't mean you're not in danger.'

'I can handle it by myself.'

'Like you were handling the meathead in the club.'

'He wasn't a problem.'

Derwent pointed at me. 'You were fucking lucky.' His voice was very slightly rougher than usual, wind on water.

'Or I can handle myself.'

'Yeah, you're hard as nails.'

I shoved his glass towards him, lifted mine and tipped it back in one go, which was sheer bravado and really fucking stupid. It hit me like a ball of fire, surging into my stomach, destroying me from the inside. My stomach turned itself inside out, twisted itself into a knot, and I wasn't going to get away with it, not this time. I spun round and ran, a hand clamped over my mouth. I didn't let go until I'd slid to my knees on the bathroom floor and stuck my head into the white porcelain bowl, smelling whisky on my breath and a ghost of bleach and the metallic odour of shame before everything I'd had to drink flew back up into my mouth and splashed into the limpid water below.

I'd been sick often enough lately to know there was no point in rushing things. I stayed in the bathroom, one hand to my head, the other draped across the loo seat, waiting with my eyes closed until the stomach cramps eased, until I'd stopped bringing up anything at all except saliva, until I started to feel more normal. There was a tinge of euphoria to the aftermath, a giddiness I never got used to. I got to my feet and rinsed out my mouth in the sink, splashing the water onto my face and neck. As soon as I buried my face in a towel I wanted, quite passionately, to stay in it for ever. To sleep, standing up if necessary. To opt out of any further conversation.

He was standing outside the bathroom when I opened the door, leaning against the wall, his hands in his pockets. The smile was gone. He looked drawn, and angry.

'Maeve.'

Derwent never called me by my first name except in the direst emergencies; when he thought he was dying, or that I was.

'Don't,' I said. 'It's not what you're thinking.'

'Oh, right. Then I'll stop worrying about you.'

'You don't need to worry.'

He looked down the hallway, away from me. 'Someone has to. You can't pretend there's nothing going on. You can't pretend you don't need to face up to reality.' He looked back at me, hurt. 'I knew you were being irresponsible but I didn't know just how bad things were. Why didn't you tell me?'

'There was nothing to tell. I—'

'You need to grow up, Kerrigan. Fast. And don't try to lie to me. I know what's going on.'

'Do you?' I folded my arms.

'It's obvious. You look like shit. You've stopped drinking

caffeine and alcohol. You were drinking tonic water at the pub tonight and pretending it was gin. Everything we see and everything we do makes you feel sick. You're taking risks because you want to hurt yourself, so it's not technically your fault if everything goes wrong.'

I tilted my head to one side. 'If what goes wrong?'

'What are you? Two months along?'

I couldn't help it. I laughed.

'Does Rob know? Is it even his?'

I shook my head, still laughing, knowing it was hysteria as much as amusement. Derwent walked away, into the sitting room, wounded but dignified in a way that I wasn't.

Time to be serious.

I followed him.

'Sit down,' I said.

'No, I—'

'*Sit.*' I walked towards him. 'You don't get to come to my home and shout at me when you know nothing about what I was doing or why. Sit down and shut up, and I'll tell you. I owe you that much.'

'But—'

'Not one word.' I pointed at the sofa and eventually, like a dog, he went and sat down.

'I'm not pregnant.'

'But—'

'No. It's my turn to speak. I'm not pregnant.' I picked up my bag and emptied the contents out on the floor, kneeling beside it so I could look for the foil blister strip. I found it and waved it at him. 'See this? Omeprazole.'

He frowned. 'I don't—'

'I have a stomach ulcer. This is my medicine. Twice a day, every day. Side effects include nausea and dizziness, unfortunately for me.'

The frown deepened.

'Think about it,' I said. 'It makes sense. I can't stand to drink tea or coffee or alcohol because they irritate my stomach. I hadn't been feeling great for a while – stomach pains, indigestion, the usual – but I started throwing up a few weeks ago. I had a ton of time off last month for doctors' appointments. Liv can tell you.'

'You didn't say anything to me about it.'

'There was no reason to. We weren't working together.' I flicked the edge of the pill strip with my thumb. 'I thought I was really ill.'

'You don't look after yourself,' he said automatically.

'All my own fault,' I agreed. 'That and the stress. Oh, and the painkillers I've had to take in the last couple of years. Turns out they're not good for you.'

'Fuck.' He put his hands over his face and let his head fall back against the sofa. 'I thought—'

'Sorry.' I was grinning when he looked back. 'You can be godfather if you like.'

'To the ulcer.'

'I call it Una.'

He chuckled, and it was genuine. 'An ulcer.'

'I know.'

'I was so sure.'

'Not this time. Thank God. I checked. They checked. No baby on board.'

'It would be one way to get Rob to come back,' Derwent observed, and I couldn't quite bring myself to laugh along with him. I concentrated on gathering the things I'd tipped out of my bag, shoving them back in it without particular care.

'You miss him.' This time it wasn't a question.

'Yeah.'

'Why?'

I sat back on my heels. 'What do you mean, why? I love him. He left me. It's been two months since I heard from him and I have no way of contacting him.' Which was driving me crazy.

'He was bloody lucky he ran away before I found out what he'd done to you.'

'Why, because you'd have beaten him up?'

'Or I'd have told your brother where to find him. I bet he'd have wanted a word.'

'Because of course poor Maeve needs some man or other to come along and make everything better.' I was shaking, I was so angry. 'I don't need someone to rescue me all the time. You don't get to defend my honour or whatever it is you tell yourself you'd do if you only had the chance.'

'What he did to you—'

'Was nothing,' I finished.

'He raped you.'

'*No*. That's not what happened.' He had been devastated by the death of a colleague and was seeking comfort. I had been trying to forget about the teenagers who threatened me – something I hadn't even shared with him. He had been drinking, so he missed the signals that I didn't want to sleep with him. I had let things go too far before I said as much. I had plenty to feel guilty about, I thought, and I'd have told Rob as much if he'd only waited around to hear it instead of disappearing out of my life. 'He didn't rape me.'

'You told me what happened and it was exactly that.'

I stood up, feeling at too much of a disadvantage when I was looking up at him. Much better to stand so I could glower at him from a height. 'We were in a relationship. He was entitled to think I wouldn't reject him.'

'He was entitled to *nothing*.' Derwent slammed his fist down on the arm of the sofa. 'He didn't have your consent to do what he did. He didn't ask.'

'He didn't need specific consent. Was he supposed to ask permission every time? We were living together.'

'Listen to yourself. Do you even hear what you're saying?' He took a deep breath, forcing himself to be calm. 'Being in a relationship doesn't hand him a golden ticket, Kerrigan. He still needed to know you were willing. And you weren't.'

Derwent blurred and I blinked, holding on to my composure because I was too proud to cry.

'He stopped when I told him to.'

'He should never have started. I know you don't want to think less of him, and I know you don't want to see yourself as a victim. Christ, I've worked enough domestic violence cases to last me a lifetime, I know you don't want to admit it to yourself.'

'I hadn't told him anything about what happened to me when I was attacked. I didn't warn him to be careful with me. I wasn't honest with him.' It poured out of me: everything I had to apologise for. Everything I wanted to say to my absent boyfriend, and I was saying it to the wrong person. 'It was my fault,' I finished.

'That's what they all say.'

'You don't know what you're talking about.' My voice was so cold the words splintered with ice.

'No, you don't know how to see Rob as anything other than Mr Perfect. Why the hell do you think he ran away? *He* knew what he did.'

'He left because I let him down. If I could just explain to him—'

Derwent was shaking his head. 'He doesn't deserve you and you don't owe him anything. I don't know why you want him back, Kerrigan. He raped you, he lied to you, and then he cheated on you. Do you really imagine the story ends with happy ever after?'

It was too much, too close to the truth. Too close to what I wouldn't allow myself to think. Because yes, he had done some things that needed to be forgiven, but I would do that, and more, if it meant I'd get him back.

When I could speak, I said, 'You should go.'

'Kerrigan, listen—'

'No. Not any more. You've said enough.'

'Yeah, I probably have.' He was calm, reasonable. He'd said what he wanted to. He'd laid the charges and if I was devastated by the explosion, he didn't care. The conversation was over; he'd moved on. He looked at his watch and pulled a face. 'Look, do me a favour. Let me stay here.'

'*What*? No. Absolutely not.' I wanted him out of my space, out of my head. No one made me feel as bad as Derwent, ever. No one made me question myself like he did, and it was the fact that I liked him when he wasn't picking me apart, that I trusted him when he wasn't undermining me, that I wanted his approval even when I told myself his opinion was worthless. I tried not to think about what he'd said but I'd heard it, and I knew the words were branded on my memory, a permanent scar.

'On the sofa, I mean.'

'No.'

'Come on. Please.'

'If this is more of your hero complex coming out—' I began.

'It's not for your sake. I mean, I don't mind keeping an eye on you. But that's not the issue.'

'Why, then?'

'It's late. I'm tired. I don't have anywhere to go except a hotel, and I just want to get some sleep.' He stretched, wincing.

'You have a flat,' I pointed out. 'Why can't you go there?'

'I'm not living there at the moment.'

I blinked. 'You live alone. Did you have a fight and kick yourself out?'

'Not quite. I'm letting Melissa Pell's mother stay there with Thomas.'

'*What*?'

'She wanted to stay somewhere in London so they could be near Melissa. She had nowhere else to go. They couldn't afford a hotel. She was going to have to take the kid away otherwise.'

'That's awfully nice of you.'

'Isn't it,' he said, in a tone that indicated the subject was closed. I wished I could manage that. 'So can I stay?'

My absolute outrage had faded to a dull ache and I was honestly too tired to argue with him any more, especially when even I had to admit it wasn't his fault the love of my life had disappeared.

'No more lectures.'

He grinned, knowing he'd won. 'Fine. Not a word.'

'You can stay. There's a bed in the spare room.'

'Thanks.'

'Don't thank me. You've done the same for me.'

'And more,' Derwent said, ruining it. He stood up and was suddenly too close to me. It came as a surprise to me that he was taller than me when I wasn't wearing shoes. I stepped back and turned away, heading for the door of my bedroom and peace. Derwent crossed the room to turn the television off. Before he did, he said, 'Anyway, I like to think this will annoy your little buddy Swain.'

I smiled in spite of myself. 'Why do you think I said yes?'

Chapter 18

I woke up, groggy and confused, to the sound of thumping dance music. It was dark outside and I scrabbled for my watch: half past six. I presumed that was morning. I also presumed it was Saturday: the weekend, but still a working day to those of us who were handling the Murchison House fire. There would be time off after a few days, when the initial heat of the investigation had cooled like the fire itself. I put a hand to my face, rubbing the sleep away. There hadn't been much sleep: if tossing and turning was an Olympic sport I'd been putting in enough practice to have a decent shot at making the team. Derwent's words kept repeating, along with my absolute inability to counter them with anything meaningful. I felt I'd let Rob down, and myself. I wasn't in denial. It was more complicated than Derwent could know. He hadn't been there when everything had fallen apart.

But he had picked up the pieces of me that were left behind.

And the only reason he had to make me feel bad about it was because he cared.

Or, I reminded myself, climbing out of bed to see what

was going on, because he enjoyed making people suffer for their mistakes.

I dragged on a dressing gown and pushed open the bedroom door, squinting against the bright light.

'Bloody hell, Kerrigan, you look rough.'

'I could say the same to you,' I snapped. Derwent was prowling around the living room in pants and a vest, to my complete lack of pleasure, and indeed surprise. 'Can you put some clothes on?'

'None to put on. Everything clean is in the car. You're going to go and get it for me when you're dressed.'

'Brilliant.'

'You're not a morning person, are you?'

'How did you guess?' I dragged myself into the kitchen, ostentatiously avoiding Derwent, and filled the kettle, more out of habit than anything else. I generally didn't manage more than a couple of mouthfuls of tea these days. As I set it down to switch it on, he came up behind me and braced his hands against the counter on either side of me, trapping me. I stiffened, outraged, and turned to find his face inches from mine. The music was loud enough that I didn't have to whisper. The neighbours would be livid. But not as livid as I was.

'What the actual fuck are you doing?'

'You have to assume Swain has video. He did the last time.'

'He did then, yes, but he doesn't now.'

'Okay.' He pushed himself back and looked down at me with a mocking smile.

'Don't do that again.' I said, unnerved.

'I wasn't trying to upset you.'

'I'm not upset.'

'I didn't touch you.'

'I know. I just like my personal space.'

'Sorry.' He patted my head in a fraternal, wholly irritating way. 'You know I wasn't trying it on. You're not my type. No offence,' he added.

'Believe me, I'm perfectly aware of your type, and I'm quite happy not to be that kind of girl.' I frowned at him. 'What were you doing?'

'I was trying to make him jealous.'

'Just being in the flat overnight is enough.' I leaned past him to get a mug and a teabag.

'He might be watching. It's not convincing if I don't come near you.'

'There's absolutely no need. Rob and I picked this place because there's no view. No windows overlook us on this side. He can't see in and he doesn't have any hidden cameras.'

'How do you know?'

'I got Kev Cox to come round and look for anything that shouldn't be here. Cameras are hard to hide. If there was something here, he'd have found it.'

'But you think he has sound.'

'I know he does. There are things he knows that he must have heard. Conversations I've had.'

'On the phone?'

'In person.'

'Just here in the flat?'

'Everywhere.' I shivered. 'I know he's listening to me but I don't know how.'

Derwent considered it. 'I'll factor it in.'

'To what?'

'My plan.'

'What plan?'

'The one I'm formulating. Don't worry.' He smirked at me. 'I'll tell you everything you need to know when you need to know it.'

'Sorry, who invited you to be involved?'

'You obviously need help.'

'I think not,' I said stiffly, pouring water into my mug and stabbing the teabag with a spoon to force the flavour out, too impatient to wait for it to steep.

'Don't worry. It'll still be risky as hell and you'll still be bait.' He tilted his head, considering me. 'I know you love danger.'

'That's not true.'

'I bet it felt good to beat that guy up last night. I bet you got a kick out of it.' He picked up my hand and examined the bruising across my knuckles from my fight with Mr Blue Shirt. 'You got the better of him. Didn't that give you a thrill?'

'Not getting hurt gave me a thrill,' I said, yanking my hand away to pour milk into the mug. 'Not having to explain my actions to response officers made me happy. Other than that—'

'Bullshit. You have a competitive streak a mile wide. Look at your hit rate for solving crimes. That doesn't happen by accident. You love to win.'

'Not me.' I shook my head. 'It's too early in the morning for this.'

'And that.' Derwent hooked the mug out of my hand. 'It'll just make you throw up. Have some water instead.'

'Oh, come on,' I said with real disgust. 'It's bad enough that you're in my flat. Now I have to get permission for everything I eat and drink?'

'I don't like sick.' He took the mug over to the sofa and sat down, sprawling across it. 'Want to hear the plan for the day?'

I was hunting through cupboards, trying to find something to eat for breakfast. 'Yep.'

'We're going to the hospital to see Melissa Pell.'

I slammed a door shut and stared at him. 'Are you out of your mind?'

He shrugged. 'Possibly. What's the problem with interviewing Melissa?'

'Um, off the top of my head, the fact that Una Burt will have a rage stroke if she finds out. It's not our case. She's not dead, for starters.'

'But other people are, and someone tried to kill her.' Derwent clicked his tongue. 'Come on, Kerrigan. Be more creative. She's a definite lead on the whole arson. Someone deliberately targeted her. Someone went out of their way to harm her. She was bashed over the head.'

'So was Armstrong, and he's the person we're supposed to be investigating.'

'I don't care about Armstrong.'

'I know that,' I said patiently. 'But DCI Burt does.'

'You know how much that matters to me.'

'Yeah, and it's moronic. Why are you giving her an opportunity to make you look bad?'

'That's not what I'm doing.'

'Oh really? You know she wants you to step out of line so she can get rid of you. Just wandering over to someone else's investigation and getting involved is exactly the kind of thing she'd mind. And you know, she'd be right.'

Derwent was looking increasingly disapproving. 'Kerrigan,' he snapped, and it sounded like a whip cracking.

'It's stupid and reckless to load the gun and hand it to her. There are leads to chase up for Armstrong – people we need to talk to. Let's do that and get it out of the way. Then you can concentrate on Melissa Pell. Assuming Chris Pettifer doesn't mind.'

'He doesn't get to mind. He doesn't outrank me.'

'Oh sure. Pull rank. That never gets people's backs up.'

'I don't have to care, though.'

'Yes, we all know you don't care what anyone thinks of you.' I'd picked up my phone and was listening to my voicemail, to the calls I'd missed the night before. 'Huh.'

'What's up?'

'Elaine Lister wants us to come to Armstrong's office. She's got some things she wants to show us.' I listened to the low voice, and to her slightly stuttering delivery. She sounded unsure of herself. 'She says she misled us yesterday about some things. Unintentionally,' I added.

'She must have lied about something and she thinks we'll find out about it some other way. Or she wants to complain to us about John Grey without him being around. I don't think there's much love between those two. It won't be important.'

'Possibly not, but we should go and talk to her.'

'You could do that on your own,' Derwent said. 'You don't need me.'

I held up a finger, listening to the next message. 'Una

Burt wants me to let her know where you are and what you're doing, and don't think I'm going to lie for you. You're coming with me.'

Derwent closed his eyes briefly. 'There's no escape, is there?'

'Sorry. Other people want Armstrong's death to be solved, even if you don't care about what happened to him.' I spun my phone on the counter top. 'I was thinking I should speak to Claudine Cole in person. If I go to her flat, I might spot someone who answers the description of the woman who was with Armstrong.'

'Knowing you,' Derwent said, 'you'll run into his murderer as soon as you set foot on the Maudling Estate.'

'That's me. Lucky.' I gave him a tight little smile.

'Can't have it both ways, Kerrigan. You're shit-hot at your job and ambitious, or you wander around tripping over killers.' Derwent's eyes were bright. 'You're never going to get promoted if you don't shout about your achievements.'

'I'm not like that.'

'Then get like that. Being modest is going to get you left behind.'

I shook my head, irritated. 'Anyway, don't you want me to find Armstrong's killer? If his murder is solved, you'll be free to pursue Melissa Pell.'

Derwent frowned. 'Pursue her attacker.'

'Obviously. That's what I meant.'

'Kerrigan,' he began, pained, and I cut him off.

'If we go to Westminster first, I can go on to the Maudling Estate and you can go to the morgue.'

'Why don't we do the estate first and then split up?' Derwent asked.

Because I don't want you anywhere near Claudine Cole. I couldn't think of a polite way to say it. He got there on his own anyway.

'You don't think she'd like to talk to a white male in a position of authority.'

'No, I don't. I think she'd assume you were like all the other coppers who'd let her and her community down.'

'I'm not.'

Debatable. 'It's just something else to overcome. We're not starting from a strong position with Claudine Cole. I don't think we should take any risks when we're dealing with her.'

'What about MI5?'

'I've requested any information they can share with us. I wouldn't hold your breath for them to rush it through.'

Derwent sighed. 'Right. We'll do it your way. You go to see Mrs Cole on your own. Are you going to warn her you're turning up?'

'No.'

'Risky.'

'I know. I don't want to annoy her but I also don't want anyone from her organisation to disappear because they know I'm coming.'

Derwent frowned. 'Do you want me to get someone else to go with you? Liv, maybe?'

'Why?'

'Because the Maudling Estate is no place for a woman on her own, even if she's a copper. Maybe especially if she's a copper. And you know that better than I do.'

'Thanks,' I said. 'But I can manage.'

He drained the last of the tea from my mug and set it down on the table. 'Tell you what, Kerrigan, keeping you out of trouble is a full-time job.'

'For what it's worth,' I said, 'that feeling is absolutely mutual.'

Geoff Armstrong's office was in Portcullis House, the great block of charmless metal and concrete that lurked by Westminster Bridge, in sorry contrast to Pugin's golden, ethereal Houses of Parliament. It was quiet as we walked through it, deserted on a Saturday morning when the MPs were all engaged in constituency business.

Armstrong had been dead for about forty hours and the small set of rooms he'd occupied were already in a state of upheaval. A trolley stood outside in the corridor, loaded with boxes of files and miscellaneous clutter such as a desk lamp and a photograph of Armstrong with a senior American politician. Derwent picked it up and looked at it.

'How did he get to see her?'

'He was good at making himself look important,' I said, taking it out of his hand and putting it back on the pile. 'And from what I know of her, they had a lot in common. No benefits, no public medical care, no safety net. Only the strong survive.'

'What happens to the kids?'

'Their parents should look after them. And if they can't—'

'They shouldn't have them.'

'Armstrong didn't have any children,' I said. 'Why do you think that was?'

'You saw Cressida. Those weren't childbearing hips.'

'She did not seem to be the maternal type,' I agreed.

'They didn't want children.' The voice came from the doorway to Armstrong's office, where Elaine Lister stood. From her pallor and the purple shadows under her eyes, I guessed she hadn't slept since the last time I'd seen her. Her hands were grey with dust. She held them in front of her, crossed at the wrist, well away from her clothes. 'Geoff didn't believe in having children for the sake of it, he said. He thought it was an indulgence in a world that was already overpopulated.'

'And his wife didn't mind?'

'She was pleased. She didn't want to lose her figure. Or her freedom.'

'They were well matched, then,' Derwent observed.

'I don't think they had very much in common at all, but they wanted the same things out of life. If that's a good marriage, they had it.'

It didn't sound like my idea of a good marriage, but what did I know? And Derwent's longest relationships could be measured in weeks, not months. We weren't in a position to judge the Armstrongs.

Which was fine, because Elaine Lister was happy to oblige. 'I suppose it will make it easier for Cressida now that they had separate lives. She's not going to miss him as much as I will.'

I blinked and Elaine caught it.

'I suppose that sounds strange, but he was my professional life and he was my best friend. He was at the centre of everything I did. Of course I'm going to miss him. And who is going to want to employ me at my age?'

'You probably shouldn't worry about that now,' I said. 'Just get through the next few days and things will seem a lot clearer.'

'I hope so.'

'What was it you wanted to show us, Mrs Lister?' Derwent asked gently. 'You mentioned on the phone that you'd misled us about something.'

'Yes. You'd better come in.' She led us into the office, where there were more boxes of files and cupboards standing empty.

'Are they making you move out already?'

'I wanted to get on with clearing the office.' She was the sort of person who needs to have something to do to feel alive, I thought. She almost smiled. 'And I wanted to get it done before John came in on Monday. I can't bear him. Always interrupting me, or talking over me. The only reason he ever spoke to me was to get ideas that he could present as his own. Eventually I stopped talking when he was around.'

'Did Mr Armstrong get on with him?' Derwent asked.

She pulled a face. 'I think Geoff thought John was useful. But he was wary of him. He knew John was only working with him because he was a rising star. John would be the first out the door if anything went wrong for Geoff. He likes success. What is it they call people like that? Star fuckers, isn't it?'

It was a shock, somehow, to hear her use bad language when she seemed so restrained otherwise. She noticed the flicker of surprise I couldn't hide and smiled.

'John Grey brings out the worst in me, I'm afraid.

218

He has no heart and I think he sold his soul years ago.'

'So Armstrong and Grey had a purely professional relationship.'

Elaine nodded. 'Of course, John is gay. Geoff didn't really approve of that. He made him promise to be discreet. It's not that Geoff was homophobic exactly but a lot of his voters would have views on homosexuality. Geoff opposed gay marriage, gay couples having children by IVF – all of the things that homosexuals seem to see as their rights these days.'

'And John Grey didn't mind that?'

'He viewed it as politically expedient to oppose these things. I have no idea what his personal opinion was or is. You'd have to ask him.'

'Did they ever argue?'

'All the time,' Elaine said calmly. 'But not about personal matters.'

'Is that what you wanted to talk to us about?' I asked. 'John Grey?'

'No.' She sat down on one of two low chairs and I took the other one. Derwent perched on the edge of the desk, which meant that we had to look up to him, just the way he liked it.

Elaine Lister cleared her throat. 'I wanted to speak to you again because – because I may not have been entirely truthful about Geoff.'

'In what respect?' I was careful not to sound shocked or surprised, and indeed I was neither. It was so common in a murder case for the victim to be an angel, perfect in every way, until reality supervened.

She looked down at her hands. 'I told you he wasn't

having an affair. But – well, I don't *know* he was. But there was something strange going on.'

'What can you tell us?' I asked.

'It started about two months ago. He had me clear three hours every Thursday. No calls unless it was incredibly urgent. No meetings, no appointments. Nothing could come between him and his Thursday afternoons.'

'Did he give you any explanation?' I asked.

'That he was going to the Maudling Estate for a meeting of Claudine Cole's group.' She looked up. 'But I rang. I was – suspicious, I suppose. They don't have meetings on Thursdays.'

'Strange thing to lie about. It's easy enough to check,' Derwent said. 'We'd have found out.'

'I know. That's why I told you.' Elaine said it as if it was perfectly reasonable.

'That makes us wonder, you see, if there's anything else you've been hiding about Mr Armstrong.' Derwent's voice was quiet but firm. 'Anything you don't think we'll find out, so you're keeping it hidden.'

She flushed, biting her lip.

'It's normal for you to feel loyal to your employer – your friend,' I said. 'But the best way to help him now is to tell us what you know. We want to find whoever killed him and we need your help for that.'

'Whoever set the fire, you mean,' Elaine Lister said.

'I mean whoever killed him.'

Her lips were bloodless. 'But I thought – you said he fell out of a window. He jumped.'

'That's how it looked initially.'

She leaned back in her chair. 'I— give me a minute, will you?'

'Would you like a glass of water?' I suggested.

'No. I'll be all right.'

'It's a shock,' Derwent said.

'Well, yes.' She started to look a little brighter as her intellect took over from her emotions. It was a problem to be solved now. 'You know, it never made sense to me that he would kill himself. Geoff wasn't that sort of person. He didn't run away, ever.'

'It looks as if he died after the fire began,' I said. 'We think he was pushed out of the window.'

'So we really need to know who he was meeting there, and why.' Derwent leaned forward. 'If there's anything you can tell us about it, please, now is the time.'

'I don't know. He didn't tell me. But every Thursday morning he sent me out to the cashpoint. The one by Westminster tube station. I got out two hundred pounds for him. And he didn't have it by Thursday evening, because a couple of times he asked me to lend him twenty quid if he was getting a taxi somewhere.'

'Did he usually ask you to get cash out for him?'

'From time to time, but only if he was really busy. I just thought he wanted to make sure it was done. If he wanted to be certain of anything, he asked me to look after it.' She saw the look on my face. 'His work was so demanding, it was easy for things to slip his mind.'

And he was a giant man-baby who couldn't even be bothered to organise the cash to pay off his lover. I nodded sympathetically. 'He really relied on you. Was it always two hundred pounds?'

'When it started, it was a hundred and twenty. It went up, over time. It was two hundred for the last couple of weeks.'

'And when did he start asking you for the cash?' Derwent asked.

'Two months ago. About the same time he told me to clear Thursday afternoon in his diary. I'd assume the two things were connected,' she added with a wry smile.

'Me too,' Derwent said.

'Did you ever hear him making mysterious phone calls?' I asked.

'No, but there were text messages. I held his phone for him if he was doing a public engagement, and there would be messages from a number I didn't recognise. Just, "okay" or "great" but it was spelled out with an eight – you know, the numeral.' She gave a little shudder. 'I used to say, "your teenager has been in touch again" and he'd laugh.'

'Do you think it was actually a teenager?' I asked.

'No, no. If it had been, he wouldn't have found it funny. No, it was just someone he'd picked up.' For a second, her expression was pure distaste. 'It's so common but it was still a shock to me when I worked it out. And he didn't try to hide it from me. He never talked to me about it, but he must have known I knew what he was doing.'

'He trusted you to keep his secrets,' I said.

'That's not all I kept. I thought you'd like these.' She reached behind her and lifted up a heavy box file from the floor. It was too full, bulging against the catch that held it shut. 'These are the threats that came in by email or on the Facebook page or Twitter or by post. Anything written down. We got phone calls too but I didn't record them. I logged them with a brief synopsis of what the caller said but it's not all that accurate, I'm afraid. Most of the threats were emailed.'

'You said Armstrong told you to throw it away,' I said.

'Yes, but I didn't say I did it.' She handed it to me. 'I hope there's something useful in there.'

Whether there was or there wasn't, going through it was going to keep me busy. And I couldn't expect any help from my senior officer, I knew very well, glancing up to see a distant look on his face. He didn't need to tell me the paperwork was all mine.

Chapter 19

I parked in an empty space outside Murchison House, reversing into a spot between two vans. My meeting was in Elton House, the third high-rise tower on the Maudling Estate, but outside Murchison House the parking spaces were still taped off for the emergency services. The building was closed to everyone except the fire investigators, the scene of crime officers who were following up on our inquiries, and the workmen who were starting to make inroads into repairing the structure for the residents. Days after the fire, the building looked worse than ever, dark-streaked where the smoke had stained it, with gaping ugly holes in the walls where the fire had clawed its way out. The sky was concrete grey, the few trees bare and black. There was no colour in it, no life. I couldn't imagine anyone wanting to move back into Murchison House, but choice was a luxury. It didn't take me very long to decide against putting the Police on Duty notice on the dashboard of the car. It looked like a police officer's car anyway: there was no point in putting an actual target on it.

I headed into Elton House, my collar turned up against

the chill, and took the stairs rather than risk the rattling lift. Claudine Cole lived on the sixth floor and I was glad I was on my own, without Derwent, who would have taken the stairs two or three at a time and complained when I got out of breath. And Liv – she would have struggled to keep up with me. She was too fragile for this, too vulnerable to be back-up. I preferred to be alone. Without wanting to, I thought of her pale face floating in the comforting gloom of the pub, the look of disappointment and surprise in her eyes. I knew she was worried about me, and I knew that, unlike Derwent, she would hold back until I invited her into my world, my problems. They were alike only in that they were both my friends, I thought, then checked myself, because Derwent wasn't a friend.

Except that, now and then, I recognised that the way he spoke to me was as close as he could come to telling me he cared. He had added me to the small group of people he would defend with his life, without question, and I knew he was pleased to be able to insert himself into my struggle with Chris Swain. I just wasn't sure that was something I should be glad about. Derwent had a trick of amplifying any situation he found himself in. If anyone was going to turn Swain from a grenade to a nuclear bomb, it was Derwent.

On the other hand, I'd been trying to provoke Swain for months, and I'd got no closer to him than before I started. So maybe I needed Derwent.

I arrived at Claudine Cole's door and took a second to let my heart rate slow. The door was decorated with a red and a white paper rose intertwined, the symbol of her campaign. A banner underneath read 'Justice for Levon', red letters on white satin, the whole thing slightly dingy now. He'd died in August, shot by an armed officer who'd chased him into a stairwell, convinced he was a gunman. A violent gang had just killed a twenty-year-old a few streets away and the area was flooded with armed officers on the lookout for a gunman. Mistaken identity. An easy mistake to make, maybe, when all teenagers seemed to wear the same trainers, the same jeans, the same oversized hoodies that shadowed their faces.

An unforgivable mistake, when you knew Levon Cole, who had never been in a gang in his life.

I squared my shoulders, took out my warrant card, and knocked on the door. A murmur of voices and the door opened. It wasn't Claudine Cole who stood there – I would have recognised her instantly, with her beautiful oval face, her braided hair, her huge, shadowed eyes. Instead, a slim black man stood in front of me, his expression unwelcoming behind heavy, dark-framed glasses. His hair was cropped, showing off the fine shape of his skull. He wore a thick cable-knit blue jumper and grey flannel trousers, like a student in the 1960s.

'Can I help you?'

'DC Maeve Kerrigan, Metropolitan Police.' I held up my warrant card and slid my foot across the threshold in the same moment. It was a mean trick, but a useful one. 'I'd like to talk to Mrs Cole, please.'

'With regard to what, exactly?'

'With regard to the fire in Murchison House.'

'That has nothing to do with Claudine.' He started to close the door.

'I know. I'm not suggesting that she was involved. I just really need to speak with her about Geoff Armstrong, the MP.'

The man stopped. Not looking at me, he said, 'What about him?'

'He was one of the victims of the fire.' It wasn't the time to go into the details of how he'd actually died, I judged. 'I need to follow up on a few things he said to people about what he was doing here on the estate. He was a regular visitor, apparently, and he said it was in order to support Mrs Cole's work.'

A laugh began deep in the man's stomach, spreading through him until his entire body was shaking. His head was thrown back as he struggled for air. 'Geoff . . . Armstrong . . . of all people . . . What a complete and total cock.' He wiped his eyes, calming down. 'No, it was nothing to do with Claudine.'

'I'd like to speak to her.'

'I've told you—'

'And I'd still like to speak to her.' There was a conversation going on somewhere in the flat, women's voices, and I strained to hear how many people were there. On and on it ran, water over stones, and I thought I could pick out Claudine Cole's low tones among the babble. 'Is there a meeting here this morning?'

'A meeting? Nah. Just a group of friends.' The man put his palms together, long fingers folding against one another. His soft voice was pure north London. 'Not somewhere you need to be, Miss Detective.'

'I'm sorry,' I said. 'I know you'd prefer it if I could leave you alone. I'd prefer that too. But I really do need to speak to Mrs Cole and if I can just come and talk to her now, I'll make sure she's left in peace.'

'Didn't you call already? She spoke to you.'

'That's right. I didn't get your name, sir.'

'No, I didn't give it to you.' He gave me a long, hostile look. 'I think you should leave now.'

'Better me on my own now than a gang of us in a couple of days' time.' I hated using bullying tactics but there was no way round it. 'You know we'll be back because we have to be. This won't end here and now. And I'm not looking for an argument with Mrs Cole. I don't want to upset anyone.'

'You being here is upsetting for all of us. We've met the Met before.' He turned his head and spat, the gobbet of saliva landing in the hallway, right beside my foot.

'I'm aware of that.' This wasn't going my way. I'd tried charm, I'd tried threats. Time for honesty. 'Look, I know I'm part of the Metropolitan Police and you and Mrs Cole have every reason to be hostile towards me because of that, but it's a big organisation. There are a lot of police officers working under the same name, and some of them are pretty shit at their jobs. Not everyone is in the game for the right reason. I have no way of convincing you that I'm one of the good guys, but I hate what happened to Levon. It shouldn't have been that way, and the officer concerned made more than one mistake when he shot him. He didn't follow the correct procedures and he's been suspended ever since it happened, quite rightly in my view.'

'It'll all get covered up and forgotten about. That's why the Police Complaints Commission haven't released their report. They're waiting for the public to lose interest so they can forgive and forget.'

'I don't think that's true. I don't know why it's been delayed but there are a lot of police officers who want to see that report published.'

'And a lot who think we're overreacting.'

'As I said, it's a big organisation. We carry the same badge, but that's where it ends.'

'You'll say anything.' The man's voice was harsh with contempt.

'It's what I believe.' *When all else fails, tell the truth.*

Incredibly, it worked. Not on the man, but on the person behind him.

'Let her come in.'

'Claudine—' the man protested.

'Let her come.' Claudine Cole turned away. I didn't wait around for the man to argue back. I dodged past him and followed Mrs Cole into her sitting room. The layout of her flat was similar to the burned-out flats I'd toured in Murchison House, and the effect was weirdly disorientating. I knew I'd never been there before but it all seemed familiar to me. Maybe it was too much time spent around grief, too. The air was tight with it, and suppressed anger, and the utter disillusionment of a mother who did everything right for her child and still lost him in the cruellest way possible. Levon Cole's face looked back at me from every wall, every surface that could hold a photograph frame. Every moment of his life had been recorded until a trigger-happy cop pressed stop.

There were three women in the room apart from Mrs Cole and me. Two of them were middle-aged, the third

229

young, and I looked at her with interest but she wasn't the woman Mrs Hearn had described coming and going from Armstrong's flat. She was plump, her face round, her hair a cloud of dyed red curls. She glowered, an expression that I saw on the faces of the women beside her.

'I'm sorry for interrupting,' I said. 'I won't be here for long.'

'No, you won't.' It was one of the middle-aged women who'd spoken, a gaunt black lady with a lot of grey in her hair. Her friend had a very similar expression on her face, although she was built on a large, solid scale.

'It's all right, Barbara. Really.' Claudine Cole sat down in a chair near the window and put a hand to her head. She looked exhausted. 'I spoke with you on the phone.'

'I know. I'm just following up.'

'If there's something you want me to say, you'd better tell me what it is. You can't expect me to guess.'

'I don't want you to say anything more than the truth,' I said.

'I already did. Geoff Armstrong was never involved with us. He never came to a meeting of Justice for Levon. And there wasn't a meeting the other night when the fire started.' She made a helpless gesture with the hand that had been pressing on her temple. 'So I can't help you, I'm afraid.'

I was still standing in the middle of the room. There wasn't an empty chair and I didn't dare ask for one. I left my notebook in my bag: I'd remember what she said anyway. 'You said he made overtures to you a couple of months ago and you weren't interested in his support.'

'He wanted to apologise to me for things he said about Levon on the television. Armstrong said he hadn't done what he was told so he deserved to die.' Her voice was flat: Claudine had run out of emotion a long time before. I remembered Armstrong saying it, although he had been a sideshow to the main event, a distraction. We had been trying to work out why police officers were dying; Armstrong had been trying to hold the media's fickle attention. I hadn't cared what he thought then. Now it seemed hugely important to understand him better.

'Did he apologise?' I asked.

'Eventually. He didn't accept at first that Levon had no reason to trust the police, even though he had done nothing wrong.'

'At first?'

'I talked to him. I made him understand how this community feels about the police. I shared the statistics about black males being stopped and searched for no reason, about racial profiling of offenders, and the Met's bias against black teenagers.'

'Did he listen?'

'He seemed to. He told me it was easier to change the institutions than the minds of young people. But he was still a racist. Still a hostile individual, always looking for common ground with the white middle classes. He didn't care about black kids who were never going to vote for him or his kind. He thought we should be grateful to the police for hounding our children.'

'Did anyone else speak with him?'

'We all did.' Barbara folded her arms. 'We put him in his place.'

'Did he form a – a friendship with anyone on the estate, do you know?'

The young woman snorted. 'I wouldn't have thought so.'

'He came here every Thursday,' I said. 'He met someone in Murchison House.'

The four of them stared at me, shocked expressions on their faces, and I thought none of them was faking. It was news for them, which was bad news for me.

'Who?' Claudine asked.

'I don't know. He kept it a secret from everyone. According to a witness, the person he was meeting was a black woman, and those meetings began after he visited the estate in connection with the fatal police shootings that took place here in September. So you see why I'm wondering if he developed a relationship with someone involved in your campaign, Mrs Cole.'

'If he did, which I doubt, I certainly wouldn't hand them over to you.' Her voice was diamond-hard. The other women exchanged looks but Claudine Cole held my gaze, her face impassive. 'I'm sure you would like to pin his death on someone involved in my campaign. That would be quite the publicity coup for you. It would discredit us, which is something that the Commissioner would dearly like.'

'Anyway, none of us would have touched him,' the young woman said. 'He was a horrible, disgusting person. And he was ugly.'

'What if he paid?' I asked.

'His money wouldn't be any good here.' She sounded definite. But Barbara's eyes had flickered, then dropped to her lap. Something had added up for her, something seen and not understood until now – which meant there was something for me to know. The frustration walked along my spine with spider feet.

Claudine lifted her chin. 'We've told you what we know. Now I'd like you to leave.'

'If you think of anything,' I said, slightly hopelessly, 'here's my card.' I held it out. None of them moved to take it. A hand came from behind me and snapped it out of my fingers: Claudine's bodyguard. I had forgotten him, which was unwise, and I hadn't heard him move, which was unsettling. Derwent would have been livid with me, and rightly.

'Mrs Cole asked you to leave,' he said.

'I'm going.'

He was standing much too close to me, so close I could see the fine grain of his skin. There was something strange about his eyes behind the glasses and it took me a moment to realise what it was: he had no eyelashes. He jostled me as I stepped past him, hard, and I could have arrested him for it if I'd wanted to, for assault on a police officer, if I'd been being aggressive. If I wanted to leave them feeling intimidated and violated, all over again. I put my hand to my belt where my baton sat, my sleek extendable Asp, snug in its holster. I flicked open the Velcro on it so I could take it out quickly, but I left it where it was.

And I was right to wait. One shove was enough to relieve his feelings. He stood, breathing hard through his nose, holding himself back with what looked like a tremendous effort.

I walked out of the flat, feeling the air crackle with hostility as I went. I didn't blame them for hating me. I represented the Metropolitan Police.

For once, I wasn't proud of that.

Chapter 20

I really didn't want to spend any more time on the Maudling Estate than I had to. In my mind I was already back in the office as I ran down the stairs and out across the car park. But I stopped beside the car, looking up at Murchison House, thinking about what a good opportunity it was and how turning my back on it was cowardly at best, unprofessional at worst. I squared my shoulders and went into Murchison House, ducking under the police tape. Somewhere high above me there was the sound of hammering. Otherwise the building was as silent as a tomb. My heels sounded too loud on the concrete floor as I ran up the stairs, counting off the floors. On the eighth floor I stopped to get my breath back and to look at a stain on the wall: dried blood, I thought. It was about five feet off the ground, and there was a further smear on the door that led into the hallway. I pushed it open carefully, and stepped inside. The hall was dark, lit only by the open staircase at one end. I took out my torch and flashed it around, seeing a dry and flaking substance on the ground. I squatted down beside it and caught a whiff of old vomit that made me turn my head away. This was where Melissa Pell had been attacked, I thought, standing up again. This was where she had been sick after her eye socket was fractured, an injury so painful that she'd passed out almost immediately. If the SOCOs hadn't photographed this scene, they needed to.

I went back into the stairwell and further up, reading the usual graffiti on the way. Long dark streaks marked the places where water from the firemen's hoses had poured down the walls and steps, as destructive in its own way as the fire. It felt as if the building was about to be demolished, the charges laid, the fuses lit. The hammering got louder the higher I went and I was ready to explain myself to anyone who challenged me, but there was no one on the tenth floor when I leaned into the hallway and looked up and down. Someone had swept a path down the middle of the corridor but I still walked with care, on tiptoe, missing my boots as the sludge that still covered the ground seeped into the leather of my shoes. The wind whined through the devastated flats and I shivered.

The door to flat 103 was open. I walked in, imagining what it had been like before the fire. An empty room. A bedroom with a double bed in it. No pictures on the walls. Nothing personal. A blank space to be filled with a secret fantasy. I crossed to the window, debris and glass crunching under my feet. Someone had put a piece of plywood across the gaping hole, leaving a gap at the top and the bottom. I peered over it, at the yard where Armstrong had landed. They had taken the broken bin away. From up here, the fence for the industrial estate looked close. I frowned, thinking about the physics of throwing a small, comparatively heavy object from a height. It didn't look as if Armstrong had thrown the phone very far at all. If it had been further away from the fence, it might never have come to light. A broken mobile phone wouldn't mean much to whoever found it outside their factory unit, if they found it at all.

Armstrong had been tall. I remembered his body as it lay on the slab in the morgue. He'd looked fit for his age, softer than a young man but still muscled. I couldn't see him being so feeble about throwing away his phone if that was what he was determined to do.

If he'd thrown it away himself, of course.

I took out my own phone and left a message for Kev Cox, aware of how loud my voice sounded in the hush of the abandoned building. The problem with Armstrong was that no one would admit knowing anything. The man was toxic, in death as in life. At least the phone couldn't lie to us.

When I'd hung up I looked out again, at the long drop. All too easy to imagine Armstrong's body tumbling through the air, a dead weight falling to a shattering impact. My knee nudged some broken glass from the window frame over the edge and it bounced and skittered down the building. It was before noon but the November light was flat, lifeless as dusk, and the glass fragments disappeared into the gloom. The effect was hypnotic. I caught myself leaning too far forward, off balance, and pulled back before I tipped over the edge.

And heard something behind me. It was a shift in the air, a whisper of movement that had no obvious source when I whipped around. The scorched room was empty, the doorway beyond it blank. I listened, eyes wide, my heart thumping. The hammering had stopped. The wind keened. I breathed as shallowly as possible. My phone was in my hand but I swapped it for my radio. I had access to the full might of the Met with one touch of the emergency button that way, and a GPS location for anyone who responded, which would be everyone. My other hand went to my belt, looking for my Asp, and found air. I looked down, unable to believe it. I'd had it earlier. I thought back to the car, to Mrs Cole's flat, to walking up the stairs in Murchison House. It had been on my belt then, hadn't it? I remembered the weight of it. Or I was imagining that I remembered it. The images spooled in my mind: crouching down on the eighth floor to look at the pool of dried vomit, or off balance as Claudine Cole's bodyguard knocked into me, when I'd opened the Velcro that kept it in place. And he'd backed off suddenly – too suddenly? Because he had got what he wanted?

And yet it didn't matter where or how I'd lost it. It was gone.

I took out my torch instead, a heavy one with a rubber grip. It wasn't standard Met issue. Like most police officers, I upgraded my kit whenever it was necessary, because what the bosses deemed good enough was hope-lessly inadequate on the street.

And I was feeling fairly inadequate myself. I had been a decent response officer in my time but I was out of practice. I was also lacking in the basic amenities such as CS spray or, better yet, a Taser. I crept across to the doorway, moving as quietly as I could, testing each place I put my feet before I trusted my weight to it. I kept my thumb on my radio's red button. When I reached the doorway I listened again, then peered around the frame as slowly and cautiously as I dared, half-crouching, ready to defend myself.

The room was empty, as it had been before. Nothing had changed. Nothing moved. The door stood a couple of inches ajar, showing me a sliver of empty hallway outside. I eased myself upright, feeling stupid, breathing again. There was nothing to fear here except shadows. I shoved my torch into my bag and headed for the door. I reached out to pull it open, and my fingers just grazed the latch before it jerked out of my reach and slammed shut. The wind, the logical part of my mind told me as terror caught in the back of my throat. I scrabbled for the latch, my nails dragging through the soot that coated the back of the door, leaving white furrows in the grime. The latch turned in my hand but the door didn't move; it didn't shift so much as a millimetre when I tugged on it.

Locked.

Stuck.

Deliberate.

Accident.

I could have argued with myself all day and it wouldn't have made any difference. It really didn't matter how it had happened. The result was the same. I was trapped. I put my ear to the wood, trying to hear if anyone was moving around outside. All I could hear was my own blood shuttling around my body at a pace too rapid for comfort. The glass in the peephole was dirty brown from smoke damage and there was no way to see through it, to see who was standing on the other side of the wood, if anyone.

I stood for a second, trying to calm my racing thoughts. If someone had locked me in – *if* – they wanted me in here, on my own, unable to escape. If they'd wanted to attack me, they had their choice of locations. There were plenty of places to lurk in the deserted tower block, many of them out of earshot of help. So an attack wasn't the ultimate goal.

So I should calm down.

And I should get the hell out of flat 103.

But in case it was an accident, I'd try to do it without using my radio. I didn't want to call for help because I'd wandered into an unsafe building unannounced and got stuck. Derwent would never let me live it down. I'd be buying doughnuts for the team for ever, the price paid for rank stupidity at work.

Fear of embarrassment was probably going to get me killed one of these days.

I started to rap on the door with my hand, then switched to the base of the torch, swinging it as hard as I dared against the wood. There were people in the building, I knew. People who wouldn't mock me for getting locked into an unattended crime scene.

No matter how hard I listened, I didn't hear the sound of the cavalry arriving. I hurried over to the other side of the flat to look out of the window. Down below – far down below – a hard-hatted builder with a plank over his shoulder was walking through the bin yard. I leaned out of the window and yelled.

'Hey! Up here! Bit of help, please?'

It took two or three goes to get him to look up, probably because builders were more accustomed to shouting
at women than to having women shout at them. He tilted
his hard hat back and stared.

'I've got stuck in flat 103. The door won't open. Can
you get someone to let me out?'

Vacant staring. He couldn't hear me, or he didn't speak
English, or he didn't care.

I tried again, and this time I added, 'I'm a police officer.'

Maybe that was what made him put the plank down
and walk away, and maybe it wasn't. Minutes passed,
slowly. I paced up and down, slithering a little where the
floor was uneven. The cold in the flat was starting to get
to me, making me shudder. That and the fear, but I wasn't
admitting that to myself. More time passed and I scolded
myself for assuming the builder had disappeared because
he was coming to help me. Possibly he'd gone home.

A noise in the corridor made me whirl around, my
heart thudding again. Safety or danger. Rescue or attack.
I took up a position a long way back from the door,
holding my radio and my torch.

'Hello? Miss?'

'In here,' I called, not getting any closer to the door.
'Can you help me?'

Something scraped on the outside of the door and there
was a clatter, followed by a thud. The door burst open
and the builder half-fell into the room. He was young,
fair, and extremely surprised to find me standing in the
burned-out flat.

'Are you okay?' His accent was strong, but I didn't
know where he was from: a couple of years ago Poland

would have been a safe bet but he could have been from pretty much anywhere in Eastern Europe.

'I'm fine.' I held up my warrant card. 'I'm investigating the fire here.'

'Okay.' He shrugged, obviously puzzled. 'Well, now you can go. Door is open.'

'Thanks. Thank you for helping me.'

'Okay.' A faint smile, but a wary one.

I walked out past him, into the hallway, but then paused. 'The door . . . Did you see what was keeping it from opening?'

'Stopped.'

I frowned. 'What do you mean?'

'Someone put wood under.' He pronounced it 'voad' and it took me a second to work out he was indicating the spar of burned wood that lay on the floor in the hallway.

'This, you mean?'

'Yes. Is under. Like this.' He showed me, pulling the door closed and shoving the wood underneath so it was jammed in place. 'No one can open with wood like this.'

I felt unease prickle over my skin. 'So it was deliberate. Someone locked me in.'

'Yes, I think so.'

'Damn it,' I whispered. 'Okay. Thank you again.'

'Okay,' he said again, with a more confident smile. 'Be careful.'

'I will.' I picked my way down the hall, into the stair-well, feeling anything but safe. Who had trapped me? Someone who wanted to tell me I was neither safe nor welcome on the Maudling Estate. Claudine Cole's body-guard? Someone else? Not my tormentors from before:

they would have come into the flat and shut the door and taken their time with me.

And I hadn't seen them once since I'd been investigating the fire. I needed to forget about them. They had almost certainly forgotten all about me.

I went down the stairs so fast I felt dizzy, counting off the floors one by one. Every sound that echoed through the building made me jump. I edged open the door to the hallway on the ground floor before I pushed it all the way back, in case someone was waiting there. I looked through the glass panel in the door that led to the car park too, peering out. There was my car, not far away.

Get in, drive off.

Think about who needs to know about this later.

I shoved open the door and ducked under the police tape again, striding towards my car with the key already in my hand. I checked my surroundings as I went, hoping that it looked casual. I was trying to spot any movement in the car park, anyone lurking in the shadows, but I didn't want them to know I was looking. That I was running scared was not what I wanted to convey to anyone watching. A police car went past on the main road, the siren wailing, blue lights flashing, and I felt encouraged. Help wasn't all that far away, if I needed it.

I was so busy looking around me that I got all the way over to the car before I noticed there was anything wrong with it. I stopped dead a couple of feet away from the driver's door. Suddenly I didn't care if anyone was watching me. I was too busy staring at the frosted glass that edged the gap where the window had been, and the shower of glass fragments that covered the driver's seat.

In the light of my torch, the glass in the window frame glinted ice white. In the driver's seat, the glass wasn't white any more. It was coated in a glutinous dark red substance that shone dully. I could smell it, too.

Not paint.

Not ink.

Blood.

Blood that was soaking into the upholstery, dripping off the steering wheel, splattered on the windscreen.

And in the middle of the entire mess, thrown contemptuously once it was of no further use, was my Asp. Whoever had done this had used my own weapon to break the window.

I took out my phone and I called Derwent, listening to the purr of the ring tone, dreading the voicemail message. Nothing was ever as beautiful as the sound of his voice when he picked up.

'Yeah.'

'Josh?' I was shaking, I found, and I could hear it in my voice. Maybe Derwent could too, because it only took that one word for him to stop sounding bored.

'What's wrong?'

'My car. Someone's vandalised it. At the estate.'

The shrug was practically visible. 'Is that all?'

I closed my eyes for a second. 'No. No, it isn't.'

'What else?'

I told him, limping through the story: the flat, the door, the builder, the wood, the glass, the blood.

My Asp.

The blood.

My fear.

The blood.

The words tumbled out of me, faster and faster, and I knew I was just reacting to the shock of it all, to the fear, to the fact that I felt I was falling apart and I couldn't quite hold myself together.

'Okay,' Derwent said when he could get a word in. 'That's enough. I've got the picture. Where are you now?'

'Standing beside the car.'

'Stay where you are, then. I'll come.'

'Okay.'

'You should be all right there. I won't be long, and you're in a safe place.'

I hung up without saying what I was thinking, and it was what I was meant to think, which made it all the more upsetting that I couldn't stop myself from repeating it, over and over again.

There's no such thing as a safe place any more.

Chapter 21

Derwent came, because he'd said he would, and he didn't come alone. I was expecting Kev Cox to be with him because the car needed the attention of a scene-of-crime officer and Kev was the best there was, so Kev's van was a welcome sight. I wasn't expecting to see the car behind Derwent's, or Una Burt getting out of it. The wind flattened her hair against her head and she looked tired as she came towards me.

'Are you all right?'

I nodded.

She looked at the car and frowned, and I couldn't tell if it was because she was angry with me, or someone else, or just concentrating. 'Tell me what happened.'

This time, I wasn't quite as hysterical while I explained where I'd been and what I'd done. Derwent came and stood beside Burt, the two of them hemming me in, probably without meaning to. Kev was already working on the car behind me.

'Why did you go into Murchison House?' Burt asked.

'To have another look at flat 103.' I remembered the phone, the message I'd left for Kev. It felt like hours ago.

'And you didn't see anyone.'

'No.'

'You didn't hear anything suspicious.'

'Lots of noises but I thought it was the builders.'

Derwent bent down and peered through the shattered window. 'How did you lose your Asp?'

'I have no idea. But when I was interviewing Claudine Cole I had a bit of trouble with a man who was in her flat. He jostled me.'

'And took it?' Derwent wheeled around. 'Which flat is Claudine Cole's?'

'Stop,' I said, slightly desperately. 'I don't think he did. I've been trying to remember and I think it was there when I was running down the stairs afterwards. But I'd undone the Velcro strap on it and I don't remember doing it back up again. So it would have been possible for it to fall out of my belt. It probably happened when I was on the eighth floor.'

'Basic error,' Derwent growled.

'It shouldn't have mattered.' I was shivering. 'Anyway, that wasn't the point of what just happened here. That was just an added extra.'

'What was the point?' Una Burt looked at me. 'In your view.'

'Making us feel we're not welcome here.' It wasn't what I believed but it sounded right and it surprised no one.

'We should talk to this man who hassled you. What was his name?'

'I don't know.'

Burt's eyebrows shot up. 'You didn't ask?'

'I was more concerned with speaking to Mrs Cole and

her friends about Geoff Armstrong. Priorities,' I added, knowing it was one of DCI Burt's favourite words. I caught a gleam of amusement in Derwent's eyes and wanted for one brief, awful moment, to laugh. 'Anyway, I don't have any reason to suspect him and I'd rather we didn't speak to him until we have some evidence against him. He's not the type to admit to a crime just because you ask him about it, and I don't want Mrs Cole to start refusing to cooperate with us over Armstrong.'

Burt looked interested. 'Did you get anywhere?'

It was like clambering back on to solid ground to talk about something that was nothing to do with me. 'They said he'd never been to a meeting here but when I mentioned he might be paying someone for sex one of them got very shifty and quiet. And the others definitely knew more than they were letting on. Not Mrs Cole – I think she's completely wrapped up in the campaign and grieving for Levon.'

'So what are you going to do?'

'Talk to the neighbourhoods officers and see if they are aware of any prostitutes answering to the description Mrs Hearn gave us. We'll find her.'

Burt nodded. 'Okay. Let's get this scene tidied up. We'll need to get hold of the CCTV from the car park.'

Kev surfaced from behind the car. 'I've got a flat-bed coming for this.'

'Is it worth it?' I asked, slightly faintly. 'It's just some vandalism.'

'I think it is.' Burt walked off towards Murchison House and I knew she would be retracing my steps, checking it out for herself, seeing what I had seen. Meticulous.

Painstaking. Controlled. Everything that Derwent wasn't, and yet they were both good police officers.

Even so, once she was out of earshot I turned to Derwent. 'Why did you bring her along?'

'She saw me leaving the office. I had to tell her where I was going.'

'I still don't see why she needed to be here. Did she think you were lying?'

He didn't laugh. 'She was worried.'

'Oh. Were you?'

'About you? Not even a little bit.' But he put his arm around my shoulders and held on for a second, solid and reassuring. 'Don't try to downplay this, Kerrigan. You must have been scared out of your mind.'

'I wasn't pleased,' I said levelly. 'But at least it's not my own car.'

'Who gives a shit about the car? I'm worried about you.'

'There's no need.' I stepped away from him, probably because I wanted more than anything to lean against him.

'You told Burt it was vandalism. What do you really think?'

'I think I know who did it.'

'Tell me.'

'Swain.' His name almost choked me. 'He's targeted my car before. He knows I'm working this crime. He was watching me. This is a message.'

'Maybe. Maybe not. That's why it's worth investigating it properly. I want to know where the blood came from for starters.'

I shuddered. I'd kept my back to the car ever since the

others had arrived. I didn't want to look at it any more. It had been violated, and even though it was a work car rather than my personal vehicle, I felt as if I'd been harmed too.

'Come on,' Derwent said. 'Before Burt comes back. We have somewhere else to be.'

I blinked at him, my mind blank. 'Where's that?'

'Wait and see.'

Our destination was a house in a narrow street near Elephant and Castle, away from the traffic that thundered around its huge roundabout at all hours of the day and night. Derwent checked the time, which was getting close to two in the afternoon. 'He might not be up yet.'

'Who?'

Instead of answering, Derwent thumped on the door with all the authority of a police officer who isn't going to be ignored.

'There's a bell,' I pointed out.

'It's not working.'

There was an incoherent yell from inside the house, which I took to mean that someone was coming to the door.

'You've been here before,' I said.

'I have.'

And that was all I was getting, I could tell. I stared at the side of Derwent's face, which conveyed only that he was sublimely unmoved by me glaring at him. Behind the door there was a noise I couldn't interpret followed by an enormous thud that made the door vibrate in its frame. There was a clatter and the door opened to reveal a young man – a boy? – half-dressed in unbuttoned jeans and a t-shirt he'd obviously dragged on to answer the door. He yawned, squinting at us.

'Oh. What do you want?' He sounded neither surprised nor particularly outraged to have had to get out of bed for us.

'A chat.' Derwent headed in and went up the stairs as if he knew where he was going. I looked at the boy who bowed and gestured at the stairs.

'After you.'

I looked around as I went up, seeing evidence of a fairly typical multi-occupancy student house – empty wine bottles and beer cans in the sitting room, clothes drying on radiators, a bathroom at the turn of the stairs that I fervently hoped I would never have a reason to use. But it was a big house, the fittings expensive under the surface layer of dirt and untidiness, and it would have cost an arm and a leg to rent. I scented privilege along with the previous night's curry and felt almost as uneasy as I'd felt on the Maudling Estate. I didn't belong here either.

Derwent was in the front bedroom when I got to the top of the stairs on the first floor. It was a large room but it felt cluttered because it was full of computers and wires and external disk drives and things I didn't even begin to recognise. That was about as much as I could see in the dim light that filtered through the curtains. Derwent edged around the bed and pulled one curtain back. The weak winter sun poured in and a cloud of dust motes filled the air like smoke.

'That's a bit extreme, man,' the boy protested. He leaned against the door frame, yawning again.

'When was the last time you saw daylight?' Derwent asked.

'Yesterday? Wait, what day is it today?' He had a husky, hurried voice with the casual dropped consonants of the public schoolboy who's learned to tone down their accent. He was all sleepy eyes and tousled hair and if I'd been nineteen or twenty I would probably have been yearning for him to notice I existed. 'What time is it?'

'Two fifteen.'

He groaned. 'I need coffee. Do you want some?'

'Not if you're making it.'

'I'm fine, thanks,' I said, slightly more polite than Derwent.

'Wait a sec, then.' He wandered out and I leaned back to watch him slide down the banisters and jump off at the bottom, which explained the shattering thump that had preceded him opening the door.

'Who is that?'

'A useful resource.' Derwent leaned against the wall. 'Have a seat.'

I looked around and saw a chair buried under a heap of dirty clothes. 'Do you know what? I think I'll stand.'

'Wise.' Derwent shook his head, disapproving. 'Students. How can they stand the squalor?'

'They have better things to do than housework.'

'Like you, you mean. Your place will be like this in a couple of months' time.'

I peered into a mug that was sitting, forgotten, on a bookcase and saw grey fur blooming in the bottom. 'I'm not that bad.'

'Not yet.'

A series of thuds announced the return of the boy, who was taking the stairs three steps at a time while carrying a mug of black coffee.

'Better?' Derwent asked.

'I will be.' He sat down in the chair at the desk and spun round, running his fingers through his chaotic hair. 'Sorry. I've only had about five hours sleep.'

Derwent raised his eyebrows. 'Partying?'

'Working.' He smiled. 'I forget what time it is when I get into it.'

'Charlie, this is my colleague Maeve.' To me, Derwent said, 'Charlie Brooke. My go-to guy for all things involving technology.'

'How do you do?' Charlie jumped up and held out a hand for me to shake, confirming my instinct that he had been brought up to be polite.

I smiled at him, then looked to Derwent again. 'So . . . why are we here?'

'To talk about Chris Swain.'

Charlie was lolling in his chair but now he sat up straight. 'Oh. *Oh*. This is her?'

'Yeah,' Derwent said. 'Maeve Kerrigan.'

'*Oh*.' He drew the word out. 'I didn't know. I should have recognised you. Sorry, I'm not awake yet.'

'Why would you recognise me?' I was suspicious.

'Um – I have seen photographs of you before.' He was blushing.

'Which photographs?'

He cast a look in Derwent's direction, appealing for help. Derwent pulled a face. 'Not the kind of photos you show your mother. Some of the ones Swain took.'

'Just for research,' Charlie said quickly. 'I didn't *look* at them.'

'Forget it. I try to,' I said lightly, though I minded. I minded a lot.

'Have you got your phone on you?' Charlie asked.

'Yeah.'

'Both of you? Give.' He held out his hand to me and I gave him my phone after a nod from Derwent, who put his down on the desk.

'Got a tin-foil box ready?'

Charlie glowered at him briefly. 'That wasn't my plan. But as it happens, if you ever need to make your own Faraday cage you *can* start off with tin-foil and a wooden box. It's not as mad as it sounds.'

'I'll keep that in mind.'

Faraday cage? I was lost already.

Charlie fiddled with my phone, switching it off. 'I'm going to put them in DFU mode. DFU means device firmware upgrade.'

'That means nothing to me,' Derwent said.

'You don't need to understand it.' Charlie put my dead phone down and picked up Derwent's. 'Basically, if you have malware on your phone that makes it look as if it's powered down when it's still active and vulnerable to remote tampering, this stops it from working.'

'Remote tampering,' I said. 'Like what?'

'Switching it on again secretly? Using it as a microphone to hear your conversations? Using it as a GPS locator for you? Your phone is constantly shedding information about you and your whereabouts. Generally, that's useful. There are good reasons for having GPS active on your phone. It's just a matter of stopping anyone else from getting that information.'

'How do I do that?' I asked. I was fairly sure I'd just found out how Chris Swain was bugging me and it made me feel sick.

'Switch to a phone without internet capability? Like a vintage one? But that only works for calls and text-only SMS.'

'Not appealing.'

'I can install anti-virus software on your phone that will keep track of any nasties and get rid of them for you.'

'If that's what you want,' Derwent said to me. 'I know you want to get Swain out of your life but letting him know where you are is the point, isn't it?'

I nodded, feeling sick. My phone sat on the desk, looking like a threat. There was nothing in my life that Swain hadn't touched in some way. He was like dog shit on a shoe, smearing everything, impossible to get rid of.

'Are we safe now?' Derwent demanded. 'Can we talk?'

'Yeah. Sorry.' Charlie swivelled on his chair and threw Derwent a charming smile. 'Safety first. Especially given who we're talking about.'

'What do you know about Chris Swain?' I asked.

'I've been following him around the internet for Mr Derwent here.'

'Since when?' I looked at Derwent who had a shifty expression on his face.

'A few months.'

'A few months,' I repeated. 'And I didn't know about it.'

Derwent shrugged. 'The Met weren't making much progress in tracking him down. Seemed like it was worth getting Charlie on the case.'

A grin lit up Charlie's face. 'It was no hardship, because Swain is a legend. His online name is Aktaion.' He said it as if it was supposed to mean something to me, as if it was the equivalent of Shakespeare or Darwin. 'He's the man. He's a total hero to hackers, cryptographers, cypher-punks – anyone who knows about how the internet works. He used to run a few forums before he dropped off the face of the earth and they were immense. I mean, key. They were a place where people could come together and make history, and I'm not exaggerating. Like, one of the main projects was developing a fully encrypted micro-blogging site that was going to be a game changer globally, completely independent of government control, completely safe to use. And then, nothing.'

'I believe that was her fault.' Derwent smirked at me.

'It was his own fault. No one made him bug my flat and drug me and try to rape me.' I frowned, shaking my head. 'Look, I understand about one word in ten of this. He was a computer genius. That much I knew. Are you saying he disappeared on the internet as well as in real life?'

Charlie nodded. 'There were rumours that he was back from time to time. He was supposedly living in Ibiza for a while with a lot of other hackers. Then he went to Morocco, they say. There were hundreds of people pretending to be him at one time or another – Son of Aktaion, The Original Aktaion and that kind of thing. But they weren't him. He was using a different identity and no one's come close to doxxing him.'

'Which means?'

'Sorry. Identifying who he is in the real world.'

'How did you know it was him?'

'I've been following him ever since Mr Derwent asked me to find him.'

'I thought it was impossible. I asked the Met's computer guys and they said—'

He gave me a pitying look. 'Yeah, he's *technically* untraceable. For them. For starters, the places he hangs out online aren't on the surface web.'

'The surface web,' I repeated.

'Oh. You don't know what that means.' He took a deep breath, obviously trying to reach back to the most basic way of explaining it, as if to a child. Or maybe a pensioner. I was feeling more ancient by the second. 'If you go looking for something on the internet where do you start? Open Safari or Internet Explorer and then use Google or another search engine?'

I nodded.

'That's only going to give you results from the surface web. Anyone can see it, anywhere. But if you look with an encrypted browser like Tor, you're going to see a whole different set of results. Websites, blogs, forums – all hidden from your average internet user, all encrypted, all untraceable.'

'Except by you.'

Charlie gave a modest shrug. 'Not everyone is me.'

'Is it illegal?'

'Not at all. Tor is funded by civil liberties groups and the US government, if you can believe that. Anyone who knows about it and downloads it can use it.' He took a quick slurp of coffee and set the mug down on the extreme edge of his desk. 'There are huge, boring arguments about people's right to privacy on the internet that I can't even be bothered to start explaining but it's legit. And to be fair, a lot of the stuff on there is perfectly legal. If you're a political activist in a state that targets dissenters, you'd be bloody glad there was a way to communicate with your allies without being seen.'

I could see the point. 'Why doesn't everyone use it?'

'People are idiots. They give away information about themselves every time they touch a device that connects to the internet and they don't have a clue. They use social media to tell the world what they want to buy, where they are, where they've been. If I was interested I could give you your home address in about a minute.'

'Just by knowing my name?'

'Not even.' He rummaged on a shelf and produced a small black box. 'This is something I made from a few bits and pieces that are widely available. It cost me about thirty quid, and it was easy. It read your phone as you passed. It's got a list of all the WiFi networks you've ever visited. The most popular ones will be your work network and your home. Your phone connects with them daily, or close enough. I can tell you where you get your morning coffee. I can tell you how you travel to work. I can get your email address. I can probably get a picture of you too if you're on Facebook or Instagram. And you have no idea. I just have to be close enough to be able to read your phone and pick out your information from everyone else's.'

'It's that easy?'

He nodded. 'I mean, being able to skim people's data has useful applications beyond stalking. You guys would love it. You don't generally believe anyone has the right to privacy.'

'If you're not doing anything wrong, you don't need to worry about being spied on,' Derwent said. 'I know what happens on these encrypted sites. Child porn, drug-dealing, terrorist chit-chat. Nothing that should be allowed to be secret.'

Charlie ran his fingers through his hair. 'Well, I mean that's a whole other argument about what the police should and shouldn't be allowed to control.'

'Everything. We should be allowed to control everything.'

'Can we get back to Swain?' I was hugging myself. 'Do you know where he is?'

'Not to the nearest mile. But I know he's in London. Or somewhere nearby. He's here a lot.'

I'd known it already but it still hit me hard. 'God.'

'I don't know why he's come back to London. Everyone knows he's wanted by the cops. He must really need to be here.'

Every word hit me hard. 'I imagine he has his reasons.'

'Does he ever contact you by email or text?'

'He writes letters. By hand.'

'Old school,' Charlie said, admiring. 'Not much we can do about that.'

'So what can you do?'

'Well, Mr Derwent said you were prepared to let him come to you.' He looked nervously at Derwent. 'Is that right?'

'I wish he would,' I said with controlled violence. 'I want this to be over, one way or another.'

'There's only one way it's going to end,' Derwent said. 'Don't worry about that.'

'So we can't get at his phone or electronics, but we can use yours. He's probably watching what you put on your phone but I've got surveillance programmes he won't spot. I can put the monitoring software on Mr Derwent's phone.'

'So you can see everything I do with my phone?'

'And where you go.' Derwent raised his eyebrows. 'Is that all right?'

'What if I lose my phone? What if he takes it away or turns it off like you did?'

'Thought of that.' Charlie held up something that looked like a USB memory stick. It was about the size of a pack of chewing gum and plain black, without markings. 'This is a Chameleon. It's a nice small GPS unit. If I text it, it sends back your location. Keep it on you, in your bag or your pocket. If you're worried about having it taken away, get some wig tape and stick it somewhere invisible.'

'I'll help.' Derwent's grin went ear to ear. 'I can think of a few places to try.'

I glowered. 'You can't help yourself, can you?'

'To be honest, I don't try,' he admitted.

'Leave me your phones and I'll install what I need to,' Charlie said.

'Do you need my password?' I asked and got raised eyebrows in return. 'Oh.'

'How long do you need?' Derwent asked, checking his watch.

'Not long. Half an hour? You can wait downstairs. Watch TV, have a cuppa, make yourselves at home. You won't be in anyone's way. No one else is up yet.'

'How many of you live here?' I asked, curious.

'There's seven of us. Proper little commune.' He grinned. 'We still haven't worked out whose job it is to clean the bathroom.'

'I'm not volunteering,' I said. 'Even to say thank you for helping me.'

Charlie ducked his head, embarrassed. 'I'm just good at this stuff. I do this kind of thing for Mr Derwent because I like helping people. I like to give something back.'

'I'm grateful,' I said, glancing at Derwent so he knew he was included in the thanks. And I meant it.

Chapter 22

After our side trip to Charlie Brooke's house, Derwent drove north of the river, to the hospital.

'I want to see what's happening with Becky Bellew. All they told me on the phone was that she was still in intensive care, which is hardly surprising. I want to know if she's improving or not. And I want to have a word with Carl Bellew if he's there. I still haven't got to the bottom of what that family do for money and I think it's important.'

I nodded. 'I'll have a word with Debbie again. She might be more forthcoming now she's had a bit longer to think about it.'

'And I want to see Melissa Pell.' He said it so smoothly someone who didn't know him might have thought it was casual.

'Why's that?'

A one-shouldered shrug and he swore under his breath at the driver in front who had braked suddenly.

'I suppose you want to know when she'll be released from hospital so you can go home,' I said.

'There's no rush.'

'Because she'll be leaving London, more than likely. Going off to live with her mother for a while. Where's she from? Lincolnshire? That's quite a long way, isn't it?'

'My only interest in her is because she's part of this case.'

'So, nothing to do with her being beautiful and needy.'

Derwent reached over and put the radio on, turning the volume all the way up so it drowned out my voice. I turned it back down again.

'Okay. All right. I'll stop.' Safer subject. 'How did you find Charlie Brooke in the first place?'

'Long story. I did a favour for him once.' Derwent's mouth curled up at the corners, remembering, and I decided I didn't want to know what the favour had been. It was safe to assume it had been semi-legal, if not out and out against the law. 'He's a good person to know. You'll never meet anyone else that clever.'

'How old is he?'

'Twenty-one. He's got a doctorate already.'

'He seemed so normal,' I said. 'Just an ordinary kid.'

'Anything but. He owns that house. Bought it himself.'

'Huh.'

'And he bought a house for his parents.'

'That must have been nice.' I thought of my parents, who had just about finished paying off the mortgage on their small, modest south London house, a house they'd never liked, a house that my mother occasionally looked at and said, in a lost and baffled way, *I never thought we'd stay here for ever*. I'd never understood that. I'd always thought they made their own choices, and so they had, now that I was grown up I realised those choices were limited to what was possible. Going back to Ireland wasn't – not really. Not when they had had jobs in London. And even now, when they were retiring, they couldn't go without leaving their own family behind. I wondered what they would say if I gave them a house in Ireland. Knowing my mother it would be something like, *are you trying to get rid of us?*

'We're never going to be buying houses for anyone, are we?' Derwent's thoughts had been parallel to mine.

'I don't know,' I said. 'With the amount of overtime you make me do, I should be a millionaire.'

'What else would you do with your time?'

I thought for a second and came up with nothing. 'I don't know. Clear out the fridge? I should really get a hobby.'

'Why bother? Nothing's going to make you happier than working, believe me.'

'Are you trying to tell me you're happy?'

He shrugged. 'As happy as I get.'

'Wow. That's really sad.'

The car turned into the hospital multi-storey car park and Derwent leaned out of the window to rip the ticket out of the machine. He threw it at me without looking. 'Parking's on you.'

'Temper, temper.'

He braked, hard, by the doors that led into the hospital's reception. 'Get out.'

'Oh, come on.'

'I have to look for a space. No point in you coming too. Especially if you're going to be annoying.'

'Me? Annoying?' But I did as I was told. There was a

time to push Derwent and there was a time to back away slowly. This was definitely the latter. 'I'll try to find Debbie Bellew.'

'Text me when you track her down.'

I slammed the door and watched him drive off, the tyres complaining as he took the turn to the ramp too fast. Any traffic officer would have pulled him over for driving like that. I was tempted to do it myself. Then again, if driving while angry was an offence, Derwent would be on a permanent ban.

I was halfway across the reception area when I noticed a bald head I recognised: Young Kevin. He was sitting on a low chair, his head in his hands. I went over to him.

'Sorry, I hope you don't mind me asking if everything is all right. Is Mrs Hearn okay?'

He lifted his head to show me eyes swimming with tears. 'What?' He seemed dazed and there was no recognition in his eyes.

'I'm the police officer who spoke to Mrs Hearn yesterday. Is she all right?'

'She's had a stroke.'

'Oh no.' I sat down on the chair beside his, genuinely upset. 'When?'

'Last night. I've only just found out. I came to see her and they said I couldn't at the moment because she has to go for a scan. They're doing tests . . .' He trailed off and shook his head. 'I don't even know. I don't understand half of the words they used. And they won't tell me much anyway because I'm not family, although you'd have a job to find anyone closer to her than me.'

'I remember,' I said. 'But she'll be all right, I'm sure.

She's in the best place, isn't she? Quick treatment helps a lot with a stroke, as far as I understand it.'

'She can't talk at the moment. They don't know if she'll be able to speak again. They said it was maybe the stress from the fire, or it could have been something that was going to happen all along.' He wiped his eyes again. 'At least she wasn't on her own in her flat. Who knows when she'd have been found? Small mercies.'

'Absolutely.' I patted his arm consolingly. 'You know, I'm sure she'll recover very quickly. I'll find out what I can for you when I'm upstairs.'

'Thanks. I appreciate it.' He gulped. 'It just hit me so hard. Reminds me of my own parents all over again.'

I looked up to see Derwent striding towards the lifts. He was taking the quickest possible route to Melissa Pell's room, I thought. There was tension in every move he made. 'Look, I have to go. Will you be here for a while?'

'I'm not going anywhere until I know she's all right.'

'Then I'll see you later.' I hared across the lobby and caught up with Derwent just before he disappeared through the lift doors. He frowned, making space for me to join him.

'Why aren't you upstairs?'

I filled him in on Mrs Hearn and what had happened to her. He listened, still frowning. 'Good thing you got a statement from her yesterday, isn't it? Interviewing a cabbage isn't much fun. And we wouldn't know anything about Armstrong's girlfriend.'

'Is that it? No "poor lady"?'

He looked around the lift with elaborate care. 'She's not here. And neither is anyone who cares about her. So no, I'm not going to pretend I care about someone I've never met.'

'God forbid you should waste a molecule of oxygen on being pleasant.'

'My thoughts exactly.'

The lift stopped at the sixth floor and Derwent pressed the button to hold the doors open. 'This is you. Intensive care. Go and talk to Debbie.'

'What about you?'

'I'm going to see Melissa Pell on the floor below.'

'Hold on a second. What about Carl Bellew?'

'What about him?'

'You said you wanted to talk to him.'

Derwent shrugged. 'Wanted is too strong a word.'

'Excuse me,' I said, addressing Derwent's crotch. 'I want to talk to Inspector Derwent, please. Could you let him use his brain again?'

'Kerrigan, do as you're told.' This time he didn't sound amused.

'No.' I took his elbow and dragged him out of the lift. 'Quite seriously, if Una Burt finds out you've abandoned the Bellews to sniff around Melissa Pell, she will start disciplinary proceedings. And I can't blame her.'

'I think Melissa is the reason the fire happened in the first place.'

'If that's the case, Pettifer and Mal will find that out.'

'They couldn't find their arses with both hands.'

'That's not true. They are good police officers and they work hard. They've gone up to Lincolnshire today to interview Mark Pell.'

'I looked him up.'

'Where? You didn't run him through the box, did you?' If Derwent had used the police national computer database illegally, for his own purposes, he would be in serious trouble.

'Relax. Open source search only. I found some local news reports about him and his business. Smiling smug fucker.'

'You have absolutely no reason to be jealous.'

'I'm not.'

'She hates him.'

'I know.'

'And she wouldn't look at you twice. She's not keen on men in general and policemen in particular.'

His eyebrows drew together. 'I know that too.'

'I realise your technique is to pick off the sick and the slow but cruising hospital wards for sexual partners is a new low.'

'That's not— look, just leave it, Kerrigan. You've made your point.' He walked off, in the direction of intensive care and Debbie Bellew.

I knew I'd hurt his feelings. I also knew that he was pushing his luck with Una Burt and he needed me to save him from himself. The end justified the means, as Derwent himself would have said. I had only treated him the way he would treat me in similar circumstances.

But I wondered if it made him feel sick when he did the wrong thing for the right reasons, or if that was just me.

We ran into a brick wall in intensive care, in the shape of a nurse at the reception desk who was adamant that we couldn't speak to Debbie Bellew.

'She's with her daughter and I'm not going to interrupt. The poor woman is exhausted.'

'Okay.' Derwent wheeled around and started to walk off, but I grabbed him. I wasn't going to give up so easily.

'It's a police matter. We wouldn't ask if it wasn't important.'

'I can't.' She leaned forward, dropping her voice. 'I had to get the doctor to prescribe Mrs Bellew some Valium earlier. She's in no condition to talk to anyone.'

'Why is she so upset? Is it Becky?'

The nurse nodded. Her good, honest face was troubled. 'We'll know more in a few hours but it doesn't look good.'

Derwent's mouth tightened. I felt it too. There was something awful about a child dying, something sharp that never seemed to lose its edge for any of us. There was no tragedy like it. That was a wrong we could never put right. There was no such thing as justice for someone whose child had died in violent circumstances, no punishment harsh enough for the person responsible for that death.

'What about Carl Bellew?' Derwent asked. 'Is he here?'

'He's been here today.' The nurse looked disapproving. 'He didn't stay very long.'

'Do you have an address for him?'

She looked through the papers on the desk until she found it on a sheet of paper. Derwent checked it against his notebook and handed it back with a nod of thanks to the nurse. We walked out of intensive care together, past the PC on duty. It wasn't either of the two we'd encountered before but a solid, useful-looking man in his thirties who had, pleasantly, checked our IDs before he allowed us in. I had no doubt that Debbie and her daughter were safe, but then the damage was done already. And I wondered how long it would be before we ran out of man-hours to spend on guarding the patients who were left in the hospital. It was the kind of thing that Una Burt did – thorough, dogged professionalism – but it was expensive and hard to justify when there wasn't an obvious threat.

'The address she had for Carl Bellew is the brother's,' Derwent said. 'He must be staying there. Presumably his kid and his mum are there too.'

'Poor Louise,' I murmured.

'Who?'

'The other daughter-in-law. She didn't seem all that happy with Nina Bellew.'

'Who would be?' Derwent rubbed his chin thoughtfully. 'Maybe Louise would be a good person to talk to.'

'I'll put her on the list.'

Derwent pushed open the door to the stairs and we walked down one flight together. He stopped beside the door but didn't open it. He was looking down at his feet, mutely miserable. It wasn't something I was used to seeing on his face. I sighed, despising myself for being a soft touch.

'Look, I want to go and check on Mrs Hearn. I told her neighbour I'd find out what I could. So if you wanted to come with me, I don't suppose it would be a bad idea for us to drop in on Melissa Pell too. I did interview her before. She might have remembered something useful.'

It was like rattling a dog's lead when it's given up on being taken for a walk. He straightened up and looked at me with surprise.

'I thought—'

'It just seems to make sense, that's all.' I opened the door and went through it quickly, not wanting to be thanked. Derwent was right behind me.

'If you go—' He broke off and I glanced at him to see he was staring at a man who was walking past us, hands in his pockets, head down. A man who was utterly un-remarkable, at least to me. Derwent was giving him a good long look, a police officer's glare, turning as the man was level with us, not even trying to be subtle about it. The man was past us, he was gone, and I took a breath to ask Derwent what was wrong.

Too late.

Without any warning, Derwent grabbed the man by the collar of his jacket, dragged him off balance and slammed him into the wall, face first.

'What the—' I began and abandoned it because Derwent wasn't going to answer me, not when he was growling threats into the man's ear.

'What are you doing?' It was a doctor, outraged in scrubs. 'You can't behave that way here. I'm calling the police.'

'We are the police,' I said, because I had to give the impression that I trusted Derwent and this was all completely professional and above board. 'It's all right, sir.' And to the visitors, patients and staff who were slowing, staring, starting to gather into a crowd, I uttered the immortal line, 'Move along, please. Go on about your business.'

They did, but with much muttering and curious, greedy looks in our direction. The man was spreadeagled against the wall, hands flat on the plaster, his face still pressed against it with the full force of Derwent's weight on the side of his head. He wasn't fighting. He wasn't resisting. He was waiting.

'What are you doing?' I whispered and got an irritable hunch of Derwent's shoulders as an answer. When the corridor was empty, or as close to it as it was going to get, Derwent released his hold on the man but stayed right in front of him, watchful. He looked as if he was hoping the man would give him an excuse to hit him.

'Turn around. Slowly.'

The man did as he was told, holding his hands up at shoulder height. He looked amused, wary and – strangely – unsurprised. He was neatly, boringly dressed in a navy jacket, a red jumper and jeans. They were expensive clothes, though, and the watch on his wrist was a heavy stainless steel one. He wore a platinum wedding band and his hands weren't shaking, which was remarkable, because mine were and I'd just been watching what had happened to him. A red mark on one cheek showed where he'd hit the wall hard. He was square-jawed and handsome, with blue eyes and a smirk I knew Derwent was itching to smack off his face.

'What's the problem?' he asked.

'What are you doing here?'

'Visiting my wife. I didn't know that was against the law.'

I stepped forward and patted him down, retrieving his wallet and checking his driver's licence. 'Mark Pell.' And it made sense as soon as I read his name: why he looked familiar, why Derwent had reacted with such violence. His eyes were just like his son's.

'Your turn,' Pell said. 'I'd like to see some ID.'

Derwent took out his wallet and flashed his warrant card in Pell's face for the briefest moment. 'How did you know she was here?'

'Your colleagues told me.'

'You mean the two detectives who've gone up to Lincolnshire to interview you today?' I said.

'Oh dear.' Mark Pell didn't look remotely perturbed. 'I seem to have got the dates confused. I hope I haven't inconvenienced anyone.'

A muscle was flickering in Derwent's jaw, a sure sign of trouble. 'Did you see her? Your wife? Did you bother her?'

He frowned. 'No. Your officer wouldn't let me in. Apparently I'm not on the list.'

I raised a silent cheer for whatever PC had sent him packing.

'So why are you still here?' Derwent asked.

'I want to see my son.' Pell let his arms fall to his sides. For the first time, there was an edge to his voice. 'I have a right to see him. His mother took him away from me three months ago and I haven't laid eyes on him since.'

'Stay away from him.' Derwent leaned a little closer. 'I mean it.'

'You don't get to say that to me unless you're enforcing a court order I don't know about.' Pell blinked at Derwent, all innocence. 'And there's no reason for there to be a court order. Whatever Melissa told you about me, don't believe it. I'm sorry to say she's a liar. Unreliable. I've been investigated time and time again and no one has ever charged me with anything. I've been in custody three times and they let me go immediately because there was no evidence I'd done anything wrong.'

'Except Melissa's statements to the police,' I said.

'Except those.' He sighed. 'I understand that you have to take it seriously. I hate the thought of domestic violence. I know you must investigate it, but really, Melissa just wasted police time and precious resources. She's a fantasist. Paranoid. I've been very concerned for her welfare and for my son since she left me.'

'Did you try to find her?'

'I hired two private investigators, one after another, and they came up with nothing.' He frowned. 'I wanted the police to help me but they wouldn't. It wasn't a priority for them, they said, because there was no evidence that either Melissa or Thomas had come to harm. Never mind the fact that Melissa is a few sandwiches short of a picnic. And then I find out she's in London, living in a sink estate. God knows what Thomas saw while he was living there. If anyone needed proof Melissa was insane, that's it, surely. Leaving a good life, a beautiful house and a loving husband to hide out in a dangerous, drug-in fested sewer.'

'Yeah, she must have been desperate,' I said, and got a quick, vicious look from Pell that made me as sure as I could be that Melissa had been telling the truth all along.

'Did you know she was in London?' Derwent asked.

'No.'

'Give me the names of the investigators you used.'

'Why?'

'Because I want to know what they told you.'

'Nothing. Like I said.'

'I want to read the reports they sent you.'

'I didn't keep them.'

'That's why I want to talk to the investigators myself.'

Pell breathed out slowly, keeping his anger under control. 'Fine. I'll give you their details if you let me look at my phone.'

'Be my guest.' Derwent watched him tapping through screens on his iPhone and asked, 'Where were you on Thursday?'

'Not setting a tower block on fire.' A glance at Derwent. 'Do you really think I'd be that stupid? That reckless?'

'I have no idea.'

'My son was in the tower block. Would I risk his life?'

'People don't always see the consequences of their actions,' I said. 'You might not have known the fire would take hold as it did. Melissa was attacked while she was evacuating the building. That makes us suspicious that she was the arsonist's target.'

'I'm sorry,' Pell said, handing his phone to Derwent to copy down the investigator's details. 'It wasn't me. I know it would be a neat answer for you, but I wasn't anywhere near London on Thursday.'

'Where were you?' I asked.

'At home.'

'With anyone?'

'No. I was alone.'

'So, no alibi.'

'I didn't know I'd need one.' Pell looked at Derwent. 'Finished with the phone?'

275

'Yeah.' He gave it back to him with elaborate care. 'Now get out of here. I don't want to see you hanging around the hospital. Thomas isn't here and he isn't going to be either. And Melissa doesn't want to see you. So walk away and don't come back.'

Pell stood for a moment, not moving. 'Are you going to see her?'

Derwent nodded.

'Can you give her a message for me?'

'Depends on what it is,' Derwent said gruffly.

'Tell her I love her and Thomas. Tell her I'll never stop. Tell her I'll never give up.' He blinked, hard, nodded at us, and walked away. I waited until he was out of sight.

'He was wearing a zip-up jacket.'

'Not black, though.'

'The stairwell was dark. Debbie could have made a mistake.'

Derwent nodded. 'But that arsehole wouldn't do his own dirty work. He'd find someone to do it for him, wouldn't he?'

'Risky,' I observed. 'If you're going to break the law, you're better off doing it yourself. You have a much bigger incentive to hide what you've done than a hired goon would. And it's hard to find a decent goon when you want one.'

'Yeah. Worth seeing if we get any ANPR hits off cars registered in Pell's name. I'll tell Pettifer.'

'A wasted trip to Lincolnshire.' I shook my head. 'Pettifer's not going to be on his side any more.'

'If only Pell knew. He'd be shaking in his shoes.'

'Are you going to pass Pell's message on?' I asked, curious.

'I've forgotten it, I'm afraid.' Derwent's eyes were wide with innocence. 'Do you remember what he said?'

'Not a word,' I lied.

Chapter 23

Melissa Pell was looking a lot better than she had been the last time I'd seen her. Her face was still a rainbow of bruising but a day had given the swelling time to go down, and her delicate prettiness had reasserted itself. She was dressed in leggings and a sweatshirt, and was sitting in the armchair by her hospital bed, watching her son. Thomas was playing under the bed with some cars, humming engine noises and talking to himself. Melissa's mother sat on the window sill, looking like her daughter in thirty years' time, albeit with an uncompromising haircut. Her expression was worried, and when we walked in through the open door she jumped, putting a hand to her throat.

'You scared me.'

'Sorry.' Derwent looked across to Melissa, who was sitting very straight in her chair, her eyes wary, and it was to her that he said, 'I didn't mean to alarm you.'

'I gather I have you to thank for giving Thomas and Mum somewhere to stay.' Her voice was brittle.

'Don't mention it.' He smiled. 'Really, don't mention it. I don't think my boss would approve.'

'It's very kind of you.'

Derwent brushed that remark away like a fly. 'Mrs Pell—'

She held up a hand to stop him. 'Melissa.'

'Melissa,' he repeated. 'It's good to see you up and about. Are you feeling better?'

'Much.' She smiled at us. 'Getting back to normal.'

'I'm glad,' Derwent said soberly. He tapped the end of the bed with one hand and I could tell he was miserable, that he didn't want to be in the room, that he certainly didn't want to have to say the sentence that was about to come out of his mouth. 'I'm sorry, but I need to tell you that I've just had occasion to deal with your husband.'

'Mark? Deal with him? What do you mean?'

'I spoke to him outside the ward.'

It took her a second to get there. 'You mean he was here? In the hospital?'

Derwent nodded.

She stood up, panicked. 'I have to go. I have to get out of here.'

'You're not well enough,' her mother said, also standing up. She put a restraining hand on her arm. 'Please, Melissa. Don't upset yourself.'

'You don't understand, Mum. We can't stay here.'

'No, wait. It's all right.' I went over to her and put my arm around her, taking over because Derwent was apparently rooted to the ground. It made me wonder if I was wrong to think he was attracted to Melissa. His usual technique was all about getting into women's personal space, making eye contact if not physical contact with them. I would have expected him to exploit her fear with ruthless efficiency. But his expression was as closed off and severe as it had been the previous time I'd seen him with Melissa, and he didn't attempt to comfort her. Maybe he'd been telling the truth when he swore his interest in her was purely professional.

Melissa was actually shaking with terror. I tried to reassure her. 'We made it clear to him that he's not welcome here. He shouldn't be back. We saw him after he'd tried to get into the ward and the policeman on duty didn't let him in, so you were safe then and you're even safer now.'

We had spoken to the constable on our way past to reinforce the message. It was the one I had told off before, and he had been genuinely delighted he'd got it right.

'He said he was her husband but I told him he wasn't on the list.'

'The only list he's on is my shit list,' Derwent had said, and bounded through the door in a good mood that had mysteriously evaporated the second he got into Melissa Pell's hospital room. There was no hint of it in his face now.

'You're safe while you're here, but I don't want you leaving the ward.' He dropped his voice. 'And I know this is difficult but I don't think Thomas should be here. Mr Pell was hoping to see him and I imagine you don't want that to happen.'

She nodded, her eyes big and shadowy with fear, but she sat down again. 'I don't want Mark anywhere near him.'

'I'll take him and your mum back to my place in a bit.'

'What if Mark follows you?'

Derwent smiled. 'He won't. And if he does, I'll lose him. I know a few tricks.'

He usually drove as if he was trying to lose a tail, but I wasn't going to tell Melissa Pell that.

'You should be out of here soon, anyway,' I said, sitting down on the edge of the bed near her. 'You look so much better.'

'I think they're going to release me tomorrow. The doctor said he wanted to keep me in one more night. We'll have to find somewhere safe to go.' Melissa looked at her mother and bit her lip. 'I can't think.'

'There's no hurry,' Derwent said. 'Stay at my place for as long as you need to. He'll never find you there.'

'But you can't just move out.'

'Don't worry about me. I have somewhere to stay for as long as I like.'

Which was, presumably, my flat. I twisted around to raise my eyebrows at him and got a cool look in return. I suppressed a groan and turned back. 'Melissa, can I just ask if you've managed to remember anything else from the other day? Before or after the fire?'

She shook her head.

'Nothing more about being attacked?'

'No.'

'I've been taking a look at the crime scene and it looks as if someone pushed you against the wall on the eighth floor.'

'How do you know?'

'There was blood on the wall.' I was acutely aware of Thomas, who was sitting under the bed having a conversation with a toy car. He didn't seem to be listening, but

I couldn't tell and I didn't want to upset him. I chose my words carefully. 'And then there was a pool of dried vomit in the eighth-floor hallway.'

She nodded, slowly. 'The nurses said my clothes were covered in sick when I came in. That's why I'm wearing these lovely things.'

'I'm sorry. I thought they were the right sort of thing given that you're in hospital.' Mrs Moore sounded deeply hurt. 'I didn't realise I'd got it wrong.'

'They are, Mum. They're fine. I wasn't complaining. They're much better than a hospital gown,' Melissa said quickly. She tried to smile. 'They're all I've got, anyway.'

'I've asked one of our forensic officers to go over that scene to see if we can find any clue as to who attacked you,' I said. 'In the meantime, try not to worry. Just concentrate on getting better.'

Behind me, there was a thud. I whipped around to see Derwent had dropped to one knee, his face twisted in agony. He was holding his chest and groaning. Slowly – infinitely slowly – he slid sideways until he was lying on the floor.

Under the bed, there was a gurgle of pure joy. A small hand appeared clutching a plastic gun. 'Peeoo. Peeoo.'

Derwent's body jerked twice as imaginary bullets hit him. 'Aaaah . . . I – I'm going . . . Goodbye, world . . .'

'Oh, Thomas,' Melissa began, but she was starting to smile.

'No.' Derwent tilted his head back so he could look at her upside down. 'He got me. Fair and square. I'm a goner.' Then, 'But I'm not finished yet.' He pointed an imaginary gun at Thomas. 'Hands up, kid. I'll take you down if it's the last thing I do.'

Thomas's response was more muffled giggling and some more shooting. Derwent dropped his weapon, let his head fall back and died for the next ninety seconds, gasping and groaning and rolling around in fake pain. Thomas came out from under the bed to watch, jumping up and down with pure glee as Derwent got as far as agonal breathing and a fine attempt at a death rattle before he gave up the battle.

Melissa and her mother applauded and I couldn't help grinning. Thomas went over to him and jumped on his chest. 'Wake *up*.'

This time there was nothing fake about the noise of pain Derwent made. 'God, Thomas, what do you weigh?'

'Don't know.'

'It's like having an elephant on my chest.'

'No!'

'Okay, not an elephant. That would be ridiculous. A baby elephant.' He tickled Thomas briefly, which made the boy scream with joy, then moved him onto the floor and stood up, dusting himself off.

'Time to go, I'm afraid.' He had gone back to the brooding reserve, as if the other version of Derwent – the playful, loving one I'd never seen before – had been a collective hallucination.

'Come and kiss me goodbye,' Melissa said to Thomas, and he ran into her arms, scrambling up into her lap. She held on to him tightly and I felt very strongly that I was intruding. I got up and moved to the door, where Mrs Moore was checking through her handbag in a worried way. Derwent stood waiting, and when Thomas slid down he put out a hand, which the boy took. He nodded to Melissa Pell.

'Remember, no wandering around the hospital. If you need to leave the ward, take the police officer who is outside the door with you.'

'Okay.' Her voice was faint and I knew she was holding on to tears that she didn't want to shed in front of her son.

'It'll be all right,' Derwent said. 'I promise.'

She nodded blindly, turning her head away, and the four of us walked into the hall, leaving her alone.

As soon as we were outside the door, Mrs Moore stopped and leaned against the wall.

'Are you all right?' I asked, afraid that she was ill.

'I want to talk to you.' She looked down at Thomas. 'Not in front of – you know.'

Derwent nodded and started towards the lift, towing Thomas. The little boy was chatting away to him about his cars, oblivious to any tension. Mrs Moore waited until they were out of range.

'I wanted to ask about Mark. You saw him. How did he look?'

It was a strange question in the circumstances and I struggled to answer it. 'I – I don't know. Normal? I've never seen him before.'

'Did he seem upset? Angry?'

'Yes. Both.' In all fairness, I had to add, 'But anyone would have been. DI Derwent pinned him up against a wall.'

'*Poor* Mark.' It burst out of her. She looked up at me,

guilty. 'I know it sounds strange to say that. But I liked him and I can't help feeling sorry for him.'

'Even though Melissa says he hurt her?'

'Oh, of course all of that is *awful*. I was devastated when she left without saying where she was going. It made me realise she had to be absolutely desperate. I wish I'd believed her when she told me about Mark, I really do. I could have helped her.' She pressed her finger-tips to her lips as if she was trying to hold the next thought in, but it fought its way out. 'Even now I can't quite imagine it. The things she said he did. He's so *nice*.'

'Abusers can be. They can be very charming.' I wasn't getting through to her. 'Those are the most dangerous of all. They're good at manipulating people, and they don't like to lose.'

'But Mark, of all people. He was such a good husband and father. It seems cruel not to let him see his son. His only child. If someone had taken Melissa away from me when she was three, I would have killed with my bare hands to get her back. I almost feel it's justifiable for him to be angry with her.'

'He was violent long before she left. That's *why* she left.' Mrs Moore's failure of logic was beginning to trouble me a lot. I could imagine her arranging to meet Mark Pell. I could imagine her finding a public place where he could see his son – speak to him, even. 'We have to consider Mark as a suspect in this case, so he needs to stay away from Melissa. But even if he had nothing to do with the fire and the injuries she's suffered now, he brutalised her for years. You know what Melissa had to endure. He abused her physically and emotionally. He cut her off from her friends and controlled everywhere she went and everything she did. She is terrified of him for a reason.'

'Thomas misses his father,' she said quietly. 'I know that. He loves him very much.'

Deep breath. 'I think it's very caring of you to be concerned about Mark and his relationship with his son but your priority has to be your daughter, her safety, and her child's welfare.'

Mrs Moore blinked a few times, rapidly, stung by the note of reproof in my voice. 'You don't know my daughter. She's very convincing – of course she is. And charming. But – well, she is a bit of a drama queen.'

'You think she's exaggerating,' I said, trying to sound calm and reasonable and unemotional even though my anger was scorching.

'I love my daughter dearly but I know what she's like. I brought her up. Every bruise was a broken bone. Every graze was a life-threatening injury. She never had a head-ache that wasn't a brain tumour.'

'Whether she has a tendency to exaggerate or not, there are medical records of her injuries. There's evidence. You don't have to take her word for it.' *Even though you should . . .*

Mrs Moore looked down at the ground and nodded. 'I shouldn't think about it. I should just do what Melissa wants me to do.'

'I think that's for the best. You know, now that Mark is aware of their whereabouts, the situation is different. He can gain access to Thomas through the family courts. They can make a ruling on custody and visitation rights.

The courts may not have a great reputation for taking the side of the father but they do try to do what's best for the children. Mark can wait a little longer to see his son.'

She nodded again, but she wouldn't meet my eye.

'Mrs Moore, please don't get in touch with Mark Pell. Don't tell him where you are, or where you're staying. If he manages to contact you, don't tell him anything about Thomas, even if a question seems innocuous. You can't take any chances.'

'I understand what you're saying.' She looked down the empty corridor. 'We'd better catch up with the others. I don't want them to leave without me.'

They were waiting by the lift. As soon as we appeared, Thomas pressed the button to call it.

'Nicely done,' Derwent said. He glanced at me for a moment, trying to gauge what Mrs Moore had wanted, and I shook my head very slightly. *Later.*

In the lobby, I turned to Mrs Moore. 'Do you think it would be a good idea for Thomas to go to the bathroom before he gets in the car? In case the traffic is bad?'

'Oh, yes, he should. Definitely.'

He pouted. 'I don't need to.'

'Don't be silly, Thomas.' There was an edge in her voice that I didn't like: she was tense about something. Warring loyalties. Irreconcilable obligations. I was willing to bet Mark Pell had been in contact with her already. I was tempted to take her phone away. Or – why not? – take Thomas away.

Derwent looked down at Thomas. 'Go on, mate. Do what you're told. Better safe than sorry.'

He was still reluctant about it, but he went, holding his grandmother's hand. I went too, checking the bathroom was empty before they used it, paranoid that Pell would be lurking behind a door. When I came out, I hurried across the lobby to Derwent and he frowned at the look on my face.

'What is it?'

'You need to take the rest of the day off.'

'What? Why?'

'You need to keep an eye on Thomas. I think Melissa's mum has been talking to Mark Pell.'

He swore quietly. 'Why would she do a stupid thing like that?'

'She likes to think the best of people.'

'But—'

'Except her daughter, who's just a drama queen and probably exaggerating.'

Derwent's face darkened. 'For fuck's sake.'

'I know. Try not to get annoyed with her. I just don't think we can trust her not to tell Mark Pell where she is, and where he can find Thomas.'

'She might have done that already.'

I shook my head. 'He was hanging around the hospital because he didn't know where else to go. He wanted to see Thomas, remember? And Melissa, but we know she's safe upstairs.'

'So you think he'll go back to Mrs Moore?'

'That's what I'd do. If he can get the boy, he can get Melissa to come back to him. She'd never leave him with his father, even if it cost her dearly.'

Derwent nodded. 'He'd make a good hostage.'

'If you're in the flat you can keep an eye on him. Melissa will be out tomorrow. She can take over from you then.'

'All right.' He was watching the bathroom door, knowing that they would come out any minute. 'You'll have to cover for me with Burt. She'd never agree to me minding the boy instead of investigating Armstrong's death.'

'What should I tell her?'

'I don't know,' he said, irritable as ever. 'Tell her I had a headache. Pretend I was with you. Does it matter? Lie.'

Easier said than done. 'Don't drop me in it,' I warned him. 'I'll tell you what I tell her, and you have to back me up. She'll punish both of us if she finds out I lied for you.'

He nodded. 'What are you going to do with the rest of the day?'

'See if I can find out anything more about Mark Pell and where he was on Thursday afternoon. I want to know what car he's driving too so you can keep an eye out for it near your place.'

'Good girl.' He straightened up. 'They're coming back.'

'Okay.'

'Let's get going,' Derwent said with a wide grin, guiding Mrs Moore and Thomas towards the car park.

Mrs Moore twisted so she could see me. 'Aren't you coming too?'

'I need to make some further inquiries here,' I said, and I meant it; I'd completely forgotten about Mrs Hearn until I saw Young Kevin sitting in the corner of the lobby staring unseeingly at a poster for flu vaccinations. 'DI Derwent will look after you.'

'Oh.' She gave him an uncertain look. He planted a hand in the small of her back and pushed her in the right direction, and I appreciated it as a technique when it wasn't me he was pushing around. It might not have been respectful, but it was certainly effective.

I went back towards the lifts and pressed the button. The lift came quickly and I stepped inside, but stopped when I heard a hoarse voice calling.

'Hold the lift. Wait a second.'

I complied, holding the doors open so Debbie Bellew could slip through them. I could smell cigarette smoke on her clothes, her breath. I couldn't blame her for needing a break, if the nurse was to be believed. She was drawn, her eyes sunk in her head, and she didn't look at me.

'Mrs Bellew.'

She jumped a mile. 'What – who?'

'I'm Maeve Kerrigan. I'm a police officer. I spoke to you before.'

'Oh.' She looked thoroughly confused. 'What do you want?'

I remembered what the nurse had said about Debbie being on Valium and decided it wasn't the right time or place to ask her about Carl. 'Just saying hello. How's Becky?'

She shook her head and I couldn't tell what she meant. The lift juddered to a stop on the second floor and a woman with a walking frame faltered on. When the doors closed, Debbie looked at me.

'What do you want?' The same question as before. I tried to look unthreatening.

'Nothing. I'm just checking on one of the other victims of the fire. Mrs Hearn.' I would walk down from Intensive Care, I'd decided, rather than leaving Debbie Bellow on her own in the lift.

A shrug: no recognition of the name.

'She's an elderly lady – she lived on your floor. Flat 104.'

'I never noticed her,' Debbie said dully.

'She noticed you.' Debbie stared at me and I felt I had to explain. 'She had a security camera over her door. She watched everyone coming and going.'

'Oh. Right.'

'But she's had a stroke.'

'Oh.'

'So I wanted to check on her.'

It was absolutely clear to me that Mrs Hearn's health and well-being meant nothing to Debbie Bellew, and why should she care? She was wholly absorbed in her own private hell. Not for the first time, I contemplated the reality of my job: by the time I turned up, it was too late to put things right. Catching the person or people responsible for Becky's injuries wouldn't help Becky, or her mother. Essentially, everything I did was irrelevant.

We reached the sixth floor and Debbie stepped out of the lift like a sleepwalker, walking away from me without so much as a goodbye.

Chapter 24

I was waiting for the police officer who'd dealt with Melissa Pell's domestic violence complaint to call me when Chris Pettifer and Mal Upton arrived in the office, looking thoroughly fed up. I waved at them. 'Fun trip?'

'Waste of time,' Pettifer growled, walking past me.

'I know.'

He stopped. 'How?'

'You went to interview Mark Pell, didn't you? But he was in London. We saw him at the hospital.'

'Are you sure it was him?' Mal asked. 'Maybe it was someone who looked like him.'

'I checked his ID.' I told them what had happened, and that Derwent had warned him to stay away from the hospital, Melissa and his son.

'Is there any chance he was telling the truth about getting the days confused?' Mal asked. Sweet-natured himself, despite his time in the police he hadn't yet acquired the cynicism about human nature that the rest of us carried around like a shield. 'It is Saturday,' Mal persisted. 'Maybe he thought we were coming to see him on Monday instead of today.'

Pettifer snorted. 'No chance.' He threw himself into his chair and nudged his computer mouse. The screen lit up and he stared at it for a second, then groaned. 'Oh *shit.*'

'What's wrong?' Mal came to look over his shoulder and started laughing straight away.

'What is it?' I was trying to see.

'I left myself logged in on the system. Some absolute bastard has changed the operating language on my computer.'

I rolled back from my desk, feeling my mood lift. 'To what?'

'I don't even know. What's the one with the little circles over the letters?'

'Norwegian?'

'Maybe. What am I supposed to do now?'

Mal was trying, not very successfully, to hide his amusement. 'Change it back?'

'I don't know how to do that when the screen's in English.' Pettifer shook his head, livid. 'When I find the prick who did this, I'm going to tear him limb from limb.'

'It could have been worse. They could have sent out an email from your account to everyone on the team.' I nipped back to the safety of my desk, hiding behind my monitor, waiting for the penny to drop.

Mal had got as far as opening his emails. He gave a delighted snort. 'Bloody hell, Chris. You could have told me.'

'What? What is it?' Pettifer thundered across the room and read the message out loud. '"Dear all, I will be embarking on gender reassignment surgery in the new

293

year. From now on I would like to be addressed as Lisa."
I do not believe this *bullshit*.'

'I know the team are going to be one hundred per cent behind you, Lisa,' I said. 'This really doesn't come as a surprise to anyone.'

'Speak for yourself,' Mal protested. 'Hours in the car today and not a word.'

'Stop laughing and tell me who did this.'

'I don't know,' I said, and shrank as Pettifer glared at me. 'I really don't know. The email was sent this morning and I wasn't in the office.'

'Who was?'

'I can't tell you that either. I wasn't here,' I reminded him. But Derwent had been, and it was absolutely in line with his sense of humour. I didn't think I'd mention that. 'You should probably check to see who else was copied in.' Such as the Met's Commissioner, the most senior police officer in the entire force.

Pettifer's howl of outrage was probably audible in every London borough.

My phone rang and I snatched it up, relieved for a number of reasons to have an excuse to bow out of the conversation that was about to take place.

'Maeve Kerrigan.'

'This is Karen Samuels. You wanted to talk to me about Melissa Pell.' She sounded middle-aged and slightly hesitant.

I pulled myself together, Pettifer's tribulations forgotten. 'Thanks for getting back to me. You responded to a domestic at Mark and Melissa Pell's residence last year, is that right?'

'Yes. I spoke to your colleagues about this already.' The first hint of a defensive note in her voice.

'I know. I just wanted to check a couple of things.' I had the report in front of me, the many pages of questions that we had to ask in cases of domestic violence.

Has the current incident resulted in injury?

Are you very frightened?

What are you afraid of? Is it further injury or violence?

Is the abuse happening more often?

When it happens, is the abuse getting worse?

Has _____ ever attempted to strangle, choke, suffocate or drown you?

Does he do or say things of a sexual nature that make you feel bad or that physically hurt you or someone else?

Melissa's answers were back and forth: yes, she was injured. Yes, she was afraid. No, the abuse wasn't happening more often. No, he had never strangled her. The picture I got was of someone who was being controlled, manipulated, terrorised, but within limits. And that frightened me more than anything else. Mark Pell was that very rare thing: an offender who knew when to stop. He didn't get carried away. He didn't get caught up in his own excitement. He didn't lose his temper.

He simply taught his wife to fear him. And he taught her that no one would believe her when she told them she needed help.

'Melissa seems to have been very cooperative with you.'

'She was.'

'But Mark Pell wasn't charged with anything. He didn't go to court.'

A heavy sigh. 'We removed him from the premises and

took him into custody, but it was decided not to proceed with the case against him.'

'It was decided,' I repeated. 'Who decided?'

'My skipper. He knows Mark quite well. They're friends.' There was a world of disapproval in her voice, and fatigue, and the frustration of working in a small town where everyone knows everyone else. 'He felt that there was no evidence linking Mr Pell to his wife's injuries. Especially given her history of mental health issues—'

'What issues?'

'A suicide attempt.'

'A serious one?'

'Well, she didn't succeed, so your guess is as good as mine. But she did try. She threatened to throw herself off a bridge one night and two of my colleagues talked her out of it.'

'When? Around this time?'

'No, four years ago. Before she had the little boy.'

I was doing sums. 'Was she pregnant then?'

'Yes. She had already been diagnosed with depression. Her GP had her down as a high-risk pregnancy because of her medical history. Apparently the hormones can make it worse when you get pregnant. I'd never heard of that. I thought it was after the birth you had to worry.'

'Did she say why she wanted to kill herself?'

'No. But she had a spell in the local hospital. It was tricky, you see, because she didn't want to take any medication, being pregnant, and there weren't all that many resources available to her.'

'So what happened? They kept her in for a bit and then let her go?'

'That's my understanding, yes. She got very good care and support for the remainder of her pregnancy. I saw her around town now and then. I used to talk to her about the little boy. I thought she was a lovely lady.'

'Did she ever complain to you about her husband again?'

'Not in so many words.' A pause. 'She didn't trust us, really, after what happened.'

'Her social worker believed her.'

'Yes, I know.'

'Did you?'

A longer pause. 'Mr Pell is very convincing. But I had reservations about it, put it that way.'

'Were you surprised when she ran away?'

'Not in the least.' Crisp, confident, no doubt about that one.

I was playing with the cord of the telephone. 'Look, off the record . . . should I be worried about Mark Pell?'

'In what way?'

'He's in London. I saw him at the hospital. Do you think he might pose a threat to Melissa?'

'I wouldn't trust him for a second.' She sounded definite.

'Do you think he could have started the fire in the tower block?'

'I couldn't say.' An unhelpful answer and I let a silence develop, waiting her out. 'It's a big leap, isn't it? A bit of domestic violence is one thing, but arson on a large scale? I can't see it. And it's reckless. He's not a reckless person. If he'd found her, I don't know why he wouldn't just terrify her into coming back to him.'

It was a good point. 'Okay. Could he have commissioned someone to start a fire in the tower block if he decided that was the way to go about getting revenge? Is there anyone in your area who might do that sort of thing for a bit of cash?'

She considered it. 'I can think of one or two characters, yes. Do you want their details?'

'Yes, please. And if you can tell me what car Mr Pell usually drives, that would help too.'

I noted down the details and thanked her. 'You've been very helpful.'

'Can you give Melissa my best wishes? And little Thomas?'

'I will.'

'I wish we could have helped them.'

'It's not always possible, is it?'

'Makes you wonder what we're here for.' She hung up and I listened to the silence on the line for a second. She wasn't the first police officer I'd met who was disillusioned with the job, fed up with picking up the pieces, of not being allowed to stop trouble before it started. I put the phone down and looked up my new targets on the PNC. The men Karen Samuels had suggested certainly had extensive criminal records. I emailed their details to Colin Vale, who was sitting with his headphones on, in a world of his own, lips moving as he watched his computer screen with unwavering concentration.

'Hey.' I nudged his arm and he jumped, then paused the footage before lifting the headphones off.

'I haven't got as far as the CCTV from today if that's why you're here.'

'I wouldn't make it a priority,' I said easily. 'It's about suspects for the arson.'

'Oh.' He brightened. 'What have you got for me?'

'Two candidates. Check your email.'

He had a look, frowning at the screen, and the picture of a bull-necked, bald-headed man that had appeared. 'Hmm. No one like that. Let's have a look at the other one.'

The second mugshot was of a thinner man, with the dead-eyed stare of the very intoxicated.

'Maybe.' Colin shuffled through some printouts on photo paper beside him. 'This guy.'

I peered. It was an image taken from the other side of the car park, of a man with a dark jacket and jeans entering Murchison House. The camera angle showed his back but he had turned his head slightly so you could see pale skin and dark eyebrows. There was nothing to say it wasn't the man in the second picture, but not much that you could be certain about.

'Is that the best you've got?'

'From the car park, yes. But I've also got hold of the footage from the eighth floor of Murchison House.'

'Melissa Pell?'

'Exactly.'

'You can see her being attacked?'

'Oh yes. The lighting is horrible,' Colin warned me as he handed over a bundle of images. 'But we can probably sharpen them up a little if you find a good suspect for me. We can get an expert in facial mapping to work up the measurements.'

I was shuffling through the pictures. They were like a

flip book, a crime occurring in front of my eyes. An empty corridor. The door opening. Melissa falling through, shoved from behind to land on her knees. A figure following her, grabbing her by the hair, smacking her head off the ground. He stood over her, looking down, gloved hand to his face, and then ran away.

'The angle isn't great, is it?' The camera was high up, looking down on them, so they were foreshortened. The fisheye effect didn't help, distorting them further. It was hard to judge the man's build: he looked bigger in comparison with Melissa than in the image from the car park.

'Do you recognise him?' Colin asked.

'No.' He was wearing the red baseball cap, pulled low over his face, and the smudgy image didn't give me anything like enough detail to see if it was someone I knew. I went back to the shot of him looking at Melissa lying on the ground in front of him. 'Is he touching his mouth?'

'Looks like it.'

'And then the door handle.'

'DNA?'

'You'd have to hope so.' I handed Colin a list. 'Here's some vehicle information for you from possible suspects. Makes, models, number plates. Worth checking on CCTV and ANPR from the area.'

'Fantastic.' Anyone else might have been sarcastic. Colin was genuinely delighted. 'I'll get on with it straight away.'

I rang Kev and left him a message, knowing that he would probably, almost certainly have thought of swabbing the door handle on the eighth floor. There was no harm in being sure. When I hung up, I turned and caught myself before I swore in surprise. Una Burt was standing beside my desk.

'I want a word with you.' She stumped off towards her office and I followed, catching Mal Upton's eye as I went. He made a throat-slitting gesture and I tried not to laugh, pulling my face straight just in time as Burt glanced back at me. 'Where's Derwent?'

'He's trying to track down Carl Bellew, the dad from flat 101.' It was technically true. It was on his list, anyway. 'We're still trying to work out if Bellew was involved in some kind of illegal activity that he ran from his flat.'

She frowned, fiddling with a pen on her desk. 'Why is Bellew hard to track down? Don't you have an address for him?'

'He's living with his brother, according to what he told the hospital. But we really need to talk to his wife or his sister-in-law. We both think the brothers are too scared of their mother to tell us anything.'

'Okay. What else have you been doing today?'

I blinked, discarding all the information I couldn't possibly share with her, which was practically everything. 'Um . . . finding out what I can about whoever vandalised the car. And I've just been talking to the police officer who dealt with Melissa Pell's domestic violence complaint.'

'Why?'

'I've just been helping Mal and Chris Pettifer out.'

'Don't you have enough to do?'

'They had a futile trip to Lincolnshire today to see Mark Pell, who's currently in London. It's a good thing you have the coppers in the hospital still because that was the only reason he didn't get to terrify Melissa today.'

'That's something, I suppose.' She sat down at her desk, looking exhausted. Her face was puffy, especially around her eyes, and there was no colour in her cheeks. 'How many patients have we still got in the hospital?'

'Three. Melissa, but she's being released tomorrow. Becky is still in intensive care and it doesn't look good.'

Burt rubbed her eyes. 'Who else?'

'Mrs Hearn, the very useful witness from flat 104. Unfortunately she's had a stroke.'

'A bad one?'

I nodded.

'Is she going to be able to help us identify Armstrong's girlfriend?'

'I'd be surprised. I managed to get to talk to one of her doctors but I couldn't get much out of him. He didn't seem to think she'd be leaving hospital in the foreseeable future.'

'Damn. I can't give her a permanent police minder.'

'Do you need to?' I asked tentatively.

'I don't know. I can't be sure.' Burt squeezed the bridge of her nose, closing her eyes again. 'I don't want to make the wrong decision. I don't want her to come to any harm. Any more harm, should I say.'

'She's given us what she can.'

'But whoever started the fire doesn't know that. If they think she's a valuable witness, she could be in danger.'

It struck me that it was rather to Una Burt's credit to value the elderly lady just as much as any other potential victim.

'We're making progress,' I said.

'Of a sort.'

'Colin's got some visuals.'

'I've seen them.' She shifted in her chair. 'Where are we on Armstrong?'

'Um . . .' I tried to think of anything I'd found out that she didn't know already. 'Still trying to track down the girlfriend.'

'It would be very nice if you and Derwent could make that a priority instead of wasting time on other inquiries.'

'It is a priority for us.'

'Then I would like you to start acting like it.' She took a moment. 'I'm getting a lot of hassle from the bosses about Armstrong. I need a result.'

'We'll get there.'

'I admire your optimism.' She leaned back. Almost to herself, she said, 'It would make it so much easier if I didn't feel Derwent was actively working against me.'

'He's not,' I said quickly.

'He does what he wants, when he wants. He is irresponsible and unreliable. And he likes winding me up.'

None of it was deniable. I sighed. 'I know he's not the easiest person to manage, but he is a good police officer. That's why Godley wanted him on the team.'

'And that's what has kept him here.'

That and the fact that Una Burt was caretaking and didn't have a say over who stayed on the team and who left. I didn't think I'd point it out.

'I don't think,' Burt said steadily, 'that it's unreasonable to expect a senior officer – an inspector – to be capable of following orders.'

'No, it's not.'

'And I don't think it's unreasonable to want my team to behave in a professional manner.'

I stared at her, unsure of what she wanted me to say.

'I know everyone is missing Charlie. I know I'm not like him.' *Charlie.* It was always jarring to hear her refer to Superintendent Godley that way.

'You're doing a good job,' I offered lamely.

The response came back straight away, in an irritable tone of voice. 'I know. But that doesn't matter if we don't get a result.'

'We're doing our best,' I said. 'Even Derwent. If you ignore the smart remarks, he's working harder than anyone.'

'That is precisely what makes him so frustrating.' There was a glimmer of humour on her plain face. 'Thank you, Maeve. Now go and find me something on Armstrong.'

I left Una Burt's office wondering why it was that I'd allowed myself to adopt Derwent's hostile attitude to the DCI. She had all the subtlety of a sledgehammer but she was dedicated and tougher than any man had to be. She'd made her way up through the ranks through sheer determination. If I had any sense, I would try to be just like Una Burt, instead of worrying about being liked, or judged. I would keep my head down and work hard and unleash the ambition I generally wouldn't admit to possessing.

But I thought about all that Una Burt had sacrificed to get to where she was – all that she continued to sacrifice, in her lonely journey to the top – and I wasn't sure I had it in me to do the same.

Chapter 25

I woke up on Sunday morning to the luxury of an empty flat. Derwent had stayed at his own place, wary of letting Melissa Pell's mother have as much as a moment to herself. I didn't know how he'd explained his sudden need to spend the night there when he'd promised to leave the flat to them for as long as they needed it, but that was his problem. Also his problem: explaining to Una Burt where he'd been and what he'd been doing, if she asked. I'd texted him briefly to tell him what I'd said about his whereabouts and that was as much as I could do.

So why I was worrying about it, I couldn't say.

For once, there was nowhere I had to be. I made myself a cup of tea and drank one mouthful before I abandoned it, but at least it was my choice this time. I curled up on the sofa, staring into space, listening to the Sunday morning silence pressing on the windows. My phone was on the table in front of me. If Chris Swain was listening to me, he was going to be bored.

And so was I. I got up and roamed around the place,

restless. There were things to do – laundry, cleaning, tidying – but I couldn't settle to any of it. Waiting for something to happen was sheer, bloody murder.

I would have welcomed an actual bloody murder.

When my phone rang, I raced across to snatch it up, excited as a gun dog running to retrieve a shot bird. 'Kerrigan.'

'I've just had a phone call from the hospital.' No preamble: Derwent at his most abrupt. 'Becky Bellew died this morning at six.'

My mood swung from high to low in seven words. I sat down, feeling like the worst person in the world. 'Poor little girl.'

'Yeah. Well, she wasn't going to have an easy time of it, was she?'

'No. But—'

'I know.' It was all he said, but I knew what he meant. 'So what now?'

'Well, there's no point in trying to speak to Debbie or Carl Bellew. We won't get near them.'

I didn't want to anyway. Talking to grieving parents was an art in itself, but it was something no one enjoyed. You did it when you had no choice in the matter. 'So . . . Louise Bellew?'

'I'd say it's our best chance to see her unaccompanied, wouldn't you? They're not going to want the other kids to be hanging around. Maybe the brother but the little girls would be a pain in the arse. They'll leave Louise at home with the kids.'

'Then that's where we should go.'

'I'll pick you up in twenty minutes.'

'Half an hour,' I wheedled.

'Twenty minutes.' He was gone.

It was easy to see from the outside why Louise Bellew had laughed at the idea of accommodating her husband's brother and his family. The house in Eastfield Lane was modern, small and aggressively tidy. It was a neat little townhouse, all red brick and white detailing, and it was about two minutes from the Maudling Estate on foot. Neither son had ended up very far from their mother, it seemed. The entire front garden was paved and three cars sat on it, all expensive, fast saloon cars. Derwent gave a low whistle. 'I'd have that one.'

'The Audi?' It was a heavy A6 S line in black. 'Why?'

'It would go like shit.'

'So would the Impreza,' I observed.

'I think I've grown out of Subarus.' He sounded sorrowful.

'It had to happen sometime. You're a bit old for them now.' That made him glower at me. I hurried to change the subject. 'What about the BMW M5? That's a powerful car.'

'Yeah. Look at the Audi, though.'

'You're drooling.'

He pulled himself together. In fact, I was glad he was talking about the cars. He'd been quiet on the way over, uncharacteristically so. He hadn't even complained that I'd kept him waiting. He had arrived a couple of minutes ahead of time so it wasn't technically my fault, but that had never stopped him from being grumpy about it before. I wondered about it – about whether it was Becky Bellew's death that was upsetting him, or something else.

'Come on.' Derwent had a good long look at the Audi as he went past it, humming appreciatively under his breath, but he was all business by the time he knocked on the door. Standing right outside the house it was possible to hear jangling music coming from inside, and a television, and a child screaming in rage. Derwent raised his eyebrows at me meaningfully and I shuddered.

'Hold on. Hold on. Just wait, Tanz.' Louise pulled the door open as far as the chain would allow. She looked surprised, and then wary. 'What is it?'

'Police, Mrs Bellew.' Derwent held up his ID. 'We met before.'

'I know who you are.' It was the same high wispy voice I'd noticed before, unexpected given her size. *Don't notice me. Don't look at me.* The brothers had both chosen meek women to marry, apologetic for the mere fact of their existence. I could understand why they hadn't wanted to find someone like their dear old mum.

Louise was watching us, wary. 'What do you want?'

'To have a word with you, if we might.'

'Carl's not here. No one's here.'

'You're here,' I said. 'And we wanted to talk to you.'

'I don't know nothing.' She was very fair and her complexion was telling me everything I needed to know: a guilty flush across her cheeks and neck, raw pink eyelids from crying. Her nails had been immaculate the last time I saw her, but now they were in a state: chipped, peeling, broken. This was a woman under considerable stress.

Just the kind of witness we could bully into cooperating.

I felt a tiny twinge of guilt. She was an easy target. I knew Derwent sensed it too, but he was more than happy to exploit it.

'Please. We could really use your help. It might be vital in helping us locate the people who did this to Becky.'

Her eyes went wide. 'Do you know who done it?'

'We have some leads we're pursuing.'

Behind Louise, a child wailed. She flinched.

'Mummy . . .'

'Not *now*, Tansy.'

The grizzling started low and ran up through the octaves, getting louder by the second.

Louise stared dully into the distance above our heads. 'Oh for God's sake.' She slammed the door and Derwent and I looked at one another: had we misjudged it that badly? Then there was a clatter as she undid the chain.

'You'd better come in.'

She went ahead of me down the narrow hallway, tugging her sweatshirt down over shapeless jeans. The kitchen was immaculate, full of the kind of gleaming surfaces I associated with ads for cleaning products I would never buy. The two little girls were in the corner playing with a toy kitchen, squabbling over a saucepan they both wanted.

'Lola. Tansy. Quit it now.' Louise bent down and grabbed the saucepan, holding it above their heads. 'I'll take it away if you don't shut up.'

'No, Mummy, give it back!'

'Please, Mummy.'

She held it for a moment, then gave it to one of the girls. I hadn't yet worked out which one was which. They were dressed the same but one was fair and one dark.

'Are they twins?'

'Yeah. They're nearly four.'

'Twins are hard work.'

'Yeah.' She half-smiled, then rubbed her forehead, as if she was regretting her moment of weakness. She slid into a chair at the table. 'Sit down.'

I took the chair nearest hers, leaving Derwent to sit at the end of the table. 'Thanks for talking to us. I know it's not easy. We're obviously very sorry about Becky.'

'It's dreadful,' she whispered. 'Poor little girl. Only seven years old.' The tears were welling in her eyes and she reached for a box of tissues, setting it on the table with a clatter.

'She was very ill.'

'Never had a chance.' Louise blew her nose noisily. 'Debbie's going to take it hard, not that I blame her. I'd kill myself if anything happened to them two.'

The two little girls were playing more quietly, faces turned towards us. Listening.

'That's why we want to find whoever started the fire,' Derwent said. 'In case they do it again.'

Louise got up and put the used tissue in the bin, flinging herself back into the chair with more force than was strictly necessary. 'I don't know how I can help. I wasn't even there.'

'We'd just like to ask you some things about the family,' I said. 'General questions. It's background information, really, but there's no one we can ask at the moment. We don't want to disturb Carl and Debbie.'

'You could talk to Rocco.'

I didn't want to talk to Rocco. 'Where is he?'

'I don't know.' She picked up her mobile phone and stared at it. 'He hasn't been in touch.'

I was aware of Derwent shifting in his seat beside me. *Get on with it. We might not have long.*

'One of the theories we have, Louise, is that the arson attack was aimed at your brother-in-law and his family. But obviously that would be quite a serious thing, wouldn't it? They'd have to have upset someone a lot.'

She nodded, not looking at me.

'So we were wondering if you could tell us if there's anything we should know about Carl, or the family. Is there someone with a grudge against them? Someone they haven't mentioned to us because they want to sort it out themselves?'

'I don't know.' Her voice was practically inaudible.

'What does Carl do for a living?' I asked.

Her eyelids flickered. 'I can't remember . . . I don't—'

'You don't remember what he said when we talked to him at the hospital?' Derwent asked the question gently. 'Because whatever he told us wasn't true?'

A nod.

'Is it drugs?'

'What? No!' Her mouth hung open for a moment: genuine offence. 'They would never have anything to do with drugs. No way.'

'We have to ask,' I said. 'Looking at the cars outside. Looking at the contents of the flat. It was a tower-block flat in a mainly council estate and it was kitted out like Buckingham Palace. Where was the money coming from, Louise? What paid for this house?'

'Rocco works hard. Both the boys do.'

'Doing what?'

She was crying again, tears sliding down the sides of her nose. She sniffed a couple of times, struggling for composure. 'I don't want to get in trouble.'

'With who? With us?'

She managed a wobbly laugh. 'No.'

'With them?' No answer. I pressed on. 'We can protect you. We can hide the fact that you were our source of information. Even if what they're doing is illegal, that's not our concern.' *At the moment.* 'We want to know why someone might have attacked the flat. Debbie seemed to suggest that Carl knew more than he was letting on about that.'

'Did she?' Her eyes went wide with surprise. 'She said that?'

'She did. But we didn't get to talk to her again and now really isn't the time to press her on it. You're the only chance we have to work out what happened here. If your husband and brother-in-law are engaged in criminal activity of some kind, it could explain why the fire was started. It could lead us to the people responsible. We're not trying to trap them. Our focus is on finding out who started the fire that ended Becky's life. I know it's hard to think that Carl and Rocco might have to bear some responsibility for what happened but that's not why we're asking.'

'It's not them.' She gave a half-hearted shrug. 'Well, it is them. They work for *her*.'

'For . . .' I prompted.

'For Nina.'

'Doing what?' Derwent asked.

'They're her muscle.' She sniffed. 'Nina's got her own business. She's a loan shark.'

'A money lender?'

'Yeah. She has been for years. You know how it goes. You borrow twenty quid, pay back thirty by the end of the week. Borrow a hundred, pay a hundred and fifty. Only no one ever pays it back. Not all of it.'

'Has she got a lot of customers?' Derwent asked. 'It takes a lot of twenties to pay for cars like the ones you've got outside.'

'I don't know how many people she's got on her books. She has a notebook in her handbag and a lot of cash. She keeps the books in her safe with the rest of the money.'

I looked at Derwent who nodded slightly. The firefighters had located the safe but, somehow, we hadn't got around to giving it back to Nina Bellew yet. That was looking like a good decision.

Louise sniffed again. 'I know Carl and Rocco are out every night calling on people.'

'Intimidating them?' I asked. 'Hurting them?'

Louise wriggled. 'They're big lads. They don't have to hurt anyone to make people take them seriously. You know how it is. You have to make people take responsibility for what they've borrowed.'

And the debts mounted up and up, with no way of paying them off, as Nina Bellew sat and calculated her profits.

'Is that why they lived on the estate?'

Louise nodded. 'Nina likes to be among her people. That's what she says. She likes to keep an eye on them.

She's famous in the estate. Everyone knows Nina. It's like a joke. If you say you want something, someone will say, "Ask Nina."'

She liked to see the people who were struggling so she could offer to help them out, I thought. She liked to get chatting to the hopeless, the helpless, the needy. She liked to see where the money was going. She liked to know who'd collected their benefits and might have some cash to spare to chip away at the mountain of debt she'd built in front of them.

'Has she ever been arrested for illegal money lending?'

'No. No one ever complains about her. Too scared. But she was inside before. She was arrested in the sixties.'

'What for?'

'Prostitution,' Louise smirked. 'And robbing her customers. Where do you think the money came from in the first place?'

'I looked her up,' Derwent said. 'She doesn't have a record.'

'Oh yeah. She gave you the wrong date of birth,' Louise said carelessly. 'And the wrong surname. She uses that name and date of birth when anyone asks.'

'Damn it,' Derwent began and I quelled him with a look. We had more important things to discuss with Louise.

'Money lending is a risky business,' I said. 'You don't make friends doing that.'

'They've had a bit of trouble now and then,' Louise admitted. 'But nothing like this.'

'What kind of thing?'

'Fights. Someone keyed Carl's car once and he was

livid. But mostly people stay away from them. They're scared of Nina. She's got no soul, that woman, and she's got Carl and Rocco under her thumb. They'd do anything for her. Whatever she said. And she'd say anything to get her hands on money.' She looked frightened. 'Listen, don't get me wrong. Rocco's done nothing too bad. He's not the violent one.'

'But Carl is?'

'Carl . . .' She shivered. 'He just doesn't think. He does what she wants him to do. If that's smashing someone's face in, he does it.'

'Has he done that? Smashed someone's face in?'

'It's just an example,' Louise whispered, shrinking a little. 'I don't know. Don't ask me anything else.'

'We'll follow it up.' Derwent nodded at me and we got up to go.

'Please don't tell them I told you about it. She'd kill me. Literally kill me.'

'We won't say a word,' Derwent assured her.

'We'll say it was an anonymous tip-off. Very useful,' I said. 'Surprisingly common.'

'As long as they don't find out.' Louise hugged herself, still terrified.

'If anyone tries to hurt you, call 999.'

'I don't need the police. I've got Rocco.'

'Do you think he'd take your side against his mother?' Derwent asked and Louise's face crumpled.

'I don't know.'

'Well, we will, I promise you. So if you feel threatened, call us.'

A nod, but I wasn't sure she meant it. They weren't

the kind of people to want anyone else to interfere in their lives. I recalled that Carl had carried his injured daughter down ten flights of stairs rather than waiting for paramedics or firefighters to help. Louise wouldn't call us. Our best hope was that Rocco would look after her. I didn't have a lot of faith that would be the case. So that left making sure no one found out Louise had talked to us. I looked at Derwent.

'Time to go.'

Outside the house, Derwent knocked on the roof of the Audi. 'Ruined it for me.'

'Why's that?'

'Now it just looks like other people's misery.'

'That's exactly what it is.' We got into the car and I sighed. 'You realise what this means, don't you?'

'What's that?'

'There was a good reason for someone to target the Bellews. That means they have to stay on our list of possible targets.'

'So?'

'So now we have no shortage of suspects, most of them living on the estate. We haven't narrowed anything down. The investigation has just got a lot more complicated.'

'We're not dealing the cards,' Derwent said. 'We just have to play them.'

'You, me and as many spare officers as Una Burt will allow us.'

'If any.' He groaned. 'I'd better give her a call. Let her know the good news.'

'Please be nice.'

'Me? I'm always nice.'

'Seriously.' I put a hand on his arm to stop him from making the call. 'She's under a lot of pressure. Go easy.'

Derwent frowned at me. 'What's going on? Are you sucking up to her for any particular reason or just to annoy me?'

'I feel sorry for her.'

'Why?'

Because she has to try to manage you. 'She's finding this investigation hard, I think. No point in making it worse for her.'

'Very considerate of you.'

'And I don't want you to give her a reason to leave all the legwork up to us. Tracking down Nina Bellew's clients is going to be a pain in the arse.'

'You heard Louise. Nina has records. We just have to persuade her to cooperate with us.'

'Let me put it this way. Your chances of getting anything out of Nina Bellew are about the same as your chances of charming Una Burt. So don't burn any bridges. We don't have any to spare.'

Chapter 26

I walked into the office on Monday morning and threw my notebook onto my desk from far enough away that eyebrows went up all around the room.

'Problem?' Liv asked.

'Don't ask.'

'Derwent? Una Burt?'

'Not this time, actually.' I sat down and swivelled on the chair, too irritated to sit still. 'The Met's task force on money lending won't let us talk to Nina Bellew about her clients.'

'Seriously?'

'They've been collecting evidence on her but they're not ready to arrest her yet. They don't want us to tip her off.'

Liv pulled a face. 'But if they've been collecting evidence . . .'

'Oh yes, they have lists of people she's screwed over, which we are more than welcome to consult. But those people are the ones prepared to talk to the cops. What we're looking for is someone so angry that they're taking the law into their own hands. And they wouldn't own up – not if their actions brought about the deaths of four people.'

'So what?'

'Dead end. There's nothing else I can do about Nina Bellew unless and until some new evidence turns up. I've asked the neighbourhoods team who cover the Maudling Estate to see if they can find out if anyone was talking shit about the Bellews – making threats, that kind of thing. Or if anyone is looking especially guilty, I suppose, since Becky died.'

'You might get a tip-off.'

'We might indeed. After all, who cares about two prostitutes and a politician? At the end of the day, they're all whores. But an innocent kid is different.' Derwent had arrived, without so much as a whiff of sulphur to warn us. He eased himself onto the corner of my desk and began to browse through my in-tray.

Liv's nose was wrinkled with disgust. 'Is that what you think? The trafficked women don't count as victims?'

'That's not what I think, no.' He said it pleasantly – politely, even – which was how I knew he was blazingly angry.

'Because they didn't deserve to die that way. None of them did,' Liv said.

Derwent glanced up, as if he was surprised she was still talking to him. 'Listen, I couldn't give a shit about Armstrong but I'd go a long way to find whoever put those girls behind a locked door and left them to burn.'

'I might be able to help you with that.' Una Burt stumped across to us, holding a cardboard folder. 'Today's the day for test results. They've been busy at the labs over the weekend.'

I sat up. 'Anything useful?'

'First things first.' She opened the folder. 'The blood in your car was not human in origin.'

'What was it?' I asked.

'Pig's blood.'

'Very funny,' Derwent said. 'Pig's blood because you're a cop. Nicely done.'

The memory of that smell in the car suddenly filled my nose, my mouth. I gagged, then turned it into a cough. Derwent shot me a look that was concern mingled with amusement.

'All right, Kerrigan?'

I nodded, coughing some more, gesturing to Una Burt to go on, for someone to say something, anything that might take the attention off me.

'Did they get any DNA off the car or the Asp?' Derwent asked.

'Nothing. No fingerprints either. He or she wore gloves.'

'What about CCTV?'

'The car was parked between two vans.' Una shook her head at me. 'Never park in a blind spot. You should know better.'

'I didn't know the car was going to be vandalised,' I protested.

'Well, you made it easy for them to do it unobserved.'

'Sorry.' I knew it was a joke but it still hurt, just a little. I believed with all my heart that it had been Chris Swain's handiwork, and I hated being his victim. I hated being two steps behind him all the time. I hated falling into his traps, especially when I should have been more careful.

'I've got to say I think it's unlikely that we'll find out who did it without DNA or CCTV.'

'I thought that might be the case,' I said. 'What about Melissa Pell's attacker?'

'Not great news. Obviously it's not a straightforward case of swabbing a weapon or something where you'd expect to find a very limited number of DNA profiles. This is a door that was in a public area of a very busy tower block and it's been in use for days since the fire. They've recovered multiple DNA profiles from it so far and it's taking time to separate out the one we want. They are working on cross-matching the profiles they've recovered against people with previous convictions. They've promised me it's a priority.' Una Burt's lips thinned slightly. 'I made it clear that it was our priority too.'

'Is that it?' Derwent said. He didn't bother to keep the disappointment out of his voice.

'No. The pathologist has been in touch. She swabbed Geoff Armstrong to try to recover useful DNA. She also noticed his eyes were irritated so she asked the lab to check for chemical residue.'

'And?'

'Capsaicin. Pepper spray,' she added.

'So Armstrong got pepper-sprayed, punched, strangled and then pushed out of a window.' Derwent whistled. 'What the hell did he do to deserve that?'

'That's what I'd like you to find out from his girlfriend.' Una Burt licked her finger to leaf through the pages in the folder. 'The DNA results are back.'

'Did they get an ID?' I asked.

'Yes. Yes, they did.' She had a strange expression on her face. 'They queried it, though.'

'Why's that?'

'Because they weren't sure the DNA profile was the one we were looking for.'

I frowned at her. 'Why not?'

Instead of answering me, she handed me the sheet of paper and let me look for myself. I read it through twice. 'Oh. *Oh.*' I looked up at Una Burt, who nodded.

'It explains some things, doesn't it?'

'If you've quite finished making orgasm noises, maybe you could share the news with the rest of the class,' Derwent said irritably.

I handed him the sheet of paper and stood up. 'Time to go and talk to Armstrong's girlfriend, I think.'

'But—'

I shrugged my coat on. 'Exactly.'

Another identical hallway in another identical tower block and I had déjà vu all over again. Visiting the Maudling Estate was like a recurring nightmare I couldn't shake off, the kind of nightmare where you try something different every time, and it works out just as badly as the time before and the time before that. But at least this time I wasn't on my own.

I just wasn't sure yet if that was going to be a help or if it was going to make things much, much worse.

'Is this it?'

I nodded and stood back as Derwent rang the doorbell.

'Who is it?' someone called from inside. A pleasant voice, I thought.

'Police,' Derwent shouted back.

A long pause. Then there was the sound of locks being turned, a chain taken off the door, a bolt slid back. The door opened slowly and a dark-skinned woman blinked at us, her manner languid rather than nervous. She was tall and slender, elegant in a dark blue knitted dress that clung to her body, her hair long and straight and silky. She looked Derwent up and down first, then switched her attention to me for a brief moment. She lowered her long eyelashes to hide the expression in her eyes but I caught it anyway: loathing.

'Justine Rickards?'

'Yes?'

'DI Derwent, DC Kerrigan. We'd just like to ask a few questions regarding the fire in Murchison House.'

'I don't know anything about that. I'm sorry.' She started to close the door.

'Just a few questions.' Derwent put out a hand and pushed the door back, hard, and for a second she resisted. She stared into his eyes, implacably hostile, and I felt a chill: there was murderous anger, if anyone wondered what it looked like. Then she shrugged and stood back.

'I was going out. You'll have to be quick.'

Derwent didn't say we would be quick. He didn't say anything, but walked past her into the flat.

'Are you coming in too?' she asked me. I was hanging back. I didn't want her behind me.

'Please, go ahead. I'll shut the door.' If you didn't know better, you'd think I was just being polite. Justine Rickards knew better. She narrowed her eyes at me again, then went ahead of me to the living room, her carriage as perfect as if she was walking down a catwalk.

'You can sit down,' she said to Derwent, who was standing with his hands in his pockets, looking around. The room was neat but not expensively furnished; if I had to guess, I'd say Justine spent her money on clothes and make-up, not her flat. 'You're making me nervous, standing there.'

'Sorry.' He sat on the small sofa and I decided not to sit beside him. I had too much experience of being squashed into a corner by Derwent and his long legs. I took a seat at a small table, leaving Justine to sit in an armchair in the corner. She sat like a *Vogue* model, her feet drawn back demurely to one side, an elbow propped on the arm of the chair.

'What can I do for you?'

'We wanted to ask you about Geoff Armstrong.'

She blinked twice, very fast. 'Why?'

'Did you know Mr Armstrong, Ms Rickards?'

'By reputation.'

'What do you mean by that?'

'I knew who he was. And I knew he wasn't popular around here. He's come up in conversation once or twice.'

'Do you work with Claudine Cole on her campaign?' I asked.

She didn't even look in my direction. 'I know Claudine. I wish her all the best with her work.'

'That's not really an answer.'

She sighed. 'I don't work with her in an official capacity, if that's what you mean. I'm not volunteering to go into schools or campaign with her. But I help out if she needs me. I do a little secretarial work for her now and then.'

'Do you have a job?' Derwent asked.

'I temp.'

'For an agency?'

'Sometimes.' She frowned. 'What has this got to do with Geoff Armstrong?'

'We've been looking for someone who was in a relationship with him. Someone who spent Thursday afternoons with him in a flat in Murchison House.'

'And?' She gave a one-shouldered shrug, irritated now. 'You're not looking at me, are you? He's not exactly my usual type.'

'The lady with him was described as an elegant black woman, about five foot ten, mid-thirties. That description fits you,' Derwent said.

'Why thank you.' She swept the long eyelashes down on to her cheeks, flirting like a film star, Dorothy Dandridge resurrected on a north London estate.

'Are you saying it wasn't you?'

'Of course it wasn't. I never met the man.' She stood up. 'Is that everything?'

'No, it's not. Do you know this man?' Derwent handed her a printout of a custody photograph: an old picture of a young man with a line shaved through one eyebrow and a sneer on his face. 'Dean Rickards.'

She sat down again, staring at the page. 'Yes. Yes, I do.'

'Who is he?'

'My brother.' It was a whisper.

'Does he live here with you?' I asked.

'Sometimes.'

'Where is he now?'

She shrugged, shaking her head. 'I don't know. I haven't seen him for days.'

'Is that unusual?'

'No. Not really. He comes and goes.' She looked from me to Derwent. 'Why are you asking me about Dean?'

'Dean's DNA is on our system for some drug-related offences he committed in his teens.'

'Stupid boy.' She tried to smile. 'He was an idiot when he was a teenager. But he put all that behind him.'

'Does he have a job now?' Derwent asked.

She shook her head. 'I help him out.'

'Where does he live when he's not with you?'

'With friends,' she said vaguely. 'I don't really know who. We lead separate lives.' She pulled herself together with a visible effort. 'Why are you asking about Dean, anyway?'

'We found his DNA on Geoff Armstrong's body,' I said. 'On his face. On his hands.'

'Maybe he met him. Maybe he sneezed on him.' She laughed. 'This is ridiculous. You're making something out of nothing. Dean didn't know Geoff Armstrong.'

'His saliva was found on Mr Armstrong's genitalia,' I said.

She opened her mouth to argue, then shut it again. 'I don't – I don't understand. There must be some mistake.'

'There's no mistake. Geoff Armstrong was engaged in sexual activity with Dean Rickards on the day he died. We think Geoff was paying him for sex.' Derwent's words were brusque but his manner was matter-of-fact, direct, unsensational. This was what had happened and it shocked none of us, except possibly Justine.

'Oh my God,' she whispered. 'Dean, what were you doing?'

'You didn't know?' I allowed myself to sound slightly puzzled.

'I had no idea. None.'

'I met Dean the other day,' I said. 'In Claudine Cole's flat.'

'He helps out sometimes. Like me.'

'He was acting as a kind of bodyguard for her. He was pretty hostile towards me.'

She looked at me for a moment, then rolled her eyes away. 'I can't imagine why.'

'Do you know what else I noticed about him?'

'No, darling, I don't.'

'He didn't have any eyelashes. None at all.'

Another frown. 'So?'

'I used to police around Vauxhall when I was a street copper. I got to know a lot about two things: the security services and gay culture. You've got MI6 on one side of the road and a load of gay nightclubs on the other, which I'm sure is a coincidence.'

'I'm sure too,' Derwent chimed in, grinning.

'I used to see the drag queens on their way into work at the Vauxhall Tavern. I got friendly with a few of them. They were nice guys. I could barely recognise them when they were dressed up, and not just because they looked different. They were different people in drag. I remember one of them telling me that he had no eyelashes left because he'd worn false eyelashes for so long and the glue had ripped his own out one by one. They hadn't grown back. He said I should always look at men's eyelashes, that it was more of a giveaway of who they were and what they did than long nails or feminine features.'

'I'm sure that was very helpful for you.' Justine's voice was raw but she was still in command of herself.

'You wear false eyelashes, don't you, Justine?'

She straightened. 'Lots of people do.'

'Yes, and lots of people wear wigs like yours.'

She tucked her hair behind her ear, self-conscious. 'I like to change my look.'

'Do you know what we rely on when we're trying to identify people from photographs? Not noses, not chins – those can change if you gain or lose weight or if you do your make-up differently or just because people get older. But ears don't change.' I leaned over and took the picture of Dean Rickards out of her hand. 'Dean's ears are just the same as yours, Justine. Exactly the same, down to the shape of the lobe.'

'We're siblings.'

'No, you aren't.' I tapped the picture. 'If I get a facial recognition expert to compare this image and a picture of you, you know what the answer will be. And if we test your DNA I can prove it to any jury's satisfaction. You are Dean Rickards. It was you I saw in Claudine Cole's flat, where you were dressed as a man. It was you who spent every Thursday afternoon with Geoff Armstrong. It was you he paid for sex. It was you who was with him last Thursday and it was you who punched him in the face hard enough to leave a bruise. You were the last person with him before he died.'

She didn't move for the longest moment – she didn't even blink. Then she sighed. 'I didn't hurt him. He was fine when I left him.'

Derwent leaned forward, propping his elbows on his knees. 'Tell us exactly what happened, Justine. Don't leave anything out. We need to know how you met and what you did.'

'Everything?'

'All of it.'

She put a hand over her eyes for a moment, struggling to keep her composure. Her fingers were trembling.

'Can I get you something? Water?' I asked.

'Don't pretend to care,' she spat. 'You don't care.'

Derwent caught my eye and shook his head, very slightly. *Don't argue with her.*

'When did you meet Geoff Armstrong?' he asked.

'Just over two months ago. After the police van got shot up on the estate.' She took a deep breath. 'He approached me. I wouldn't have gone near him. He wanted to know what it was like to grow up here. We had one short conversation about it and at the end of it he tried to kiss me.'

Derwent's tone was matter-of-fact. 'Did you know you were—'

'What? That I was what?'

'Transsexual.' Repeated diversity training courses were really paying off for Derwent.

'No. He had no idea.'

'When did you tell him?'

'After I let him kiss me.' She looked at Derwent, challenging him. 'After I let him feel me up.'

'How did he react?'

'He was shocked.' She laughed. 'He was terrified someone would find out. He gave me five hundred quid. I didn't even ask him for it. I wouldn't have said anything anyway. But he said he wanted to make a gesture.'

'And you took the money.'

'I'm saving up.' She cupped her chest. 'I had my boobs done last year but I haven't done the rest. I've found a really good surgeon in Thailand. He does these operations all the time. I don't want to have it done here and get something that looks weird and doesn't work properly.'

'So you're not . . .' Derwent trailed off, floundering.

'I'm halfway through the process. Would you like to see?'

'That won't be necessary.' He looked down, embarrassed, then back up at her with a rueful grin and she loved it, sitting a little taller. Treating her like a woman was the best way he could have gone about winning her trust.

'Did you contact Armstrong again?' I asked.

'No. He called me. I didn't know who it was at first. He said he couldn't stop thinking about me and he wanted to meet me again.'

I could believe it. She was fascinating, graceful, feminine in every way. The other day, in her heavy jumper that hid her implants, wearing masculine glasses, she had been playing dress up. Dean was a character she'd been playing. Justine was the real person.

'And you agreed because you needed the money.'

'I'm not a tart.' She was defensive, straight away. 'I

330

said no at first. Then he kept calling. He begged me for one more chance.'

'So you arranged to meet.'

'I didn't want him in my flat. I knew 103 in Murchison House was empty because I knew the girl who used to live there. It was supposed to be renovated before the next tenant came along and I still had a key so it seemed like the obvious place to meet.'

'And what happened?'

'Do you want the details of that too? Everything we did to one another? All the filthy little tricks I showed him?'

'No.' Derwent was patience personified. 'I want to know what arrangement you came to that meant he was here every Thursday with a roll of banknotes in his back pocket.'

'Oh.' She leaned back against her chair, looking tired. 'I never charged him but he liked to give me a gift at the end. He wanted me to have nice things. He brought me presents sometimes. Wine, food, bits of jewellery. Underwear. The kind of things rich men give women. Because that's how he saw me. He didn't know Dean. He didn't want to know.'

'So it was more than a business relationship to both of you,' I said.

'Very much more.' Justine laughed, but there were tears in her eyes. 'I fell in love with him. Stupid, wasn't it? We were so different. I was everything he was supposed to hate. He was kind to me, though. He saw me the way I wanted people to see me. I think he liked that I wasn't one thing or another – that turned him on. But he still wanted me to have my operation. He wanted to be the first, afterwards. He offered to pay for the whole thing but I turned him down. I thought – I thought he would find it hard, afterwards. It's a big operation. It takes time to recover.' Her lip curled. 'Geoff wasn't made to be a nurse.'

'But you still loved him,' I said.

'He worshipped me. That's hard to resist when you've grown up being called a freak and a pervert and getting beaten up at least once a week.' She caught herself. 'Anyway, that doesn't matter. What matters is that we had feelings for one another.'

'Did you talk about him leaving his wife? Going public?'

'I did. He didn't. He was terrified we'd get found out. He wouldn't even leave the flat with me in case anyone saw him.'

'Even when the building was on fire?'

'Even then. He was getting dressed . . .' The tears filled her eyes again. 'I was mean to him. I did hit him.'

'Why?'

'He called me a stupid bitch for opening the door when there were people in the corridor.' She shrugged delicately. 'I don't like being spoken to that way.'

'Understandable,' Derwent said. 'What else did you do?'

'Nothing. I warned him to hurry up and he said he would. He told me to go. That was it. I waited for him outside to make sure he was okay but he didn't come out. In the end I rang 999 and told them he was there and where to look for him.'

I made a note: that was the anonymous call that had come in about Armstrong.

Justine looked miserable. 'Do you know what really hurts? He chose to die rather than risk anyone finding out about us. He said he loved me but when it came down to it he was too ashamed of me to save his own skin.'

Derwent shook his head. 'That's not what happened.'

'How do you know?'

'He was murdered.'

'What?' She dug her fingernails into the arms of her chair, eyes wide. 'What happened?'

'That's what we're trying to find out.' Derwent opened his folder, consulting Dr Early's report on Armstrong's injuries. 'So you did hit him.'

'Once. Here.' She indicated her jaw.

'You didn't spray him with pepper spray?'

'No.'

'And you didn't strangle him.'

'No.'

'He was conscious when you left.'

'He was putting his clothes back on.'

'Did you see anyone strange when you were leaving the flat? Anyone hanging around?'

She took a moment to think. 'I mean, it was chaos in the hall. Pure chaos. People coming and going, there was smoke, it was dark, the lights weren't on – I don't know if I'd have noticed anyone.'

'Did you shut the door after you?'

She nodded. 'Definitely.'

'Would Geoff have answered the door if someone knocked on it?'

'I really doubt it. He was terrified of being discovered. I mean, that was part of the thrill. But he would have shat himself if someone tried to get into the flat.'

'Unless he was expecting them,' I said, thinking out loud. Derwent frowned at me, not following, and I waved a hand at him. *Not now.*

'Is that everything you know?' Derwent asked Justine.

'Everything.' She took a deep breath and let it out. 'It feels good to say.'

'And you've been completely honest with us.'

'Completely.'

'And you have nothing to hide. You didn't harm Armstrong.'

'He was fine when I left, I swear.' She looked from Derwent to me. 'You have to believe me.'

'What I don't understand,' I said, 'is why you went back to dressing as Dean. If you didn't do anything wrong, what did you have to hide?'

'I was ashamed,' she said quietly. 'Not of being trans. Of sleeping with Geoff. I didn't want anyone to know – not after he'd let me down. He was so bothered about his reputation he didn't seem to realise people would have judged *me* for sleeping with *him*. He thought he was the only one with something to lose.' She half-smiled. 'I loved him, you know, but he wasn't half a dickhead sometimes.'

Chapter 27

'Why didn't you arrest her?' Una Burt was looking for something on her desk, rifling through piles of paper and emptying folders. To say she was impressed by what we'd found out from Justine Rickards would be an exaggeration.

'Why didn't you arrest *him*?' Chris Pettifer said.

'Her.' Derwent stared him down, daring him to argue about it. 'And for what?'

'Killing Armstrong.'

'Because there's no evidence she did.' Derwent folded his arms, casual in shirtsleeves, outwardly relaxed. If I'd been Pettifer I would have been feeling nervous, though. There was an edge to Derwent's voice that I recognised as a red flag. 'She was with him. She saw him regularly. She was paid to meet him even though, according to her, she'd have done it for free. She left him alive and she had no reason to kill him. So tell me why I should have arrested her, because I'm not seeing it.'

'She gave you a story about Armstrong and you swallowed it because you're not interested in finding out what happened to him.' Una Burt paused for a second, reading the page in front of her, then put it in the bin and kept searching. 'She came up with an ingenious explanation for the large sums of money Armstrong kept transferring to her. Do we have any evidence she wasn't blackmailing him?'

'If he'd gone to the papers and said, "Geoff Armstrong is a hypocrite who tried to kiss me even though I'm black and a transsexual and I live on benefits and I'm everything he claims to despise", he'd have got a hell of a payday,' Pettifer said.

'But she didn't do that,' I said. 'And can you stop calling her *he*?'

'You two are so politically correct,' Pettifer said. It was certainly the first time Derwent had ever been accused of that and he took offence.

'She's more of a woman than anything you've ever shagged, mate.'

'That's enough.' Burt sat down but she was still hunting, distracted. 'It was worth much more to Justine Rickards to keep Armstrong on the hook. Regular payments are better than a one-off.'

Derwent raised one eyebrow. 'Do you really think Armstrong would have let Justine suck his cock if she'd been blackmailing him?'

Burt's head snapped up, her mouth tight with irritation. But she conceded the point. 'Possibly not.'

'Look, everything she's told us fits in with what we know,' Derwent said. 'She left him getting dressed. He was half-dressed when he died. She admits she punched him. He had a mark from that. She didn't know anything about the pepper spray and why would she have needed it? They were the same height and I reckon she's stronger than most women, even though the hormone treatment would be taking the edge off her. She could have taken him in a fight. He didn't hit her back when she punched him.'

'So who did need pepper spray to subdue him?'

'Someone who wanted to kill him,' I said. 'Someone knows he's there. Someone starts a fire. Maybe they pretend to be a firefighter when they knock on the door. He opens it, gets hit with the pepper spray, which incapacitates him. Then he's strangled and thrown out the window. We're meant to assume he jumped or fell while trying to escape the fire.'

'How does Justine fit into that?' Una Burt asked. 'She was there too.'

'It's possible she was in on it.' I looked at Derwent. 'Did you believe she loved him? I'm not so sure.'

'He didn't strike me as a particularly lovable person,' Derwent agreed. 'But then again, Justine was trying to distract us from the prostitution angle.'

'Or maybe she didn't want us to think of her as a possible suspect. She's part of a community that had no love for Armstrong – quite the opposite, in fact. And she's an angry person.' I remembered how she'd jostled me, how she'd looked at me with total disdain. There was something ruthless about Justine. She'd had to hide the real her while she grew up; she'd had to fight to become what she was. That required strength of character and determination and an ability to dissemble. 'She could have set him up.'

Derwent glowered at me. 'Got any evidence?'

'Not yet.'

'Then go and get some,' Burt said crisply. She shooed us out of her office and we straggled back to our desks.

'Tea?' Pettifer suggested.

My stomach lurched and it wasn't just because Pettifer made legendarily bad tea. 'No thanks.' I sat down, feeling exhausted, and sick, and miserable. I'd slept badly. Derwent had been back in my flat, since Melissa Pell was out of hospital and staying in his place. I should have felt safer to have him with me but it bothered me that he was there, knocking things over in the bathroom, opening drawers, watching me, *judging*. It bothered me a lot more when he got up at a quarter past five and slammed the front door on his way out for a run that had ended with muddy trainers in my hall and a sweaty, rain-soaked Derwent stretching in front of the television while I tried to eat a piece of toast and ignore him.

I leaned back in my chair and frowned at Derwent, who was standing near my desk, staring into space. 'Why are you being so nice about Justine Rickards? It's not like you to be so understanding.'

The corner of his mouth twitched. 'I feel sorry for her.'

'Really?' *You're capable of that?*

'She must have been miserable for her whole life. Still is, probably. I can't imagine what it would be like to hate yourself. I've never wanted to be anything other than what I am.' He drew his shoulders back, standing tall. 'There's nothing better than being a white man, is there? Especially an Englishman.'

'Yep. That's the kind of thinking that won the Empire,' I said acidly.

'All right, half-breed.'

'One hundred per cent Irish, thanks.'

'Genetically. But you were born here. What does that make you?'

'It makes me tired of this conversation.'

Instead of answering, Derwent sank to the floor in front of my desk. I sat in silence for a second, then broke.

'What are you doing?'

A grunt. 'Thinking.' Another grunt.

I stood up to see what he was actually doing. 'Push-ups. Of course.'

'It helps.' He was rattling through them and it pained me to admit that his form was good, his back flat. 'Gets . . . the blood . . . flowing.'

'You're not in the army now.'

'Thank God.' He paused in the up position, holding it for a moment, then stood up, tucking his shirt in. 'What are *you* doing?'

'Going through the threats against Armstrong that Elaine Lister gave us.'

'Anything interesting?'

'I'm learning some new vocabulary.' I sat down again, staring at the piles of paper that had spread across my desk. 'I'm trying to organise it by date first. Then thematically. I'll say this for him, he pissed off a lot of different types of people.'

'Who votes for someone like that?'

'People who want to shake things up. People who don't trust the main parties, the career politicians who always say the right thing. People who love a character.' I rolled my eyes. 'People who shouldn't have the vote.'

'Have we got Armstrong's phone records yet?'

'I've requested them from the phone company. The techs are still trying to get something out of Armstrong's phone. They never found the SIM card.'

'Chase up the phone company.'

Phone calls made and received, numbers we could link to people we knew or those who hadn't cropped up in our investigation yet, records of text messages although not their content, not unless the phone could be persuaded to give up its secrets . . . It could make Armstrong's last moments three-dimensional for us, shade in the background, make him live again for long enough to find out who ended his life.

All that from a phone.

The irony wasn't lost on me that Chris Swain was using mine in much the same way: to know what I did and where I went, who I was communicating with, and how. And he probably knew much more about me than I could ever find out about Geoff Armstrong. We had to stay within the law, by definition. We had to fight to get every scrap of information that might help us. The playing field was by no means level but we still had to win.

I got off the phone after a long journey through buck-passing middle managers to someone who promised me that yes, it would be today, or tomorrow at the latest, they understood it was urgent, they would do their best. Frustration knotted my stomach. I needed to eat something, I thought, but I couldn't think of anything that didn't make me feel sick. I found half a cereal bar in my desk drawer and picked at it. I was thinking about whether I'd ever be well again, whether being sick like this was a response to the way I lived – whether my job was, in fact, killing me. Then again, most of the stress and worry in my life was outside of work, when I had nothing to distract me from the shadow Chris Swain cast across my life, or when I was alone, replaying the last minutes of my relationship with Rob, changing what I said and did. There were times when concentrating on my job felt like sanctuary.

Conclusion: I just wasn't very good at having a life.

Derwent knocked on my desk, interrupting me mid-gloom. 'We're wanted.'

I looked around to see Una Burt waiting at the door of her office as Colin Vale went in after a man with dark hair. I recognised the people-trafficking expert, though it took me a little longer to remember his name: Tom Bridges. And Kev Cox was already inside, standing by Una Burt's desk with a folder. I followed Derwent across the room, my misery shelved for the time being in favour of curiosity. Pettifer and Mal Upton were right behind me. The small office filled up quickly and felt more than crowded with eight of us in it. I found a filing cabinet to lean against, judging that Derwent would disapprove of me sitting in one of the two chairs by the desk. Bridges took one, Colin Vale the other. Pettifer and Derwent battled briefly for the window sill and Derwent, of course, got it.

'What have you got, Kev?' Burt asked.

'It's about the door on the eighth floor.' He flipped open his folder. 'Quite a few DNA profiles, as you'd expect, and I don't think it's too surprising to anyone to hear that we were able to attach the profiles to individuals who are known to the police.'

'Not on that estate,' Derwent said. 'They should give them CRO numbers at birth. It would save time.'

'Kev sent the list to me.' Tom Bridges looked around, checking that he'd met us all before and he didn't need to explain who he was. His expression changed very slightly when he got to me, interest narrowing his eyes and I looked down at the carpet. When I looked up again, Bridges was addressing Burt but, inevitably, Derwent was watching me.

'I had a scan through the names and records and one of them jumped out at me,' Bridges said. 'Ray Griffin. He's a local fixer for a gang of Albanians who've been running a people-smuggling operation across Europe for the last five years. They are some bad lads.'

'The kind of people who'd have three girls locked in a flat on the Maudling Estate?' I asked.

'Exactly that kind.' He took a photograph out of a folder and held it up. 'This is Ray.'

Ray was maybe thirty, with dark hair, a square jaw and a wide neck, his mouth a little bit slack in the picture. I was wary of reading too much into a custody photograph but he looked blank, as if there wasn't much going on behind his small eyes.

Colin leaned in, staring at the image intently. 'What do you think, Maeve?'

I bent to see, holding up a sheet of paper to cover half the picture so all we could see was a square jaw, an ear, a hint of downturned mouth and a wide neck. 'That looks like the guy from the hallway to me.'

'Scientific approach,' Pettifer commented and I glowered at him.

'Did you look at the CCTV, Chris? Or did you assume that was someone else's job?'

'Colin hadn't shown it to me.'

'You didn't ask.' Colin said it in a matter-of-fact way.

'We got skin cells and saliva from him. You were looking for someone who touched his face,' Kev said. 'He fits on that front. Scientifically, I mean.' He caught my eye and grinned.

Pettifer turned to Burt. 'I've never heard of this guy before. He's nothing to do with Melissa Pell. If he did attack her, what possible reason did he have for doing it?'

'Can we connect him with Mark Pell?' Burt said.

'Maybe?' Pettifer rubbed his head. 'I don't know.'

'If we can get something on Mark Pell, we should do it,' Derwent said. 'I don't like him.'

'Should we pick Ray up?' Mal said. 'No harm in asking him if he knows Pell, is there?'

'I don't see that we have much to lose,' Una Burt said. 'Do we have a good address for him?'

'We've got his last known address from his probation officer, his ex-girlfriend's house in Woolwich and we've got his mum's address. He's well known to my colleagues. They're fairly sure we'll find him,' Bridges said. 'I'd start with the Woolwich address, myself.'

'Ex-girlfriend, though.' Derwent gave Bridges his best chilling look. 'Why would he hang around there?'

'Two kids.'

'Fair enough.' Derwent was quick enough to drop an argument when it looked like a loser. He turned to Burt. 'What's the plan, boss?'

'We'll split up into three groups. There are enough of us to go to all three addresses at the same time. I don't want him getting a tip off from his mother and disappearing on us.'

'Anything we should know about? Any form for carrying weapons?' Derwent asked Bridges.

'Known to carry a knife on occasion. No firearms that we know of. He's a big guy, over six foot.'

'Stab vests, then,' Derwent said. 'We can get TSG support. They'll put in the doors for us.'

They'd also be armed with Tasers, which was a lot better than turning up empty-handed.

'Right.' Burt cleared her throat, reasserting herself. 'I'll go to Woolwich. Josh, you take the last known address. Chris, you go to the mum's house. I'll sort out the TSG support and we'll try and execute these warrants as soon as possible. So no wandering off.'

The last bit was transparently aimed at Derwent, who was looking restless. He stood up and stretched. 'Can't wait.'

'Can I come too?' Bridges was tapping his fingers on his kneecap. I recognised the hunter's instinct that made a good cop; I knew it because I had it too.

'Of course. You can join any of the teams.' Burt smiled at him in a distracted way.

'Can I look at the file?' I asked Bridges as everyone began to shuffle out of the office.

'Of course.'

I took it with me, stopping at the nearest desk so I could lay it flat and leaf through it. Bridges came to stand beside me, looking over my shoulder.

'Small time stuff.'

'He doesn't look like a master criminal,' I said. He looked like a violent but dim-witted goon, good for beating people up, including his ex-girlfriend. He'd been inside most recently for armed robbery, but he was the kind of criminal who spent half his life behind bars without fear or remorse. Like a long commute, it was the price he paid for doing what he loved. The idea of prison as a deterrent would have made him laugh.

'Thanks for sticking up for the trafficked women the other day.'

I looked up, surprised. 'Oh – when Belcott was being vile about them, you mean? Not a problem.'

'It's not the first time I've encountered that attitude to sex workers.'

'Everyone needs someone to look down on. Belcott has to try very hard to find someone inferior to him.'

Bridges grinned at me. 'You like working with him, then.'

'I put up with it.' I shut the file and handed it back to him. 'He's a twat and he always has been. Now and then I tell him what I think of him.'

'Poor guy.'

'He deserves it.'

I started to walk away but Bridges called after me. 'Which address are you going to?'

'Oh – probably the last known address.'

Mal looked up. 'Do you want to come with us? The mum's in Stepney.'

'Um . . .' I looked across at Derwent, who was on the other side of the office, talking to Colin Vale. 'I think I'd better not.'

'Don't you want a break?' Mal said, dropping his voice so Derwent couldn't hear.

'That would be nice. But it's more diplomatic to go with him.' Besides, I didn't like to think what kind of trouble Derwent would get into without me.

'That's where I was thinking of going,' Bridges said. 'To the last known address, I mean.'

'Don't feel you have to put yourself through it,' I said quietly. 'Most people wouldn't volunteer to spend time with Josh Derwent if they didn't have to.'

'He's a charmer.'

'There are those who think so.' It baffled me too.

As if to prove the point, Derwent glanced over and frowned at me. 'Get a move on, Kerrigan. Kit up. If we make a quick exit, we can grab a sandwich on the way.'

'I'm okay.'

Derwent shook his head. 'No. You need to eat.'

I glowered. 'I said I'm fine.'

He moved a little closer, so he was right in the middle of the room, but if anything his voice was louder when he said, 'You didn't manage much breakfast this morning. I almost sent you back to bed.'

It wasn't my imagination: the room went quiet. And Derwent knew exactly what he'd done, his expression more innocent than a choirboy's. Bridges' phone rang and he walked out of the office to take the call. I watched him disappear through the door and turned back to Derwent, raising my eyebrows.

'*Really?*'

'Sorry.' He couldn't have sounded more insincere if he'd tried. He swaggered off towards Una Burt's office, pausing to whisper into my ear, 'He's not what you need at the moment. You have enough problems.'

'So you didn't notice his wedding ring?'

Derwent looked amused. 'Would that stop him? Or you?'

'We know you have no principles whatsoever, but don't assume everyone else behaves the same way.' I was dizzy with anger: how typical of Derwent to misinterpret Bridges' interest in me. 'Piss off, *sir*.'

'Just trying to help.' He disappeared through Una Burt's door. I went to Mal's desk.

'Can I change my mind about coming to Stepney?'

'Yeah.' He looked past me to where the back of Derwent's head was visible in the boss's office. 'I mean, if you're sure.'

I didn't allow myself to think about the consequences. What I knew was that it had taken a long time but I had finally reached my limit.

'Trust me,' I said. 'I'm certain.'

Chapter 28

Ray Griffin's mother's house in Stepney was in a small street of 1950s council housing, in-fill building to replace Victorian slums that had been blasted off the face of the earth during the Blitz. We stopped around the corner so Pettifer could brief the TSG officers who had come along to support us. The TSG were the muscle of the Met, big men who specialised in knocking down doors and quelling violent protests. Their van was squatting on the pavement in front of us, the white livery tinted orange in the streetlights. It was mid-afternoon and the sun was gone for the day, the sky darkening by the second. The air was icy, and the rain that glinted on our windscreen was gritty with sleet.

Mal twisted in the passenger seat to talk to me. 'Are you okay?'

'Fine.' I was finding it hard to stay awake, if anything: Pettifer liked to drive with all the windows up and the heating on full, so the car was stuffy.

'You seemed a bit annoyed earlier.'

'With Derwent?' I pulled a face. 'I shouldn't let him get to me.'

'He was sort of implying you're living together.'

'He sort of was.' I hugged myself, trying not to yawn. 'He's staying with me at the moment.'

Mal nodded as if he understood, but the expression in his eyes was pure confusion. 'Does that mean you and Rob have broken up?'

'It's – it's complicated.' It came back to me with a shock that Chris Swain might be listening to our conversation through my phone. 'I'm not really sure what's happening.'

He sighed. 'Look, I know this is out of line and I completely understand if you and Josh are together, properly, but if it's a casual thing and it comes to an end, maybe . . . you could circulate an email to interested parties?'

'Such as?'

'I'm not even going to pretend I mean someone else. Sorry. I'm really bad at this but I—' He hesitated, then finished in a rush. 'I like you.'

Mal was so absolutely the opposite of every man I'd ever been involved with – rumpled, shaggy, gentle, awkward – that I couldn't wrap my head around what it would be like to be with him.

'I think Una would have a view on me working my way through the team.'

'Does she know about you and Derwent?'

'No.' I bit my lip. 'You know, there's really nothing for her to know. He's – well, it's not serious.'

'I always wondered if you'd get together.'

Never, I thought. *Never ever*. It would be like sticking my head in a hornets' nest: briefly interesting, perhaps, but a terrible, stupid mistake I would regret.

But because I couldn't be sure Swain wasn't listening, I had to find a way to suggest we were engaged in a passionate affair, without actually saying so or throwing up in my mouth. 'We know each other very well. You can't lie to one another when you spend so much time together.' It was, in fact, true.

Mal nodded. 'Sorry for asking about it. None of my business.'

'That's okay.'

'Just when he said that at work. It made me wonder and then I had to ask.' He smiled. 'I was pretty sure there was something going on when he made Bridges back off.'

I closed my eyes briefly at the memory: the purest embarrassment. 'I don't think it was necessary. Bridges wasn't flirting with me.'

'Maybe not. But you do get a fair bit of attention.'

'I'm not married and I don't happen to be a lesbian. That means a lot of men will consider their chances, especially in the Met. There aren't a lot of single straight women around. You know that. There are three women on our team and Liv is very happy in a long-term relationship with another woman. Una Burt is the boss. That leaves me.'

'Yeah, it's just statistics.' Mal grinned at me. 'I'll try to remember.'

Without my noticing, Pettifer had come back. He yanked open the driver's door and I jumped.

'All right, you two. We're ready.'

I uncurled myself reluctantly, feeling chilled as I got out of the car into the teeth of the rain and wind. Head down, I walked around the corner, half-listening to Mal and Pettifer as they talked tactics. Somewhere out there on this dark, cold evening, Chris Swain was living, breathing. Watching. Listening.

Hating.

He was hunted too. He knew the police wanted to speak to him, even if he didn't know about Derwent's unofficial attempts to track him down. He should have been nervous. He should have been looking over his shoulder, not drawing attention to himself by scaring me and vandalising my car. But he was arrogant, and obsessed. Anyway, it was different for him. He was choosing that for himself, coming to London, putting himself in harm's way. I'd done nothing and yet I was caught up in his sinister little games. He could stop, if he liked. I couldn't make him leave me alone. At least, I hadn't managed it yet.

The house was part of a terrace but there was an alleyway that ran behind the gardens, so Pettifer sent a group of TSG officers and Mal around to the back.

'We don't want him to run off before we've had a chance to talk to him, do we?'

They went quietly, keeping low, and as soon as they were in position Mal radioed through to tell us. The longer we drew this out, the better Ray Griffin's chances of noticing that something was going on and trying to escape. Pettifer rang Una Burt.

'We're ready when you are, boss.' He listened for a second, then nodded to the TSG sergeant. 'When you're ready.'

I'd seen it done before but there was always something impressive and slightly terrifying about watching the TSG gain entry to a house and search it. Four of them were between me and the front door, big men standing shoulder to shoulder. I caught a glimpse of Griffin's mother when she opened the door, a small woman with her hair scraped back into a high ponytail, her face tight with anger.

'He's not here. I don't know why you're looking for him here. He's not been here for weeks.'

They ignored her, filling the house with broad shoulders and loud voices. Pettifer and I followed, standing in the hall while the TSG guys thumped up the stairs.

'They'd better not be making a mess up there.' Mrs Griffin's arms were folded. One foot tapped meaningfully in a fluffy slipper. 'Why do they want him, anyway?'

'We're just making some inquiries,' I said.

'He ain't done nothing wrong. Not since he came out of prison last time. He's promised me.'

'Then he's got nothing to worry about,' Pettifer said, with that heavy police humour that made people think we were arrogant. Maybe we were. It was often the cockiest boxers who won their fights.

Suddenly there was a lot of noise from upstairs: officers shouting orders and a deep voice swearing a blue streak.

'There's a surprise,' Pettifer said calmly. 'He was here after all. Fancy that.'

Mrs Griffin's mouth was puckered like a cat's backside. 'You should leave him alone. He's simple. He gets himself mixed up in stuff and it's not his fault.'

The TSG sergeant rattled down the stairs, looking pleased with himself. 'He was hiding in the loft. Looked as if he'd been there a while. He had a mattress up there, and a camping toilet.'

'Naughty Ray.' Pettifer grinned indulgently. 'Bring him down. I'll call the boss and let her know.'

'You'll need a van to transport him,' the sergeant said. 'He's not what I'd call a model prisoner.'

Upstairs, Ray was screaming. 'You're breaking my arm – you're breaking my fucking arm, man. Get off me.'

'This is police brutality,' Mrs Griffin said. 'I'm going to make a complaint.'

'Good for you.' Pettifer bounced out of the house, his phone to his ear. There was nothing like being the ones who struck gold on a raid.

'We'll need his phone,' I said to the TSG sergeant. 'Can you check if you've got it?'

'He didn't have one on him.'

I turned to Mrs Griffin. 'Any ideas?'

'Fuck off.'

'Right.' I snapped on some gloves. I was good at searching, and glad to have something to do. 'I'll find it myself.'

We took Ray Griffin straight back to the office – with his phone, which I'd located in the toaster – and dumped him in a secure interview room. Dave Kemp and Mal stayed with him while we waited for a solicitor so we could interview him. Griffin had kicked off at the house, and in the back of the van, but once he was in the interview room he calmed down. He looked defeated, as if the fight had gone out of him.

As it happened, all the fighting was happening one floor up, where Una Burt and Derwent were toe to toe.

'You should let me interview him,' Derwent said.

'Why would I do that? I'm perfectly able to handle it myself.'

'You should be supervising, not involved. You're in charge, not one of the troops.'

'I'm aware of that.' Pure acid. 'I don't see the two things as incompatible. And as you say, I am in charge, so I decide what happens. I will be conducting the interview myself.'

'He's not going to tell you anything.'

'Why not?'

Derwent struggled for a moment to say why and I could see the thoughts crashing around in his head: you can't charm him with looks like yours; he won't be scared of you; he'll go no comment all the way and you don't have any people skills so you won't be able to coax him out of it. 'I just think I have a better chance of making him talk.'

'Right. Well, I do not. You can watch the interview if you like and I'll be grateful for any suggestions you may have but I am going to take the lead on talking to Griffin. I'm going to have Tom Bridges with me too because he knows more about Griffin's past and his associates. I don't have room for anyone else.'

'But—'

'No.'

Pettifer poked his head around the door. 'Boss, the solicitor's here.'

'At last.' She picked up her folder and walked away without another word to Derwent.

'Did you really think she'd give you a shot?' I asked.

'If she wasn't so full of herself, she'd have left it to me.'

'Oh, I see. It's her ego that's the problem.'

'She's not a good leader. She likes the spotlight too much.'

'Whereas you're just a willing foot soldier.'

He frowned at me. 'That's exactly it. I'm not in it for the glory.'

'But you won't admit that anyone else is capable of doing as good a job as you.'

'That's because I have long experience of people being shit at their jobs.'

'You can't say that about Burt.'

A muscle flickered in Derwent's jaw. 'We'll see.'

For once I was squarely on Una Burt's side. I hoped she'd prove him wrong. I went into the meeting room where there was a TV that linked to the interview room, and found a place to sit between Colin Vale and Liv. Derwent swaggered in, all attitude, and gave me a hurt look when he realised I wasn't planning to sit next to him. I ignored it. I'd had enough of him taking advantage of other people's better natures.

The first half-hour of the interview made me want to drop my head into my hands and groan. Burt pawed at Griffin like a lion trying to coax a tortoise out of its shell; there was no subtlety to it.

'Where were you on the 28th of November between midday and midnight?'

'Were you on the Maudling Estate?'

'Have you ever been on the Maudling Estate?'

'Do you own a red baseball cap?'

And like a metronome, without inflection, without

surprise, the answer came back. *No comment. No comment.*
As I'd suspected from the custody photograph he wasn't
the brightest guy but he knew enough to say nothing,
and there was damn all we could do with that.

I looked across at Derwent once. He was staring at the
television screen with the kind of intensity that could
melt glass. I gave him credit for one thing: it gave him
no pleasure at all to be proved right when it meant we
were getting nowhere.

For God's sake, Una, get it together.

As if she'd heard me, she leaned forward. 'Do you
know a woman called Melissa Pell?'

A frown: this wasn't a question he'd anticipated. 'No.'

'Ever heard the name before?'

'No.'

'What about Mark Pell?'

He made eye contact with her for a second, with
nothing but blank incomprehension. 'No.'

I glanced at Derwent to see what he thought. He was
completely still, not blinking, barely breathing, like a
sniper with the target in his sights.

Burt opened a folder and took out the CCTV stills Colin
Vale had collected for us.

'This is you, isn't it, Ray?'

'No comment.' But his eyes tracked down from the
spot on the wall where he'd been staring so he could look
at the images.

'He knows it's him,' Vale said softly.

Burt leaned forward and leafed through the images
until she got to one from the eighth-floor camera. 'This
is you. And this is a woman named Melissa Pell. This is

you attacking her and I'd like to know why.'

The solicitor leaned in to see the images, her expression carefully neutral. She was a young woman, blonde and bubbly by nature, and I saw a reaction she couldn't quite hide when she saw how the man came after Melissa Pell, the casual savagery that had left her unconscious.

'Melissa was in hospital for days after this. She had some very serious injuries. That, straight away, is grievous bodily harm, and that's you committing it.'

'It's not me.'

'We recovered your DNA from the crime scene.'

'It's mistaken identity.'

'It's nothing of the kind. You are a career criminal and we've got you on camera attacking a defenceless woman. That's enough to get you back in prison for a very long time, even without the rest.'

He licked his lips. 'The rest?'

'You do realise, don't you, Mr Griffin, that this is evidence that you were on the Maudling Estate?'

No answer.

'And you do realise that we're looking for the person responsible for setting the fire that devastated Murchison House? Four people died, Mr Griffin. One of them was a little girl. Two of them were young women who were locked in a flat and left to die. That's murder, pure and simple.'

'The fire was nothing to do with me. I just—' He bit his lip and shook his head.

'You just what?'

'Nothing.'

At a nod from Burt, Tom Bridges took over, his voice

calm and matter-of-fact. 'You work for Sajmir Culaj, don't you?'

Ray went as red as if he'd been scalded. 'No comment.'

'That's a fact, though, isn't it, because that's why you went to prison last time. It's been proved in court, so there's no point in going no comment.'

Griffin pressed his lips together, as if he was physically trying to restrain himself from answering.

'Do you know what I know about Sajmir Culaj? I know he's moved away from wholesaling drugs. I know what he makes most of his money from these days.'

'Is that a question?' the solicitor asked.

Bridges frowned. 'Let me put it a different way. Do you know where the money's coming from, Ray?'

'No comment.'

'Big money in moving people across borders, Ray. Make them pay to get into the country, make them work once they're here. Slavery – that's one word for it. Trafficking people. Women. Children. Using them as domestic servants. Using them as free labour. Using them for sex.'

'I don't know anything about that.' It was a mumble.

'What do you know about flat 113 in Murchison House? What do you know about the women who were living there? They died there, Ray, didn't they?'

Ray's eyes started watering. He sniffed, blotting them with the back of his wrist.

'You were at your mum's house, Ray. Hiding. You knew someone was coming for you – you just didn't know if it would be the police who got to you first or if it would be Culaj's guys. You're probably quite glad it was us.'

'No.'

'Because you've got a big problem, haven't you?' There was nothing aggressive in the way Bridges said it; they could have been friends talking in a pub. 'You were supposed to look after those girls and they ended up dead. Culaj isn't going to be very happy with you. If I were you, I'd start talking, even if it means you're going to end up in prison for a bit. Let's face it, you're going anyway for the attack on Melissa Pell. Prison looks like the safest place you could be until Culaj forgets about you.'

Ray blinked miserably. 'It was an accident. It wasn't supposed to happen that way.'

'That's done it,' Colin said beside me. 'Got the bastard.'

'What wasn't, Ray? What happened?' Bridges asked. 'Did you start the fire?'

'No. Absolutely not. That was nothing to do with me. I was just supposed to go and make sure the girls were all right.'

'The girls?'

'In flat 113. They weren't allowed to go out on their own. Sometimes they needed food or whatever. I didn't have anything to do with them working. I just called in now and then, when Sajmir asked me to. He didn't like having the same people going too often because the girls would try to get friendly with you and he didn't want that. I wasn't supposed to talk to them.'

'How many girls were there?'

'Three.'

'Three. Are you sure?'

'One black, one blonde, one brunette.'

'Names?'

He shrugged, his face completely blank, and I felt utterly furious that he hadn't even wondered if they had names, let alone what the names might have been.

'Do you know anything about them? Where they were from?'

'The black girl was African.'

'Africa's a big place,' Bridges said. 'Narrow it down for me, fella.'

'I don't know. Sorry. The other two were from Russia.'

'Definitely?'

'That's what I thought. They sounded like it.'

Derwent was shaking his head slowly, unimpressed. Bridges clearly felt the same way, because he abandoned the attempt to find out anything about the girls.

'So were you there when the fire started?'

'I was in flat 117. Sajmir used that one as a kind of office. I was just hanging around, you know. Watching a bit of telly. I didn't have anywhere else to be. I wasn't in a hurry to go and see the girls. Then the alarms started going off.'

'What did you do?'

'I rang Sajmir. I didn't know what to do.'

'What did he say?'

'That I should get the girls out.' Ray closed his eyes, breathing hard. 'I tried.'

'You can't have tried very hard,' Una Burt said coldly. 'They burned to death.'

'That wasn't my fault.' He was crying again, openly this time. 'I opened the door and the one with fair hair rushed me. She kneed me in the bollocks and then she ran. I shut the door on the other two to chase after her.

I didn't mean to lock them in. I thought I'd be able to get back to them. I was afraid of what Sajmir would say if I just let her get away. I thought I could get her back and then collect the other two and we could all go to one of Sajmir's other houses together. I didn't want to get in trouble.'

I could imagine it all too clearly: Ray panicking, the smoke filling the air, the situation spiralling out of control as the girl made her break for freedom. Ray could really only handle one problem at a time. Chasing after her must have seemed like the logical thing to do. But he'd left the other two girls to die in horrible circumstances, in terror, in pain. He'd condemned them to a death no one would ever wish on their worst enemy.

'So you ran after the missing girl,' Bridges said. 'Did you catch her?'

He shook his head. 'I thought I had. I thought it was her.' He tapped the picture that was still in front of him: Melissa with her fair hair hanging down. 'I caught up with her and I roughed her up a bit. I didn't hit her hard or anything. It was just to teach her a lesson and make her behave.'

I risked another look at Derwent, who was completely still except for a thumb that tapped on the desk in front of him. Una Burt had made the right choice, I thought. Maybe Derwent thought it too. Bridges was objective, and calm, and highly effective. Derwent was likely to be none of these things in a room with the man who had fractured Melissa Pell's eye socket.

On the screen, Ray Griffin sighed. 'But then I realised it was the wrong girl. By the time I got down to the ground floor, there was no sign of the one I was looking for. And then I went to go back up but the firefighters had already arrived and they stopped me. I didn't know what to do.'

'You didn't think of telling the firefighters about the two women you'd locked into their flat?' Una Burt's voice dripped with hostility. 'Or the one you'd left unconscious on the eighth floor?'

'I thought they'd find them.' He squeezed his eyes shut. 'I never meant for anyone to get hurt. I thought it was going to be all right. And then I realised I'd fucked it up. The blonde girl ran away. The other two died. I hurt this woman and I didn't even mean to. But it was all just an accident. A mistake.'

'For fuck's sake.' Derwent got up and walked out of the room, as if he couldn't bear to listen to any more.

On the television screen, Ray Griffin was still talking, as if he couldn't stop, now that he'd started. As if explaining it would make it all right.

'It wasn't my fault. You have to believe me. None of it was my fault.'

Chapter 29

'Planning on going home soon?' Derwent stood by my desk, jangling his car keys.

I checked the time: later than I'd thought. 'In a while.'

'I'm going now.'

'Okay.'

'So I can give you a lift.'

'Why?' If I sounded suspicious, it was because I was.

Derwent blinked at me, innocent. 'Because we're going to the same place, and it's freezing out, and whatever you're doing can probably wait until tomorrow.'

It was a peace offering, I realised, because he'd behaved like an arse all day. And he was right; I wasn't doing anything urgent. Ray Griffin had gone through the CCTV images with Colin Vale and identified the fair-haired girl for us, so at last we had a face to look for, and a description, and we'd circulated the image as widely as we could even though we were days too late: ports and airports, police and hospitals. She was our best chance of identifying the dead girls, and prosecuting Sajmir Culaj as well as Ray Griffin. More than that, she was on her own, running for her life with nothing more than the clothes she stood up in. Finding her was a priority. But I wasn't going to be able to do that from my desk. And I needed to get some rest.

I pushed my chair back.

'Okay. Thanks.'

He twirled his car keys around his finger. 'Good. I'll see you downstairs. Don't keep me waiting too long.'

Leopards, spots, etc. I rolled my eyes behind his back and got on with packing my bag.

Derwent was waiting in the car park behind the office, his coat collar turned up against the cold.

'You weren't wrong about the weather.' I ran across, shivering, and opened the passenger door to put my things in the foot well. 'Why aren't you in the car?'

'I want a word. Is your phone in your bag?' I nodded and he slammed the door shut. 'Just in case Swain is listening.'

'Talk fast.' I was jumping from foot to foot, trying to stay warm. The temperature had dropped like a stone, the sky bright with stars even in central London.

'I wanted to talk to you about what happened earlier, with Bridges.'

I frowned at him. 'You were out of line. There was no need for it.'

'I was trying to look out for you.'

'By giving everyone on the team the impression that we're shagging? You didn't have to yell about it.'

'Sorry.' He didn't look all that bothered and I felt myself getting angrier. He had no idea of the implications of what he'd done.

'It's all right for you. You don't have anything like a

good reputation. Sleeping with me would be a massive step up for you.'

There was a glint in his eye. 'I've been congratulated more than once today.'

'For fuck's sake.' I was trembling and I couldn't tell if it was pure rage or the cold. 'You know what people are saying about me. You know the conclusions they're drawing. You know what they'll be calling me behind my back.'

'When this is over, I'll explain it was nothing.' He said it carelessly, as if it was that easy.

'No one will believe you.'

'You're worrying for no reason.'

'You just don't realise that there's a different set of standards for women. You get a pat on the back and I get judged. You're my boss, for God's sake.'

'I'm sorry,' he said again, and this time he sounded more like he meant it. 'I just wanted to get rid of Bridges for you.'

'He was being pleasant. And if he had been trying to flirt with me, I would have been capable of dealing with it by myself. It was none of your business.'

'You need looking after, Kerrigan.'

'Not by you.'

'Who else is going to do it? You'll never ask for help. You're like a feral cat. You don't know how to trust anyone.'

'Trusting people is a quick way to get hurt.'

Derwent whistled. 'And people say I'm a cynic. Don't you trust me?'

'I trust you to cause trouble.'

He grinned. 'That'll do.'

I'd had enough. 'Can we get into the car now?'

'Not yet. We need to talk about Swain.'

'What about him?'

'We need to push him further. Make him angry. Make him reckless.'

I frowned. 'What do you have in mind?'

'I have a few ideas.' He leaned against the car. 'Look, just go with it. Pretend it's undercover work. Whatever happens, it's not personal. What we're doing is a means to an end.'

'What are we doing?' I asked, wary.

'Wait and see.' There was a spring in his step as he went around to the driver's side of the car.

It was a bad sign, if ever I'd seen one.

Derwent parked in the car park underneath the apartment building, where there was no mobile phone reception at all.

'Right.' He looked at me sideways. 'Ready?'

'To do what?'

'To have some fun.'

And that was all I was getting. I followed him into the lift and up to my floor, where he stood back to let me open the door. He'd taken out his phone and he nodded to me to do the same. Then he pushed me into my bedroom.

'What—'

'Shhh.' He took my phone out of my hand and put it on the table by the bed, covering it so the camera was out of action. I put my hands on my hips and frowned at him.

He winked. Then he started to unknot his tie. 'I've been thinking about this all day.'

'Huh?'

'I know you've been thinking about it too.' The pitch of his voice had gone down. He sounded not entirely like himself, or at least not as I usually heard him. And despite myself, I felt it in the pit of my stomach. He raised his eyebrows expectantly.

I cleared my throat. 'Yes. Of course.'

His widest grin. He shrugged off his coat and tossed it onto a chair from a distance. Then he kicked off his shoes and let them fall to the floor.

I whispered, 'What the hell are you doing?'

'You're so beautiful.' He pointed at me and mimed taking clothes off. I shook my head. He glared. *Come on.* 'Take your top off. Let me look at you.'

With a sigh, I unbuttoned my coat and let it fall at my feet, then pulled off one shoe after another. Derwent gave me the thumbs-up. He threw himself onto my bed, wriggling to get comfortable as he took out his phone. Charlie Brooke had certified it as clean as well as loading it with spyware for Derwent to use on me. He thumbed through screens, looking for something, and gave a little hum of satisfaction as he found it. In a hurried, breathless voice he said, 'Oh God.'

I leaned over to see. A first-person shooter game was on the screen, with zombies lurching towards us. My eyebrows went sky-high. Derwent shrugged. He patted the bed beside him and waggled his eyebrows. I rolled my eyes. *No way.*

He groaned, his attention back on his phone. 'Fucking

hell, Maeve.' He made a *hurry up and get on with it* motion without looking at me.

I knelt on the bed beside him and whispered, 'I know you're enjoying this.'

He didn't so much as glance at me. Instead, he gave me a very earnest shake of his head that meant the exact opposite. Then he said, loudly, 'You're incredible.' He put one foot on the floor and moved so the springs began to creak rhythmically. 'Oh, Maeve. That's it.'

I closed my eyes for a second and shook my head in sheer disbelief that I was even considering joining in. Then I gasped. 'Oh, *yes*.'

Derwent snorted with amusement. I opened my eyes wide and looked meaningfully at him.

'Sorry,' he mouthed. In a low but distinct voice he said, 'Tell me what you want me to do to you, Maeve.' The grin widened. 'In detail.'

As if. 'Just . . . don't stop.'

And he didn't, for quite some time. I contributed a few sighs and moans while trying not to catch Derwent's eye, although he was far more interested in his phone than in me, and once, when the zombies got him, he forgot what we were doing and started swearing at his game. After a few minutes I started thinking about how ridiculous this situation was, got the giggles and couldn't stop. Derwent grabbed hold of me and pinned me down with his hand over my mouth, shaking his head in such disapproval that it made me much, much worse. He talked himself to what sounded like a shattering imaginary climax while he checked the weather forecast and his email. Towards the end he rattled the headboard so it banged the wall, faster and faster, which made me laugh so hard I was weeping. Derwent sighed, annoyed.

Pull yourself together.

I tried. I really did. I just had to hope the little mewling sounds I was making could be confused with passion.

When he'd finished, Derwent flipped a pillow over my face and rolled away. I knocked it off and took a few deep breaths, getting control of myself before I looked at him again. It felt good to laugh, for once. It felt like a good alternative to shivering in the dark, afraid of what unseen malevolence might be waiting for me. I felt lighter. Happy, almost.

'That was amazing.' Derwent clambered off the bed and stretched, yawning silently. He sounded reverent and looked completely unmoved. 'You're amazing, Maeve.'

I propped myself up on one elbow. 'You too, Josh. I never knew it could be that way.'

I saw him lose it, just for a second, but he caught himself before he actually guffawed. 'Are you hungry?'

I thought about it. 'Yes, actually.'

'I'll take you out for dinner.'

'You don't have to.'

'It's the least I can do to thank you for putting up with me.' He picked up his shoes and coat and disappeared down the hall, and I realised I had no idea if he meant it or if it was just meant for Chris Swain to hear, and nothing to do with how Derwent really felt at all.

We went to a little family-run Italian restaurant near the flat, so warm and noisy on a freezing Wednesday night that my face flamed and my ears rang as soon as we went inside. The waitress beamed when she saw me, but then she noticed Derwent. Her face fell and she showed us to a table with cold, unsmiling efficiency.

Derwent watched her walk away. 'Who pissed on her pasta?'

'I used to come in here a lot with Rob.'

'Oh.'

'Yeah.' I felt acutely uncomfortable, in fact, to be sitting at a table opposite the wrong person. 'Maybe this wasn't the best choice.'

Derwent grinned at me. 'Don't worry. I can cope. Anyway, this is perfect.'

'What makes you say that?'

'Too noisy for anyone to overhear us or Swain to listen in so I don't have to bother with any of that lovey-dovey shit.'

'Heaven forbid.'

'This is all about making him think we're a normal couple.' Derwent looked at me over the top of the menu. 'I know he's a twisted little fuck but I bet he'd give his left nut to take you out to dinner. He probably threw a party when you and Rob split up. If anything is going to make him crazy it's seeing you move on from Rob to someone who's still nothing like him, and someone who's in your life all the time. Someone who's entitled to be around you the way he'll never be.'

I nodded, feeling my spirits slump at the thought of Swain and how I made him feel. 'Look, can I ask you a favour?'

'You can ask.'

'Can we not talk about Swain?'

He looked surprised. 'Okay.'

'And can you just be nice?'

He put down the menu. 'I'm always nice.'

'You're always trying to get a reaction and it's exhausting.'

Derwent frowned. 'I like the suggestion that it's all me. You come out fighting every time. What do you expect?'

'Oh, I see. It's *my* fault.'

'You don't help yourself.'

'If you think I'm going to let you walk all over me for the sake of a quiet life, you're dead wrong.' I leaned on the table and propped my head up on my hand. 'But I don't have anything left for this. Not tonight. Can we just have a nice meal and a pleasant conversation?'

'Of course.' He retreated behind his menu again, and I thought I'd probably hurt his feelings, but I couldn't let that worry me.

When the waitress came, he exerted himself to charm her and referred to me as 'my colleague' about a hundred times. She went from scowls to smiles and then, inevitably, blushing giggles before she had finished taking our order.

'Well done,' I said as she headed for the kitchen. 'Another one bites the dust.'

'I thought you'd want me to make it clear to her that we weren't together. If you let Rob come back, you can come in here without worrying about what she thinks of you.'

'Yeah.' If I let Rob come back. If he ever tried to come back. And I knew from Derwent's tone what he would think of me if I did let Rob back into my life, whatever the waitress's opinion might be.

'Let me guess,' Derwent said. 'You don't want to talk about that either.'

'Not really.'

'Okay.' And for once it was that easy. He starting talking about something else: an anecdote I'd never heard before about something ridiculous he'd done when he was a probationer. That led to another anecdote, and somehow we actually managed to have a conversation that wasn't full of spikes and pitfalls, that flowed without either of us bristling into defensive mode, for the rest of the meal. I ate pizza and wished my ulcer would allow me to drink red wine and felt like a human being for the first time in a long time.

When we were finished, the restaurant had emptied around us. Derwent paid at the till, talking to the waitress for a good long time. He came back smirking.

'Did you get her number?' I whispered.

'Nah.'

'You're slipping.'

'I didn't ask.' He pulled his coat on. 'I've got other things on my mind at the moment.'

'What things?'

'Things *I* don't want to talk about.' He shoved his hands in his pockets and grinned at me. 'Anyway, I don't need her number. I know where she works.'

He would never change, I thought. He was consistent, if nothing else. Somehow, though, his behaviour had lost its capacity to shock me. It was just too predictable to be outrageous.

The cold air was a slap in the face after the heat of the restaurant. I ducked my head, burying my chin in my coat as I walked beside Derwent. We didn't have far to go, at least.

'Hold my hand.' Derwent held out his hand to me.

'No, thanks.'

'Hand, Kerrigan.' It was his *don't argue with me* tone of voice and I pulled my hand out of my pocket reluctantly, wishing that one of us had thought to wear gloves so we weren't skin to skin. He tucked my hand and his into his coat pocket, palm to palm, fingers interlaced. 'That looks better,' he muttered.

I walked along beside him, matching his stride, acutely uncomfortable. It was like wearing the wrong size of shoes: all I could think about was how strange and wrong it was to hold hands with Derwent, of all people, and how much more intimate it was than lying on a bed with him making sex noises.

'All right?'

'Yeah,' I said, thinking *not really, no*. But it was the sort of thing that would inflame Chris Swain, infuriate him, make him reckless and, crucially, careless, and it was worth doing if he was near enough to see. If I'd learned one thing about Chris Swain in all the time he'd been chasing me, it was that he was usually watching.

We turned the final corner before the entrance to my building and Derwent swung me around, into a doorway. He stepped very close to me and put his face against my neck. I felt his breath on my skin as he whispered, 'Pretend you're enjoying this.'

I shivered, unsettled. He was leaning on me, crushing me. His lips brushed my neck. I knew it amused him to see how far I was prepared to go. There was always that sadistic undertone, mild but definite. An endless staring contest. *Who'll blink first?* He rested his cheek against mine. Velvety stubble brushed my skin and it tingled. Like an allergic reaction, I thought.

He tilted his head as if he was going to kiss me and I jerked back, hitting my head on the wall behind me. The pain brought tears to my eyes and I caught my breath.

Derwent frowned down at me. 'Kerrigan?'

I pushed him away and walked to the door of my building, my head down. He followed, not saying anything. In the lift, I stood on one side of the small space and he leaned against the other wall, watching me. I didn't look at him then or outside my front door as I fumbled to get the key in the lock. I went straight to the bathroom without taking off my coat and locked myself inside. I leaned against the door, my throat aching from the effort of not weeping.

'Kerrigan?' He was on the other side of the door, inches away.

'Give me a second.' I put my hand over my mouth to stifle the sob that was breaking through and I couldn't explain why I was so upset, except that I felt fatally, cruelly compromised. I would never have chosen to have Derwent touch me like that. It was confusing and unsettling: wrong. A violation, with the best of intentions.

It was as if Chris Swain was syphilis and Derwent was the mercury cure. Both were, in their own way, damaging to the point of being lethal.

Choose your poison, I thought, splashing cold water on my face once I'd managed to stop crying. Except that there was no choice. Not really.

I turned the tap off and dried my face and as I emerged from the towel I heard Derwent's phone ringing. I listened, not moving, as he had a brief conversation with whoever was on the other end. Then I heard him come towards the door and I unlocked it before he had time to knock on it. He looked at me and he must have known I'd been crying, but with uncharacteristic restraint he didn't mention it.

'That was Una Burt.'

'And?'

'They've found the girl.'

Chapter 30

She had made it to Kent before she ran out of luck.

'They picked her up at a truckstop near Ashford,' Una Burt told us the following morning. We were waiting for Dave Kemp and Ben Dornton to return with her from Dover, where she'd been held in custody overnight. 'She was looking for someone to take her to the Continent but she hasn't got a passport and none of the truckers would risk it.'

The penalties for helping illegal, undocumented migrants to cross borders were harsh and getting harsher all the time. I wasn't surprised she'd found it hard to find a professional driver to take her.

'Bad luck,' I commented.

Burt shrugged. 'She was making a reasonable amount of money off them. When the officers searched her she had over a thousand pounds on her in cash.'

I whistled. 'That's a lot of work, isn't it? What's the going rate for prostitutes these days?'

'You can't expect me to answer that without someone jumping to conclusions,' Derwent said.

'I promise you, it wouldn't make me think less of you.'

The way Una Burt said it expressed very clearly that there was no way for her to think less of Derwent than she did already. His eyebrows twitched together, a brief acknowledgement that she'd hit home.

'Anyway,' I said quickly, 'if she was earning that in tens and twenties, she's been working constantly since the fire. Or she nicked it from someone.'

'Or both,' Derwent said. 'A lot of punters won't make a complaint about being robbed. Too embarrassed, and too afraid of getting in trouble for using hookers.'

'I want to know where the money came from,' Burt said. 'And I want to find out what she knows about the other girls in the flat. And obviously I want to know what she saw the night of the fire. Anything else?'

'We need to get her to confirm Ray Griffin's version of events.' Derwent shrugged. 'Maybe it's me being cynical but I don't know that I believe in someone like him making a full confession.'

'He's hoping to be charged with manslaughter rather than murder. No intent to harm, according to his version of events. His solicitor says he'll plead guilty to manslaughter.'

Derwent pulled a face. 'We'll see what the CPS make of it. They won't be keen if the girl gives us a different story about what happened.'

'Do we have a name for her?' I asked.

'Not yet. Her fingerprints aren't on the system. We'll circulate them through Interpol and see if anything comes up in another jurisdiction.'

'I take it she's not saying anything.'

'Not yet.'

'Who's interviewing her?' Derwent rocked back and forth on the balls of his feet, playing it cool. He might as well not have bothered.

Una said, 'I was thinking of doing it. With Liv, or you, Maeve.'

'You think she'll respond better to women?' Derwent shook his head. 'No way. She's been told what to do by men for months, maybe years. She won't respect you. She'll think she can get around you.'

'You don't think you're going to be able to intimidate her into talking, do you?' Una shuddered. 'Spare me.'

'Take Kerrigan with you, then.' Derwent grabbed my arm and literally pulled me forward. 'Liv's all right but Kerrigan is better. She'll get inside the girl's head.'

'Thanks,' I said, surprised.

'Wouldn't say it if it wasn't true.' He levered himself off the edge of the desk he'd been sitting on and walked off. I was glad he hadn't waited to see if Una Burt took his advice. She'd have loved to disappoint him.

'Well?' She raised her eyebrows at me, challenging me. Give Liv an opportunity to shine, or act as if I was entitled to take her place? What was the right choice? Ambition or holding back? Liv needed to recover her reputation after being on sick leave for so long. It would make her more confident.

But then again, her career wasn't my concern, even if we were friends. Someone like Derwent wouldn't think twice.

What it came down to, in the end, was the case.

'Let me do it,' I said quietly.

'You think I should pick you over Liv?'

'She's a good interviewer.' I hesitated. 'I'm better.'

Una nodded, slowly. 'All right. But you'd better prove it.'

I walked away from her feeling like Judas. But I didn't feel as if I'd done the wrong thing, even when Liv glanced up from some paperwork and smiled at me, all unknowing. I loved her, but I was better.

Nonetheless, when Ben Dornton walked into the office and nodded to Una Burt, I felt my heart begin to thump. I stood up to join them, aware that Derwent was watching me.

'We've got her in interview 1.'

Una Burt nodded. 'Let's give her a cup of tea. Make her feel at home.'

'Did she say anything on the way here?' I asked.

'Not a dicky bird.' Ben shrugged. 'We did try.'

'Do you have her property?'

He handed me a plastic bag. 'Knock yourself out. All logged and checked by the custody sergeant in Ashford.'

I flattened out the bag: cigarettes, a lighter, a fold of crisp banknotes with a paper band around it, some coins, a SIM card, a badge with a kitten on it, a short, blunt pencil, an open pack of chewing gum. No ID of any kind. 'Did she have a phone?'

'Nope.'

'Dumped it?'

Dornton shrugged. 'Maybe. Maybe she didn't have anyone to call.'

The interview room was cold when I walked in. The girl sat at the table, her head down. Her hair was similar in colour to Melissa Pell's, but hers was dry from bleaching, the ends ragged and broken. She glanced up when I sat down at the table, beside Una Burt, and I felt a jolt. She was younger than Melissa, and me, but her eyes looked a hundred years older. She was tiny in a zipped hoodie and jeans, and her legs jigged constantly under the table.

'All right,' Una Burt said. 'Do you need an interpreter?'

She shook her head briefly.

'Just to explain why you're here, we have a few questions for you about the fire in Murchison House last week. You're not under caution at this point. We want to speak to you as a witness.'

Her thin face was wary, like a fox's.

'Could you tell us your name? Or a name we can call you?'

'Drina.' One word wasn't enough for me to place her accent. It thickened the consonants.

'And a last name?'

She shook her head, very definite.

'Where are you from, Drina?'

'I want to stay here. I want to claim asylum.'

Una Burt took it on the chin, even though it was a complication we could have done without. 'We can try to help you with that. At the moment we're just trying to establish how you came to be in this country with no documents.'

She shrugged.

'You were working as a prostitute, is that right?'

Another shrug, this one less certain. Drina suspected a trap.

'The men who brought you to the UK – they made you work as a prostitute.'

A nod, quick and furtive. 'Not my choice.'

'When did you come here?'

'I don't know.' Her eyes flicked around the room as if she was looking for a clue, and I realised that she was wary of committing herself. Claiming asylum was a difficult process, full of traps for the unwary. We'd be lucky to persuade her to be specific about anything.

'You're safe now,' I said. 'We're just asking you a few questions, okay?'

A nod.

'Maybe we could talk about the flat,' I suggested. 'How long had you been there?'

'Two, three months.'

'Did you work there?'

'No. They took us. We went in a car to another place. Other girls there. Lots of different girls. It was nightclub.'

'Name?'

'I don't know,' she said levelly, and I knew she wasn't going to give us a single word that would help us if she could avoid it. 'We were in back of club. Other girls were dancers, or hostesses – this is the word? But we were in back rooms.'

'What did you do in the back rooms?' Una asked and was rewarded with a look of frank bemusement.

'The men came there.'

'Many men?'

A nod.

'English men? Albanians? Russians?'

'All different.'

'Did the club have a logo? Branding?' I tried again. 'A picture they used on everything?'

'Birds. Two. Like this.' She held her hands up as if they were darting at one another.

'Any particular type of bird?' Una Burt asked.

She pushed her lips out, puzzled. 'Black. I don't know.'

Tom Bridges might be able to help us identify a particular club, if he knew of one associated with Sajmir Culaj. Drina was being more helpful than I'd expected.

'What about the other girls in the flat?' Una Burt asked. 'Do you know their names?'

'Elizabeth, she was the black girl. And Maggie. Magda, I think, but they call her Maggie because it's easy.' Drina sniffed. 'Always a name that people can say. Makes it easy.'

'Surnames?'

'No.'

'Can you tell me anything about them?'

'No.'

'Drina,' I said quietly. 'Do you know what happened at Murchison House after you ran away? Do you know what happened to Maggie and Elizabeth?'

Her eyes were wide. 'No.'

'They died, Drina. I'm sorry.'

'How?'

'They were locked inside the flat and they weren't rescued in time.'

She took a little panicky breath. 'I thought—'

'What did you think?'

'Nothing.' She looked down and I could practically see the walls going up between us, the barriers she was determined to erect between herself and her past. *Shut it down, lock it out: if it doesn't touch me, it doesn't matter.* Make someone desperate enough and you can separate them from their very humanity.

Which meant it was time to have a crack at reuniting Drina with hers.

'Is there anything you can tell us about Elizabeth and Maggie?' I asked. 'We'd like to find out who they were, even if we can't do anything else for them now. We'd like them to have names. We'd like to tell their families what happened.'

She looked up at me and there was something like surprise in her eyes. And whether it was a coincidence or not, her English suddenly improved, the syntax smoothing out, the words coming more easily.

'Elizabeth was from Liberia. She had a little sister there.' Drina swallowed. 'That's all I know. She missed her. She wanted to go home.'

'And Maggie?'

'We didn't talk.' And that was all I was getting.

'What happened the day of the fire?'

'Nothing. It was day like any day. Waiting for evening. We went to club late, at ten, eleven at night. So day was for rest. We didn't talk much. We stayed in bedrooms. Was better not to talk.'

'Were you afraid they were listening to you?'

'Of course,' she said, surprised. 'They knew what we do. Always. Maggie would not speak to me for this reason. We were both beaten, when we tried to talk.'

It was no kind of life they'd endured.

'What happened on the day of the fire?' Una asked. 'Anything different?'

'It was just the same. We were waiting. Then I noticed the smoke.' She swallowed. 'We started to try to get out. We were screaming for help. And the man came.'

'This man?' I showed her Ray Griffin's picture.

'Yes. He had been before.'

'What happened then?'

'I was scared. We were afraid. I thought he would not let us leave if we asked him. We were never allowed to leave unless it was time to go to the club. And he didn't know what to do, I could see. I kicked him and I ran.' Her bottom lip trembled. 'I thought other girls were coming too. Behind me.'

'He locked them in.'

'Stupid,' she whispered.

'Did you know he was chasing you?'

She nodded. 'I went down one floor then through the door. I thought I could hide. He was on the stairs. There was much smoke – I thought he would go past me.'

'But the fire was burning on the tenth floor,' I said.

A vigorous nod. 'So much smoke. Smoke everywhere. I waited for as long as I could and then I ran down. I didn't see the man again. I went outside and I ran as far as I could. I thought they would come after me. I couldn't wait.'

'Did you see anything strange on the way down? Anyone behaving oddly?' Una asked.

'Just scared people.' Drina tried to smile. 'I was thinking of myself. Only myself.'

'It's understandable.' Una pushed her chair back. 'We'll write up a witness statement based on what you've told us and get you to sign it.'

She shrank a little. 'I don't want to go to court.'

'We might not need you to,' Una said briskly. 'There's a very good chance this man will plead guilty before the trial gets under way. But if we need you to give evidence, please do. The men who did this to you and Maggie and Elizabeth don't deserve to get away with it.'

'But—'

'We can protect you from them. I promise you. There's nothing to fear.' Una's voice rang with sincerity, which was unsurprising, since she believed it wholeheartedly. I wasn't so sure she was right.

And I wasn't so sure the interview was over.

'Hold on a second.'

Burt had got to her feet. She sat down again, looking at me with surprise. Drina was back to looking wary.

'In your property – the things they took out of your pockets and bag in custody – there was a SIM card, but no phone. Where did the SIM card come from?'

'I don't know.'

'Is it yours?'

I could see her thinking, trying to work out how damaging it would be to tell the truth. 'No,' she said eventually.

'Whose is it?'

'I don't know.'

'Three people died last Thursday. One of them was a man, a politician. Geoff Armstrong.'

'I don't know him.'

'I can show you a picture if you like. Medium height, grey hair. Mid-fifties. Ringing any bells?'

'I don't know.'

'We found his mobile phone in pieces near the tower.

Someone had thrown it out of the window. But we didn't find his SIM card.'

Drina had the glazed look of a trapped animal. It made me think I was right. I made sure I sounded certain when I went on.

'If we examine the SIM card in your property, are we going to find out it belonged to Geoff Armstrong?'

She shook her head, stunned.

'Someone killed him, Drina. Someone strangled him and threw him out of a window, and if you've got his SIM card you're going straight to the top of my list of suspects. This is your chance to get in first. Do you want to tell me what happened? The truth, I mean?'

She thought about denying everything, thought about it for longer than I would have liked, but in the end she said something that sounded true to me. 'I didn't kill him. He was already dead when I went in.'

Una Burt stiffened beside me but she managed to hide her surprise when she spoke. 'Go on.'

'I was in the corridor on the tenth floor. The smoke was terrible. I was coughing, choking. I crawled to the door because I could see it was open. I thought I could hide in the flat for a few minutes by the window. But when I went in, I could hear crying.'

'What did you do?'

'I went in further. I wanted to get to the window and I wanted to see what was happening. There was a woman there, crying. And the man, he was on the floor. His eyes were open but he was dead. She asked me to help her. She wanted to get his body out of the window but she couldn't lift him.'

Oh, Justine . . . I hated that she'd lied to us. I hated even more that I'd believed her.

'And you did?' Una Burt raised her eyebrows. 'Didn't you have other things on your mind, like escaping from the fire and the man who was chasing you?'

'Of course. But she needed help.'

'And you needed money,' I said quietly. 'Lots of it. You had no cash, no cards, no ID. You took whatever cash you could find from him, didn't you?'

'He didn't need it any more. Anyway, he didn't have much. Ten, fifteen pounds.'

'You missed two hundred pounds in his back pocket.'

She clicked her tongue, annoyed. 'I should have checked. The woman threw the phone away. She dropped the SIM card and I picked it up. I meant to get rid of it.'

'Did you? Or did you mean to keep it? The SIM card would have told you who he was, wouldn't it? Knowledge is power. The more you knew, the better you could exploit the situation.'

Drina blinked at me, all innocence. 'I just forgot to throw it away.'

'You left his watch and his signet ring – why?' Una asked. 'They were valuable.'

'I only wanted money. A watch, a ring – people can say, "Yes, that belonged to my father." People remember watches and rings. Money has no owner.'

I nodded. 'And you wanted more money, didn't you?'

'I don't—'

'The woman gave it to you. You had over a thousand pounds in cash on you when the police picked you up at the truck stop. New notes. If you'd earned it from

387

prostituting yourself, it would have been in fives and tens and twenties, not consecutively numbered new twenties.'

She bit her lip. 'I needed to get away. She owed me. And she was rich. She could help me.'

I was thinking of Justine Rickards, of the money she'd been saving for her operation. 'What was the woman's name?'

'I don't know.'

'Where did she live? On the estate?'

'I don't know. We took a taxi to a hotel near a motorway. She paid for the taxi and for a room for three nights. She came back after two nights with money. I didn't think she'd come, but she did. I didn't see her. She put it under the door.'

'Did she give you a way to contact her?'

'No.'

'Describe her.'

A shrug. 'I can't.'

'Height.'

'I don't know.'

'Hair colour.'

'She had a scarf over her head.'

'Skin colour.'

A shrug. 'White.'

'White? Are you sure?' I didn't mean for my voice to be as sharp as it sounded.

'Yes. Of course. Like you.'

Justine Rickards was light-skinned, but there was no way on God's earth anyone could have confused her skin with my sun-hating Irish complexion.

'White,' I said.

'Yes, this is what I'm saying, white.'

'Eye colour?'

'I didn't notice.'

I sighed, frustrated. 'Age?'

'Old.' She looked at Una. 'Same as you, maybe.'

The chief inspector's mouth twitched. 'Right. Thank you.'

'If I showed you a photograph of her, would you recognise her?' I asked.

'I don't think so.'

'Drina,' I said. 'This is important.'

'I'm sorry.' She didn't sound it. 'I can't say anything more.'

Whether she couldn't or wouldn't, there was no budging her. I persevered for a little while and got nowhere. When I emerged from the interview room, Derwent was waiting outside the door.

'That was nice work.'

'Sort of.'

'Where does it leave us?'

'Looking for a white woman who wanted Armstrong dead. Someone who carried pepper spray. Someone who was made murderously angry to discover he'd been sleeping with someone else.'

'His wife.' Derwent stuck his hands in his pockets. 'He'd warned her to arm herself. I never believed she didn't know exactly where he was. There's vague and there's wilful ignorance.'

'Go and see her,' Una Burt said. 'Put her under pressure.'

'Two minutes,' I said. 'There's something I want to check first.'

Chapter 31

The house looked empty. The curtains were drawn at all
the windows, even though it was mid-morning, and there
was an indefinable air of abandonment to the place.
Derwent rang the doorbell for a good long time, his eyes
on me throughout, as if it was my fault that no one was
answering. Eventually, I saw a figure approaching the
door. It was the housekeeper who'd been making soup
the last time we visited the Armstrongs. She looked terrified when she saw us.

'We wanted to speak to Mrs Armstrong, please. Is she
here?' Derwent asked.

A nod and she stood back to let us come in, her hands
plucking the little apron she wore. The sound of footsteps
on the stairs made me look up. Elaine Lister was running
down the steps. She stopped when she saw us.

'Oh. I thought it was a delivery or the press again.'

'No. Just us.' Derwent frowned up at her. 'Where's Mrs
Armstrong?'

'She's in bed, I think.' Elaine came down another step.
'She hasn't been feeling too well.'

'Can we see her?'

'Is it just an update on the case?'

'Yes,' Derwent said easily. 'We just need a quick word with her.'

'Unless it's urgent, I'm afraid—'

'We really do need to speak to her,' I said, not having the patience to negotiate with Armstrong's secretary any longer.

'Of course.' She gave me a tight-lipped smile. 'I'll get her to come down.'

'No need.' Derwent took the stairs two at a time, arriving at Elaine's side before she had time to protest. 'We can speak to her up here.'

'Oh. I'll just go and see.' Elaine looked at the house-keeper, a look that sent the woman scurrying back to the kitchen. Then she led us up the stairs, not hurrying, until she reached a closed door. 'Wait here, please.'

She tapped on the door, then went in without waiting for an answer. I looked around, noting the paintings on the walls, the oriental rugs, the general air of wealth and privilege. It felt like a glamorous sort of prison to me, with paid warders to control every aspect of the inmates' lives.

The door opened again. 'You can come in, but not for long.'

The room was dark. It smelled sour, as if the windows hadn't been opened for a long time. Cressida Armstrong was in bed, sitting up against some pillows. She looked thinner than on our previous visit, and the half-closed eyes made me think she was dopey with drugs.

'Can we have some light in here?' Derwent asked and Elaine opened one set of curtains, the heavy oyster-coloured silk sweeping back to reveal an elaborate, highly feminine bedroom.

'Mrs Armstrong. Can you hear me?'

'Yes, of course,' she muttered. Her words were slurred.

'What's she on?' Derwent asked Elaine, his irritation obvious.

'Whatever the doctor prescribed. She was anxious. She was finding it hard to sleep.'

'Cressida, are you listening to me?' Derwent sat down on the edge of the bed. 'Cressida, I need to talk to you about Geoff.'

'He's gone.' She dragged her eyes open with an effort. 'He's left me. All alone.'

'She wasn't like this the other day,' I said in a low voice.

'It took a while to sink in. She enjoyed the attention at first. The excitement.' Elaine looked at Cressida. 'Then she realised what it meant.'

'Cressida, do you have a mobile phone?' Derwent asked.

'In my bag.' She gestured at a handbag that was on a chair near the bed.

'Can I look at it?'

'Of course.' Her eyes closed again, her head tilting back. Out of it.

Derwent pulled on some gloves and went through the bag, his movements deft and careful. The first thing he took out was a small can of pepper spray, which he put on the table by the bed. He set her mobile phone beside it and pointed at the pepper spray.

'That's not legal.'

'Geoff bought it for her. She wouldn't have known

anything about it being legal or illegal. You can take it away if you want.'

'I will,' Derwent said. He levered off the cap and looked at it. 'As I thought.'

'What? What did you think?' Elaine asked.

Derwent ignored her. He checked the phone was switched on and had reception, then nodded to me. I took out my phone and dialled the number I'd noted from Armstrong's phone records, the records that had finally turned up about ten minutes before we left the office. The three of us stared at the bedside table, at the phone. Cressida was miles away, floating on a chemical cloud of bliss. The room was so quiet, everyone could hear the purring sound from my phone as the number I had dialled rang, and rang, and rang.

The phone on the bedside table didn't so much as beep.

'What are you doing?' Elaine asked.

'Checking to see if Mrs Armstrong was in contact with her husband before he died.' I sighed. 'No luck.'

'What number did you dial?'

'The last number he called.' I shook my head at Derwent. 'Out of luck, I'm afraid.'

I could hear the regular tread of someone climbing the stairs, not quickly. There was a tap on the door and the housekeeper's worried face peered around it. She held out a phone to Elaine Lister. 'You left your phone downstairs. Someone called you. Just now. I thought it might be urgent.'

I thought Elaine was going to smack it out of her hand. She lunged towards the housekeeper and I stepped in the way, shoving her back against a chest of drawers.

Framed photographs toppled over and Cressida opened her eyes.

'That's interesting,' Derwent said, having taken the phone himself. 'That's your number, Kerrigan.'

'Imagine that,' I said flatly.

'Elaine Lister, you are under arrest for the murder of Geoff Armstrong on the twenty-eighth of November of this year. You do not have to say anything unless you wish to do so, but it may harm your defence if you fail to mention when questioned something you later rely on in Court. Anything you say will be used in evidence.'

'This is insane.' Elaine twisted in my grip, trying to get free.

'We can work out exactly where the phone has been, you see. And when. We can put you in the flat with Armstrong when he died.' Derwent looked at Elaine and his expression was cold. 'We've got a witness.' Who was probably not going to cooperate with us. 'We've got you on CCTV.' An image so smudgy that she was truly unidentifiable, her head hidden with a scarf. Derwent moved on to more solid ground. 'We've got the cashier's stamp and initials on the cool grand you dropped on paying off your little accomplice, so we can work out which bank you got it from and check their CCTV to prove the money came from you. Your money, your bank account, your partner in crime who's in custody even as we speak. We have your phone. And Cressida's pepper spray has never been used. It's still sealed. I think we'll find that yours, on the other hand, *was* used. And it was used on Geoff Armstrong himself, just before you killed him.'

'Fuck you,' Elaine spat. She tried to struggle away from me but I held on to her.

'Why did you do it, Elaine? Tell us. We know everything else, and we can prove it. You loved him, didn't you?' Derwent's tone was calm. Conversational. Reasonable, even. 'Why did you kill him?'

'Why were you even there?' I frowned at her, as if she puzzled me. As if I thought she was pathetic. 'He didn't need you. He didn't want you. So why were you there?'

The words tore out of her. 'I wanted to help him. I wanted to rescue him.'

'Did you start the fire?'

'No. No, of course not. I followed him there. I always did. It wasn't safe for him to be there. I waited downstairs, in case he needed me. And then he did.' Her face was glistening with sweat and tears and her nose was running. She couldn't have looked less attractive, less heroic, less like the image of herself she'd had as she charged up the stairs to the rescue. 'I heard the alarms. I saw the smoke. I called him and he wasn't going to leave. I mean, I could see flames. It wasn't just a little fire. It was breaking windows, bursting through the walls. He was in terrible danger.'

'And you went to rescue him.'

'I wanted to help him get out. I saw *her*.'

'Her?'

'The black *bitch* he was fucking. *She* ran away. She *left* him. She can't have cared about him at all.'

I didn't think it was the right moment to explain about Armstrong and Justine and their arrangement.

In the bed, Cressida stirred. 'What did she say? Who?'

Elaine ignored her, thankfully. She was absorbed in her own difficulties, her own sacrifices.

'I went to save him, even though it was dangerous.'

'And he didn't appreciate it,' I said quietly. 'He shouted at you.'

'He called me a moron.' She sobbed, once. 'I had the pepper spray in my hand. I don't know what I was thinking. It just made me so angry that he spoke to me like that. I've given him *everything*. I was risking my life for him. I sprayed him with it and he was completely furious.' Tears filled her eyes. 'The things he said. He shouted. I couldn't bear it. He was kneeling down at my feet, rubbing his eyes, and I put my scarf around his neck and pulled. I wanted to make him take me seriously. I wanted him to be scared of me. I wanted him to know how angry I was. I wanted him to realise he couldn't speak to me that way.' She blinked. 'It was only supposed to scare him. But then – then he died . . .'

She broke down, weeping and raging at us, at Cressida who was struggling to understand what was going on. The housekeeper wept too, in the hall, sitting on a chair with a hand over her mouth. Reluctantly, Derwent handcuffed Elaine for our safety and her own, with her wrists in front of her. Something about being handcuffed made her calmer, as if it made it all real in a way it hadn't been before. I helped her down the stairs as Derwent called for a van to transport her to the nearest police station. He phoned Una Burt too, to give her the good news, and he wasn't standing quite far enough away from the house as he spoke, the ring of triumph all too audible to me. Elaine Lister shivered like a puppy beside me in the hall. I watched her in a great gilt-framed mirror that hung on the wall, not quite able to stare at her directly. She was gulping air in a way I recognised.

'Are you all right?'

'I think – I think I'm going to be sick.' She jumped up and I stood too. 'There's a cloakroom here – if I might – Oh, *God* . . .'

It was a tiny room, a sink and a lavatory and nothing but a framed print on the wall. I let her go in and stood outside with the door open, listening to the too-familiar retch and spatter.

Derwent came through the front door and raised his eyebrows. 'Escaped, has she?'

'Being sick,' I said, glancing at Derwent. *Better here than in the van*, we were both thinking, and we thought it for a second too long. I heard the crack and tinkle of glass breaking and I knew what it was before I even turned around: she had used the handcuffs to smash the thin picture glass to long, cutting shards. I moved as quickly as I could, hurling myself through the doorway, and it was too slow but I was never going to be fast enough to stop her.

I got a hand to the rigid bar that linked the cuffs and dragged it down with as much force as I could muster, pulling her hands down, away from her face, yanking her into the hall to sprawl on the carpet. I put my foot on the cuffs, holding her hands down as Derwent carefully drew a four-inch piece of glass out from between her fingers.

'She's bleeding,' he said. 'Check her.'

I turned her over, not seeing any injury. Her eyes were closed, her face shuttered. As I bent over her she coughed fat droplets of blood that splattered against my cheek, my neck, my shirt.

'Oh shit.' I forced her mouth open as wide as I could and peered in. Her mouth and throat were filling with blood. 'I think she swallowed some glass.'

'Right.' Derwent bent down and gathered her into his arms. He carried her out to the car, at speed. She was limp, semi-conscious or pretending to be.

I ran to open the back door. 'Should I call an ambulance?'

'No point in waiting. We've got blue lights too.' He laid her on the back seat and straightened up. 'Sit in the back with her. Stop her from falling off the seat if you can. And don't let her get away with anything else.'

I put a hand to my head, distraught. 'I'm sorry, I—'

'Not now,' he snapped and I had to be content with that, and the murderous look that accompanied it.

If you ever want to know what true fear is, I highly recommend being in a car driven by Josh Derwent on a blue-light run. I gnawed through my bottom lip, hanging on to Elaine Lister for dear life as we cut through the north London traffic like a scalpel. It took us three or four minutes to get to the hospital, the one where the burn victims had been, with the sirens screaming all the way. I cradled Elaine, who was silent except for an occasional cough that racked her body. I sacrificed my jacket to cover her mouth, to catch the spray of blood that each cough forced out of her. Her breathing was shallow and a gurgling sound accompanied every breath: her lungs and airway filling with blood, I guessed, and I didn't mind how fast we went or how many close calls we had on the way, as long as she didn't die in my arms. Derwent swung in through the ambulances-only entrance and pulled up outside the A & E department, jumping out of the car almost before it had stopped.

'Bit of help here, please,' he shouted, summoning paramedics who lifted Elaine and transferred her to a trolley, checking, assessing but most of all moving her as fast as they could towards proper medical care. We went with her, as far as we were allowed to go, Derwent fumbling with his handcuff key as the triage nurse tutted at the cuffs.

Elaine was our prisoner, still.

When they moved her to surgery we went too, occupying one of the rooms for relatives. Una Burt arrived with Chris Pettifer and Mal Upton and Liv and pretty much everyone who wasn't doing anything else, and they listened while I explained how it was I'd managed to allow a murderer enough space to harm herself just minutes after she'd confessed. Derwent neither damned me nor defended me until Chris Pettifer made a crack at my expense.

'She did all right.' Derwent didn't look in my direction. His focus was all on Pettifer, on putting him in his place. 'She got the situation under control quickly and safely. Couldn't have asked her to do much more.'

Liv patted my hand, unseen by everyone else, and I was grateful for the support. Somehow, brusque though it was, what Derwent had said meant more to me than anything – more than Liv's sympathy, or Una Burt's muttered reassurance.

It felt like an endless wait until the surgeon was finished with Elaine Lister, in a room that got increasingly stuffy. Derwent went out at one point, too restless to sit still, and I went after him. He was striding down the corridor, away from me.

'Hey,' I called.

He looked back. 'What do you want?'

'Thanks for sticking up for me.'

'It's all right.'

'No, really. I – I made a mistake. I know I did.' I caught up with him. 'But you were kind about it and I appreciate it.'

'You did make a mistake. But so did I.' Derwent shook his head. 'Never cuff them in front, no matter how meek and mild they seem to be. I know that. You know it too. If she'd been cuffed with her hands behind her, we wouldn't be here now. We'd be home and dry.'

'*My* home,' I said. 'Don't get too comfortable.'

'Technically, it's your boyfriend's home. Your ex-boyfriend, I mean.' Derwent raised his eyebrows. 'Do you even pay rent?'

'That's none of your business,' I said, stung. 'And if you don't move out soon, I'm going to start charging *you* rent.'

'I make a valuable non-monetary contribution to your life and don't you forget it.'

'I wish I could.'

He flashed a grin at me that lit up his face for a second. Then he dismissed me with, 'I'll see you later.'

'Where are you going?'

'Coffee,' Derwent said, walking away.

'I drink coffee too.'

'Don't follow me.'

'But—'

'Don't follow me. I mean it.' He turned to frown at me. 'Stay. Good dog. Stay.'

I stood and watched him until he was out of sight. It shouldn't have surprised me that Derwent wanted to be alone.

After all, he was one hundred per cent full-blooded diva.

Chapter 32

I lasted another fifteen minutes in the waiting room before I began to fantasise about killing everyone around me, slowly. Ordinarily I would never have followed an example set by Derwent, but it seemed to me he had the right idea. I slid out of the room without saying anything to anyone about where I was going. I wasn't altogether sure myself.

I wandered through the familiar corridors and stairwells until I reached the ward where the fire's victims had been. Only Mary Hearn was left now. The police officer's chair outside the door was unattended. I stood and looked at it for a moment, wondering when Una Burt had given the order to stop guarding Mary Hearn. When she had outlived her usefulness? When Una had run out of hours to spend on guard duty? When the case had moved on? When it had become clear to me – and I presumed everyone else – that we had made no progress whatsoever on identifying the arsonist? It was unlikely that we'd track them down now, I thought. All the secrets of Murchison House – all the sorrow, and pain, and hidden hurt – had drifted away from me like smoke, to dissipate against the clear blue winter sky. The building would be repaired. The flats would fill up with new residents, or the old ones bravely returning. Everything would be the same as it was before, except for the Bellews, and Geoff Armstrong, and the unknown women who had died there.

I went through the doors and headed over to the nurses' station, where a middle-aged nurse gave me a not particularly welcoming look. I held up my ID.

'I just wanted to check up on Mary Hearn. How is she?'

The nurse's manner warmed slightly. 'She's much better. She's talking to us now. Much more like her old self.'

'Is she still mentally all there?'

'She's still sharp as anything.' The nurse half-smiled. 'She doesn't let us get away with much, I can tell you.'

I smiled, relieved. 'That's a sign she's on the mend.'

'It is. Mind you, she'll need to do a lot of physio. The stroke affected her left side. She's very weak. She won't be running any marathons for a while.'

'Can I see her?'

'Of course. She's in room 310. Her daughter is with her at the moment.'

I had started to move away, but I stopped. 'Her daughter?'

'Yes, she's just arrived. I think she was abroad or something. She got here about two minutes before you did.' The nurse smiled up at me. The smile faded from her face. 'Is everything all right?'

'She doesn't have a daughter. Which way is her room?'

She pointed to the left and I ran, almost crashing into

a doctor as I rounded the corner. I ignored him, skirted a patient who was edging along on a walking frame, and hurled myself into room 310.

It took me a second to orientate myself: the curtains were drawn around the bed and the window blind was down so the light was dim. I slid between the curtains and saw a figure bent over the bed, standing between me and Mrs Hearn. From the end of the bed it looked innocent – touching, even. But Mrs Hearn was trying to struggle, her legs moving weakly under the covers. The woman didn't look around even when I shouted, '*Get back!*'

She was intent on what she was doing, the effort vibrating in her arms and across her shoulders. When I got close enough to grab her I could see her hand was over Mrs Hearn's mouth, her fingers pinching the old woman's nostrils closed, cutting off her air. I got hold of her wrists and elbowed her back from the bed, pushing her through the curtains so I could pin her against the wall as I shouted for help. It wasn't long in coming: the nurse from the desk had followed me. She exclaimed in horror at the sight of Mrs Hearn, her eyes closed, her lips blue, her cheeks sunken. The nurse pressed an alarm button that brought running feet from all over the ward, and competent medical staff who swung into practised routines to knock Death's hand off Mrs Hearn's shoulder.

As they worked on her I struggled with my prisoner, who was desperately trying to get free, and I hadn't the least idea what was going on but I'd recognised her as soon as I laid hands on her. She was shorter than me, and thinner, and her hair had loosened so it fell into her eyes, and none of that helped her. She raked at my face, her nails gouging my skin even though I jerked my head back. I got tired of that very quickly and kicked her leg as hard as I could, knocking her off balance enough for me to get her onto the floor where she was easier to control. I knelt on her shoulder, trying to stop her from fighting without hurting her. A solidly built male nurse squatted on her legs, which helped. I needed both hands to hold her wrists behind her, since my cuffs were two floors down in the waiting room near the operating theatre.

'Get off me,' she howled. 'I can't breathe. I can't breathe.'

'That's a lot of shouting for someone who can't breathe,' I observed. I was trying to see how the doctors were doing with Mrs Hearn. The bed was surrounded by people in scrubs barking observations and instructions at one another, and all I could conclude was that they were still trying to keep her alive, so there had to be a chance they'd succeed.

'You're killing me,' the woman sobbed.

'Nope. Arresting you.' And I did just that, reciting her rights, all the while wondering what the hell was going on.

Eventually some security staff arrived and took over for me, so I could call Una Burt. I was still out of breath from fighting the woman, and my cheek stung like a bastard.

When the chief inspector answered her phone, she sounded irritated. 'What is it, Maeve? Where are you?'

'I've got one in custody,' I said, trying not to pant. 'Room 310.'

A short pause. Then, 'What for?'

'Murder.' I looked at the bed, where Mrs Hearn was shaking her head slowly and trying to talk. 'Actually, make that attempted murder.' On the floor, Debbie Bellew snarled and fought. I touched my face, where it hurt, and my fingertips came away red. 'And assault on a police officer. Let's stick that one on the charge sheet too.'

I had a brief reunion with the police constable who'd been guarding Mrs Hearn: he was one of the response officers who turned up to transport my prisoner to the nearest police station.

'I don't believe it. All that time waiting for something to happen, and the second I leave it all kicks off.'

'Which suggests you were doing a pretty good job,' I pointed out, as Una Burt came to stand beside me, looking shattered.

'Who is she?'

'Her name is Debbie Bellew,' I said. 'She's the mother of one of the fire victims.'

'What was she doing here?'

'I have no idea.'

'Good thing you happened to come along today.'

'Yes, it was.' I said it soberly. It was just luck that Mrs Hearn had survived; luck, and a determination to cling to life that I admired. It wasn't as if she had all that much to look forward to, in my view, but she was a fighter, and she hadn't given up yet.

Derwent appeared in the doorway, scowling darkly. He paused to take in the whole scene: the response officers, the prisoner, the milling medical staff who were now pretty much just gawking, the dressing on my face.

'I leave you on your own for five minutes, Kerrigan. Five minutes.' He bit his lip, which could have been concern, if I was thinking the best of him. 'What's under the bandage?'

I unpeeled the tape to show him: three scrapes that a nurse had cleaned quickly, but more thoroughly than I could have wished.

It wasn't concern that had him biting his lip after all. He'd been trying not to laugh. It broke out on his face as a wide, wide grin. 'Did they give you one of those cone collar things to stop you scratching at it?'

'Ha ha,' I said acidly.

Una Burt frowned at Derwent. 'Where did you spring from? Where were you?'

'I was just—' he broke off as Mrs Hearn made a low, groaning sound. They had propped her up against some pillows, at her request, and a nurse sat beside the head of the bed, watching her carefully. She looked frail, and bruised, and above all confused. 'Is she all right?'

'For someone who just nearly died,' Burt said tartly. I wondered if she'd noticed his neat sidestepping of the question about where he'd been when I needed him. I had noticed it and filed it away for a future discussion.

'Who – who is she? What did she want with me?' Mrs Hearn's voice was slurred at the edges but she was coherent.

'It's your neighbour from flat 101,' I explained.

Debbie gave a wail that made the hairs stand up on the back of my neck. She was writhing in distress.

'Take her away,' Una Burt said to the uniformed officers.

'See if you can get her assessed by someone in mental health before you take her to the police station, though. I don't want her having to come back here to be sectioned if this is where she needs to be.'

'No. Not yet.' Mrs Hearn squinted across the room. 'What's your name?'

'Debbie.' She twisted her body. 'Let me go. I have to go.'

'I saw you.' Mrs Hearn nodded. 'Before the fire.'

'No!' Debbie screamed the word, then started sobbing. 'I have to go. Take me away. I don't want to be here any more.'

'You saw her?' I was concentrating on Mrs Hearn. 'Where did you see her?'

'On my television. In the hallway.'

'Debbie went out to do some shopping,' I said to Una Burt. 'That's why she wasn't in the flat.'

'Shopping.' Mrs Hearn nodded. 'But she stopped on the way.'

'Shut up. Shut up.' Debbie was shaking her head. Her limbs were trembling. '*Shut up.*'

'She was in the cupboard. The storage whatchamacallit in the hall. I saw her.'

'Are you sure?' Una Burt demanded.

'Oh yes. I wondered, you know. Strange place to be.'

'What was she doing in there?'

Mrs Hearn blinked slowly. 'I don't know, dear. I couldn't see.'

I turned to look at Debbie, at the tears that streaked her face. 'Mrs Bellew . . . were you in the cupboard?'

A storm of sobbing was my answer.

The smoke alarm had been disabled.

Something had started a fire in or near the store cupboard, a space full of chemicals and flammable material.

Debbie had been haggard with worry about the cause of the fire.

Debbie had tried to find out what we knew about how the fire started.

Debbie had tried to divert attention from herself by hinting about her husband's business.

Debbie had worked out there was one possible witness to what she'd done.

I had *told* her there was one possible witness to what she had done.

'Were you smoking in the cupboard?' I asked.

'I can't . . .'

'Mrs Bellew, tell me the truth. Were you smoking in the cupboard?'

'No.' It sounded weak and she knew it. 'Maybe. I put it out, though. I made sure it was out. It couldn't have been me who started the fire. Not me. I was careful. I was *careful*.'

Between one thing and another, it was hours before I was finished with Debbie Bellew. It made me tremendously sad to have to take her to the local police station and sit with her while we waited for a solicitor, and then to interview her about what she'd done the night of the fire. I spoke to Andrew Harper, the fire investigator, who confirmed that an unattended cigarette and the cleaning products in the cupboard could have caused a fire that should have been easy to put out, if it hadn't gone on for long enough to spread inside the building's ventilation system.

'Get as much information from her as you can about what was in the cupboard and where she put the cigarette when she had finished smoking it. We can create a similar set-up at headquarters and work out what went wrong.'

'To stop it from happening again.'

'In an ideal world,' Harper said. 'But you can't account for circumstances. People will always make mistakes. Accidents will always happen.'

It was true. And you could go mad, I thought, if you were doomed to go back through the ifs of this case for ever, as Debbie Bellew undoubtedly would. Four people had died but if the smoke alarm had been working, or if Debbie had noticed her cigarette wasn't out, or if she'd waited until she got to the car park, or even if the lift had been working in the first place none of it might have happened. One action in the chain of events led to another and the consequences, for Debbie and her family, for the girls we knew as Elizabeth and Maggie, and for Geoff Armstrong, had been catastrophic.

And Debbie knew it. She'd thought about little else since the fire. Now she was grieving for her daughter, and suffering the added burden of guilt and shame. But that didn't excuse what she had tried to do to Mrs Hearn. It didn't begin to excuse it.

I dragged myself out of the police station and took a taxi back to the office to dump the paperwork. The lights dazzled me through the sleet that battered the taxi's windows. The streets were empty, glassy with rain.

Debbie would be in court the following morning, a first appearance to remand her in custody. I wanted to be there. I was superstitious about not going to court. It was too easy for everything to go wrong when your back was turned.

I felt like death as I walked into the building, heading for the lift rather than the stairs. I was too tired to walk straight, let alone climb stairs. My face hurt. My feet hurt. I was freezing, too, because Elaine Lister's blood had done for my jacket and I'd left my coat in Derwent's car. A thin blouse was not enough clothing to keep out the cold on a chilly December night.

The place was deserted, the lights mostly off. A cleaner was vacuuming in Una Burt's office. He was a sad-eyed man who didn't even glance in my direction, or at the boards that lined her room, or the pictures and maps and notes that covered them. Incurious, because it was in his interests not to see what we saw every day. We could have been selling insurance, as far as he was concerned. An office was an office. And the fact that it was filled with other people's nightmares wasn't his problem.

I left my things on my desk and stretched, feeling my joints complain. Too much sitting. Too much stress. Too many sudden movements.

Too many fights.

What I needed was a drink, and someone to hold me, and talk me down from the unhappy, uneasy ledge I'd clambered onto in the course of the day. My nerves were raw, my mind buzzing even though I was tired. I needed peace. I needed comfort.

What I needed was Rob.

What I got was a clatter as Mal Upton pushed open the door and knocked over the cleaner's mop. He stared down at it, surprised. 'How did that get there?'

'I think someone knocked it over,' I said.

He made heavy weather of picking it up again and sticking it in the bucket so it was balanced. 'What are you doing here?'

'I just finished dealing with Debbie Bellew. Your turn.'

'Getting things done,' he said vaguely. 'I was just going.'

'Me too.'

'Can I give you a lift home?' His face was comically earnest, and hopeful, but at the same time I sensed he was braced for disappointment.

'That would be brilliant.'

'Really?' He beamed. 'Great.'

'I can't invite you in,' I said, recalling a little too late that Derwent would be there.

He leaned on a desk, dislodging a stack of files that slid across the surface like a fan opening. 'I was just offering you a lift.'

'I know.' I thought about trying to explain that I'd been being friendly instead of treating him like a free taxi service but I was too tired, too worn out. I picked up my bag. 'Are you ready to go?'

'Yeah.' He reached over and grabbed his coat, which got stuck on the arm of his chair and a few seconds of awkwardness and swearing passed, while I tried to pretend I hadn't noticed.

We went down the stairs to the car park and I was half asleep as I walked over to his car, yawning widely and uninhibitedly. At least Derwent kept me awake, I thought, even if that was because it was hard to sleep when you were dancing on a razor blade. Mal was peaceful. Unchallenging. Quietly adoring.

I needed to learn how to put up with that.

Mal drove to the exit and tapped in his code in to open the gate. He let his car roll forward as the gates started to move. It was a VW Golf; it didn't need a lot of space. He judged it perfectly, flashing through the gap while the gates were bare inches from the car, and he glanced at me, and grinned, and the side of the car caved in. The side pillar went, the windscreen exploded, the car crumpled like paper, the airbags blew and I was swinging sideways, weightless in my seat, knowing I'd land soon and that when I did, it would hurt. The seconds stretched for hours. I looked beyond Mal, trying to work out what was happening, squinting against the lights of the car that had crashed into us. It was a Range Rover, a tank that had a weight and height advantage over us, and the engine roared as it drove Mal's car sideways, swung it around and slammed us into a brick wall. The front of the VW disintegrated, effectively, with a sound like the end of the world, and we came to a stop.

The Range Rover's engine noise changed as the driver put it into reverse. It moved back, metal grinding on metal, and Mal's car juddered as it released us like a cat bored with a dead mouse. I felt deafened, numbed. I could smell something acrid and chemical, something that made me think we should get out of the car and not waste any time about it. Somehow, I couldn't coordinate undoing my seatbelt and trying the door. It was easier to wait for someone to rescue me. Someone would come.

Mal was silent beside me. I tried to look at him but my head weighed a hundred tons and it wouldn't move, and besides, I was so tired.

My door opened and a man leaned in, undid my seat-belt, slid a hand under my knees and behind my back, and lifted me out.

'I'm all right,' I said, when I manifestly wasn't, and my rescuer ignored me. He carried me a short distance as the icy rain stung my face and hands, and then I was inside a car, on the back seat, sheltered. Safe. The car door shut.

Rescued.

I looked out of the window at the heap of incomprehensible metal that the VW had become, and missed the moment that my rescuer climbed into the driver's seat of the car. The outside world began to move, the misshapen wreckage disappearing into the darkness, and I looked down at my hands, at the cable tie that was cutting into my wrists, and then I looked at the back of the driver's head and I knew him.

I knew him.

It wasn't rescue, after all.

Quite the opposite.

Chapter 33

The Range Rover proved one thing: if you wanted a car that could annihilate another vehicle in a crash and then drive away, it was worth the money. It passed through the empty streets at a reasonable pace – not fast enough to ping any speed cameras or attract the attention of a traffic car, but quickly. I tried to keep track of our route but there were few enough landmarks as we went north and out through the endless, featureless London suburbs. All I could tell was that Chris Swain had a destination in mind and knew his route well enough not to need a map, or sat nav, or anything that might have given me a clue about where we were going and where we might end up. London was huge, epically sprawling, and yet it didn't seem long at all before we were out of the reach of the orange streetlights, cutting through darkness on what looked like country roads. He wasn't using the main roads, I realised, with their ANPR cameras and CCTV and other drivers. He was effectively invisible on the narrow lanes that ran parallel to the major routes, the old highways that had been superseded by multi-lane motorways.

I sat still in the back of the car, my eyes half-closed, as if I was barely conscious. I didn't try to talk, or escape. The cable ties were impossible to break and I had nothing to cut them. I was thinking as fast as my sluggish brain would allow, thinking about whether I still had my phone in my pocket or if I'd dropped it into my bag – my bag which was probably in the wreckage of Mal's car. I couldn't remember, and it seemed terribly important even though I was miles away from being able to call for help.

What I mainly thought about, however, was Chris Swain and what he was planning to do with me. I thought about what I knew about him, and how I might use that against him.

I thought about what I might do to survive.

After a stretch of time that I couldn't quite measure, the car slowed, turned down a side lane and bumped along an unpaved track for a hundred yards or so, to an open gate. He drove into an unlit space beside a low building, the wheels bumping over cobbles.

'Where are we?' I asked, and was ignored.

He got out, locking me inside the car, and disappeared into the building. A security light came on, flooding the yard with white light that made me squint. It went out once he went inside but it had done its work: I had no night vision at all now. It was like being blind for a few seconds. I felt a bubble of panic rise up from the pit of my stomach, from the part of me that wasn't rationalising and planning and considering – the part of me that knew I was in danger. Panic was unproductive.

Fear was not my friend.

Light leaked out from behind the curtains and I got a

better impression of the building: a low farmhouse, one storey, a simple, small house. The door opened and he was briefly silhouetted against the light: he was bigger than I remembered, as if he'd been putting on muscle. He had a full beard now and it blurred the outline of his face, hiding the weak jaw I remembered. He started to cross the yard and the light came on again. This time I was expecting it, and I shielded my eyes so I could watch him. His hands were empty. He moved with absolute confidence towards me and I waited because I didn't have much of a choice about it.

The door lock clicked and he pulled it open. The cold air took my breath away. It smelled of farmland, of animals and grass. We had to be somewhere in Hertfordshire or Bedfordshire, I thought, but I wasn't sure and anyway, it didn't matter. He reached in and I held my hands out of the way to let him get at the seatbelt release, cooperating. I wanted to get into the house. I had a better chance in the house to put some space between me and Swain. He let the seatbelt zip back into its holder and took my wrists in his hands, just above where the cable ties cut into them.

'No fighting.'

I shook my head.

'And no shouting. There's no one to hear you, but it bores me.' His voice was flat. Unemotional. He should have been excited, or edgy, but he wasn't. Dead calm.

I looked into Chris Swain's eyes and I knew, without a shadow of a doubt, that his intention was to kill me. Whatever happened before that, it would end with my death. I could fight. I could try to run. I could cooperate.

I could do whatever he wanted and play whatever games he liked.

He would kill me in the end.

He drew me out of the car and got behind me so he could walk me over to the door. I dragged a little, limping, looking around at the barns that formed two sides of the yard. They seemed to be empty, unused. It looked as if Swain was operating alone, which didn't surprise me. He wasn't the kind to share. At least that meant I only had him to deal with, though. He was quite enough on his own. He kneed me in the back of the thigh.

'Hurry up.'

'It's my leg,' I said. 'I must have hurt it in the crash.'

He clicked his tongue in irritation and I stopped feeling scared for one glorious second of pure rage. That took me inside the house, where I stopped. It was just as cold inside as in the yard. I looked around at the big brick fireplace, the faded sofas, the dried flower arrangements in the window.

'This is nice.' I was striving to sound calm myself. It would unsettle him, I thought, if I wasn't scared. 'Not exactly your style, I'd have thought, but nice.'

'It suits my purposes.'

'A farm?'

'It used to be a farm. There are no animals here any more.' He shoved me forward, towards the upright chair that stood in the middle of the room. 'Sit.'

I sat. He busied himself with more cable ties, passing them around my elbows and through the back of the chair so my arms were pulled back. It was agony.

'Please. I can't sit like this.'

He ignored me in favour of lighting the fire, fussing around with firelighters and kindling, poking at it as the flames sullenly refused to catch. The wood smoked and I coughed without meaning to, but I saw it irritate him. He gave up after a while, leaving the fire to its own devices, and disappeared into the small kitchen off the living room. He came back with a glass and a bottle of Scotch and sat on the sofa opposite me.

'No thanks,' I said.

'It's not for you.' He poured himself a generous measure and knocked it back, hissing as it hit home.

'Dutch courage?' It sounded bitchy. Somehow I couldn't stop myself from mocking him. It would have been so much more sensible to be pleasant.

'Shut up.' He poured more whisky into his glass and sat back, eyeing me. 'What happened to your face?'

'Don't you know?' I shook my head slowly. 'You must be slipping.'

His mouth was tight with annoyance and he hid it behind the rim of the glass as he took a sip.

'My turn for a question. What's the plan?'

'What do you mean?'

'The plan. You have a plan, I know that. Part one worked very well. You got me. So what's part two?'

'You'll see.' Another sip.

'That's just rude,' I said. 'Discourteous. You're the one in charge, Chris. You're the one who's running this show. I just want to know what to expect.'

'Patience.' He was smirking now.

'All right,' I snapped. 'Fine. If you don't want to talk

about that, we won't talk about it. But since we're here, face to face, after all this time, I would like to know one thing. You owe me that much.'

He laughed. 'I don't owe you shit.'

'I disagree.' I pulled my shoulders back, trying to get into a more comfortable position. 'And it's not a difficult question to answer, I think.'

'All right. Ask.'

I looked at him levelly. 'Why me? Setting aside for the moment that you're insane, what is it about me that made you decide to ruin my life?'

'Ruin your life?' he repeated. 'You've done that yourself, Maeve. I can't say I'm impressed with the choices you've been making. I thought you'd try to trade up after the last one, but you just moved on to the nearest available cock, even if it happens to belong to your boss.'

'Derwent?' I laughed. 'Yeah. That's exactly what happened. But let me tell you, it's worth it.'

'I don't want to hear it.'

'Oh, you do. You can't stop yourself.' I smirked. 'Do you know what I've discovered? It's kind of a turn-on to think of you wanking yourself raw while we're fucking.'

'Stop,' he said, violently, and I did, for a moment. Then I tried again.

'Will you tell me why you're doing this?'

'I don't know.'

'Bullshit. That's not a good enough answer. You don't go to these lengths and not know why.'

He started to smile. 'I think you've just answered your own question. Look at you. You're still fighting. You don't ever give up. You don't know how.'

It was true, I had to acknowledge. 'It's not in my nature.'

'I like challenges, Maeve. I like to go places I'm not supposed to go. Hacking is the same kind of thrill. Breaking the unbreakable. Getting through whatever defences they think they have. Using their strengths against them. Getting my own way.' He smiled and I felt a chill. 'You're the one thing I couldn't crack, no matter how I tried. Anyone else would have broken a long time ago.'

'I don't know how,' I said simply. 'I don't know what I would have to do to give in.'

'You're not scared of anything. I trapped you in the tower block and you got yourself out. The car – you didn't give a shit about it. I was watching. You just called your boss, as if all you needed was a lift.'

'It wasn't my car,' I said. I didn't want to think about how scared he had made me. How unsettling it had been. How deeply shaken I had felt. If he thought I wasn't afraid of him, I was happy to let him keep thinking it. 'I knew it was your work too. You're very predictable, Chris.'

He laughed, and there was something jittery about it. He was nervous. 'You didn't predict this.'

I shrugged. 'I knew you'd come for me one day.'

Chris sipped his drink, smiling to himself. 'I looked up your name, you know. Maeve. She was a great warrior queen of old Ireland. Your parents named you well.'

I snorted. 'I hate to break it to you but I was named after my granny. She kept chickens and she made bread every day and prayed a decade of the rosary every time she had a spare five minutes and her house always smelled of soup. She was a lovely person but she was no warrior queen, mate.'

He looked discomfited. 'It's appropriate. That's all.'

'You're right, though. Names can be revealing,' I said, relenting. 'Especially the names we choose for ourselves.'

'What do you mean?'

'Aktaion.' I let the word hang in the air for a second and I saw him react, his pupils widening in shock. 'I've been finding out more about you, too. I looked it up – the name you called yourself. It's from Greek mythology. He was the hunter who saw Artemis bathing, wasn't he?'

A nod.

'That's how you see yourself. A brave hunter. And you like to look, especially if you can get away without being seen. The women you raped didn't even know you'd done it. You drugged them. They weren't awake while you used their bodies. They were barely alive.' I frowned. 'And I'm sorry if I don't see the challenge there.'

'I didn't want to hurt anyone.'

Didn't. Past tense. We'd come a long way from that, I realised.

'You didn't want to get caught.'

'I liked being in control. I liked being able to do what I wanted without asking permission. I liked not having to beg.' He sneered. 'You women. You're all the same. You moan and you complain and you demand. You spend your lives making us crawl to you, as if you're something special.'

'I'm sorry. Were you saying something? All I could hear was a high-pitched whine.'

His face darkened. 'Someone in your position shouldn't try to make me angry.'

'I've never tried to have any effect on you at all,' I said quietly.

He sat and sipped his drink, glaring at me.

'Do you know what I think? I think you did those things because you don't believe that anyone could ever love you. You don't believe that anyone would want to be with you because of who you are.'

He snorted. 'Great. Psychoanalysis.'

'Far from it. Common sense.' I smiled. 'Do you know what people really think of you? They worship you. You're the high priest of this weird little world of yours. If you want love, you just have to show your face online.'

His jaw clenched. 'What do you know about my world?'

'I made it my business to find out about it. About you. About what you set in motion. If you're staring at me, you have to expect me to look back.'

'And what did you find out?'

'It's shady, isn't it? The secret side of the internet. Selling drugs and weapons and information. Hacking and hiding in the name of freedom.' I shook my head. 'It doesn't contribute anything useful to society. It allows people to indulge their secret obsessions. Things they'd never admit in the cold light of day. People like you pretend it's all right to abandon morality, as if you're flying a flag for something bigger than yourselves. Freedom of speech. Freedom to behave however you like. It's childish, Chris. It doesn't impress me. And that's before you even start thinking about the pornography. I've looked at the images. I've seen more than my share of kids being hurt. Women being tortured. Animals. It gets more and more extreme, doesn't it? What was once shocking becomes

423

mundane. You want to see more. You want to be shocked. You want to be thrilled. And it's all secret. No one will ever find out.' I stared him down. 'You're harming people. *You*. You might not be in the room with them but you are a part of the process that put them there. You're the one who makes it worthwhile to rape and kill little kids.'

'On the contrary. My websites provide a safe space. They allow people to explore their darker desires safely. It takes away their need to experiment in real life. The images you've seen – most of them were made years ago. The same ones do the rounds over and over again. Those kids are grown up by now, or long gone. It's over. There's no one to rescue. There's no one to blame any more.'

'Is that how you make peace with yourself?'

'I don't have to. I don't need to argue with you about it.' He tilted his glass to finish his drink, then set the glass down on the table. 'I'm glad we had this chat. It's been very interesting. I wish we could spend longer talking.'

'I'm not going anywhere,' I said drily.

'You're going into the other room.'

I felt a chill ghost over me. 'What's in the other room?'

Instead of answering me, he smiled, and stood up.

Fuck. I felt the adrenalin begin to hum in my body, uselessly. He took out a box-cutter, a sharp little thing that sliced through the cable ties around my elbows without difficulty. I gasped with relief as the tension across my chest and shoulders eased. He hauled me to my feet, keeping a tight grip on me. I wavered, off balance, weak as a kitten.

'Walk.'

'Where? Which way?' I looked down at him – I couldn't

help that since I was taller than him, but I could have avoided looking haughty about it and I didn't bother. 'If you're going to order me around you could make more of an effort to be clear about what you want.'

He shoved me away from him so I stumbled and almost fell. 'What I want' – he pushed me again – 'is for you to go into that room.'

I went. At least, I limped as far as the doorway. He had put the light on and I saw the set-up straight away: the bed, mainly, and the restraints that hung from the bedposts and the things he was planning to use on me and the cameras to record it all, so he could play it again and again. So he could share what he did across the world and get the praise he craved.

'You're going to wish I'd drugged you,' he said in my ear. His breath tickled my neck. 'You're going to beg me to knock you out. Then you're going to beg me to put you out of your misery. When I kill you you'll be glad to go.'

'Chris . . .' I felt the panic start to hit me, the almost uncontrollable urge to run. I backed away from the room and collided with Swain. I shrank away, catching my breath, as if I'd touched something white-hot.

'I don't know if this can possibly live up to the antici-pation,' Swain hissed, 'but let me tell you this: even if it's only half as good as what I've imagined, it'll be worth it. I've been watching you for years and I have planned every second of what's about to happen to you and I am going to take my time.' He spaced out the last three words. *Take. My. Time.*

I pivoted on the leg I'd pretended to injure and kicked

him as hard as I could on the knee. I could have wished for heavy boots for some added heft but he wasn't a natural fighter and he wasn't expecting it and I could see it hurt. He fell back, shocked. I didn't waste any time following up my kick because I would lose a fight, sooner or later, and losing wasn't an option. I plunged past him into the sitting room, and I didn't have time to make for the door. He'd recovered too quickly, jumping in front of it, blocking my exit. I backed away, towards the fireplace.

'No you don't, you little bitch. You're not getting out of here. This is the end of the road.'

'I couldn't agree more.' I bent and picked up the poker, weighing it in my hands. *Never cuff anyone in front.* Derwent had been right about that. 'As if I was just going to run away after all you've done to me.'

For the first time I could see doubt in his face.

'What did you say? "Even if it's only half as good as what I've imagined, it'll be worth it."' I lifted the poker and looked at it, then at him. 'That's pretty much how I feel too.'

'What do you mean?'

I took two steps forward and swung the poker with as much force as I could, hitting him in the left arm. There was a horrible crack as his humerus broke, and he cried out, his eyes wide with pain.

'When are you going to work it out?' I smiled at him sweetly. 'You're not in charge here. You never have been.'

And the door opened behind him.

Chapter 34

'What took you so long?' I demanded.

Derwent was breathing hard, as if he'd had to run, and his shoes were coated in mud. 'Couldn't make it up the lane. The car got stuck.'

'How annoying.'

'Tell me about it.' Derwent turned and eyed Chris Swain, who was edging away from him. He was holding his arm, and he was white with pain. 'Where are you going?' Derwent asked, interested.

'Nowhere.'

'What happened to your arm, fella?'

'I did it.' I waved the poker apologetically. 'I don't know what came over me.'

'Kerrigan.' Derwent's voice was gravelly with amusement. 'I didn't know you had it in you.'

'It's surprising what you can do when you try.' I nodded at Swain. 'He's got a box-cutter.'

He was trying to get it out of his pocket as I said it, his fingers trembling.

'I'd better take that,' Derwent said, and did, easily. He made Swain look small. All of Swain's toughness had faded away. It had been a pure illusion and I thought the person who had been most taken in by it was Swain himself. 'We haven't been introduced, have we? I'm Josh Derwent and you're a piece of shit.'

'Look,' Chris said, passing his tongue over dry lips. 'I'm sorry.'

'*Now* you're sorry. Now that *he* turns up.' I shook my head. 'That's sexist.'

'I'll go. You'll never see me again. I promise.' Swain looked at me. 'I'll leave you alone. I swear it.'

'Bit late for that, to be honest.' Derwent took out his handcuffs. 'Give me your right hand.'

'Are you arresting me?'

'Did I say I was arresting you? Give me your right hand.'

Swain held it out, shaking as if he had a fever. Derwent snapped the first cuff on.

'Turn around.'

'I can't put my other arm back.'

'You can, you know. It'll hurt, but you can do it.'

'I can't. I really can't.'

'Let me help,' Derwent said, and pulled it back so he could cuff Swain's wrists together. Swain yelled at the top of his voice, a horrible bubbling sound.

'Now, now. You told me not to bother screaming, remember?' I moved across to let Derwent cut the cable ties off my hands. I stayed out of range of Swain's feet although I didn't think he had any fight in him. He was a wreck, pale and sweaty, his eyes darting around the room in pure desperation.

'What are you going to do with me?' he whimpered.

'Well, first of all, I'm going to enjoy this moment.' I smiled. 'Do you remember what happened to Aktaion in the myth? Artemis turned him into a stag. He was a hunter but then he became prey, and his own hounds tore him apart.' I reached behind me to unstick the Chameleon from the hollow of my spine, wincing a little as the tape pulled my skin. I showed it to him. 'I've been wearing this for days. I got this from one of your most devoted disciples. You taught him everything he knows about encryption software and how to get around it. You showed him how to follow people like a shadow in real life and on the internet. He followed you for us. He knew where you went and what you did.' I leaned in. 'How does it feel, Chris? How do you like being watched? What does it feel like to be my prey?'

'Fuck you,' he said, his voice low and venomous, and Derwent smacked him on the back of the head.

'Language.'

'You can't hit me.'

'I can do whatever I like.'

'You're a police officer.'

'Did I say you were under arrest?' Derwent looked at me and laughed. 'He thinks this is official business.'

'You're the one who hates playing by the rules, Chris,' I pointed out. 'We should be free to do what we like to you, shouldn't we? We're not going to be restrained by society's expectations.'

'You'll get in trouble.'

'I don't think so. I'm pretty sure we can lie our way out of it.'

'If anyone finds out,' Derwent said.

'We can forget all this now.' Swain looked from Derwent to me. 'I won't tell anyone. I won't complain. I'll go.'

'I wish you'd stop talking,' Derwent said. Then he looked at me and raised his eyebrows. 'Well?'

I stood and thought. I allowed myself to think about what Swain had done to me. I allowed myself to feel all the anger, all the fear, all the hatred that had soured in me over the years that he'd been my stalker. I turned my back on my training. I needed to speak a language that he would understand.

'Go and look in the bedroom,' I said to Derwent. 'See what he'd planned for me.'

He went. He stood in the doorway where I had stood, and he looked, and he understood and it shook him. A muscle flickered in his cheek but he sounded eerily calm when he spoke.

'What do you want me to do?'

'I want you to kill him.'

Derwent looked at me and his face was completely blank. His eyes, though – his eyes burned like fire.

'It's the only way,' I said. 'It'll never stop otherwise.'

And Derwent nodded. 'All right.' He shrugged off his coat and jacket, and started rolling up his sleeves.

'What? No!' Swain was sobbing. 'You can't.'

'I can't do it myself. I'm not strong enough,' I said. 'You are.'

Derwent nodded again. He went across to where Swain was trying to curl himself up into a ball, weeping and pleading.

'Have some dignity,' Derwent said, his voice low and almost sympathetic. 'Die like a man.'

'You can't . . .'

Derwent's mouth tightened and he dragged Swain to his feet. 'Come on. Outside.'

'I won't go. I won't.'

Derwent had plenty of experience with manhandling reluctant prisoners. He'd said Swain was going through the door and through the door Swain went, although both the door and Swain sustained some serious damage in the process. Swain staggered into the yard, Derwent right behind him, and the security light came on. Their shadows stretched across the ground as Swain fell, got to his feet, tried to run and was caught. It was almost too easy.

I stood in the doorway, watching. I felt nothing. Nothing at all. Not satisfaction. Not pleasure. Not horror.

I was numb.

Derwent dragged Swain across to a stone trough in the corner of the yard. I hadn't noticed it before, but it was full of rainwater. The water was green with algae and an unhealthy yellow scum covered the surface. Derwent pushed Swain to his knees, then looked at me, a gladiator awaiting the thumbs up or down from a fickle empress.

'Are you sure?'

'I'm sure.' My voice didn't shake.

Derwent twisted his hand in the back of Swain's hair, and Swain was crying now, great racking sobs. That was despair, I thought, and I felt no pity for him.

The muscles flickered in Derwent's arms as he

plunged Swain's head under the surface of the filthy water and held him down. Swain bucked and fought but he didn't have a chance, not against Derwent. The water slopped around, sliding down the sides of the trough as Swain twisted, his feet drumming on the ground, and Derwent turned his head and stared at me, never taking his eyes off me, until I nodded. He lifted Swain's head and the air rushed back into his lungs with a loud whoop. Swain was trembling, his eyes wide with terror, as he panted for oxygen. There was a stain spreading on the back of his jeans. Derwent looked down, breathing hard himself from the effort of keeping Swain under the water. His face twisted in disgust. He threw Swain away from him to sprawl across the dirty cobbles.

'Now you know the meaning of shit-scared, you little prick.'

Swain grovelled, weeping, unmanned quite completely. Derwent stepped over him, standing with one foot on either side of his body.

'You don't tell anyone about what you've been doing to Kerrigan. Do you hear me? Not now, not in interview, not in court. You weren't stalking her. You weren't following her. You weren't obsessed with her. You wanted to get revenge on her because she set the cops on you, but it was no more than that, do you hear me? And it ends. Now.' He lifted his foot and very deliberately pressed the sole of his boot into the side of Swain's head, leaning more and more weight on him as Swain screamed. Derwent held him down against the cobbles for a little longer than I might have, then stepped away from him. He took a second before he turned to me.

'Are you all right?'

I nodded. 'Nicely done.'

Derwent sketched a salute. He looked drawn, utterly exhausted but more in spirit than physically. Swain hadn't put up much of a fight, even in what could have been his death throes.

'What is it?' I asked.

He was about to tell me when a car cut down the lane beyond the farm, moving fast. Blue lights bounced off the farmhouse.

'The cops. Good timing,' Derwent said casually. He bent down and picked up Swain by the scruff of the neck. 'Nothing happened here except that I arrested you. Whatever else you say, no one will believe you.'

Swain closed his eyes and nodded, and Derwent prepared to face the police officers who were picking their way through the gate, their faces taut with tension.

'It's all right. We've got him.'

'What happened?' The officers were Thames Valley police, which answered one question of mine: we weren't in Hertfordshire.

'It's a long story, but this is very much a wanted man,' Derwent said, pointing at Swain.

The superintendent stared at him, appalled. 'What happened to him?'

'I think he tripped,' I said.

'It was more of a stumble.' Derwent blinked at the superintendent, all innocence, and the superintendent nodded, understanding enough to know that he shouldn't ask any more questions.

'That was unlucky. We'll get him cleaned up at the nick.'

'No hurry,' Derwent said, and smiled.

It was a long time before we got back to London – a long night of giving statements and having my injuries photographed and talking: talking to the officers who'd taken Swain to the police station, talking to Una Burt, talking to the doctor on duty who had been very interested in how Swain broke his arm and had asked a lot of questions to see if I had concussion after the car crash. The one person I didn't get to speak to was Derwent. Not after he pulled me to one side when they were still loading Swain into the van to transport him to custody.

'Are you all right?'

'Yeah,' I said with a lopsided smile. 'You know how it is. I'm not sure how I feel about what we did.'

'What I did.'

'What I asked you to do,' I said. 'It's not on you.'

He shook his head very slightly. 'It wasn't hard. The only thing that worried me was whether I'd be able to stop myself in time.'

I blinked, surprised. 'You wouldn't have killed him for me.'

'No.' His face was bleak. 'Maeve, when he crashed into you – he killed Mal. Mal's dead.'

I stared at him. 'He can't be. The airbag deployed. He was right beside me and I'm not even scratched. You must be wrong.'

'No, I'm not. He broke his neck.'

'No,' I said, angry with him now. 'You've made a mistake. The airbag went off.'

'He's dead.'

'Stop *saying* that. It's not true. It's not.' Because if he was dead, it was my fault. If he was dead, it was because I had put him in Swain's path.

If Mal was dead, I had as good as killed him myself.

Chapter 35

They bury you quickly, in most cultures, or burn you, or conduct whatever ritual it is that sets your spirit free. There are good, practical reasons for that, but the main one, it seemed to me, was to get it over with. It was ten endless days before they laid poor Mal to rest, halfway through December, too close to Christmas. We tried, all of us, not to take up too much room in the little church but the whole team wanted to be there, and so did most people who'd worked with him, and somehow Mal's family almost disappeared among the police officers. His other family, I thought, and ached for him, and for them, and for everyone who was going to miss him. I was going to miss him and I was only starting to realise how little I'd known of him.

I hadn't known he was a Catholic.

I hadn't known he had always wanted to be a police officer. I hadn't known he wore a police costume all weekend, every weekend the year he was six.

I hadn't known he had worked as a lifeguard for three summers when he was a teenager and saved two people from drowning.

I hadn't known that he received a commendation for bravery when he was a probationer, for tackling a man who was waving an axe around Kilburn and shouting about Jesus.

I hadn't known he had five devoted friends from school who had each made him be their best man because he was so good at it.

I hadn't known he was on such good terms with his ex-girlfriends that all of them came to his funeral, occupying a pew together and weeping uninhibitedly for a decent man they had loved, once upon a time.

I hadn't known he had two sisters and a dog that adored him, that was so devoted that the priest had allowed the family to bring it to the funeral service. The dog was a spaniel with curly ears and wistful eyes. It looked up at everyone who passed, hoping. Needing Mal to be alive, somehow.

Not understanding.

And to be honest, we all felt that way. There was no understanding it. No accepting it. I sat in a pew with Derwent on one side of me and a grim-faced Chris Pettifer on the other and every part of me ached with sheer misery. I wasn't the only one there who felt a sense of loss, but I was the only one who felt responsible.

The familiar words of the funeral service comforted me a little. I had been to many funerals in my time, for work and with my parents, who saw it as a point of pride to attend as many funerals as possible, and it was a well-worn ritual. I concentrated on that (*eternal rest, grant unto him O Lord*) and not on the look on Mal's mother's face (*let perpetual light shine upon him*) or the way his sister broke down during the reading she attempted (*may he rest in peace*). Derwent was silent beside me. He didn't join in with the ragged singing or the responses. I had to resist the urge to lean against him, to collapse on him and let him support me.

Anyway, I wasn't sure he'd hold me up.

It wasn't that he blamed me, necessarily. Not as much as I blamed myself, at least. But we still hadn't really talked about what had happened, because of logistics as much as anything. I hadn't been at work and he hadn't been in my flat. He had moved out as soon as he got back to London, packing his things in a businesslike way. There had been no discussion about it. There had been no question of him staying. The need for him to be in my home was at an end. Wanting him there was illogical. He couldn't have comforted me.

No one could.

But I was very much aware of being alone.

The burial was to be in a cemetery near the church. The family had asked if the other mourners would stay away from the graveside. When the service was over, the police officers gathered outside. There was a guard of honour as Mal's friends and his father carried the heavy coffin out of the church, staggering a little under its weight, their faces anguished. I stood alone in the crowd, near the back, holding in the tears.

I didn't deserve to cry.

Once the coffin was in the hearse and the family had taken their leave, the police officers broke up into groups to talk. Liv cut through the crowd and fetched up beside me.

'There you are. Are you all right?'

I nodded. 'As well as I can be.'

She squeezed my hand, all sympathy. 'No one blames you.'

'They all know what happened,' I said in a low voice. I was aware of the looks I was getting. My ear was attuned to the sudden silence that fell on people's conversations when they noticed I was nearby.

I might have been the same way myself, if it had happened to someone else.

'No one will think about that soon. They'll forget.'

'It doesn't matter,' I said, because it didn't. I deserved it. I wished I could suffer more for what had happened to Mal.

I would have given a lot to change what had happened, and I couldn't, and it killed me.

'I'm going to go, I think,' I said.

'You're not coming for a drink? We're all going to the local pub in a bit. Just – you know. To honour his memory.'

To reassert that we were alive, I thought. To laugh after crying. There was nothing like the sense of release after a funeral: it was part of being human. I didn't grudge them the beers or the instinct to gather together. There had already been a police wake for Mal a couple of days after he died, but I hadn't gone to that either. I hugged her. 'Raise a glass for me.'

I walked to the car park, taking smaller steps than usual thanks to the narrow skirt of my smart black suit. Derwent was there, standing beside his car, staring into space. As I watched, he dragged his tie off, pulling at it savagely. Then he held it, irresolute.

'On.'

'What?' He turned.

'Put it on. You don't want to look too casual.'

He flipped up his collar and put the tie around his neck, adjusting it so the ends were the right length before he began to knot it. 'Too casual for what?'

'For Melissa.'

He raised his eyebrows, but he didn't deny it. 'How did you know?'

Because you need, above all else, to be needed. Because you want more than anything to be loved.

I shrugged. 'Just a guess.'

Derwent finished with his tie and smoothed it down. Almost to himself, he said, 'When you spend your time looking into the shadows, you have to remind yourself there's light too.'

I reached up and adjusted his tie for him, loosening it a fraction, tweaking his collar. 'There. You'll do.'

He looked down at me. 'Are you going to be okay?'

'I hope so.'

'Come back to work soon.'

'I will.'

He got into his car and I watched him drive away. People were beginning to drift to their cars or head to the pub. No one spoke to me as I walked back to the church.

It was dark inside, and empty, and the air smelled like the churches of my childhood: the sweet odour of incense and furniture polish. The sanctuary lamp glowed red in the gloom. There was a stand of candles near the door, in front of a statue of the Virgin Mary. I dropped a pound coin into the slot and took out a candle, holding it to one of the other flames until the wick caught. I set it into a place near the front, the little flame dancing in the draught from the open door, a light in the darkness that somehow wasn't enough to push the shadows away. I stood there for a minute, thinking about Mal. I wanted to pray for him. I wanted to tell him how I would miss him. I wanted to say goodbye.

I just couldn't find the words.

Acknowledgements

Huge thanks as ever to the usual suspects at Ebury and United Agents, particularly my editor Gillian Green for her dedicated hard work, and my agent Ariella Feiner for her superb guidance. I must also thank my wonderful family and friends for their unfailing support, and the great community of crime writers, bloggers and readers for their generous enthusiasm.

I could not have written this book without reference to *Blaze: The Forensics of Fire* by Nicholas Faith, *The Dark Net: Inside the Digital Underworld* by Jamie Bartlett, and *Stalking a City for Fun and Frivolity* by Brendan O'Connor. I am also very grateful to my husband, James Norman, for his encyclopaedic knowledge of all things legal and police-related. *After the Fire* is, of course, a work of fiction. Any mistakes in this book are mine (and some of them may even be deliberate).

Finally, my thanks to Shirley Brooke for her winning bid in a charity auction to name a character in *After the Fire*. Her son, Charlie Brooke, gave me some suggestions for how he'd like the character to be and I hope my version of a Charlie Brooke lives up to his expectations.